SHADOWS WALKING

A NOVEL BY DOUGLAS R. SKOPP

WITH A FOREWORD BY
E. THOMAS MORAN

Cover design by Norman Taber

Copyright © Douglas R. Skopp 2010
All rights reserved.

ISBN: 1439231990
ISBN-13: 9781439231999
Library of Congress Control Number: 2009902233

www.createspace.com/900001062
www.shadowswalking.com

Printed by CreateSpace.

For my teachers, my colleagues, my students, my friends....

…indifference to the sufferings that one causes…,
even if it is given other names, is a terrible
and permanent form of cruelty.

— Marcel Proust

Foreword

The famed director of the film *Shoah*, Claude Lanzmann, bitterly insisted that there can be no explanation for the Holocaust. He echoed the line from a Primo Levi story, in which an *SS* guard at Auschwitz declares to a prisoner who asks for an explanation of the misery all around him, "There is no 'why' here." Indeed, it appears that there can be no comprehensible explanation for the Holocaust. It was as indifferent to human suffering as an earthquake that indiscriminately swallows lives. But unlike an earthquake, with its blind remorselessness, the *Shoah* was conceived and carried out by human beings who could see into the eyes and hear the cries of those they willfully destroyed.

How do we then come to terms with the Holocaust? At the most specific level of historical analysis, we might infer that the majority of the German people were so intoxicated with Hitler's renewal of their national pride in the early years of his regime, and so terrified of him and his henchmen in the later years, that they simply were pushed down a brutally tragic path. Or that German society at that time was so unusually prone to accept authority and so poisoned by anti-Semitism that Hitler's fanaticism overpowered any opposition. We might consequently conclude that the Holocaust says nothing about *us* —that *it could not happen here*. We want to believe that the Holocaust does not derive from anything inherent in the human condition. We can therefore insist that the human beings who perpetrated it were thoroughly evil, so unlike us that we need not give their behavior any more thought than we expect predatory animals to show kindness to their prey. We confidently proclaim that *we* would never, could never, do what *they* did, nor would those we know and love.

But the Holocaust is not the only time that human beings have been so relentlessly malevolent to other human beings. It is only the worst, most horrific of such episodes in its scale, not its kind. Human history presents us with an endless, gruesome parade of massacres and genocides. Alexander the Great, tutored as a boy by Aristotle, the author of what is arguably the most renowned text on ethics in history, burned the city of Tyre to the ground, crucified its men and sold its women and children into slavery. Hulagu Khan's massacre in 1258 of Baghdad left grizzly stacks of human heads around the city; according to some reports, the size of its population did not recover until the last century. The bones of a generation bleaching in immense killing fields stretching across the Cambodian landscape, and the images of young Rwandan men hunting down their former neighbors and hacking them to death with sun-glinted, blood stained machetes are but two of many recent reminders of genocide. The ghastly historical record is as endless as it is merciless.

When burdened by knowledge of History's villainies, we cannot evade fearful questions. Is it possible that that this barbarism reflects some capacity within all of us? How do we come to terms with the realization that genocides have not been perpetrated by depraved lunatics, with bizarre life stories and opaque eyes that can't focus, like sharks', but that they are carried out by ordinary human beings? Only if the world were starkly simple would we be let off the hook from having to contemplate things so disturbing that they resemble the calibration of evil in hell.

In facing History's record, we often feel stunned and lost. Some resort to a resigned nihilism, in which, without a fixed moral order, "all things *really* are possible," as Dostoyevsky feared. A few others might slide into a bloodlust that bellows a deadly rage signaled by an impulse in our limbic brain as a way to protect us from victimhood—or give vent to revenge. Most of us simply move on, unwilling and unable to look back and reflect on what lies behind us and in us, and which, even more terrifyingly, may foreshadow what lies before us. But in some interior chamber of ourselves, in the rational mind or in the mysterious longing of the heart, we strain for comprehension. The past and the future compel us to discover why human beings commit intentional, shattering slaughter—and then to use that understanding to subdue violence and to learn humanity.

This remarkable novel offers an attempt at answering these questions, not through analysis, but through the unfolding of ordinary lives lived in a world where horror happened on an unprecedented scale. Doug Skopp presents the Holocaust through the experiences of a Nazi medical doctor, Johann Brenner. Brenner is a fictitious character, but through Skopp's meticulous historical research, he is a composite of very real figures—doctors who should have been a bulwark against the cruelty of the Holocaust but who, nevertheless, participated in its torturous medical research and helped to perfect its barbaric efficiency. Skopp is not interested in reductive and easy interpretations. He requires that we see the world as Brenner and the others in his circle lived it.

As we struggle to comprehend Brenner's moral universe and, as easy answers are denied to us, what are we left with? Like Schopenhauer, Skopp does not want to "curse or judge but to understand." Through a novelist's eye, he reveals the skein of forces that press on an ordinary life: professional ambitions; needs for esteem and belonging; the desire to emulate or obey those charismatic and self-certain figures who would shape us for their own ends; the anesthetizing affects of family crises; the self-serving construction of historical memory; and inattention to the best convictions of the good people who love us. If we allow it, these forces can draw us into a forbidding indifference to the suffering of others.

In limpid, beautifully crafted prose, the novel weaves these themes together in ways that are rich with detail and nuance. Psychological, sociological or historical analyses by themselves can be too didactic, somehow too incomplete as our only interpretive lenses, when faced

with an event as resoundingly inconceivable in the magnitude of its pro-
tracted, insensate terror as the Holocaust. What is called for, and what
Skopp provides, is a kind of indirection—the circling around and around
until, with enough glimpses from enough different angles and enough
intricate insights, we gain awareness of how ordinary people actually
lived lives that led them to become so ultimately disconnected from the
persons they intended to be. Gradually, we acquire a sense of how indifference can take root and ossify until it defines a life—an ordinary life
of a normal human being, not merely the life of a one-dimensional beast
to whom we cannot relate: the life of a person we might know, even as
we know our own. This novel is powerful in the way it constructs this
awareness and in the unexpected, haunting, and richly symbolic unfolding of its final moments.

Shadows Walking could only have been written by a person like
Doug Skopp. By the acclaim of admiring friends, colleagues and generations of students, he is a quintessentially gentle and profoundly good
man. Yet he has spent much of the last twenty-five years staring into the
smoldering pit of suffering that is the Holocaust. In his case, this is not
the reflection of a morbid preoccupation or obsession. It has been an act
of bravery. He has sought the understanding the world needs, but may
not want. His work has led him away from the human tendency to easy
condemnation of others, especially those who commit terrible wrongs,
which, as he has tried to teach and implies here, only lays the foundation
and the deluded justification for more futile hatred and more genocides.

Skopp's sorrowful but determined quest has led him to understand
tragedy in its deepest sense. Tragedy in which the divided individual human heart can engender the destruction of others, as it leads to its own
destruction. In this ancient understanding of tragic destiny, well-mean-
ing, idealistic individuals can become the authors of the collapse of the
world they share with others. This is, paradoxically, an insight that can
lead human beings on a journey toward a cautionary understanding of
human responsibility and prepare them for the arduous construction of
the essential ethical strength to stand against an inward drift to indifference. The demands of ethical courage require us to engage in a perilous

trek around our own ambitions and fears and to open our eyes "to the child dying at our feet," as Nikos Kazantzakis vividly portrayed.

Skopp opens us to the possibility that empathy, not retribution, lights the only hopeful path to justice. To some, this path, no doubt, seems unnaturally demanding and emotionally much less satisfying than a calculated, formal spasm of assault on a despised person or group whom we judge to be the cause of our discontents. Such spasms of assault frame the disconsolate record of history. But, the more worthy injunction implied in this novel is to understand and overcome our own human capacity to allow a frozen darkness to engulf our hearts, leaving us as lost in the ice of indifference as the inhabitants of Dante's Ninth Circle of Hell. Finally, this awareness requires that we be acutely attentive to the good people in our world who possess the moral clarity to save us from failure in this task, and who can redeem us if we do fail. We must learn to recognize that, like Johann's wife, Helga, these individuals may not be dominating or overpowering, but they are as necessary to the meaning of our lives as a lover who whispers truths in a quiet voice.

Perhaps the mosaic of subtle understanding that Doug Skopp offers is, in the end, the most for which we can hope. But his intention is just that—to leave us with some hope and a decent purpose—in respect and compassion for others—to which we can commit ourselves.

E. Thomas Moran, Ph.D.
Director, Institute for Ethics in Public Life and
Distinguished Service Professor
State University of New York at Plattsburgh

CHAPTER ONE
1946: Trials

Johann Brenner climbed inside the first boxcar he could find in Berlin's train yards as the city was falling to the Russians. When the train headed south, toward Nuremberg, he cursed his luck. But he knew it could have gone east, deeper into the territory held by the Soviets, or into Russia itself. He knew that the war would soon end. If only the train were not bombed before he could jump off.

His false papers afforded him a new identity, a new life. He wanted to go west, to Karlsruhe, where he hoped to find his wife. He was comforted by his belief that she had fled their apartment in Nuremberg to live with her sister in the *Rhineland*. He missed her, but their separation helped him forget what he wanted to forget.

As the train neared Nuremberg, he jumped. American troops captured him within minutes. They brought him to a D.P. camp outside the city and assigned him and other "displaced persons" to one of the re-construction crews at Nuremberg's Palace of Justice. But his war wounds— a leg injury resulting in an awkward limp from the First World War, and a scarred right hand, which he concealed with a glove, from the Second—made him unfit for hard labor. Instead, he worked as a cleaner inside the courthouse. He followed orders, did as he was told, and the Americans were satisfied.

When the courthouse repairs were completed, Johann Brenner—now known as Heinrich Westermann—was selected to be the head custodian in Nuremberg's Palace of Justice. He liked his title. He assigned himself the night shift: eleven to seven. He appreciated the quiet. In the vast building, he alone was awake. He had a bunk, a small desk, and a cupboard under the stairs in the basement. He took his meals during the workweek in the building's cafeteria; on weekends, he lined up at the nearby soup kitchen. Supervising the others, he felt responsible, even a bit important. Sometimes he hummed softly as he walked up and down the stairs. He alone knew that he had been a doctor at Auschwitz.

He was careful to not antagonize the other men or show any favoritism. He avoided asking them questions and answered few of theirs. Mostly in silence, they swept, mopped and polished the Palace of Justice's floors, stairs, and the various offices and meeting rooms, washed its windows, cleaned its toilets and prepared it for the trials that would begin in the late summer.

Johann took a particular interest in Room 600, the main courtroom, and assigned himself to dust and wax the defendants' dock, the lawyers' tables, and the wooden railing around the witness stand. He enjoyed smoothing the green felt over the judges' bench, arranging their chairs, tending to their pitchers of water and their glasses. He brought everything to a shining, pure order—an order best seen in the morning light when he drew back the heavy drapes. The wood-paneled walls turned to old gold. The aluminum clock numerals above the dock shone like silver. The green marble doorway gleamed. The judges' bench became a throne.

He knew that his *Vaterland* was in ruins. Millions had lost their lives. Millions more were starving and dreading the winter. And beyond Germany, millions more had been killed. Loves lost. Lives shattered. Homes bombed. The living faced chaos. Like them all, he was numbed by the war.

Debris and loose gravel covered Nuremberg's cobblestoned streets. More than ninety percent of the city had been destroyed. What remained was a tangled collection of fragments, of disconnected, painful memories and choices. Choices made before the war had consequences that led to more choices, all of them knotted and confused. Like Johann himself.

He had heard of the mayor's predictions that it would take seventy-five years for the city to be rebuilt. Walking along *Fürthstraße* toward the old city, he saw that the castle moat had been drained and tented over with canvas to accommodate as many of the homeless as possible. He saw that his lovely, beloved city, "Germany's little treasure chest," had been bombed back to the time of ox-carts. All the more startling to see visiting Americans, dignitaries and businessmen, being driven in automobiles like space ships along cleared roads from the Palace of Justice to the relatively unharmed suburbs of the city. Some were staying in what was still standing of the *Deutsche Hof*, the hotel where Hitler himself often had stood on the balcony to address the *Volk* at the annual September Party rallies. Their robin's egg blue, pearly gray or apple green automobiles looked gigantic—smooth, confident, powerful; with chrome-rimmed headlights and shiny grills; with hubcaps like silver platters and over-sized white-walled tires. Ash and sand swirled behind them. They came from a world where colors and brightness had not been obliterated. A different world than Nuremberg's dark brown and sooty black. The contrast was painful. At first, Johann stayed inside as much as he could. His basement bunk became his home.

All the same, those six months in 1945, after the surrender and before the trials began, were his most carefree since before the Great Depression. Before the war, he had expected to be a hero. Then came chaos. He wanted to forget all that. To escape the morgue of the past. To believe that what he had seen and done before his *Vaterland*'s collapse was behind him. To escape his fear of being recognized. For a while, he succeeded. Then he began having nightmares again.

In November 1945, the International Military Tribunal began in Room 600. Twenty-two of the highest-ranking Nazis sat in the prisoners' dock on the chairs that he had polished and straightened. They were on trial for "conspiracy to wage aggressive war," for "crimes against peace," for "violations of the laws of war," and for "crimes against humanity." The Russian, French, British and American presiding judges propped their elbows on the green felt cloth that he had smoothed, and drank water from the glasses that he had set so neatly at each of their places.

On that first day of the trial, he stood against the back wall, behind the visitors' gallery. He wanted to see the Nazi defendants in flesh and blood. Goering was the only one he had seen up close before, when Hitler had given a speech in Nuremberg. He remembered that warm autumn night of ten years ago: soldiers singing and goose-stepping with power and confidence; workers marching with shovels, held like rifles over their shoulders; the flames from the torchlight parade dancing in his son Paul-Adolf's eyes. He remembered how they, along with the multitude, had cheered and stretched their arms out toward their *Führer*. The next day, the newspapers trumpeted the racial laws. Paul-Adolf wore his Hitler Youth uniform to school and was so excited that he forgot his books.

Goering, despite his defiant glare, looked shabby now in the prisoners' dock. So did the others. When the opening proceedings turned toward describing Nazi medical experimentation, sterilizations and genocide, Johann began to feel dizzy and went to lie down on his basement bunk. He soon fell into fitful sleep. Hours later, he awakened thrashing and screaming. "Clean this up! Clean this up at once!" he heard himself shouting into the blackness.

After that, he did not attend any more sessions of the International Military Tribunal. He worked his night shift, which suited the other janitors quite well, and then spent the daylight hours trying to sleep. He was relieved when the Tribunal ended on the last day of September 1946. But the nightmares did not stop.

The next trial—the "Nazi Doctors' Trial"—began soon afterwards. A panel of American judges was hearing evidence against twenty-two men and one woman. All were charged with murder, torture and atrocities "in the name of medical science." All but three of the defendants were physicians.

He did not plan to attend any of these proceedings. But when one of the defendants vomited before collapsing in the prisoner's dock, the bailiff summoned him to clean it up. From then on, he was required to be present. He sat in the corner of the courtroom, just behind two photographers who were perched above him on their stepladders.

He tried to reassure himself that his fears of being recognized were groundless. He knew that he had aged. That he was stooped and gaunt to the point of looking skeletal. That he had not regained any of the weight he had lost since he was wounded at Auschwitz. The mirror in the basement washroom showed him how much his eyes were sunken and rimmed with shadows. How prominent were his cheekbones. And how, he thought, his thinning, gray hair, and the wispy moustache that he now wore made him look far older than forty-eight. 'I am a different man now,' he hoped. 'A different man.'

Most of the time during the Doctors' Trial he pretended to be asleep. Still, he could not contain his curiosity about the drama around him. Since he was not given earphones, he could not hear the simultaneous translations of the proceedings. He did not understand what the American judges and prosecuting attorneys were saying. That did not stop him from admiring their crisp uniforms, their bright brass buttons, their control of what was going on. By contrast, he thought the German defense attorneys, with their worn, baggy suits and their limp shirts, seemed confused and nervous.

He could not stop himself from glancing up into the spectators' gallery. It was easy enough to pick out the Americans. They looked well fed and healthy. 'Those hungry-looking ones must be Germans,' he thought. 'Perhaps family members of a defendant, or of one of the witnesses.' One woman, wearing a black coat, a tight-fitting black hat and a dark, heavy veil sat near the back of the gallery. When he noticed that she was staring at him, he quickly looked down at the floor. Sitting a few seats away in the same row, another woman wore the bright clothes and thick make-up that he thought must be the style of all American women, based on the movies he had seen before the war.

Many of the visitors seemed to be uninterested in the proceedings, and that made them all the more conspicuous. Some, he decided, were probably Nurembergers simply trying to get warm after a night in makeshift lodgings. But others might be in disguise, just as fearful of detection as he was. Did he know them? Did they know him?

The twenty-three defendants mirrored Nuremberg's wretchedness. He tried not to look too long at them, but could not avoid taking quick glances in their direction. The military men among them wore dusty old uniforms that looked like padded pajamas, bare of any insignia or decoration; the civilians wore shabby suits. Wearing his neatly pressed, gray janitor's smock helped him believe he was different.

Most of the defendants appeared downcast. With their arms folded stiffly, they stared blankly or looked down into their laps. Only the chief defendant, *Doktor* Karl Brandt, one of Adolf Hitler's personal physicians and the highest-ranking Nazi medical administrator to survive the war, seemed alert enough to understand the charges against him. Despite Brandt's haggard appearance, Johann recognized him immediately.

The last time he had seen Brandt in Nuremberg was in the autumn of 1939, just after the war began. As *Reich* Commissioner for Health and Sanitation, *Generalleutnant* Brandt was the honored guest of Nuremberg's chapter of the Nazi Physicians' Association, in town to give a speech about the state's concern with "mental defectives." "We must be scientific," he had said, "especially when Germany's survival is at stake. We must make hard choices and use our skills to heal our people." Johann recalled how much he had admired Brandt's certainty and self-confidence, his idealism and determination. All doctors should be like him, he thought. Fearless, uncompromising in their service to the *Volk*, worthy of respect. That evening, when he was introduced to Brandt, he had made an effusive comment about how history would not forget what was being said and done at meetings like this all across Germany. Brandt replied by raising his arm stiffly in a Hitler salute.

Now Brandt sat on trial, head unbowed, a disdainful arch in his eyebrow, sneering occasionally at his fellow defendants. His shiny black, pomaded hair, precisely parted and combed back from his high forehead, reflected the ceiling's lights. His mouth and jaw seemed hard, even rigid, as though his facial structure and musculature made it impossible for him to smile. His head and neck had a chiseled, sculpted quality, much like the Nazis' idealized Nordic hero. The small cleft in his chin added to the effect. Occasionally he glanced at the witnesses, or at the judges' bench, but mostly he cocked his head so he could stare at the ceiling or look away from the other prisoners. His every gesture displayed a man wanting to be in control of himself, a man of self-confidence, entitled to authority. Johann blanched each time Brandt turned his head toward him. But if the *Reich* Commissioner recognized him, he did not show it.

This day's testimony was about castration. On the stand stood a pudgy, balding man, who looked at least sixty, but was probably not yet thirty. After the preliminary oath, he began talking immediately in German with a Polish accent, without the hesitation or the stumbling Johann had noticed in previous witnesses. In a high voice that came in quick bursts followed by pauses and deep labored breaths, he told how he had avoided an earlier roundup of his fellow prisoners on a road-construction crew by hanging back. Those prisoners, he said, had been taken by truck to a nearby clinic for an unspecified, brief treatment they could not understand. They had come back to the work camp the same day and began working at once.

The bulbous microphone, so tall that the witness had to stretch to reach it, made a hissing sound each time he spoke a word that ended in an "s." Johann's mind flashed back to Auschwitz and an image of Aronsohn, lying on the floor. Aronsohn had had the same accent. He sank down into his chair and put his hand over his eyes, as the prosecuting attorney directed the witness to continue.

Softly, the man said, "...twenty Jews, of twenty to twenty-four years of age, were chosen. But this time the selection went by the alphabet. I was one of the very first. We were deported to Birkenau into a woman labor camp. There a tall doctor, in the gray uniform of the *Luftwaffe* arrived."

Johann winced. He sucked in air, making an almost audible whistle. In his mind, each sentence in the prisoner's testimony ended with Aronsohn's terrified scream: 'I am a man!" He sank deeper into his chair.

"We had to undress and our sexual organs were placed under an apparatus and kept there under the apparatus for fifteen minutes. The apparatus strongly heated the sexual organs..." The microphone crackled. "...and the surrounding parts, and later on those parts began to show a black color. After this treatment..."

The word "treatment" gave Johann a jolt. He shifted his feet and began to perspire.

"...we had to work again right away. After some days the sexual organs of most of my comrades became purulent and they had great difficulties in walking. In spite of this they had to go on working until they collapsed..." The witness paused for a loud, wheezing breath, then continued, "...and those who collapsed were sent," another, longer pause, "...to the gas chambers."

Johann exhaled loudly. He felt panic rise in his throat. He reached into his pocket for his handkerchief and wiped his brow. He clenched his teeth and shut his eyes. 'Take deep breaths, Johann. Slow, deep breaths. Don't faint now. Yes, the genitalia often were 'purulent.' Grotesquely, pathetically filled with pus.'

The courtroom was quiet. For all Johann knew, everyone was looking at him. But all eyes were on the witness. The heavy drapes closed out the afternoon's sunlight. They hung motionless, cloaking everything in a funereal stupor. The military policemen's absurdly shiny, white helmets reflected the ceiling lights, but the lights themselves and the very air in the room now seemed shadowy and gray.

Speaking directly to the judges, in a startlingly calm voice, the witness said, "I myself had only an exudation, but no suppuration."

Johann gasped. 'Yes,' he thought. 'Many of them only had a slow oozing of pus, not a runny discharge. He was one of the lucky ones.'

He dared to look directly at the witness for an instant before he looked down again into his lap, and closed his eyes.

"Two weeks later," the man continued, "it was about October 1943, seven men of our group were led to Auschwitz I. This distance had to be marched." Again the microphone hissed as the witness said the last phrase in his Polish accented German, "...*zu Fuss*..." He paused, turned to look at the judges' bench, and finally said, "The seven men had great difficulty in walking because their sexual organs were hurting. We were led to Auschwitz I, into the sick barracks, *Block 20*. There we were operated on."

The witness paused again, as though he had to turn another page in his mind before he could continue. "We received an injection in the back by which the lower part of the body became insensible while the upper part remained quite normal." Another, longer pause. A sigh, like a gentle wind over grasses. "Both testicles were taken off." These last words were spoken with such calmness, such resignation, so softly, even gently, that some of the prisoners in the dock smiled with the belief that the witness's tone of voice was proof that no harm had been done. Johann clenched his teeth so tightly his jaw muscles began to hurt. He opened his eyes and saw that only Brandt among the defendants was as stony-faced as before. Standing on a ladder in the corner above Johann's seat, a photographer was operating a motion picture camera that emitted a low, mechanical growl. Over its sound, Johann heard someone in the balcony crying.

After a brief pause, the witness added, in a somewhat louder voice, "There was no prior examination as to spermatic fluid."

'Yes,' Johann recalled to himself, 'until Schumann changed the protocol.'

When the witness next said, in his broken German, "I have been able to see the whole procedure in the mirror glass of a surgical lamp," Johann was confused for a moment, then thought, 'Yes, he could have seen what was happening to him. Lord!' He swallowed and hung his head.

"Also," the witness continued, now in a louder, stronger voice, "none of us were asked whether we agreed to the operation. They just said, 'you go,' and then we were sent to the operation table without the possibility of saying anything." He looked over at the prisoners' dock with an icy glare, drawing everyone's eyes that way, too. Then he shouted, "No consent for the operation was obtained. We were merely told: 'Your turn,' and sent to the operating table without a word."

Johann grimaced and clenched his fists in his lap. The glove on his right hand was beginning to tear between his thumb and forefinger. He longed to take it off, but knew he could not.

The witness slowly looked around the courtroom. "The man in charge of the sterilization and castration experiments at Auschwitz was a *Doktor* Schumann. During these operations, the doctors had white coats on. A gray uniform of the *Luftwaffe* was the only uniform I ever saw on any one of the doctors during the X-ray sterilization. This uniform had an open collar and a tie worn with it."

Johann closed his eyes again. He remembered his first meeting with Horst Schumann, in early 1940 at the asylum in Grafeneck, just five years after he joined the party. He remembered how inspired he had been by Schumann's resolute determination to do, as he had said, "whatever had to be done." Grafeneck's calm seemed to sanction, to justify, to make natural and even beautiful what took place there. Such lovely, pastoral beauty, such ordered nature. So civilized and thoughtful a place of refuge. Johann recalled the winter sunlight filtering through a light snowfall, how it softened the faces of bundled-up patients who were able to go outside and walk or be wheeled along by their attendants on tree-lined paths. He did not ask himself what those human beings might have been thinking on the day they were loaded onto a gray bus for their last, short journey. He had thought that they could not think.

His decision to help Schumann in the Nazis' euthanasia program once had been one of the proudest moments of his life. Now he thought differently, that he had let himself be captured and used by Schumann's certainty. That he was taken in by Grafeneck's placid order. By all the reasoning that had led him to that place. He could still hear Schumann tell him, in his smooth, rich voice, "We are only doing what good doctors have done through the ages—saving the patient, in this case our

Germany, from a weakening, ultimately destructive condition. But we are doing it more humanely, more methodically than it has ever been done before. Healthy German boys and girls deserve to be protected from these useless creatures."

He had been convinced at the time that the gassings at Grafeneck were essential, and for that reason, ethical and responsible. Even if he could not tell Helga, his wife, precisely what was happening there, he remembered how disappointed he was that she did not sense his satisfaction with his visit, that she did not share his enthusiasm, if only for his own sake. At the time, he had blamed it on his abbreviated account, nothing more. Only now, attending the trial, did he realize that her intuition had told her well enough what happened at Grafeneck.

From the day these trials began, he felt as though he had half-swallowed a serpent that coiled around his tongue and stretched down his throat. Each time, just when he felt he was going to suffocate or vomit, the serpent let him have another breath or two. Try as he might, he neither could spit it out, nor swallow it fully. He had once tried to examine his throat using a pencil as a tongue depressor, half-expecting to see a black, tumorous growth.

Johann looked up to see the witness trying to stop himself from sobbing. The microphone amplified the noise, making it sound like the walls were whispering. After two or three minutes, the man took a deep breath, and began to talk as though he had said all this many times before, without pause or hesitation. His testimony filled the courtroom with its smothering, dull sound: "After that I was in the hospital for three weeks. My other comrades suffered from strong suppuration as a result of the operation. We had very little food in the hospital, and we had fleas and every other possible vermin. Every third week a selection was made. Sixty percent were taken away into the gas chamber. After that, the hospital was almost empty. I, then, volunteered for work, in spite of the fact that I was still a very sick man." A pause. Another deep breath. "The only reason why I volunteered was that I was afraid of the gas chambers. I then worked with the prison tailor. The rest of the comrades still remained in the hospital." The witness looked at the judges and said, "The selection took place in about the following manner: The block leader came into the room and reported, 'All Jews stand to attention.' All the sick had to get out of their beds, even those who were very ill, and they had to fall in completely naked. We had to stand to attention before an *SS* doctor with a high service grade. This doctor, however, did not see all the sick for he had to deal with thousands of persons. He only took the chart away from each sick person, and a day later, exactly during the most important Jewish holiday, sixty percent were transported into the gas chamber. The selections were always made by *SS* doctors."

'Yes,' Johann thought. 'I was there. I did that.'

"Later on," the witness continued, "I worked in the camp and was beaten very often. Also, I had very much work. On the 18th of January, we had to cover a great distance by foot. As many of us broke down, we were loaded into cattle wagons and transported to Dachau, without food. When we arrived at Dachau on January 28, 1945, forty to fifty percent were dead."

Johann forced himself to look at the witness. He closed his eyes when the witness began to weep. But he could not shut out the man's testimony, whispering now: "I feel very discouraged, and I am ashamed of my castration. The worst is that I have no future anymore. I eat very little, and in spite of that I am getting fat."

When Johann opened his eyes and looked again at the witness stand, the man was gone. An American military policeman stood against the wall by the door in the forced relaxation of his "at-ease," looking like he had been carved of wood and painted to resemble a human being, just for effect. The courtroom was silent.

When the presiding judge declared a recess, Johann watched the twenty-three defendants file out. Sullenness enveloped them like a cloud. The dull noise of muffled conversations, chairs scraping the floor, and shuffling feet filled the courtroom. The gallery emptied while he remained seated and closed his eyes again. 'Take deep breaths, Johann. Slow deep breaths,' he told himself. 'You must not faint. You must not faint! Remember, you helped Philipp. You tried to do what was right. In the end, you tried. You tried.' When everyone had gone, he got up stiffly and limped toward the basement door.

Another janitor caught up with him. "A woman in mourning gave this to the porter. He asked me to give it to you." Puzzled, Johann took the piece of paper and said a quick "*Danke schön*." At the bottom of the stairs, he read the note: "*Meet me at 5 p.m. in the St. Lorenz Kirche. H.*" He immediately recognized Helga's handwriting.

It took him nearly a half an hour to walk to the church. When a woman wearing black near the altar heard his footsteps, she rose, turned toward him, and lifted her veil. She began to cry. They embraced, but he held her with a stiffness that she did not understand. She did not want to let him go. When he stepped back, she saw how much older he looked. His skin was sallow. His eyes were sunken. His cheeks were hollow. He had deep creases in his forehead. His lower jaw seemed larger, his lips thinner. But it was her Johann. She tried to dry her eyes.

Before she could speak, he said, "I can't believe it. You are here. In Nuremberg. Why? When did you come back?"

"I never left."

"But you wrote that you were leaving to go to your sister, to Erika in Karlsruhe."

"That was just before the big bombing. I couldn't leave after that. No trains. And too many people needed help here."

"Where are you staying?"

"In our apartment. Our building escaped the bombs without too much damage. Every building around us is leveled. Many were killed. We were lucky. Poor *Frau* Bitzer, from downstairs—remember, with her hunchback? She was staying overnight with her daughter next door. Both killed in their basement's bomb shelter. Grandchildren, too. The Barschelders from upstairs were killed in the street. He, on the spot. She died before they got her to the hospital. The Sonderbergs—both dead, under the bridge. Other neighbors, too. So many. Everywhere in the city. Thousands they say. Who can say how many? So many lost. So many."

Helga reached out to touch him and caught her breath. "But I don't understand. Why didn't you come home? What are you doing as a janitor at the trial?"

He saw her eyes were asking other questions as well.

"I thought you had left Nuremberg," he said, looking away. "I got your letter saying you were going to leave for Karlsruhe. And I couldn't bear to see what had happened to our neighborhood. To our home. I couldn't bear it. I was afraid."

Helga had never heard him admit he was afraid. "The war is over," she said. "What are you afraid of?"

"It's over for some. Never for others. What am I afraid of?" He paused. Looking toward the altar, he said, "I dare not tell you, Helga."

"Why can't you tell me? Come home now. It's alright."

"No. I cannot go with you now. Not yet. Someday perhaps. Not yet."

She saw that he was trembling. "Sit down. We can talk here." She tried to control the rage inside her. She began to tremble, too.

Most of the church's windows were missing. Overhead, huge sections of the vaulted ceiling gaped open to the late afternoon's clouds. A mason's chisel rang in a staccato rhythm from somewhere outside. An old couple prayed in one of the side chapels. Votive candles flickered wildly. He put his hands in his overcoat pockets. She tried to take them out and hold them. He refused.

As calmly as she could, she said, "I had the feeling you would not want me to speak to you at the courthouse. You looked away every time I looked at you. That's why I wrote the note. You look ill."

"Your veil. Why are you still wearing mourning? Did Erika die?"

She gasped. "No, not for my sister. For you, Johann. For you." She heard her voice rising. "You died. At least that's what the official letter said. Addressed to me, "*Frau* Widow Johann Brenner, M.D." Right there on the envelope. Widow. I didn't even have to open it to know what it would say. How it got to me, I don't know. You died in Berlin, it said. In May '45. The letter came in December. Just before Christmas. I had no reason to doubt it. You never contacted me. Your last letter was almost a year before, in January. Before the war ended."

"There was no mail service after that," he said.

"But I didn't want to go to Karlsruhe, in case you never received my letter. I stayed here. I put up your photograph in the train station. I began working at the hospital, thinking you would come there. I asked neighbors to watch for you during the day. Then the official letter."

"I left my papers on a corpse in Berlin and took his. I grew this moustache to look more like him. Heinrich Westermann."

"Come home with me."

He saw the anger in her eyes. How she had aged. How tired she was. "I cannot, Helga. No. We must not be seen together. I will be recognized."

"What have you done? What has happened to you?"

He looked away.

She stared at him. "At the trial," she said, "I hear terrible things. Today, the witness…"

"Why are you going to the trial?"

She was silent for a long time. "I want to find out what it meant to be a doctor over these years. To find out more about you. And now it's a miracle. I find you at the trial." She began to weep again. "I want you to come back to me. I want us to live our lives together again. We have lost so much. But we can still build a life together. Please. I work at the hospital. You could work there. You are needed …."

"Helga…." He looked down, and then he turned toward the chapel where the old couple were crossing themselves and leaving. 'Helga, please, I must work this out by myself." He was speaking so quietly she could barely hear him.

"By yourself? By yourself? Do you think I am a suit of clothes you can put on or off at your whim? You've been here in Nuremberg for more than a year and you never even looked for me? A year and you let me think you were dead? And now you want me to go home alone and wait some more?"

"You must understand. I can't come home with you now. I have a bed in the courthouse. I work there. I get my meals there. I cannot tell you any more. I cannot. Not yet."

"No, you don't understand. I miss you." She reached out again to touch his cheek, but he pulled away. "Johann, please...," she whispered.

"No. I've told you all I can. I am afraid. I will be recognized. If we are seen together, some neighbor or patient or former colleague will recognize me. Then it won't be easy for you either. I don't have to tell you that I was a member of the Party."

"So? From the butcher to the mayor, who wasn't a member of the Party in Nuremberg? The denazification procedures are a joke. Only the highest-ranking Nazis—and then only the ones who couldn't offer up some forged documents—have any trouble. Doctors are needed now, Johann."

"From what you have read and heard today in the trial, you must know that..."

"You can trust me...." Helga tried to look into his eyes.

"Maybe I will try to write it down."

"And I should wait? Just wait? I have waited long enough. I will go to Erika in Karlsruhe. I won't wear mourning any more. You can stay here if you like. But I won't."

"You don't understand...."

"You never thought I could understand anything. Well, I understand that you are unable to help yourself and don't want me to help you. I won't waste any more time." She began to cry.

He tried to hold her arm but she pulled free, stood up and walked away. He almost got up to follow her. But he slumped back into the pew and watched her go down the aisle. He watched her pause in the church's shattered western door, silhouetted against the gray outside, and then she was gone.

*****

When the bombs fell, Helga could not leave Nuremberg. Like everyone else, she had to live by her wits to survive. A peasant woman whose husband had been Johann's patient needed someone to write a letter to the authorities about her two missing sons. Soon others came, too, asking her to write letters or complete forms or provide medical records. In exchange, each would bring her something—a few eggs, some potatoes, a piece of smoked meat, or a stick of firewood. She bartered away clothes for a can filled with lard and a pound of hard cheese. Her dressy shoes got her a half pound of tea in a metal box. She bartered some linens and the necklace of tiny pearls she was given by her mother at her confirmation for a sack of potatoes and some charcoal briquettes. She stashed it all—lard, cheese, tea, potatoes and briquettes—under her bed because she did not dare keep it in the basement. Each day she ate only one potato, which she fried in a bit of lard in a frying pan on her stove, and a thin slice of cheese. When the cheese and lard were gone, she roasted the potato in the stove. After she traded a neighbor ten potatoes for twenty candles, she did not dare burn the candles, lest their light attract drunken soldiers or robbers. One briquette in the parlor stove each night hardly made a difference, but she imagined herself warm enough until she went to bed. She turned her mirror to the wall, not wanting to see how thin she had become. Soon, she thought, Johann will be returning. Then things will be better. For a month, she waited in the station for every train rumored to be arriving from Berlin. The letter from Berlin arrived instead.

Helga's work at the hospital gave her some distraction. She saw so many others with a harder future. Hideously burned and blinded children. Young men with stumps for legs. A woman about her age whose lower jaw had been blown off, crying tears that saturated the bandages around what was left of her chin. She tried to feed them, to comfort all of them, to say some kind words to their few visitors. Mostly, she sat beside their beds in silence, not wanting to go home to her empty apartment. More than a year had passed since she believed her husband dead.

When she saw him that day in the courtroom, she could not believe it. Was that him, sitting there in a janitor's smock? He looked shrunken. Much older. If only he would stand up, she thought. If only he would take a few steps, she would know him by his limp. When the court recessed, she waited for him to leave, but he did not get up from his chair.

Finally, she scribbled the note and gave it to the porter at the front door. 'If it is him, he will come,' she told herself.

Waiting in the church, she worried that it would not be him. What would she say? What would she do? She did not pray so much as hope. Then he had come to her. When the rhythm of his steps on the stone aisle confirmed her hopes, she stopped herself from saying "amen." Instead, she held him as tightly as she could.

She was entirely unprepared for his not wanting to go home. She refused to believe it. For more than a dozen years, while the storm was raging, she had been patient. Only when it stopped, she reasoned, could one begin to find one's bearings, make a path, and see the sunshine restore the world's familiar shapes. Eventually, the storm must end. And now, when it finally had, he wanted her to be patient and endure still more.

*****

It was nearly dark. Wind swirled dust and bits of debris at every corner. He began walking away from the church back toward the old city gate and the road to the Palace of Justice. When he found a sheltered place to sit down, he began to chew on a slice of bread that he had put in his pocket. He tried not to think about Helga.

Around him, teenage girls, women in kerchiefs, and a few old men, their faces red from the cold, were sorting out bricks from bombed-out buildings and stacking them by the narrow-gauge tracks of an improvised railway in the street. It crisscrossed the city for some eighty-miles, transporting the rubble to more distant sorting piles, a rock crusher and a new brick factory. Did the past have to be crushed before the future could be built?

One old man standing apart from the others was using the handle of his cane to snag bricks off a heap far taller than he was. When two had tumbled down to his feet, he would pick them up and carry them over to the stack he had started some twenty feet away. He worked slowly, walking back and forth with a stiff, halting gait. Johann guessed the man to be in his mid-seventies. There was something familiar about him, but he could not decide what it was. A former patient? A neighbor before the war?

The old man never looked at him, as though moving the bricks to "his" stack by the street was his only concern in the universe. He was focused on a tangle of scorched and smashed bricks, broken glass, and shards from the soot-gray slate roof. The once solid lintel stone over the doorway—with its deeply incised letters, *Volksbank*, "People's Bank"—lay cracked in three parts in the debris on the barely visible granite steps. Johann's eyes widened when realized that this was the *Volksbank* where he and Helga had kept their savings.

He began to study the old man's routine. Anything to forget the pain of his meeting with her. He guessed that there were over five thousand bricks in the pile. He divided that by the time the old man took to carry two bricks to his stack: thirty bricks per hour. If the old man worked six hours a day, six days a week—that seemed reasonable—he could move the pile in twenty-one days, finishing just before Christmas.

He had had this habit since childhood. Estimating things. Estimating time. How long would it take for a hive of bees to pollinate an orchard? How long would it take a dripping icicle to overflow a thawing flower box hanging outside his bedroom window in Pohlendorf, the town where he grew up? How many steps would it take to walk through the park on his way to the policlinic in Nuremberg, if he stayed in the middle of the path? How many more or fewer if he stayed on one or the other of its edges?

'Twenty-one days,' he thought, 'twenty-one days to put some order back the world. By Christmas. The old man is doing it. Why can't I?'

He had been a physician. He was trained to diagnose illness. He knew he was ill. Confused, miserable, lost. Broken like the buildings in this city he once loved. He knew that he needed to examine the choices he had made—to see the consequences of each upon the next, in order to diagnose his condition. He decided to write a letter to Helga.

CHAPTER TWO
𝔖𝔭𝔦𝔡𝔢𝔯𝔰 𝔥𝔞𝔱𝔠𝔥𝔢𝔡

Dearest Helga!

I fear I have lost my soul—and now you. For too long, fear has shamed me into silence. Now I must tell you what I have seen, what I have done, what I know others have done. Why I thought I was doing so much good and instead did so much harm.

I don't know where it all began. Was it in Munich while I was still studying medicine, when I first heard with my own ears the hissing hatred that has brought this ruin down upon us? Was it in the first World War? Was it still before that? Oh, my beloved, even if it all began long before we met, I must find the place and the time when I chose, when we Germans chose our terrible future.

I remember shadows. And in those shadows, spiders hatched. Venomous terrors were born. I know. I was one.

The girls, the women and the old man clearing the rubble left when it got dark. Johann stayed. Sitting on the broken lintel of what remained of the *Volksbank* in Nuremberg, he remembered a similar night some twenty-five years earlier, in Munich. He was living with his parents and finishing his medical studies at the university. His wounds from

21

the first war had healed. He thought he was well. Looking back, he knew he was not. He remembered his discontent, his anger, his fears. He remembered hearing a speaker whose passion seared into him like acid. Whose message ensnared him, not so much for its meaning as for the certainty with which it was said. He occasionally had heard similar thoughts and ignored them. But that was before the unthinkable surrender in 1918 had made him vulnerable.

*****

The war ended in disaster. It galled him that revolution and anarchy seemed reasonable to millions. He was stunned when the communists prevailed. That red flags, for him the symbol of something monstrous, hung from buildings and lampposts. He cheered when the conservatives fought back. Cheered, when the revolutionary leaders fled for their lives. Took heart, when hundreds were shot and thousands imprisoned, since he firmly believed them to be traitors and villains. Was jubilant when their red flags were trampled underfoot. He drank to the health of the bankers and policemen, small shopkeepers and military officers who were congratulating themselves on overcoming the menace. He agreed with religious leaders who declared that God was pleased.

When the terms of the Treaty were announced, he shared in the national outrage and dismay. But he had little contact with what was welling up in Germany's beer halls and basements. He knew but vaguely of the zealots, with their new flags and ancient symbols, who were desperate for the birth—or what they thought was the "re-birth"—of a heroic Germany. Like them, he had immeasurable pride in the *Volk*'s glorious past. Yes, the *Volk* was in a struggle for its survival. And yes, it was superior to the other races. All that was incontrovertible. Everything that he had been taught, read and saw reinforced his pride as a German. But he gave little thought to the zealots' complaints and proposals when he saw their handbills and placards. If they shouted that they would make theirs a world order to outlast all before it, that their ends justified any means, well, it was just a healthy enthusiasm for their cause. No more significant than fans at a soccer match, cheering on their team.

Johann did not think of himself as one of those desperate men in whom the war's anger still boiled. One of those millions to whom the war still gave meaning and purpose. If he was more on their side than any other, it was only because he shared their understanding of patriotism and loyalty. But he was too preoccupied with putting his own life back together to join their protests. He merely watched their parades, saw the fierce intensity in their eyes, and walked on. He was a man of science, studying medicine. Calm. Thoughtful. Devoted to reason. Above politics and passion. Until that December night.

He was going to meet his childhood friend and fellow medical student, Philipp Stein, for a beer in the "Golden Stork." Then back to the seminar room in the university clinic for two or three more hours' study. Philipp told him he would meet him after nine, near the jeweler's on the *Marktstraße*, around the corner from the tavern. "I want to show you a wrist watch in the shop window," he said.

When Johann arrived, Philipp was nowhere to be seen. Instead, he saw a milling crowd of twenty or so huddled before a man who stood on the front steps of the jewelry shop. Most were veterans still in uniform. One or two wore suit-coats, white shirts and black neckties under their over-coats. A yellow light, the only light still burning on the street aside from the one over the "Golden Stork," a half-dozen doors away at the corner, shone down on the speaker's head and spread his shadow over the steps and the men standing closest to him. Waiting for Philipp on the edge of the crowd, Johann could not help but hear the speech. Without his knowing how, the speaker's frenzy and the listeners' enthusiasm slowly captured him.

The speaker began softly, slowly, his voice soothing in its timbre. He started each sentence almost inaudibly, but then his voice grew louder, its cadence an hypnotic rhythm. As his pace quickened, his tone rose into a rasping staccato. He began to jab the air and gesture wildly. His eyes widened. The crowd swayed with his voice, falling and rising with each shrill exclamation. They seemed to be held up by strings the speaker had contrived to hang from above their heads. He spat out his words like sharp-edged rocks. Clauses twisted in and out, wrapped around nouns and adjectives, were laced together with prepositions and adverbs, followed by more adjectives and nouns—every word heavy with hatred. Johann felt the need to dodge when the sentences finished with verbs that were hurled like fiery torches. He winced when the speaker sliced the air with his arm, stabbed it, pierced it, strangled it with gestures that seemed to take hold of an invisible enemy and slaughter him on the spot. No one was turning away. They all wanted more, craving the thrill and power it brought them.

The speaker was shouting now, his voice shrill, his eyes wider than before. Johann remembered seeing a mangy dog on the Western front, barking fiercely into a shell hole at some unseen threat. "Why had Germany lost the War? The Jews. Who profited from the Dictated Peace at Versailles? The Jews. Why was Germany suffering now? The Jews. Why were Germans poor? The Jews. Why were Germans out of work? The Jews. Who was conniving to steal what wealth the Germans did have? The Jews. Who keeps Germany from its true destiny? The Jews!"

To each question the crowd shouted the expected answer: *"die Ju-den!""die Ju-den!""die Ju-den!"* They pursed their lips and dragged out the syllables—*Juuu-den, Juuuu-den, Juuuu-den!*—into a twisted kiss. A poisonous bite by an ancient serpent.

The speaker, a short, chalky-faced, pale-eyed, narrow shouldered man, never looked at any of them directly. He looked up at the night sky, up and down the street. He pointed his finger toward the heavens. He clenched his fist. He raised his hands above his head, like a victorious champion. And as he did, the light over the jewelry store's doorway cast a shadow that turned his face into a skull.

Johann forgot about Philipp. He forgot about going back to the reading room in the university. He forgot about his promise to his mother to come home early and get some sleep. Something inside him told him to get away. But his leg was stiff. He had only managed a dozen steps away from the crowd when he heard a loud cheer. He looked back to see the electric light burst with a popping sound, then fall to the pavement, its glass tinkling. The shop's windowpane shattered immediately afterward, and the crowd cheered again, louder than before.

At the sound of a police whistle, he walked as fast as he could until he found himself on a park bench. There he sat. Moonlight pierced the clouds at intervals, turning the world around him into black and white. The church bell struck the next hour, one solitary throbbing tone, like a cry for help cut short.

The low voices that he had heard at the edge of the *Stadtpark* had given way to snores. Occasionally, the wind would bring him the faint humming of some somber tune he could not identify, the audible longings of a sleepless old soldier. He felt the presence all around him of lost men, adrift and aimless since the war: the *Freikorps*, the "volunteer corps" that had gathered and camped out by the thousands in Germany's parks and railroad yards and fields, especially here in Munich. Like homing pigeons unable to find their homes, forced to be satisfied to huddle in a cage at the convenience of some unfathomable master. Artillery shells waiting to be used, purposeless without war to give them direction. They had forgotten or lost the futures they had promised themselves. They could not imagine themselves now without their uniforms. Could not imagine resuming whatever before the war had been a normal life. They would be soldiers as long as they lived. He counted himself lucky not to be one of them, to have escaped whatever it was that held them captive. He still lived at home. He wore a shirt his mother ironed for him each day, the trousers she mended for him, the four-button dark wool jacket of his father's wedding suit, which fit him well enough. He had a purpose in his life. He should be home, asleep in his own warm bed.

When, on the bench, he eventually drifted into a troubled sleep, he relived the nightmare of the battle in which he was wounded. He awoke with a start at the noise of a shell exploding in his dream, his head still pulsing with what he had heard by the jewelry store on *Marktstraße*. Of late he had made a point of avoiding the street demonstrations that had become common in Munich since the end of the war. Whether social-ist, communist, pacifist, anarchist, or some indefinable combination of all those passions—all made him uncomfortable. Who were these self-appointed saviors haranguing the crowds with their visions of the future? The anarchists and the pacifists were living in a dreamland, harmless enough, even charming in their childishness. More dangerous were the socialists. Good riddance to Eisner!

Just after Eisner's assassination, he had told Philipp that it had been a blessing, that Eisner's socialism would destroy Bavaria and contaminate all of Germany. Philipp seemed to agree, but not as strongly as he thought he should. Two months later, in the aftermath of the assassination, when the communists declared the Bavarian Soviet Republic, he had told Philipp, "From bad to worse. Now we're in the hands of devils. Blood-red devils!" Again, Philipp had disappointed him by not appearing to share his agitation. Sitting on the park bench now, Johann shook his head. The moonlight slanted starkly between passing clouds. A sudden wind rattled through the bushes behind him. He remembered their conversation about what had happened after Eisner was shot.

"Don't you see? Communism is insane," he had said. "An absurdity. Socialism gone crazy. Both would deprive mankind of the natural feeling of satisfaction in accomplishments. Both want to reduce us to the lowest common denominator. I'm not willing to be brought down to the level of a rag picker. The level of a sluggard good-for-nothing. A wastrel." He remembered looking at Philipp for some sign of encouragement. When there was none, he went on. "Socialism and communism block us from the acquisition and protection of beautiful things. Both deny human nature. Both deny God. Both..."

"Stop, Johann. I know what you are trying to say." Philipp raised his eyebrows into a look that he might have given a patient in the field hospital, then smiled.

Johann remembered thinking that Philipp did not take him seriously. "Let me finish," he had said. "Both would insinuate themselves between members of a family, between the proper relationship of man and wife. Both would give everyone the illusion that he or she was equally entitled to anything, no matter who had earned it. It would pit a woman against her husband." He remembered being hoarse.

Philipp took advantage of the pause. "I don't think you have a full grasp...."

Johann interrupted him. "Where would we, where would future doctors be if we are held to be equal to everyone else?"

"We're not doctors yet," Philipp had chided. "Now calm down. I might have to call a doctor."

"No. Listen. Why don't you see the seriousness of this? You're always trying to make a joke." He saw Philipp smile and could not resist smiling, too. He had wanted to go on about how doctors were specially gifted, with special responsibilities, and therefore were entitled to special rewards. But he knew Philipp was not listening, that he was amazed and bewildered by his outburst. And he remembered that he also was amazed that he had allowed himself to become so passionate. But how could Bavaria be a Soviet Republic? It was like honey being bitter!

The violent overthrow of the communists in Munich had brought him great relief. He felt some pity for the hundreds shot in the streets by the *Freikorps*, possibly by some of those men sleeping near him now in the park, but he had seen no other way to restore order. The revolutionaries had to pay the price for their foolishness. They should have known better than to try to force something unnatural on the world.

He would have said that politics was not an important a topic for him or for his classmates and professors. At best, it was the subject of an occasional conversation, easily dropped because they all shared the same assumptions and attitudes. It was proper, he thought, that their intellectual energies and passions focused on new medical procedures. If their more casual discussions concerned automobiles and airplanes, cigars, or where to go for a beer, and avoided politics and religion, that was as it should be for men of science. Politics were beneath them. Let others who were willing to get their hands dirty and their principles corrupted play those games in Germany's back alleys and smoky beer-halls.

But he did have political opinions. Where he had gained his political opinions, he could not say. He knew that some had come from his father, but he could not remember explicitly discussing politics with him more than a few times in his life. He recalled something his father said to him when he was ten or eleven: "Christianity promises us equality in the next world, not in this one. Marx was a sinner. Worse, a Jew." He could not remember now why his father had said this, or what he had replied. Just that it led him to think that political values were connected to religious beliefs. Still, his father knew that Philipp was Jewish and had encouraged their friendship. "There are Jews and there are Jews," his father said. "Little Philipp's father works hard for a living. That's what matters."

Johann learned early in his life that Philipp and his family were good Jews. And so were the Semmelbergs, who had a little general store where he and Philip bought candy. The Steins and the Semmelbergs were exceptions to the rule. He knew there were other Jews in Pohlendorf, but he knew none of them. As for Jews in general, knew what everyone believed. They had betrayed the Son of God. They were clannish and stubborn, with their different customs and peculiarities. And cheats, greedy, money grubbing. Unscrupulous. Untrustworthy. Outsiders. All this had been in the air for centuries. He gave these attitudes no more thought than breathing.

Johann also knew that his father thought all of Germany should be like their Bavaria. "If only our kings were Lutherans," he was fond of saying, "Bavaria would be heaven on earth!" His father's pride in his Lutheran heritage—"The Brenners learned their faith from Luther himself!" was another of his father's frequent sayings—was more like pride in family history than an active religious commitment. "Our Catholic neighbors are not that smart. They believe everything their priests tell them. They can't read the Bible!" But just the same, his father found an excuse for not going to Pohlendorf's tiny Lutheran church whenever he could. They were one of the few Lutheran families in the predominantly Catholic town. The men he sat with on Sunday afternoons in the tavern or on the town's square talked about their religious traditions only indirectly, when they made jokes about the town's priests or its young Lutheran pastor.

Like his father, Johann grew up thinking of himself as Lutheran, but had little to do with the church. When he was twelve or thirteen, he would have been glad to stay away, although his mother insisted that he go with her and his younger brother and sister to services each week. If he thought of himself as different from the other boys in his school, it was because they had different religious instruction and went to different churches. Thinking about such things during the war, he came to the conclusion that his friendship with Philipp may have developed because they both were non-Catholics.

And like his father, Johann would have been happy not to vote. Democracy in general fit them both like a celluloid collar—something they would have been glad to fling off at the first opportunity. When the two men did vote the first time, going together to the polls in 1921, they marked their ballots for the *Deutsche Volkspartei,* the German People's Party, primarily because of its opposition to the terms of the Versailles Treaty and because they didn't trust the socialists.

"We have to vote, otherwise the Socialists will sell us to the French," he told his father.

Afterwards, the old man said, "Louis III was not on the ballot. The whole lot can jump in the Danube for all I care. A waste of time."

Johann's political views were reinforced by his history teacher, *Doktor* Schmidt, at the *Gymnasium.* One of his fondest school memories was history class, when "Old Schmidterl" would energetically condemn anything and everything except the "noble Bavarian monarchy and the blessings it has brought to our people." The boys soon came to know this phrase as the tag end of every day's lesson, whether on the ancient Allemani or in a welcome digression on the "noble red-skinned chiefs" of America.

He also absorbed some general political ideas from his conversations with *Pfarrer* Bosch, as ardent a patriot as he was a Lutheran pastor. Johann would not have admitted that he enjoyed going to the required weekly religion class, but he admired Bosch's playful, enthusiastic nature. Bosch was just ten years older than Johann, more like an older brother.

"So, Hansl, where were you last Sunday?" Bosch asked him, as the boys were walking out of the classroom. "Might have done you some good to kneel in church."

"You think I haven't anything to do but listen to you?" Johann said, screwing up his face. "I already know what you are going say up there on the pulpit." Those boys close enough to hear him were astounded. But when Bosch began to laugh uncontrollably, they all joined in.

"All right, next Sunday, Hansl Brenner, I might invite you up to speak for me. The Lord tells us that there's wisdom in the mouth of babes. In this case, I am a Thomas."

"Watch out, *Herr Pfarrer*. I might surprise you," Johann replied. Bosch laughed even louder.

Through the rest of the week, Johann feared that he might be called up to the pulpit and even began thinking about what he would say. But Bosch gave his sermon as usual, winking once at Johann when he said that doubting would lead to faith, just as St. Thomas overcame his doubt when he saw his resurrected Lord.

When Bosch was killed in Belgium in the first month of the war, Johann could not understand why so good a man could be killed so young, in war or any other way. He remembered the gasp of the congregation and the startled look on his mother's face when *Pfarrer* Melchior announced the news. After that, he rarely went to church.

Johann remembered his childhood as though it was on the other side of a deep, unbridgeable chasm. As for heaven, he still believed what he had been taught, that it was up there, beyond the branches high above the park bench where he now sat, unthinkably far beyond the icy moon. He could still hear Bosch telling him and the other boys in religion class that this world was like a train station, that it was important to get on the right train, the only train that would go to heaven and an eternal life.

Now as he sat among the shadows in a park in Munich, he shook his head. 'I've got time enough to get on that train. I survived the war. Before I think about the next world, I've got to make something of myself in this one.'

He heard someone walking on the other side of the park's wall—on *Tegernstraße*, he thought. Footsteps mingled with the sound of whistling that rose and fell as though it was made by the wind. At some point, the sounds formed a military march that he knew but could not name.

The whistler did not know the whole tune, or couldn't be bothered with whistling all its parts. He repeated the chorus over and over, monotonous, mechanical, lifeless. After a while, the footsteps and whistling slowly vanished.

In the intervals when the wind died down, there was still no silence. The snoring of the sleeping veterans filled the night with an eerie, low buzzing. He tried to drown out the noise with his own breathing. And now someone was coming on a bicycle along the street behind the wall. The bicycle's chain clanked louder and louder, a rising crescendo of rhythmic sounds, metal on metal, then gave way, a diminuendo, disappearing around a corner, just like the whistler's. Maybe a baker's apprentice was going to work, too sleepy to do anything but pedal.

Baking would be good work, he thought. The warm ovens. The clean table. The pure flour. The living, rising dough. The smell of the baking bread. Beginning each day by making something needed. Why couldn't it be that easy for all of them? Why couldn't the world be so simple? Bakers would be bakers. Doctors would be doctors. Both would do good work, nourishing work, work that was clean and pure and sustaining and life giving. These forlorn veterans, he thought, sleeping in parks and fields across Germany want nothing more than a reason to live and do good work, just like everyone else. Why isn't it easy? When moonlight flooded over him for an instant, he smiled faintly, imagining it was so. Then the shadows on the path started shifting again.

No, if ever there was such a world, it was in the olden days, the distant past, or in the days yet to come, the distant future. It was not now. Not here. It was somewhere else, far away, on the other side of time. Like childhood, or heaven. He thought again about *Pfarrer* Bosch. Was the train that had taken him to the war and his death on the same track as the train that he said would take him to heaven? All he could do was hope that it was so.

*****

He remembered the train rides he had taken in his own life. One had taken him from his childhood in Pohlendorf to the war. Another had brought him home, wounded, a man. If there was any happy memory for him in the war, it was when he stepped on the train headed for boot camp, waving his good-byes to his family, alongside his comrades, waving to their families with the same enthusiasm. And another memory, this one bitter: his anger that Germany had not yet won the war when he came home. Two moments: one at the beginning, of excitement; and one at the end, of misery. Disappointment followed both.

It seemed like centuries since he had wanted to go to war. His schoolmates all planned to enlist together, to be in the same platoon, to serve their *Vaterland* and gain glory. Wouldn't they all look grand in their uniforms? Of course they would all get medals. Of course they would all be heroes.

None of that happened. Even their uniforms looked different from what they had imagined. Worse, he was separated from his schoolmates right after boot camp. Philipp Stein and Christian Gerstner, his two closest friends did not even pass the military physical with the rest of the class. Philipp finally had talked his way into a uniform and was sent off to France and guard duty. Christian was a frail youth who looked twelve, rather than eighteen. No one knew what had happened to him once he was drafted in the last year of the war.

After just three weeks of training—mostly drills, learning how to crawl in mud below barbed wire and machine gun fire—he found himself on a beach north of Ostend, spotting planes over the Channel. When he complained to his superior officer that he wanted to go to the front and see action, that he wanted to serve the *Kaiser* in battle, the man just laughed. "Don't worry, boy. There's action enough here. If you want to get wounded or killed, you'll have plenty of opportunity. Brawls. Exploding ammunition dumps. Truck and train accidents. Yes, your mother will thank me." Johann was not consoled.

A few days later, he thought his chance to become a hero had arrived. On a foggy, early September morning, he shouted out, "Four enemy planes coming over from the northwest! No, five! Six! Six British Bristols! No, more!" He raced over to the telegraph operator who clicked out the warning. But when they went outside and looked for the planes, all they could see was a flock of seabirds approaching the breakwater.

In October, his company was sent south, near Douai. But instead of going on to the front, Johann's unit stayed behind the rest, setting up in a bombed-out train station about five miles north of the city. He was made a clerk, armed with rubber stamps, ledger books and wire baskets. His special assignment was accounting for the wounded. All bandaged up and covered in their sheets, they looked like so many loaves of bread. Johann organized their papers, checked them off lists, stamped the lists and put them in envelopes, one for each carload. There was no end to the work.

Train after train came and went. Trains came from Germany with new troops. The men got off and marched away. The empty cars were sent back with the wounded. He heard an occasional groan or cry of pain, but most were drowned out by the noise of the engine. Back and forth, night and day. He got so that he knew without looking up what kind of engines were pulling in and how long the train was, just by listening to the clanking over the separation in the tracks outside the station window. Sometimes, empty coffins, smelling of fresh lumber, the nail-heads still shiny, would be unloaded from the boxcars, replaced by coffins smelling differently. He measured his time in trains. This was not war, he thought. This was more like the work that went on behind the scenes at an opera, moving props and adjusting the lights, dropping the curtain or making the sound of thunder. He wanted to be in the war, not behind it.

He had not carried a gun since boot camp. He had grown used to sleeping in a bunk, dry and sound, upstairs in the train station. The toilet worked. There were potatoes and cabbages and even eggs and chicken to eat, not the watery, gray stew of the trenches. Every tenth day, he was off duty. He wrote home often, and received prompt replies. He began to think he would live that way for the rest of his life.

Everything changed in the first phase of First Quarter Master General Ludendorff's desperate spring offensive. Johann was assigned battle duty in a unit in northwest France. For ten days, German shells whined overhead and fell on the enemy's trenches like a fiery waterfall. Then came gas. His unit moved swiftly out of St. Quentin toward the British line. It dissolved before them. But shattered German bodies lay here and there in no-man's-land, pointing the way. His was one of them.

He was wounded in the first wave of the assault, just a few yards beyond his trench, even before he got to no-man's-land. He had tripped over a strand of German barbed wire and fell face first into the mud. A shell exploded in front of him, just where he would have been had he not fallen. One piece of shrapnel struck him in the shoulder; another his left leg. "Superficial wounds. No need for amputation," he heard someone say through his screaming. He was one of the first to be evacuated.

He remembered clenching his teeth as someone poured alcohol along his back and on his calf. The searing pain knocked him out. He came to, propped up on a cot somewhere in a small church whose windows had been blown out by bombs.

He recovered slowly, escaping the greatest danger, blood poisoning, while others around him died in not always silent agony. His shoulder healed first. His leg was more troublesome. A jagged scar stiffened his calf muscle. The nerves were damaged, too. He might be lame for life, an orderly told him without emotion: "A limp is better than a stump."

Then everyone was loaded on a train only to be stopped a few miles away and put into another church, just slightly larger than the first, but with its windows intact. Around him men lay moaning on cots, their heads bandaged tightly, in some cases right over their eyes, or with stumps for legs or arms. One soldier near him kept his head under his blanket and whimpered like a dog. After several hours trying to endure the man's moaning, he shouted, "Will you stop it! Be a man! Be a German!" The other invalids just looked at him until he muttered an apology.

When he heard the news some three weeks later that *Operation Michael* had been a great victory for Germany, he stood up by his cot for the first time with the support of a crutch. French reserves had stopped the German advance, but not before it had gained forty miles. All praise to

God! Cheers for the *Kaiser*! Cheers for General Ludendorff! Cheers for the *Vaterland*! The war will be over soon. Germany, Victorious!

By the end of May he was on a train going back to Bavaria, a train that passed through a station just like the one where he had stamped out the papers for wounded men. From Namur, the train went slowly eastwards, moving an hour, stopping for two, then starting again. When it finally crossed the border into the Prussian *Rhineland*, he cheered with the rest of the wounded men in his railway car.

Johann was not sure that he wanted to be going home. He knew his medal would please his mother and father. His younger brother and sister would want to hold it and show it to their friends. He looked forward to seeing his family again. But he despised his cane and planned to throw it away as soon as he could. He could hear his father tell him that it was a badge of honor, an emblem of his sacrifice for the *Vaterland*. But he found it a sign of weakness, of loss.

A boy waved a German flag and handed him a newspaper through the train window during the stop in Frankfurt. It proclaimed still greater successes on the front and an imminent victory: "*Only Forty Miles to Paris*," "*General Ludendorff Confident*," "*French Troops Broken!*"

After another day's stop on a siding somewhere east of the *Frankenwald*, the train started up again. By the time they neared Munich, the newspapers were scoffing at the arrival of American troops, soft and untrained. "Imagine," Johann told another wounded soldier, "after all we have seen and done, we are going to miss Germany's inevitable triumph, marching with our comrades into Paris!" The man agreed: "This train is going in the wrong direction, away from victory instead of toward it." Soon a chant arose among all the men in the car, "Toward Victory! Toward Victory! Toward Paris!" Johann shouted as loudly as he could.

His fever returned and he was kept another three weeks in a military hospital near Munich. His mother and father took the train from Pohlendorf and visited him on each Sunday. Together they sat in silence in the hospital garden. Johann felt too tired to answer their questions.

His first day at home, eating his mother's cooking and looking out the window of his bedroom at the ancient apple tree in bloom, was happy. But everyone looked so thin. And Pohlendorf was desolate. So many women wore black. Even the bells at the *Marienkirche* sounded hollow. He went for a walk along the town's narrow streets, avoiding shadows, corners, confining spaces. He felt he was looking through the people who greeted him and wanted to speak with him. When he came home, he went straight to his bed. That night and many afterwards were terrifying. He dreaded the nightmares they would bring.

The headlines in the newspaper sustained him. The French would surrender any day now. If not in July, then in August. At the latest, by September. Then the *Kaiser* would proclaim a new holiday for all of Germany. Then, he thought, all this confusion, this gloom would disappear. The war had gone on too long—longer than anyone had imagined. But it would soon be over, and worth it.

He sat by the church in the town's square in the late summer afternoons with four other veterans—he with his cane, another with a missing foot and an empty stare, a third with dark glasses and a scar that stretched below them and around his deformed chin, a fourth with a stump just below his shoulder. They were missing the end of the war, missing Germany's long awaited victory, by a few months. Just their luck!

Three years later, sitting on the park bench in Munich in the middle of the night, he still could not comprehend how Germany could have lost the war. He remembered how he had read the impossible words, printed in red ink, at the end of October: "*Government in Berlin resigns!*" "*Mutiny erupts in the German navy at Kiel!*" "*Armistice!*" The headlines might as well have been written in blood. The exclamation points, daggers.

The trenches that his comrades had cut in the enemy's land at the beginning of the war and which they had vowed never to abandon had filled with their corpses. The train station and the remains of the village north of Douai, where he had spent nearly three years recording the boxcars of living and dead, had been re-taken. The Belgian beach near Ostend, where he spent the first few months of the war, was now quiet, he supposed, and calm except for the rhythm of the waves and the calls of seabirds on the shore.

When the November revolution broke out in Munich before the armistice took effect, he had just regained his ability to walk several steps without his cane. Two days later he read the glaring headlines: "*Kaiser abdicates! Flees to Holland!*" There could not have been more chaos in Johann's mind. 'How could the *Kaiser* abdicate? How could he flee?' Johann could not accept that a provisional government, that any German government would agree to an armistice. Even more impossible in his mind was that a red flag could fly over Munich. 'After all the sacrifice we have made for victory, now an armistice? Impossible! Outrageous!'

He had tried to put a good twist on it. An armistice, he and his friends said to each other reassuringly, well, good. "No, better than good," he had said. "We can gather our dead and wounded. Catch our breath. Then, come the spring, Ludendorff and Hindenburg will lead us to Paris. A glorious summer in Paris! It will happen. It must. Therefore, it will." His comrades, with their missing limbs and disappointed lives, had nodded and cheered, huddling in the November wind. And when he had shouted above their cheers, "Germany's destiny demands victory. Nothing less!" pigeons on the little square took flight.

*****

Those three tumultuous years had passed. His beloved, eternal Bavarian monarchy had disappeared like cigarette smoke in a railway car, sucked out an opened window. His Germany was broken. Centuries of tradition had been ground to dust. Centuries of hope and work and sacrifice lay like the chalky dirt in the gravel on the park path at his feet. Lifeless. Meaningless. His Germany had endured three years now of the cursèd peace. If the war's beginning seemed like last week, its end was not yet in sight.

Where was justice? Where was God? What evil force had caused this calamity? The *Volk* and the *Vaterland* must have been betrayed. But by whom?

He was bewildered by the radio's loud music. By the bizarre ideas he read in the newspapers. By Pohlendorf's lifeless streets and vacant shops.

37

By his parents' sudden decision, as his father's business declined, to sell their home and move to a cramped apartment in Munich. Underneath it all, he knew, was the war. It had infected everything. Everywhere a sweet-sour smell, acrid, piercing. The smell of disease and ferment. Rot and dung.

Most veterans still wore the shadow of the war more tightly than any suit of clothes. They had lost their purpose, their future. Johann hesitated to look at himself in the mirror, for fear that he, too, would have angry, bitter, or hollow eyes. He saw them begging on Munich's main streets. Some leaned on their single crutch, an empty pant-leg pinned up to the waist, and limped a few steps after each passerby. Others sat on little wheeled planks and pushed themselves along, trying to avoid the cobblestone crossings or the pits and cracks in the sidewalks. A young, blind man still in uniform was holding on to the arm of a child who was walking too quickly, trying to reassure him that there was nothing in the way. The war was not over for any of them.

Until this night, he had tried to convince himself that he was not one of these ghosts. He thought he had left the war behind, with a medal and a stiff leg as souvenirs. But his scars were deep and his memories were cutting as shards of glass. Now, if anything was clear to him, it was that the war was not like an obsolete locomotive, shut down and rusting on a siding in the corner of a railway yard. No, it was still in motion, perhaps invisible, but still moving, pulling them all along. 'What if it doesn't stop for as long as I live? How will we ever be able to get off?"

This night he could not bring himself to go upstairs to his family's apartment, to go past his parents' bedroom door and down the hallway to the bedroom he shared with his little brother. Despite the hour, his mother would hear him coming in and get up, put on her robe and offer to make him tea. "No, Mama. I don't want any tea. Go back to bed. Please." His father would snore sharply and wake with a start: "Ottilie? What is it? Ottilie? Is Johann home?" Then he'd get up too, and tea would be unavoidable.

This night more than others, he feared getting undressed and going to bed. But if he did not go home until everyone was awake and having breakfast, his mother would scold him for wearing the same clothes two days in a row. He would have to admit he had just come home, or lie and say he had put them back on by mistake. Then Rudi and Angelika would come into the kitchen and ask him silly questions, laughing and giggling, until their father shushed them and said his usual, "We do not play games at mealtime, children."

Any other time, Johann would have welcomed these familiar rituals. He had often gone home late, fallen asleep in his clothes, awakened abruptly, and then hurried through his breakfast before going off to the lecture hall. His mother's scolding had not mattered then. One morning she had teased him by saying that she appreciated how he saved her doing laundry and that the professor would recognize him more easily in the same clothes. The laughter was particularly loud, even from his father.

Near Douai, before he was wounded, he had forced himself not to give much thought to the contents of the pine coffins or the wounded men that he recorded in the train station. Each coffin, each wounded or dead soldier was a single-line entry on a list. Only when he was himself on such a list did he see how they all were at the mercy of their damaged bodies, blinded, burned, robbed of their limbs. That they needed a doctor until it was too late to need anyone but a priest or a pastor. That's when he decided to study medicine. The idea kept him sane. For several nights afterwards, he fell asleep imagining himself on a podium, receiving a medal, amidst the cheers of a surrounding crowd of grateful, healthy patients.

His father enthusiastically supported him during his studies, even though it was a drain on the family's dwindling resources. Medicine was more respectable than Friedrich Brenner's occupation as a traveling salesman of parts for fine watches to the watchmakers in his district of Bavaria. His pride and ambition for his son had begun much earlier, when the boy's teachers had said he was worthy of a *Gymnasium* education to prepare for university study, rather than the commercial or trade schooling more common among boys of his class. 'Medicine will provide my Johann with a more secure future than any businessman can expect. No one will give him a sales quota or make him compete with crooks fobbing off shoddy goods,' he thought. He had raised his son to believe in honesty and hard work: "You do this because it is right, because you must if you want to succeed. But even if you don't succeed, you will always know you have done what is right." Johann had only to look at his father to hear his words.

He had no great difficulties with his studies. He soon realized that medical school required more obedience than intelligence. While he did not excel, he worked as hard as he could and found satisfaction in his level of success. That more than anything else helped to separate him in his mind from the veterans sleeping in the park.

In that harrowing December night at the jewelry store, he had become confused again. He still wanted to be a doctor, a leader. But now, sitting on the park bench, he saw that he wanted to be told what to do, to be led.

Johann had thought he despised the herd. When his *Gymnasium* class read in Nietzsche's *Thus Spake Zarathustra* that the true man soars above his inferiors, their eyes glowed and a flush of perspiration appeared on their brows. Their teacher fanned their zeal. They all swore never to be like sheep. While a sixteen-year-old could make such promises, he now understood how simple-minded that was: not everyone could be a leader; nor should everyone want to be one. To follow a strong leader was good, too. It showed loyalty and honor, responsibility and selflessness. Leader and led joined each other in a holy, ennobling bond, each giving the other greater strength than he would have had alone. This strength, he now saw, was what he had felt in the war. In the chaos that followed the war, this lesson seemed all the more urgent.

That night at the jewelry story, he witnessed another legacy of the war. The men in the crowd seemed not to care that they were followers. They cheered the speaker's every word. He was astounded to see them give themselves up to the speaker in a kind of sexual act, letting themselves be caressed, stroked, and then brought to rapture by his power. How thrilled they were to be caught up in a common belief. And he saw how the speaker by himself, without the willing crowd, was meaningless, an absurdity. How the crowd, not the leader, held power and raised him up like a hero on their shoulders. Supporting a leader who told them what to do might be as close as those in the crowd would ever come to feeling powerful, to taking control of their destiny. Even if it meant giving up everything they believed in, and being told what they should believe from now on.

At that point in his life, Johann did not believe that Germany's problems could be blamed on the Jews. He knew some Jews were living in much worse conditions than his family or friends. And what about those Jews who were killed fighting for Germany, like Philipp's Uncle Max? Or those Jews whose philanthropy was feeding widows and orphans right here in Munich? No, it defied reason to think that the Jews were so powerful, so cunning, and so self-serving as to cause Germany's defeat. Why would they want to anyway? Blaming them was too simple.

He had tried to make this point in a discussion with his schoolmates in the first or second year of *Gymnasium*, when one of the boys had insulted Philipp for being a "Jewish traitor like Judas." It was "stupid" to think like that, Johann had said. He was inclined to think well of everyone, to judge an individual on his own merits and not to lump people together into groups. This was certainly how he remembered himself in his school days.

Still, what explained all this misery and suffering throughout the *Vaterland*? Although he did not know the answer, that night in the park Johann was struck by the possibility that others might. It would be "unscientific," he told himself, to dismiss them, even if their argument seemed absurd. Maybe some part of what they said was true. But then *why* did this way of thinking seem so unnatural, so contradictory to the way the world should be? He would have to talk about this with Philipp.

He thought back to the summers of his childhood. To the long, warm days and the slow fading of the light. To the distant, glowing sunsets on the Alps. To the contests he had with Philipp: who could throw a stick further? who could stand on his hands longest? when the evening came, who could first see all the stars in *ursa minor*? They often had climbed up into an old apple tree off a path above Pohlendorf to scan the eastern horizon as the sky darkened. The town below was a collection of miniature houses and streets, the marketplace and town square beside the *Marienkirche*, their homes, their *Gymnasium*, the tiny Lutheran church, the synagogue and graveyard on the edge of town, Semmelberg's store where they bought candy—all no bigger than the wooden model on display in the town's city hall. They could hear the evening bells and see farmers calling their cows to the barns for the milking. If the wind came from the west, they sometimes heard train whistles from Munich. One special summer evening—'was it just before my twelfth birthday?' he wondered—Philipp and he had carefully pricked each other's forefinger with his pocketknife. Two drops of deep red blood emerged on their fingertips, tiny beads, glistening. They had touched each other's palms. Then they had touched their fingertips together, clasped hands, and swore a solemn oath to be friends forever. "This is what the red Indians do. We are now blood brothers," Philipp had said. He had nodded. The apple tree had held them high above the earth. Had made them feel part of the sky itself. Like stars, growing brighter with each moment.

Now Johann looked up to see tree branches like arms dangling in the moonlight. He stared down at the graveled walkway, like a dappled gray serpent whose head might be pointing either way, to the left or to the right. Gusts of wind shook the trees. Their rippling shadows on the path made it seem to move, but Johann could not tell in which direction. He shuffled his feet to get them warm. The gravel grated as he scuffed it, the sound of tiny bones rubbing back and forth. His eyes tried to make sense of the textured shadows at his feet. Each time he scuffed his feet, the path seemed to slither away, as the moon's cold light shifted through the branches. The shadows around him were all grays, with different tones and depths, like out-of-focus photographs. He sensed that they would stretch across him for the rest of his life.

CHAPTER THREE
ꜰull of Ꜹope

We drew our zeal for perfection on earth from a common source. Science. Our arrogant belief that we would find absolute truth in science was at the heart of our ruin. We reveled in the truth of Darwin's insight. We applied his theory to human society. We championed eugenics. And fueling all our beliefs was our pride. Pride in being German. Pride in being Scientists. German Scientists.

Philipp Stein held a vision of this perfection, too. But he did not have the hatred that came over us. It drove us all the more to believe in ourselves, to pride ourselves on our objectivity. When I began to notice this hatred coursing through me, when it first rose up in my throat, Philipp and I were still young, still friends, still full of hope for Germany, for all of us. We wanted the same future. We believed in ourselves as doctors, as men of science and truth.

During the years he lived in Nuremberg, before the Nazis invaded Poland in 1939 and he went to war for the second time, Johann had many acquaintances, but few friends. He was absorbed by his work. What time he could spare, he spent with his family. If he spoke of anyone as a friend, it was of Philipp.

Another medical student once had compared them to the two inter-twined serpents on Aesculapius' staff. Philipp said that he appreciated the image and continued, with his characteristic charm, "However, there is but *one* snake on Aesculapius' staff. It's the true symbol of the medical profession. You are referring to the caduceus, with its wings and twin serpents—that's the staff carried by Hermes, messenger of the gods. Somehow, it has been confused over the years with Aesculapius' staff." With that, he put his arm around Johann: "So, you see, only one of us is a snake!"

"That's you!" Johann shot back. They all laughed.

"Well, I may remind you, then," Philipp said, folding his arms and rocking back on his heels, "that the ancients held the snake to be sacred, good fortune, Goodness itself. It was the *oroborous*—a snake with its tail in its mouth, a perfect circle, consuming itself, sustaining itself. Life coming from death. Eternity. Yes, like me, Philipp Stein, the eternal Jew!" More laughter.

"Goodness itself you are not!" Johann added.

"True enough," Philipp said. "But who among us wants to be a saint? Being a doctor is close enough."

That conversation was nearly twenty-five years before Nuremberg's destruction. At the end of another day of trial testimony, Johann recalled a more painful memory of his friend, when they were studying together in the fall of 1922.

*****

Philipp sat impatiently in the beer garden, looking at his watch and wondering if he had gotten the days mixed up. Johann had promised to meet him for their regular study session and a beer at their *Stammlokal*, the "Golden Stork." His watch showed half-past five, the appointed time, and just after he had looked at it, the bells from the *Frauenkirche* across the square confirmed it. The shadow of the linden tree at the gate fell across his table and his empty glass. Around him, groups of students and older men, probably veterans, were growing louder as they downed their beers. The insistent laughter—more like a croaking—of a drunken old woman behind him made Philipp want to turn and look, but he did not.

Instead, Philipp went back to his book—Wassermann and Kolle's *Handbuch der pathogenen Mikroorganismen*, volume three of eight. His mind began to wander. How could an eight-volume work, especially one this technical and complex, be called a "handbook"? For a giant's hand, perhaps. He flipped the pages back and forth at random. It contained a lot of the same material he had heard Wassermann lecture on in Berlin—reading straight from the text. He had to take it back to the medical school library by noon on Monday. He knew he could not finish it by then.

At the moment, he was more concerned about what would be on the *Physikum* exams about blood pathogens. He should have brought his notes from yesterday's lectures. He could have used the time to re-write them. Perhaps Johann had some ideas about potential questions. There were sure to be some on Wassermann's work on diphtheria and perhaps on syphilis.

The students sitting nearest Philipp broke into another cycle of drinking-song rituals, their fourth. At that rate, they would never make it far into the evening. His own drinking days seemed a century ago—during his last year in Pohlendorf's *Gymnasium*. That was almost six years now and beer was no longer much of an attraction. In this and other more important ways, he knew that he had changed. The war made him more serious. How could it not?

Sometime in his early teenage years he had decided that his best strategy in school would be to learn only as much as was needed and no more—just enough to not be embarrassed by the teacher on the one side, or taunted by his friends on the other. Whenever he could, he found this mid-point. Let the others in the class, especially Johann and Christian, rise above the teacher's challenges, and pay the occasional price of the teacher's disappointment or displeasure in their answers, to say nothing of the snide remarks from some of their classmates. Like almost all of them, he saw no harm in deferring to the teacher's ultimate authority. As his father said, "A good life means finding your place in God's order of things."

But even with his half-hearted effort, he was the youngest member of his class when he received his *Abitur*, the coveted "Completion Certificate" from the *Gymnasium* that qualified him for university study. With honors in both history and physics, he was chosen by his peers to give one of the commencement speeches. He chose the occasion to announce that he was not going directly on to university as expected.

"We have a duty. To our *Vaterland*! To Bavaria! To Pohlendorf! To our teachers! To our Families!" His classmates cheered. The assembled faculty smiled and nodded their approval. "We all know what this duty is. To fight for our survival. For our rightful destiny. For the glory of our *Volk*." More cheers. Fathers rose to their feet. "To join our brothers in arms." Still more cheers and applause. "Long live our *Kaiser* Wilhelm and our noble King Ludwig!" Tumultuous cheers and stamping feet set the room's chandeliers swaying.

Of course, Philipp had not convinced them to do anything other than what they had planned to do anyway. At that time, not one in a hundred thousand young German men thought of anything but going to war. He wanted to enlist with his friends and, if possible, his youngest uncle, Max, in the same Royal Bavarian brigade, hoping that they would all serve in the same platoon. The *Vaterland* needs me, he thought. It will be dangerous, yes, but wonderful. Just as the song says, "gladly fighting and bleeding for Throne and *Reich*." The tune went round and round in his head.

His classmates and Uncle Max went to war without him. The examination board was willing to overlook his age, but the medical report raised questions about his eyes, lungs and feet. He remembered their laughter when he protested, "I've got two of each. Show me who has more!" Given the *Reich*'s need for soldiers, a few weeks later they reversed their decision and judged him suitable for garrison duty. After boot camp, he was posted first to Koblenz, then to Strasbourg, then back to Koblenz and then to a little village on the border of Lorraine, just north of Nancy, all in a matter of seven weeks. He remained there, from early 1916 on to the Armistice in November 1918, assigned to a squad operating a telegraph shed at the railroad junction outside the village. The westerly winds occasionally brought him the sound of artillery fire and cannons. Nighttime brought the flash of shells on the far horizon. Occasionally he could hear the staccato noise of machine guns and battle cries.

During the last desperate Ludendorff offensive in the summer of 1918, he thought he might get into combat. Instead, he was "misplaced" when his superior officer left for the front without leaving any orders for him and the nine other men in the squad. At first they all lay low, setting up a hideaway in a disabled boxcar on an overgrown siding and foraging for food and water. After three days of this, feeling guilty, he left them, and reported to the transfer hospital in a village some ten miles away as a volunteer.

He worked as a night shift orderly in the ward. Since sleeping by day proved impossible, he forced himself to stay busy as long as he could when his shift was over. The routine consisted of admitting the injured soldiers, feeding them, changing their bandages, and moving the dead ones out to make room for the new arrivals. None of the wounded stayed longer than a week. They either died or were put back on a train to a larger hospital east of the Rhine. Rarely, one would be released for further front duty, occasioning wide attention on the ward. The soldier himself often did not know whether he wanted to celebrate or scream and run away. A few times one tried to get Philipp to give him something to produce a high fever, or help him fake some complication of his condition. He did what he could.

After he was off duty, especially in the last months of the war, he would sit for a while beside the cot of a wounded soldier. Then he would walk up the hills into the deserted vineyards above the hospital and look toward the western front. The setting October sun would almost warm his face. Ever since his first winter in the war, he felt cold all the time, even in summer. Sitting on a stairway in the vineyard with the wind rasping through the gray-green leaves and the sinking light, he could not escape the season's chill. The vines hung heavy with unpicked, rotting grapes. Here and there, a few had escaped the hard evening frosts, glistening sweet and full. The very air seemed fermented. A soft wind rustled the leaves like the sobbing in the ward.

Philipp could see no battle lines from where he sat, but he knew that somewhere not far away, men on each side were killing each other by the thousands for the right to advance a few hundred yards. If the winds were blowing steady, he thought he could smell the front, a pungent mixture of grapes, corpses, mud, gunpowder, blood, and death. It was a smell unlike anything he had ever known.

The setting sun painted the hillside and the hospital below, where the men were stretched out in their cots, row after row of them, like empty wine bottles. The blinded and mutilated pained him most. He could not find the right words to cheer them. He knew he sounded unconvincing if he told them they would recover. They may have expected nothing more than "how are you?" or "the sun is out today," but Philipp felt that he disappointed them. After a while, he learned that just sitting quietly beside a wounded man comforted them both.

He wrote home and told his mother his new address. She wrote him once, sometimes twice a week. Small packages of food or hand-knit socks or a newspaper came regularly, too, until he wrote to say she should not send anything more, but save for things the family needed. One letter brought news of Uncle Max's death in Belgium. Another told him that Fritz Kellner, his greatest school rival in Latin, had been killed, probably in a battlefield just beyond Philipp's view on the northwestern horizon. Then Georg Zoellner and Peter Ehrle. Did it matter where they died? Each letter from his mother enclosed little rectangular newspaper clippings, edged in black, falling out of the envelope to the floor. Obituary notices of the young men of Pohlendorf. Their names, a star by their date of birth and a little cross by the date of their death. And here he was, away from the front, among the crippled and the blind, sitting in a vineyard on a hillside watching the sunset over France.

The hospital was enough battlefield to last him a lifetime. Before the war, he believed he should serve his *Vaterland*. In the hospital, he saw the horrors that he had been spared. He was both grateful and guilty for not having gone into combat. Any glory he earned now, he thought, would be to honor the memory of Uncle Max and his dead friends. He decided on the spot to study medicine when the war was over. A doctor in the field hospital told him that the medical faculty at the university in Berlin was the best in Germany: "In the world, for that matter. At least it was before the war."

When he arrived home in Pohlendorf after the war, he saw Johann a few times. But he didn't want to talk about the war or politics. After reading the newspapers for a few days, he refused to look at them anymore. Everything he saw depressed him. The only way he could escape his numbness was to walk by himself in the hills above the town, until his cheeks glowed and his breath steamed. Then he would come back to his home and sit by the *Kachelofen* in the parlor, reading the books he loved when he was a child, as the stove's warmth enveloped him. Shortly after New Year's Day he told his family of his plans to go to Berlin to study medicine. His mother did not understand why he would want to leave so soon, or, if he had to study, why not in Munich. His father said through his tears, "Go, you are old enough to know what you want." And so, just two months after he came home from the war, on a snowy January dawn, Philipp boarded a train for Berlin.

He found a seat near a steamy window on a third class bench. He wanted to open it and say another 'good-bye' to his parents who stood on the platform, but it was stuck. In backwards letters he wrote, "Be strong! Be well! P!," then wiped the window clear and blew them each a kiss as the train began to move away. He saw that his mother was crying and thought his father was, too.

The train crawled north, nearing Berlin only at dusk. Then, for some reason, it stopped. Philipp asked the conductor about the delay.

"Nothing I know about. For now we're stopping here. Enjoy the view, *mein Herr*," came the response in a strong Berliner accent.

The view was a weedy embankment, wires drooping from telephone poles, gray buildings behind ragged wooden fences, and peeling signs. The pale evening sky rendered everything into an eerie silhouette that grew more indistinct as he watched. The railway car soon filled with cigarette smoke. He tried again in vain to open the window. Soon, all he could see was a red halo of light whenever a passenger took a drag on a cigarette. When he got up and walked down the aisle, the conductor waved him back.

"Go back to your seat. Everyone stays inside."

After an hour, the train lurched forward and slowly made its way through the yard, rocking this way and that as it crossed from one siding to another until it reached the dark station The conductor walked through the train shouting, "No exit. No exit. Stay in your seats, no exit yet."

Outside his window, Philipp saw what he thought were squads of soldiers on the platform, rifles at the ready. When it was clear that they would not be leaving the train soon, he closed his eyes and tried to sleep. He was startled by the sound of gunfire. Instinctively, he ducked down as low as he could. He heard a squad of soldiers running down the platform. Bursts of light and the sound of another volley, this one more muffled than the first, proved to him that he was not dreaming. He saw more rifle flashes and heard more soldiers running past. Passengers began to scream. Trembling, he pulled his suitcase down from the luggage rack, put it between himself and the window, and crawled under his seat.

When the conductor reappeared, with a soldier walking in front of him and another behind, their rifles at the ready, he announced that those who wanted to leave were free to do so, but "due to unusual circumstances," the train would be returning to Munich in five minutes. Philipp was the only passenger who got off. The train began to move as soon as he stepped on the platform.

The station was filled with soldiers. He was directed toward the only permissible exit. Outside, it was chaos. The air was heavy with the smell of burning rubber. An automobile had rammed a barricade of timbers, overturned and was ablaze. He stumbled over a placard that read, "Brothers don't shoot!" Next to it was the body of a young woman, her hair wet with blood. He saw more bodies. An officer on horseback maneuvered between them, shouting to medics running with stretchers toward a fleet of ambulances. Others were lining up the dead on the sidewalk. Philipp heard more shots in the distance. When he went to the nearest ambulance and asked if he could help, a burly guard asked him for his papers before telling him to go away. Another pushed him in his chest with the butt of his rifle. He began to run as best he could, crouching and carrying his suitcase over his head, he knew not where.

It did not occur to him that Germany's capitol might be more frightening than what he had seen in France. Having refused to read the recent newspapers, he was ignorant of the revolutionary turbulence that was boiling over at the end of the war, of the divisions between the communists and the socialists, of the death squads that formed within the *Freikorps*. Berlin was seething with revolution. Just a few weeks before he arrived, Horse Guards and military units from the garrison in Potsdam had marched on the *Kaiser*'s palace to rid it of the thousands of mutinous sailors who were camped on its grounds demanding their back pay. Thousands of working-class Berliners had rallied to protect them. Communists thought the revolution had come. But their leaders were killed and the military prevailed.

Philipp trembled in terror under a canal bridge, until he fell asleep promising himself that he would have nothing to do with violence for the rest of his life. In the morning, everything seemed normal. Barges went by on the canal. The streets were busy. He asked for directions to the university. Just a few blocks further, he was told. Was last night a dream?

He found the registration office of the university. His papers were in order. He saw a bulletin board with advertisements for student housing. One offered three single rooms, all in the same apartment building in Kreuzberg: "Clean. Quiet. Cheap." He asked for directions, and an hour later, was talking with the landlady, *Frau* Grünberg. She gave him a cup of tea, some dried apples, told him that he looked tired and that his mother would want him to eat. He smiled. One room was still available, she said, in the attic, small, but with a window that faced the canal. He took it. Later that night, sitting in a nearby café, he wrote his parents a letter telling him that he was safe: "It was a long, but uneventful trip," he lied, hoping they wouldn't read the newspapers.

The next day he registered his address with the police, then hurried to the university for a lecture on human anatomy. Unlike most students, he attended lectures every day. *Frau* Grünberg came out of her apartment to greet him on the stairway every time she heard him come in and offered him to make him something to eat, but most of the time he declined. "You aren't eating," she would say, smiling broadly, her gold tooth gleaming.

"Yes, I am, *Frau* Grünberg. I am. At the student's *mensa*. Thank you." Then he would hurry up to his room and begin reading in the used editions of medical texts that he bought in the bookstalls near the university.

Philipp studied with frenzy. No more just getting by, he thought. After going to lectures and reviewing his notes, he slept during the early evening, setting his alarm clock for midnight, then studied through the night until four or five in the morning, at which point he fell asleep for another hour or two. He ate little and lost weight. *Frau* Grünberg took it upon herself to chastise him when she brought him a basin of hot water each morning.

"You are going to be a doctor and you can't take care of yourself," she said with a motherly tone.

"I'm fine, *Frau* Grünberg. Thank you."

"You are not fine. You are crazy. Eat something and you will be fine."

"You sound like my mother," Philipp said smiling, thinking that she even looked like his mother.

"Mothers know these things."

"Thank you. I will eat more."

But he did not. He bartered some of his ration cards for candles. The low ceiling in his room acquired a sooty tone. A spider's web he had admired and spared, accumulated dust, tore loose from its corner, and collapsed. *Frau* Grünberg opened the window to air the room out after he left for the university each morning, but when he returned, it still smelled stale. Street noises and the wind combined into a rasping, aching sound that droned on, even with his window closed and the curtains drawn. The wind blew a metallic smell off the canal.

Despite Philipp's efforts to focus on his studies, the city's pace and fierceness permeated everything. He could not avoid its tensions and smells. Sometimes, he fell into a pit of doubts about the sanity of the world. The war's details slowly shrank to a pile of ashes in his memory, but its acrid smells still burned in his nostrils. He tried to forget he had been a soldier. That a bloody battle had raged less than a mile from where he was studying. But he had nightmares in which he was a skeleton marching in an army of skeletons underneath the Brandenburger Gate, all of them chained together and singing.

He tried to shake off his fears. He threw his wartime journal into the canal. He bought a new, leather-bound notebook, brushed the snow off a bench by the canal, sat down and made his first entry: "*I will put the war behind me. I will! This journal will be my witness. In it I will mark my path toward a better world, a better future, a world without violence. I renounce violence.*" Underlining his last sentence, he added, "*It leads only to more violence.*"

Early the next morning, before he got dressed, he added, "*As a physician, as a citizen of Germany, as a human being, I have much work to do. Medicine is my calling, my hope. It is hope for all of us. With rigor, with clear thinking, with persistence, with courage, we will conquer illness and maybe even death itself.*" He looked out the window toward the sun rising over snow-covered trees to the east. A thin sheet of ice on the canal glowed with the dawn. He watched as a barge broke it into shards. Then he wrote with a flourish, *This is my faith. My religion. For it, I would gladly undergo the greatest of tortures.*"

He missed his mother more than he had during the war. He missed his family; his school friends, especially Johann; even some of his teachers. He longed for peace. He discarded every tangible reminder of the war years, except photographs his mother had sent him of his family. He saw no way to resolve his pain or doubt but to immerse himself in his studies.

The winter in Berlin after the war was no grayer or colder than usual, but for Philipp, it was depressing. In his mind, the sky was filled with a constant haze that had drifted over from the west, swallowing everything in shadowy twilight. He longed for sunlight and yet denied himself any chance to have it. He avoided other students. How could they laugh? How could they be so aimless? Letters from his parents pained him, and lay unread for days on his dresser. His sleep was fitful. A new nightmare: a monster crawls out of a cesspool, breathing poison gas and laughing as little children die in its path; a blinding winter storm buries it deep in snow, but it rages up and shakes off the snow, now no longer white, but transformed into blood red gore. He awoke each time just as the monster declared himself come to rule the world.

Berliners seemed so oblivious of the war's consequences. Who was facing the fact that Germany was now irreparably changed? The city was like the mutilated patient he tried to help in the field hospital who had lost both legs to gangrene, but swore he did not need any artificial ones and insisted he could get up and run if they would only let him. How could anyone in Berlin—the generals defending themselves in the news-papers, his professors who came and went with barely a nod to their students, the mailman who was convinced that the war had not been lost—how could anyone believe that life could go on as it had before? That everything had changed? Were people blind? Or cowards, unwilling to admit the truth?

Spring brought welcome news. The Ministry of Health ordered that the medical school curriculum should be condensed, to replace the number of physicians who had been lost in the war, so he would need only four more semesters before he could stand for his *Physikum*. He wrote his parents that he would work through the summer in the university's chemistry laboratory and then transfer to the university in Munich for the remainder of his studies and take the exam there. His father wrote back, predictably, that he and Philipp's mother were proud of his spirit and determination.

But *Frau* Grünberg told him he could not have his rent money back for the fall term, since her blind husband's pension was not being paid. He guessed from his mother's letters that they were pinching pennies, too. His father, besides paying Uncle Max's widow for a few hours' work each day, even though he didn't need the help, had trouble getting paper goods for his stationary shop without payment in advance. So he decided to stay in Berlin until December. To help his parents out, he had signed on as an orderly in one of Berlin's district hospitals during the influenza epidemic that was still raging and sent his earnings home. He took more hours in the summer, cut back when the university came back into session, and stopped working only a few days before he left the city. Two years later, his father would tell him that he had put the entire amount that he had sent them in a savings account, and it was wiped out by the hyperinflation.

He resented the hospital's factory-like routines and chaffed under his constant inability to make any difference in the lives of the patients who were shuffled through its wards. He felt as though he were locked in a great engine room, mechanically interesting, fascinating for its size and complexity, but fiercely loud and unpredictably dangerous. Berlin reminded him of an anthill that he had found under a rotten piece of wood when he was a child. He was mesmerized by its mysterious energy, driven by an unseen force. But he could not imagine himself as an ant. He revisited the anthill several times over the rest of the summer, hoping to see some pattern in its frenzy. Much later, in the war, he realized that each ant did what it did because there was nothing else it could do. It was the same for him. And he knew that his time now in Berlin studying medicine and working at the hospital was like that, too, despite his sense of unease.

He forced himself to concentrate on his studies with even greater zeal. He saw himself moving more toward medical research than medical practice, away from his earlier ambition to be a surgeon. He now wanted to know everything one could know about how the human body worked and what could be done to make it work better. He saw the body as an intricate machine, whose mysteries could be unraveled piece-by-piece and part-by-part. Each step is like a conquest of a mountain. Someday, this living machine will be fully mastered. Someday, each of its parts will be so clearly and completely understood that new ones can be made. New eyes, legs, hearts. Illness will be conquered. Suffering will be unnecessary. Remembered as absurd. Life will be long and full for everyone. Doctors, most likely German doctors, will lead the way back into Eden. Death will flee before us. Walking along the city's canals, with such thoughts going through his head, he propelled himself from one day to the next.

He studied medicine in a different way than he had studied Latin or Greek in *Gymnasium*. That had been a game, the subjects only mildly interesting in themselves. Although he had always been told that doing anything less than his best was "a sin"—this from his parents, who were so irreligious that the word "sin" was rarely mentioned—he didn't have to study much to succeed. But learning about the human body in medical school was vastly more important to him than studying Latin or Greek. It was more like swimming for the shore of a promised land.

When he left Berlin for Munich at the end of the fall semester, he was more confident. He knew that he had to apply himself to his studies, but that he could relax more often, and should try to recover some of his earlier exuberance and sense of humor. Until he faced the state examinations, his last year of medical study was almost enjoyable. His renewed friendship with Johann helped relieve the tension. It reminded him of their childhood, of earlier, more innocent times in Pohlendorf. Johann always laughed at his jokes. Their frequent study breaks together were a chance for both of them to catch their breaths.

He was ordering his second beer when Johann arrived at the *Bier-garten*, full of apologies. The noisy group of students noticed his arrival with a toast: "To Friendship!" and began to sing a folk song. Philipp and Johann smiled and joined in. The setting sun balanced like a glowing ball on the ridgeline of the *Frauenkirche*'s steeply pitched, tile roof. It seemed about to roll down toward them, then rolled the other way, disappearing. The October air quickly cooled.

Johann was sweaty and somewhat disheveled. He looked ashen and tired. "Sorry. I'm coming from a meeting with Lenz. Thanks for waiting."

"You met with Lenz? What do you want with him, or he with you?"

"He's interested in racial hygiene, you know. He and Kaup, despite their feuding, want the same thing. Solid, scientific, biological evidence for social policy. I wrote a short position paper for him. Nothing special, mostly a catalog and review of the recent literature. Maybe he'll like it. The field interests me. I'm hoping for my *Praktikum* here in Munich. Perhaps with Lenz."

"You'd work for him?"

"Sure, why not?"

"I don't like him. Although I do like his concept of 'scientific racism.' And eugenics is the cutting edge, the remedy for humanity's ills. But Lenz is extreme. Then, of course, he doesn't like me either."

"Why should he not like you?" Johann asked, even as the answer came to him. Lenz made no effort to disguise his anti-Semitism. He tried to tell Philipp that Lenz left his political views outside the lecture hall and the laboratory. But they both knew that was not true.

"I suppose you're overlooking his lecture to the Munich Society for Racial Hygiene," Philipp said.

"He's a scientist," Johann replied.

"He's an anti-Semite.

"He's a scientist, able to think objectively."

"Not as far as I can see. Why didn't you give your paper to Professor Kaup? At least Kaup follows Grotjahn and is constructive in the way he thinks we should apply eugenics to society. I know what will happen to me and mine if Lenz has his way."

"Nonsense. This is science, Philipp. It's bound to be controversial. I just thought Lenz would be more interested in my paper, and besides, he's the one who might want an assistant, not Kaup. I still have not landed anything for my residency. Probably nothing will come of it anyway. Now, if you do not mind, I do not want to talk about medicine just yet. Where's my beer?"

"He's bringing it. What do you want to talk about?" Philipp asked.

"Not medicine. Or politics. Nor the economy. Or the damned French or British. Not the Americans, who've gone back into their shell. Not the Communists. Not Rathenau's murder. Not the weather. Not boxing..."

"Not your automobile!" Philipp interjected.

"I don't have an automobile."

"Well, then, it'll be easy not to talk about that."

Johann and Philipp both smiled. The waiter put down a heavy dou-ble-liter glass of beer. Johann paid.

"Okay, okay," Johann said. "I'm in a bad mood. I need to get a spot for my residency here in Munich. You don't have to worry. You're going to Freiburg. I can't leave Munich."

"Why not?"

"Well, I met a girl…"

"Aha! Love comes to Johann. Anyone I know?"

"You've probably seen her. Probably thought of asking her out, too. She works in the medical library. Helga Mueller. Tall, thin, blond, soft voice, very attractive. Wears her hair short, but not too short. She and I have been going for walks in the Botanical Garden. And we went to the carnival one night." He laughed.

"Yes, I have seen her. No wonder you don't want to leave Munich. But how do you have time to court *Fräulein* Mueller? I have my hands full just preparing for the *Physikum*. Wassermann and Kolle's little handbook here is just packed with stuff I am betting we need to know. And this is just the third of eight!" Philipp pushed the dark brown volume away from Johann's beer glass.

"I found it boring. I'm just going to skim it. On volume five now," Johann said.

"Well, it's not exactly gripping, I admit. But it's a great reference work. Why we have to know it by heart is a mystery to me. It should be enough for those medical gods that we know where to find something when we have to. I'm tired of playing these memory games. Exams. No contact with patients. I want to get out of the lecture hall. Work with patients, do some research, finally be a doctor."

"Won't be long now. Another month and the state exams are behind us. By this time next year, your *Praktikum* will almost be finished. You'll own the clinic in Freiburg. *Doktor* Hoche probably will ask you to marry his daughter—if he has one," Johann said, smiling. "And with your luck, he will. And I'll probably have to settle for some boring residency I don't want here in Munich. Then again, maybe Lenz will smile on me."

"Beware when the devil smiles on you."

"Please, Lenz is no devil. He just says things in an extreme fashion to provoke controversy. Trust me."

"I don't think so. He's got too many political ambitions. Speaking of Wassermann...."

"Can't we talk about something else besides medicine?"

"We should study, Johann. The exam's coming up fast. But all right. How about the other Wassermann. The novelist. Jakob Wassermann. Read any of his books?"

"No. Should I?"

"I think so. His latest is not a novel, but a memoir. *My Life as a German and a Jew.*"

"Why should I read that?"

"Well, I thought you were interested in Germany. And you always said you wanted to know more about Jews," Philipp said.

"I think I know enough about Germany and our Jews, thank you. What's to know? We live in Germany where there are Jews. Some Jews are good Germans—you, for example. Others are only good Jews. I doubt they are as harmful as people say, but I don't really know. They seem to be everywhere. Two Wassermanns for example. Is our Wassermann Jewish? Most likely. Is Kolle? I guess we know Lenz is not. Kaup? Grotjahn? Not likely. Old Rathenau sure was. Eisner, too, of course." Johann paused to think, then continued, "I don't know about Liebknecht, but that wild woman Luxemburg sure was, according to my father. Every country has them, it seems. Lenin, they say, is Jewish, though I've heard the opposite, too. But Trotsky is. And Rockefeller, I suppose. Warburg, certainly. All of them, either communists, beginning with Marx, or rich. I suppose there's some reason for it."

"Did I ever tell you I saw them fish Luxemburg's body out of the canal? Right near where I lived." Philipp paused to look up at the darkening sky. "So you think Jews are the cause of all the world's problems?"

"Of course not," Johann said quickly. He looked into his beer glass, talking more to it and himself than to Philipp. "Well, we live in a democracy now, do we not? Government by the people. I guess that goes with it. All kinds of people." Then, louder, his clenched fist upon the table, "But how do we make sure that everyone is loyal? The Reds do not know the meaning of the word. I don't miss Eisner and his crew one second. Maybe gunning down Eisner and Rathenau and Luxemburg and Erzberger was extreme, but they were dangerous, dangerous people. The revolution was a disaster. The communists were terrifying. We can be glad that won't happen again." Johann looked away at the students who were shouting at each other and calling for the waiter.

For a few seconds, Philipp was stunned into silence. Then, in a soft, steady voice, he looked right at Johann. "What's wrong with you? Eisner and the rest were murdered. Murdered by murderers who should be punished. Instead, these murderers are free, right in our midst, for all we know. The right wing press reveres them. The *Freikorps* killed hundreds in the streets not far from here. Meanwhile, all our so-called German patriots vilify their dead victims for every imaginable sin, and sum them all up with the one word, "Jew!" You don't believe in murder, do you, Johann? My God!"

"Of course not," he said again. "Of course I don't believe in murder! I believe in a state of laws. The old Germany was a state of laws. Where is it now? Gone. Done in by the Weimar social democrats and the communists—and you cannot deny that a significant number of them are Jews. No, I saw enough murdering in the war. Don't get me wrong, Philipp. I just think we are vulnerable now. Germany has very little strength. We can be taken advantage of. We *have* been taken advantage of. Some people are good at taking advantage of us."

Philipp backed his chair away from the table.

Johann continued. "Not just Jews. Politicians. Even generals. And lawyers, it goes without saying. And civil servants. Too many of these "modern men" have grown ruthless because of the war. The war has poisoned us. Not all of us. But far too many of us. You've said the same thing, Philipp. The *Volk* is angry and hungry and frightened. Some have turned vicious. You know that. We just have to be careful. All this confusion has to stop somewhere. Someone has to stop it." His face grew ashen again. He pulled at his collar. The dusk gave his eyes dark shadows.

Johann downed what remained in his *stein* in a deep swallow. "You and I and those of us that survived the war have to get on with our lives, all of us. Jews and non-Jews. We're all Germans, aren't we? Aren't we?" He raised his *stein* again, then realized it was empty. . "All right, I know. I probably have said too much. Excuse me. Please. I didn't want to offend you. I told you I was on edge. Let me buy you another beer."

"No, thanks." Philipp said, not knowing whether he should try to change the subject. After a long pause, he looked into Johann's eyes. What he saw reminded him of the wounded soldiers he had tried to help in France. "I don't understand you, Johann. How long has it been since we saw each other last? One week? Two? You don't seem like the person I saw last time. What's happened? The pressure of the exams? I should think you would be happier, if this Helga Mueller has any influence on you. Where's your sense of proportion? Where's your rational judgment, *Mensch*?"

Johann was about to say something when Philipp continued, "This is just like medicine. If the state is sick—I grant you it's not healthy, and you know that I'm no great friend of the communists or the socialists—but if the state is sick, if we are ill as a people, then we have to do a very careful, calm investigation of our pathology. Then, we have to prescribe a remedy that won't kill us. You seem ready to use medieval leeches to bleed the state to death. Or maybe you're advocating a kind of amputation. We've talked already about how stupid so many amputations were during the war. Barbaric. We're not going to do that again, I hope. This is the twentieth century, remember? We may not have begun it gracefully, but we'll make it up soon enough. This is medical science's century, Johann! *Our century*, soon-to-be *Herr Doktor* Brenner. Where did you get such crazy ideas?" Philipp was flushed.

"Let's drop it, okay? I'm too tired and hungry to make sense now. I didn't come here to have an argument. Want to order something? Cheese? Some rolls or a *Bretzel*? I'll go find the waiter. Have to go to the

Clo. Be right back. Don't leave." Johann stood up abruptly, grabbed his cane, and went inside the restaurant.

Philipp watched him walking unsteadily, like a man in a daze. Some of the students looked at him, too. He must be ill, he thought. Something was wrong. Perhaps he was suffering some of the recurring war shock that plagued so many veterans. He had tried in vain to get Johann to talk about what he did in the war, but soon saw that it was a touchy matter. Something terrible must have happened. His odd behavior must be a residual effect from his war experience. Extreme anxiety, made worse by fatigue, erupting involuntarily. Nerves. A precursor of neurasthenia. He told himself to look up the topic in the medical journals.

He thought about how long ago their childhood games had been. How, since the war ended, they had become pre-occupied, no, obsessed, with their studies. How they needed to be distracted from the uncertainties of their future. He knew his anxieties. Surely, Johann felt them, too. The viciousness of the war was just under the surface of everything they did. The exuberance they had hoped for at its end had been denied them. Nothing was easy or certain. They were finishing their dissertations—his in fact was finished, but he could not resist tinkering with his narrative; Johann never wanted to talk about how his was going. They were frantically preparing for the examinations. Trying to find a decent residency, with all the competition, was a full-time task, on top of their other work. He knew he had been lucky, getting a *Praktikum* at Hoche's clinic in Freiburg, but he still wished he had been taken on in Berlin. Look at the time spent trying to land that assistantship at the *Kaiser-Wilhelm*! Johann was making it harder for himself trying to find something in Munich. When did they, or any of the medical students have time to relax and talk about anything but medicine?

Philipp put the Wassermann and Kolle under his chair and waited, thinking of what to say when Johann returned. His thoughts turned to that time less than a year before, when they were supposed to meet at the "Stork." He had seen the crowd of men under the light by the jewelry store and heard their chant from far down the street. His instincts had told him to turn around and go back to his apartment. He knew that Jews had been beaten in that street before. The crowd looked and sounded rough. He never went to the tavern. Could Johann have been there? He remembered that Johann looked strange the next day in the laboratory—sallow-faced, tired, nervous. But only now, sitting in the *Biergarten,* did he wonder if Johann was among those men, if he had been shouting "*Die Juden!*" along with the rest. He had a bitter taste in his mouth.

Johann returned after some minutes. He had washed his face and combed his hair, straightened his necktie and tucked in his shirt. He smiled that open, pleasant smile that Philipp remembered from their childhood, as though they had not seen each other in years. It was almost as though they had not just had a conversation that threatened their friendship. At that moment, neither seemed willing to throw that friendship away.

"Feeling better?"

"Yes. I must eat something. The waiter is bringing bread and cheese. For you, too, right?"

"Sure. I'll stay a while longer. I told the lab assistant I'd be back by eight. But answer me one thing, please. Are you taking something for your nerves?"

"Ever the doctor," Johann said. "You'll be a good one all right. No, I am not taking any drugs. I got septicemia at the front. It's a long story. Perhaps I'll tell you sometime. They got me over it. But since then I have occasional fevers, dizzy spells. Faintness from low blood pressure, especially if I have not eaten, low pulse, dilated eyes. Syncope, most likely. That's what I think it is, anyway. Doesn't happen often. I should not have drunk my beer so quickly. It's gone now. I'm fine, really. Fine."

"Good. You had me worried. You are not usually that irrational. A bit thickheaded now and then, but I don't think of you as a fanatic. Remember Grau? Peter Grau? Now he was a crazy!"

"I'm fine, just tired."

"What you said does bother me, though." Philipp said. "I agree that many people are not paying attention to what's been happening since the war. But there are more people against something, against anything and everything, than for it. More people thinking everything is stupid or corrupt or evil than people who think things are good. More people hating. Wanting to do someone or something harm. Anti-Semites. Anti-communists. Anti-women. Anti-modern art, music. Anti-anyone-someone-does-not-like, for God's sake! Hating everything and everyone different from them. We're all in trouble if this doesn't stop. Did you see…"

Johann interrupted him. "We've suffered shocks, terrible shocks," he said, gesturing with both arms. "The war. The unjust Treaty. The damnable peace. And it is not over yet, either. Our paper money is worthless. We should never have gone off gold. Our *dear* government keeps changing its mind. Britain, France and Belgium are breathing down our necks. Foreign troops are on our soil, *our* soil, mind you, and telling us what to do! Imagine! We're treated like criminals for loving our *Vaterland*. You know what happens when you push a bear into a corner." He began to perspire.

"Don't you think I know all this? Just slow down, comrade. But violence won't…"

"Don't "comrade" me," Johann blurted back, his voice rising. "I want no part of the communists' message." Then he took a deep breath. "Of course some people are going to say extreme things. Even do extreme things. I understand why they're angry. You must too." He was proud of himself now, sounding so analytical and logical. "If you like, the *Vaterland* is like me just before, dizzy, hungry, confused. No wonder I sounded a bit wild. But you'll see." He began to speak with deliberate slowness. "The wild men will calm down. This will all pass. As you said, this is our century, the doctors' century. We will cure these dizzy spells once and for all." He forced a smile and then a laugh.

Philipp relaxed. "I hope you're right. I want to work as a scientist. I want to find the truth. As a German, I want to do it for Germany. But not just for Germany. And not just for Jews, either, no matter what the anti-Semites may believe. For everybody."

"Without question. See, I knew we agreed about this," Johann said, slapping the table. The waiter came with their bread and cheese, and more beer. The students began yet another song. High overhead, thin clouds caught the last of the evening light. The *Frauenkirche* seemed to glow. Philipp and Johann did not notice. Their conversation had turned to Wassermann and Kolle's categories of microorganisms.

CHAPTER FOUR

Not Asleep, Not Awake

Until I met you, time was a burden to me. The past was horrible. The present was cruel. And the future loomed like a monster. I felt trapped between nightmares. No matter how much I tried to help my parents or my patients, I felt useless. Powerless. Hopeless. To watch them suffer was my first glimpse of my own weakness. At the policlinic, my patients, especially the parents of those frail children, expected me to work some sort of miracle. I expected that of myself. Our professors, Philipp, the other medical students, none of us could imagine a world in which we could fail.

The three bottom steps of the front stairway of Helga Brenner's apartment building were shattered when a bomb hit the street. She had found some boards and nails to patch up the damage. But the boards were stolen while she was away working—probably by someone who needed firewood. Then she found more nails and stretched pieces of carpet over the gap, careful each time she used the stairway to stand as near the edge of the wall as she could. The back stairs were undamaged, but much darker. She climbed them slowly, fearful that someone had scavenged them also while she was away.

There was no electricity. She lit a candle stump and put it on the edge of the sink. The flame danced in the draft. It made the shadows in the corners of the room darker and more ominous. Every window in her apartment had broken panes. Wind blew around the boards she had wedged into them, and stuffing the curtains into them did not help. She had run out of rags to stuff into the cracks in the walls. She could see the sky through the hole in the hallway ceiling, where the roof's slate tiles had crashed through to the floor. It rained through the ceiling and along the wall of her bedroom. When it snowed, she thought, the floor would be easier to keep dry. Bricks from the damaged front wall lay in a heap beside the door. But the building was still standing. On either side, the apartment houses had collapsed.

Helga was cold. This was one of the days when she thought it must be warmer outside than in. The kitchen stove pipe rattled in the wind. She could put her hand through the gaps where it had been wrenched away from the wall. She moved the candle into the parlor. She trusted the parlor stove more and did whatever cooking she could there. She was shivering when she lit the stove with twigs she had gathered earlier in the fall. Only a few more briquettes were left. In a day or two, she would have to break up the box she was sitting on into firewood. Soon she would have to burn the antique wardrobe and chest she had inherited from her parents.

Officially, winter was still two weeks away and already it was colder than she could remember. Helga had taken her coat off when she came home, but now she put it back on. She made herself a cup of nettle tea. It gave off a musty smell. Its warmth kept her from crying. She took the candle into her bedroom and put it on the floor near the wardrobe. Inside hung Johann's two suits, his overcoat, and his father's old, green-gray loden coat that he could not bear to part with. There were Johann's shoes, still polished as he had left them seven years before, when he went to war. She would burn their newspaper stuffing to start the morning's fire. She opened the chest's top drawer. There were his handkerchiefs, just as she had ironed them. She had sold or bartered almost all of her own clothes, almost everything she could from the apartment. But not his things. The monogrammed handkerchiefs she had given him. His childhood pocketknife. His gold wristwatch. She had believed the letter that told of his death, but could not bear to give up what he had left behind.

That evening, Helga felt more alone than she had through all the previous months. Johann had not died! She felt betrayed, furious, knowing that he had been in Nuremberg for over a year, never looking for her, never coming to their neighborhood. She knew how stubborn he was, how unwilling to show any sign of weakness, but why couldn't he come home and help her? Why couldn't he help her, when he must have known how difficult life was for her? She knew he must have some terrible secret, that he wanted to keep from her. Who didn't have a secret now? But didn't he love her? Didn't he trust her? She had never given him any reason to think she did not love or trust him.

She began to cry. She looked at his gold watch before she put it back under the handkerchiefs. Tomorrow, she would tell them at the hospital that she would be moving to her sister's in Karlsruhe. As for the gold watch, any American soldier would be willing to buy it.

*****

Johann's parents had given him a wristwatch on his fourteenth birthday. It was a fine one—"good gold, but more important, good inside; the best jewels, gears, springs and other parts in my inventory," his father had said. It had a tiny inscription in Gothic letters on the back: *"For J.B. Use time wisely or it will use you. F.B. / O.B. 1909."* "It's what's inside, Johann, what's inside that makes it good."

"Yes, Papa."

"It's not the most expensive watch, but the most reliable. One does not guarantee the other, Johann. Remember that. The gold is not the most important part of a watch, that is just the outside. You must judge the inside of a thing, not the outside."

"Yes, Papa. Thank you. Thank you, Mama."

His mother, Ottilie, smiled her quiet smile. Fine wrinkles at the corners of her eyes and of her mouth mirrored each other. "Now put it on. Let's see how it looks," she said.

Johann wore the watch almost without interruption—to school, on his walking trips into the countryside, when he was asleep. Despite his mother's worry, nothing had ever happened to it. It was his treasure, and he cherished it. She saw that he was growing up. Not just taller than her. Serious. Determined. Already his own person.

Five years later, on his nineteenth birthday, before he went to war, he agreed to leave his gold watch home, to please his mother. "No need to tempt fate. Someone might steal it when you are sleeping." she said and gave him a hug. To replace it, his father gave him a nickel-plated pocket-watch with a hinged cover. Inside was the message, *"For J.B. Stay well. Stay true. F.B. / O.B. 1914."* Johann clipped the chain onto his belt and slipped the watch into his pocket. The gold wristwatch was put on the little table by his bed. His mother said she would not move it until he returned.

"Now, I'll make you your favorite *Linzertorte*, and we'll have a drop or two of Papa's hard cider for the occasion. We'll all sing!"

"More than a drop for me!" Johann reached to tickle his mother under her arm and she pulled away, laughing.

The pocket-watch served him well through the war. If Johann's looking at it had been able to erode its face, it would have been unreadable within a few weeks of leaving boot camp. He consulted it at every opportunity, as though it alone could confirm that time was passing. With each step he took on march, his canteen knocked against it in his pocket, making a muffled, metallic sound, a kind of time keeping of its own. Twice it fell into the mud. Once it dropped into a latrine and he had to fish it out. Even after that, it kept time. He remembered fumbling for it as he recovered consciousness after being wounded. Hearing it still ticking gave him hope for himself.

When he came home from the war, he exchanged the pocket-watch for his beloved gold wristwatch. He put it on, clumsily fastening the strap after so many years of not having to. The pocket-watch was consigned to a corner of his dresser's top drawer, resting on a fine cotton handkerchief his mother had embroidered with his initials.

After less than a week at home, he retrieved his pocket-watch. The gold wristwatch took its place in the dresser drawer. Looking at his wristwatch made him ache with a dull hurt that he could not describe. He thought he would feel better if he did not see it, at least for a while.

The war had blurred his memory of his school years. He could no longer isolate one event from another. "School" had become a great generalization; a piece of fabric boiled into a tight felt, so dense that its individual threads could no longer be seen. Mostly, Johann had liked "school," welcoming the challenges the teachers set for him and enjoying their praise when he succeeded. Occasionally he had chastised himself for glorying in the admiration of his friends and classmates, but that didn't stop him from trying to be first in everything.

Johann would have driven himself equally hard to become the best carpenter or the best machinist or the best tavern keeper. What others thought of him and his work mattered. He did not want to be ordinary. He knew he was lucky to be brighter than average, and he was driven to know how much he could achieve if he really tried.

There had been some moments of satisfaction in *Gymnasium*, especially in *Secunda* and *Prima*, his last two years. These were his "gold watch years," because he was allowed to wear his precious wristwatch to school. When he went off to war, his "pocket-watch years," he realized that he had felt the same way in school as he felt in battle. Facing enemy artillery fire, waiting for the command to go "over the top" and attack, he was on the ready to duck incoming shells. When he was in school, it seemed that the teacher would often launch an attack from a cannon pointed directly at him.

He had enjoyed anticipating and repelling the teachers' assaults. Sometimes he succeeded in shunting their attention away from the subject at hand—the class regarded him as a hero on a few occasions for such "valiant duty under fire." Or, more often, he had parried their attacks with correct answers or pithy observations. That was fun, even exhilarating. But, despite his successes in school, Johann knew he was not brilliant, that he lacked intellectual curiosity and quickness. In his own mind, he was an apt student, hard working, determined, mastering whatever was required to succeed. He did what his teachers' expected him to do. They regarded him well, knowing he was not the sort of boy who would give them trouble. Philipp, on the other hand, was quicker; when the teachers attempted to put him in his place, they often were outflanked, to Johann's secret envy and delight.

After he returned home from the war, Johann's gold wristwatch reminded him too much of the future he had promised himself. After he returned home, each bit of that future unfolded in the painful, uncertain present. Each new minute intruded on him like an uninvited, unwelcome and demanding guest. Where was his promised future now?

The past was happier: the simple, perfect world of Pohlendorf that he knew as a child. He remembered being thrilled by the arrival of guests at his parents' home. Whether they were family or his father's business associates or neighbors, they would brighten the parlor-room that his mother reserved for special occasions. Often they would bring him a toy, or a *pfennig* or two that he could add to his savings. This in turn launched him on long speculations about what he would buy and how much more he needed and when he would have enough.

After the war, Pohlendorf shriveled into itself. Many of its young men were dead. The influenza epidemic was another blow. His father's business began to fail when Pohlendorf's three watchmakers, undone by cheap, mass-produced watches, closed their doors. So did both of Pohlendorf's tailors, one of its seamstresses, two of its three barbers, its only furniture store owner, and its only livery. The town's one remaining undertaker profited for a while, but in the end, he sat in Pohlendorf's last tavern, lamenting into his beer.

Friedrich Brenner sold his home for much less than it was worth and moved his family to a small apartment in Munich. He hoped to live off their savings and what he could earn in semi-retirement. He tried as long as he could to hide his bitterness. But the future was a menacing stranger. Johann was his best hope to regain the family's financial security. Johann knew his father's expectations of him and, though anxious, devoted himself to the task.

It helped that medical school's intense requirements absorbed him. His passionately opinionated professors distracted him with their thundering cannonades and aloof pronouncements. But medical school was never a joy. It was more like a forced march through dangerous terrain. He looked forward to its conclusion and the status that would bring him. To repaying his parents for their sacrifices, to comforting them in their old age. And Helga made him feel at ease. She listened to his complaints, calmed him, helped him sort out his thoughts. She gave him strength by believing in him. He saw her nearly every day.

He was disappointed when he did not receive the assistantship at the university under Lenz, but was determined to stay near Helga in Munich. He consoled himself that his *Praktikum* at one of its neighborhood policlinics was providing him with valuable experience in the routines of day-to-day medicine. He hated learning how to cope with the state's dreaded medical insurance system, with its tangle of forms and codes. Eventually, he hoped he would have only private patients and could charge what he liked. He tried not to complain to Helga, but she sensed when he was irritated and drew it out of him.

"The state makes us into bureaucrats, paper pushers," he said.

"I know you don't like it, but what are the alternatives?"

"The state should trust us. We are the experts here. For me to waste my time documenting every patient's sneeze makes me into a clerk. Better would be for me just to check off the treatment I prescribe from a list. Then the patient brings that form to the bank or the post office, and some actual clerk takes care of it from there. The state should allow us physicians to set our own schedule of fees. Anything short of that shows that the state thinks less of me than it should. If there are corrupt physicians..."

"You know there are."

"Well, if there are corrupt physicians, let us take care of them ourselves. We can manage our own affairs. We know who is a good doctor and who is not."

Johann clung to the belief that once he began his own private practice and got out from under the state's oversight, he would gain financial security and everything else that came with being a doctor. 'Things could be worse,' he'd say aloud to himself on his walk back to his parents' apartment. But he worried about his parents, about his brother and sister, about his *Vaterland*. He worried, too, that there was a growing number of physicians, competing with each other for positions and patients. Another reason to fear the future.

In Munich, Johann's father aged rapidly. He had taken to daily shouting to anyone within earshot that he refused to read the newspapers or discuss anything with anybody. "*Wirrwarr!* Confusion! Everything is confusion!" he would mutter under his breath, over and over. Where there once had been a lively give and take between father and son, now there were only silences. And his father's mutterings, "*Wirrwarr!* Confusion!"

His mother became more talkative, even outspoken, but in a way that was just as frightening as his father's outbursts. Ottilie Brenner wondered aloud almost every morning whether there would be enough food for the winter. At the slightest turn in the weather, she would rush around the apartment stopping up drafts that only she perceived. In late June, she had begun to "lay in," as she called it, whatever she could get, whether she needed it or not. She was hoarding. Johann did not discourage her in this. He wasn't sure what to do. 'Didn't she know that all those soft cheeses and cooking apples would spoil long before the family could eat them? Didn't she realize that there wasn't enough space in the cellar to store all the potatoes she had bought by the end of August?'

Then she promised to buy another two hundred pounds from a peasant who sold her produce in the St. Martin's Church marketplace every Wednesday. Looking over the new potatoes, the two women lamented all the changes that had occurred in their lifetimes:

"Have you seen all the drunken beggars and thieves near the train station?" *Frau* Brenner asked. "There's no work even for honest people. And prices are higher than ever. Why don't they do something about the rising prices?"

"Scoundrels!" the woman replied.

"Why don't they borrow money from the French or the English or the Belgians?"

"From those foreign high-and-mighties? They won't help us, you can be sure, thanks to the damned war. I trust my potatoes more than I trust any Englishman!"

"Then they should ask the Americans. They are different. There are so many Germans in America. No German would forget the *Vaterland*. Yes, they should ask the Americans to help." Johann's mother looked around the marketplace, as though there was an American she could tell this to.

"They must do it now. Soon it will be too late!"

The "they" both women invoked was the government in Berlin. Or was it Weimar? Johann's mother did not know. Toward the end of the summer, he noticed that she grew more impatient. She spoke in a faint, lisping whisper, while chewing on her lower lip:

"Where is our *Kaiser* when we need him? Where are the men like old Bismarck? He wouldn't let this happen to Germany. Our King Ludwig would not have let this happen. He should have been *Kaiser*. Where is he?" she would ask, over and over, until she looked like she was about to weep.

Johann's father would merely respond, if he responded at all, "Don't worry, Ottilie. Don't bother yourself about things you don't understand." Johann agreed with him. A woman like his mother was not supposed to concern herself about politics. It was making her ill. Both men noticed that she was increasingly distracted, with an uncontrollable tick at the corner of her eye, and occasionally a tremor in her arm.

Johann, without much success, tried to determine the connections between these physical symptoms and whatever syndrome she was developing. He suspected some thyroid condition, but she would not go to the clinic for tests. He attempted to reassure her in a voice that sounded hollow even to himself. "Everything will be fine, Mama. You'll see. Everything will turn out fine. We're not going to starve. You'll see." His brother and sister reacted to the problem by staying away from their apartment as much as possible. Neither had his drive to succeed in school and disobeyed their parents whenever they could.

He worried more about his father than his mother or his siblings. Friedrich Brenner seemed to have aged twenty years in the last ten. Johann was stunned by how often his father lost track of time. "Is today Sunday or Monday?" the old man would ask, when it was neither. "I'll get some coal from the cellar," he had said in July, when every window in the apartment was open. "No doubt about it," he would say, "we'll be able to see the king when he drives by on his way to the palace." Johann's brother would respond, "But Papa, the king is no longer king. And the *Kaiser* is no longer the *Kaiser*. He doesn't even live in Germany. I read in the newspapers that...," only to be cut off and told to mind his tongue.

Johann wondered how his father could conduct his business affairs. But, unexpectedly, for days or weeks at a time, his father would become as lucid as he always had been, with his crisp and precise way and that disarming, kindly smile. These "good" periods grew shorter and shorter. Friedrich Brenner took to saying, as many four or five times in the same hour, "I wish I could understand it all."

Johann did not blame his father for not understanding. He knew no one who did. His professors at the university seemed lost in their own fog, with their competing theories. If they could not make sense of it, how could his father, or he? He had no idea about what should be done. His mother's hope that America would loan Germany money sounded like a good idea. But would one country loan another country money, after they had just been at war? It certainly had not honored its promises about the Treaty. Their Wilson was a swindler. Someone must have bought him off. It hurt to think how much the Germans had trusted him. How it would all work out he could not imagine.

Father and son met occasionally for a walk in Munich's *Botanischer Garten*, near the train station, usually early in the morning, when Johann was coming home from all night duty in the policlinic and his father was about to leave for a sales trip or an old friend. If Johann's father had slept well and the weather was good, their conversation was usually calm.

"Well, Papa, how did you sleep? Did you try out the flannel pajamas yet?"

"I'm too old to sleep. I don't need sleep, just rest. Sleep is a waste of time."

"Nonsense. Your body needs to restore its energies in sleep. Mine sure does."

"Well, you always liked to stay in bed, even as a little boy. How's the policlinic?"

"The same. We have more patients, more bureaucracy, and less medicine. It's especially bad for children. Tuberculosis is everywhere just now. We saw ten children last night. One died before we could get him to the hospital. Another will probably die tonight or tomorrow. The parents wait too long before coming to us. It's crazy. Being a doctor means I get to see people die. I thought I would keep them alive."

"We all die."

"But I see young children dying. Children. And cannot do anything about it. They are sickly and undernourished. Their poor parents don't know what to do. And neither do I, to be honest. Why should they live for four or five years, and then die? They bring little joy to their parents. They just take up their time. And eat. So the parents and other children have even less to eat. It would be better if they never lived. I'm sure their parents think so."

"Don't be so sure until you have a child yourself."

He wanted to change the subject. His father already knew his frustrations with his work. And it was not a good idea to ask his father about his business. Both of them knew better than share their memories of their two-storied house out in Pohlendorf, of Minna, their cook who used to make fried dough balls with honey at Christmas, of the big cherry tree and the thorny black current and gooseberry bushes in the side yard. Talking about it, just thinking about it made them both unhappy. Those days seemed like a fairy tale.

Johann did not understand why his father's business went bad at the end of the war. He assumed it was due to the economic crisis brought on by the terms of the Versailles Treaty, but he didn't know how. His father refused to discuss it. The topic was certain to bring his father's spirits further down, but what was there to talk about? Finally, Johann asked, "So, how's business, papa?"

The old man grumbled under his breath. "Not bad, considering that nobody seems to want to know what time it is anymore. No, that's not true. Nobody wants to believe what time it is. Nobody wants to take time to enjoy a fine watch. I could sell any number of cheap watches, fake gold, flashy and false. The parts might as well be made of cardboard. The watch works for a while, grinds itself to dust and stops. Good old watches, with jeweled movements that look beautiful, their gears like tiny flowers, family treasures—my Lord! People are selling them all over the place, practically for nothing. But they cost money to repair, or people don't want this or that engraving, or they're too "old fashioned" and nobody buys them. Just the Jews buy quality now."

"So you've said, Papa. But that means they are buying your parts for their watches, right?"

"No. They buy from their own suppliers. Listen, Johann, if I were a Jew, I would buy good watches, diamonds, jewelry, too. When we chase them out of Germany, they know they'll only be able to get away with what they can carry. Vermin. They've cost me enough in my business. They've cost all of us. All of Germany."

Johann did not want to talk about this, either. He did not know whether to believe his father or not. He did not know any other men who sold parts for watches. As for Jews in medicine, well, yes, there were many. Some said, too many. A fellow medical student complained that Jews laugh too much, while "good Germans" had nothing to laugh at after the war. Professor Schonauer once said in a lecture on endocrinology that the Jews had too much influence in Germany, like an "overactive, malfunctioning gland." At the policlinic, Johann heard the same complaint from his colleagues: "Too many Jews. Too many Jews in medicine. The Jews have all the rich patients. The Jews have all the money and live well, while we good Germans go hungry."

He knew that his father had not always been like this. He remembered the picnics each July that his family had with the Steins in the woods above Pohlendorf, when they celebrated Philipp's and his father's birthdays that fell in the same week. His father often told him how much he liked the Steins and how happy he was that Philipp was his friend.

In Johann's childhood memories, his father was strong, filled with good will and patience. Each afternoon, while they waited for his father to come home, his mother had read to him from beautiful books. At night, the light from the gas street lamp outside filled his room with a soft glow. Mysteries by day became dreams at night, followed by sunny mornings. If he could not go outside, there were treasures in the house to find.

The most tantalizing was his father's business suitcase, upstairs in the study next to his parents' bedroom. It was heavy and cumbersome for Johann to lift. He knew this from the one time his father had helped him hold it up by its double handle. His father had said, "Johann, you must never touch this without me. Do you understand? Never." The warning occurred each time his father let him come near it. And he nodded each time and solemnly said, "Yes, Papa, I understand." Then his father would lift the suitcase up to the desk, put it on its side and help Johann climb up on his lap. Slowly, ceremoniously, like the curtain rising in a theater, Johann's father would open it for the boy to see.

The case's dark blue-black interior brightened into a deep, shimmering, satiny Prussian blue with flashes of purple, especially as the reddening evening sky seeped inside. There were forty or more satin-lined little compartments. In one, nestling in the rich colors, were dozens of shiny, glowing little metal wheels, some notched with gears, some smooth-edged, some bigger, some smaller. In another, springs that seemed to be made of silvery-blue strands of hair, all coiled in their nests. Another contained silvery rods and pins, in which one could see elongated reflections of the light. A small compartment held tiny rubies, looking like little beads of blood or the salty fish eggs a neighbor brought to their house on New Year's Eve. A larger one had blank, white faces that looked like bright moons. Another, golden arrows of different lengths that would become the watches' hands. And, most fascinating of all, ten compartments in a row contained tiny golden numbers of different sizes, zeroes, ones, twos, threes.... Johann learned to count up to ten by looking at these numbers with his father, as they would count together in a whisper. Then his father told him how to make an 'eleven' and a 'twelve' and counted again with him as they looked at the larger numbers on the wall clock. But he always wanted to look some more at the wonders in the suitcase. No matter how often Johann was permitted this vision, it always thrilled him. And it thrilled his father to see his son's delight.

On some days, the suitcase would stay in its place at home, next to his father's desk in the den. He could recall the moment when one night in bed, after his father had told him he would be leaving early the next morning, he decided to see the suitcase by himself. The temptation overruled his fear of violating his father's commandment. After breakfast, when his mother was busy in the kitchen, he went quietly back upstairs. She thought he had gone to his bedroom to get a toy or look at a picture book. But he went to his father's study and hoisted the suitcase up onto the desk—the place Johann thought that it should be opened to reveal its magical contents—and put it on its side. But it was locked. Johann heard his mother coming upstairs and hastily swung the case down to its original place and put it back where he found it.

In the evening, when his father came home, Johann begged him to open the suitcase.

"After dinner perhaps."

"Please, Papa. I've been good all day."

"After dinner" came, and his father agreed to Johann's pleasure. When the two went up stairs to the study, there was the suitcase, just as Johann had left it. His father lifted it up to the desktop and slowly opened it a tiny crack. Johann pressed his face to the opening in order to not miss a single second of the vision. To his horror—he could recall the feeling even now, nearly twenty years later—all the tiny wheels and springs, the pins and little rubies began to rain out of their compartments and into the lid of the case. Where he had expected to see beautiful, enchanting order, there was chaos. In his enthusiasm to see it earlier in the day, he must have turned the suitcase upside-down. He could not remember how he was punished, only feeling all the more afraid because his father did not display the anger he knew he deserved.

Walking in silence with his father on those mornings through the *Botanischer Garten*, he knew that other truths must replace those he had learned as a child. But he still wanted something firm and lasting. His father's declining fortunes had begun to fade even before the war. And what about his own? Where the park's crisp grass edging should have been, there was only a ragged line of weedy growth. The orderliness, the neatness, the certainty of edges and boundaries that they both remembered from those long ago Sunday afternoon walks was missing. The riverbank was so scarred and littered that sitting there was unpleasant. Weeds smothered old flowerbeds. A branch had been torn off a small oak, leaving a jagged wound with the bark stripped down the still oozing trunk. It was amazing that more trees had not been cut down or disfigured with the desperate need for firewood.

When he saw his father off at the train station, he noticed how slowly the old man went up the stairs: how tired he looked, how the hair on the back of his neck hung over his collar like faded straw. At home, Johann found his mother outwardly in good spirits, as usual. But he knew something was bothering her when she sliced the bread extra thin and only put one sort of jam on the table, without butter. She had been scrimping for weeks on their soups and even on the Sunday stew. But she usually put two or three pots of jam on the table, perhaps some cheese or a slice of smoked meat and butter for his "breakfast" after he had been at the clinic on night duty. His brother and sister had already eaten and left for the day. Maybe she wasn't feeling well.

"You all right, Mama?"

"Sure."

"You seem distracted."

"What's that, 'distracted'? Where do you find these words, 'distracted'? I've just got a lot on my mind. Who doesn't nowadays?"

"Like what?"

"Nothing important. It's just that what little money we have is as worthless as cobwebs. Your father's always grumbling about his clients and how the world stinks. Your brother wants to play jazz piano in the city all night long and emigrate to America. Your sister says she is going to cut her hair and get a motorized bicycle! Imagine. A sixteen-year-old girl riding a motorized bicycle. And who will pay for it? A girl on a motorized bicycle!" she repeated. "Not in my day," she continued. "I know, it's not really important. But I have to have an answer for these things. Your father says to your brother and sister, 'Ask Mama.' Or at least that's what they tell me he says. I don't want to bother him with these matters. He has enough on his mind. He looks poor and doesn't eat as much as he used to. ."

"Well, let Rudi play his jazz if he wants to, but tell him he must wait until he is twenty-one before you will discuss emigration. Only one more year, but he might change his mind. And let Angelika cut her hair if she wants to, but she must wait until she is eighteen until she can ride a motorized bicycle. Lots of girls are riding bikes with motors now, Mama. Even motorcycles. She can start saving for it. You can talk with her, Mama, and with Rudi. They listen to you. As for Papa, well, I think he looks tired. And his grumbling is understandable. He's a proud man. He'll be better after he gets used to his new routine."

"You understand nothing. Nothing. There's too much change already."

So that was the problem. "May I have some cheese, Mama?"

"I'll go down to Kramer's and get some, if they have any. I gave the last slice to your father. I'll go right now."

"Stay, Mama. It's all right." He did not tell her about Helga. He guessed she knew and she would approve. But he did not want to take the chance of upsetting her.

He took up the newspaper when he went to his room. The headlines told of French and Belgian troops in the Ruhr. 'What an impossible humiliation!' he fumed in silence, this damned Treaty!' The *Reichsbank* policies, he read, were not responsible for "the disorganization of the currency and the still increasing inflation." He snorted and threw the paper on his bed in disgust. 'All right, *Herr* Rudolf Havenstein, whoever you are! And the rest of you lordly gentlemen on the Executive Committee of the *Reichsbank*! Well, then, who is responsible? One American dollar now equals one hundred million German paper marks. One month ago it was worth two million. Back in June, it was worth one hundred thousand. How absurd! Mama said it—"Money as worthless as cobwebs!" How stupid!'

He could not imagine how much two million was. How could anyone imagine it? A wheelbarrow full of money! Two wheelbarrows? There were dozens of thousands of white blood cells in a single liter of a tubercular patient's blood. Billions of white blood cells in each pale tubercular child, like the little boy he had watched die the evening before. But what did such numbers mean? Just that something had gone terribly wrong. That the natural order was undone. That chaos was a disease that must be cured.

How could his mother buy butter or bread or anything, with money so worthless? His parents' savings, if they had any by the time this hyperinflation was over, would be worth a pile of dust. 'She must be bartering,' he thought. 'Her jam! Her wonderful gooseberry jam! Or her hoard of potatoes. But what of other housewives? Surely they had jam and potatoes to barter, too. Would a quarter of a pound of butter cost a hundred thousand jars of jam, a million pounds of potatoes?' He almost laughed. He knew that his parents had sacrificed on his account so he could study, instead of going to work at fourteen and helping support the family. He wondered if he could sell anything on the black market. His watch? Would it come to that?

All this news. All this disorder. All this wasting away, this coughing, this pale, red-eyed, bony-cheeked, thin-fingered dying. He fell asleep, but it was not a satisfying sleep. When the newspaper fell off the bed with a stiff, rustling sound, he jerked up and called out, "Flares!" But he fell back asleep almost immediately.

Johann's concerns were not just for Germany. His concerns were for his family, for himself within Germany. Here he was, twenty-seven, finishing his residency, about to be fully licensed, about to achieve a goal toward which he had worked conscientiously since he had been wounded near Douai, and now he did not know whether he wanted to finish. Where could he go? Whom could he begin to help? He wanted so much to be a hero. But heroes, he thought, never had doubts. And he had many.

The only part of his life he did not doubt was Helga. They saw each other every day in the medical school library, on a break from his rounds in the university hospital or before he returned to his work at the poli-clinic. He often took her an apple or a pear from the hospital's canteen.

"You again, you thief, with a pear this time."

"I'm not a thief. I could have eaten the pear. I paid for it with my meal."

"Paid? Nobody pays for anything now. We just pretend to have money. It's not even good paper." She smiled.

"You look nice today, Helga."

"Don't I look nice every day?"

He laughed at how she knew how to draw him out of his moodiness. She always tried to calm him, to cheer him. When he was with her, he felt stronger.

"Yes, you look nice every day, but especially today!"

"I finished this dress last night. It's from material my oldest sister was going to use. But she will never use it now, will she? Poor Sonja." She started to look away.

"I know you miss Sonja. It must be hard on your parents and on your little sister, Erika, too. Sonja was too young. Someday we will be able to stop tuberculosis. Professor Knauer said it is just a matter of time, though I don't know how surgery will help. You can't cut out a person's lungs and put in new ones."

Helga took a bite of the pear, absently and without really listening to him. She had heard this before. His talk about medicine did not so much bore her as leave her feeling incapable of saying anything intelligent. Good health, she thought, should be automatic, like sunshine or flowers. When it wasn't, she felt cheated, just as she felt cheated when it rained on a day she planned to go to the countryside. Then he said something that made her listen.

"Helga. I love you. I loved you even before that night together at the carnival. I want to marry you."

She looked at him. She loved his high forehead and his clean smell, his straight teeth, his wrists, his hands. She loved his smooth voice. She loved his sense of dedication to medicine, even if she did not understand it. She marveled at his eagerness to believe he could solve every problem, at his belief that medicine would cure every illness. With her oldest sister dead and her father dying, her mother absorbed by the same concerns that absorbed Johann's mother, she needed his sense of strength and his loyalty, his promise that he would never leave her.

"I love you, too, Johann. Yes. I love you. Yes, I want to marry you, too. Soon, please. Soon."

They saw each other again that evening when the library closed. He walked her to her family's apartment, near the Chinese Tower, across from the English Garden. It was a nice walk at any time, especially near sunset. But that evening, it was enchanting. Arm in arm, or with their arms around each other's waist, they sang and laughed. Helga had asked him about his limp only once, and when he said he got it in the war and did not want to talk about it, she said she understood and would not ask him again. She was good like that, he thought. She knew what bothered him and what to say, or not to say. She never offered him advice or challenged his ideas unless he asked, 'What do you think?' Then, without sounding like she had made up her mind, she asked him to explain what he meant or what he thought should happen. She sometimes said she did not understand him, but most of the time, she said exactly what he knew was right. He once told her how important it was to him that she agreed with him, that she understood his reasons and his conclusions.

"But I won't agree with you, Johann, if I think you are wrong."

"Good. But how often am I wrong?"

They laughed out loud. Walking down the park's edge toward her home, they talked about the names they would give their children: for the two boys, Paul-Adolf and Friedrich, and for the girl, Greta and Ottilie, in honor of their respective grandparents. They talked about where they would live: not in Munich, but not in a village either; maybe Augsburg or Landsberg, maybe toward the east of Munich, nearer the Austrian Alps, maybe north—but always in Bavaria. "Nuremberg is supposed to be lovely, a real German city," Johann said. "Munich is over-crowded. Who can trust Munich, after what happened following the war? Too many vagabonds and loiterers. Too many foreigners. "Ridding the place of communists," Johann said, "was necessary, but who knows when they'll be back." Helga nodded, not so much out of political conviction as out of her desire to show agreement with Johann in everything she did not understand.

"The ideal place," he said, "would be someplace like Pohlendorf. I'll have to take you out there some time to see my family's old house. It was beautiful." Wherever they would settle, he would have a small practice, specializing, he thought, in pediatric medicine. His residency had proved to him how much he liked to work with children. He would concentrate on juvenile diseases. Tuberculosis and diphtheria were ravaging children across Germany. He would help find a cure. Helga would organize his office and do the paperwork. They would have healthy children. They would be happy.

They said "good night." Helga promised to speak with her parents about their plans. She told him to come to her family's midday meal after church that Sunday. "I will wear my gold wristwatch!" he said. They kissed quickly, both smiling, laughing at being so close to what they wanted. Johann turned and walked back toward the clinic. Helga did not quite have the courage to tell him she thought she was pregnant.

CHAPTER FIVE

𝔚e 𝔚ere 𝔖till 𝔜oung

When Philipp left Munich, I didn't envy him in the least, even though he had a prestigious residency, and I hadn't. I was confident that I would reach great professional heights, too. I had you and was to be a father. I knew I might have to work harder, but I was willing to do whatever I could, with you by my side. After all, we Were still young. Our lives were full of hope.

Johann closed the heavy drapes against the cold, overcast December morning and took his seat before anyone entered Room 600. The trial had entered a procedural phase. Discussions between the lawyers and the judges interrupted the witnesses' testimonies. He was torn between fascination and boredom.

Several spectators fell asleep during the lawyers' lengthy statements. Johann sat stiffly upright, but his mind wandered. Looking at the famous physicians in the prisoners' dock, he remembered the time when he imagined that he and Philipp would be among them, renowned for their scientific achievement, their service to the *Vaterland*, to all humankind.

Now he was serving as a janitor. Philipp was beyond help. And famous doctors were on trial for crimes against humanity.

He remembered Philipp leaving for his residency. He had walked along the platform as fast as he could while the long train moved away from the station. He could still see his friend laughing, cheerful, exuberant, leaning out of the window and waving his white handkerchief with exaggerated gestures, shouting: "*Auf Wiedersehen*, Johann! Long live medical science!"

*****

It never occurred to Philipp to leave Germany and find a residency in Austria or Switzerland. He was a German. His future was in Germany. And Germany's physicians, whether he agreed with their teachings or not, were the best. His residency was with the renowned Alfred Hoche, Professor of Psychiatry at *Albert-Ludwigs Universität* in Freiburg-im-Breisgau. A plum of an assistantship.

Philipp looked again at Hoche's cordial response to his application letter. He had decided to focus on psychiatry. It blended his interests in eugenics, epidemiology and public health. Later he planned to pursue research on the relationship between public health and mental health, with a special eye toward helping working-class children deal with the problems they faced in Germany's cities.

The morning was bright and clear as his train sped westward. Every now and then Philipp imagined he could see a peak of the Alps to the south. After a few hours, the view of rolling foothills hinted at Lake Constance beyond. Toward noon, the train's shadow shortened and shifted as the train moved through the Swabian Alb beyond Ulm. As they rounded a long curve coming into the Black Forest, he could see the locomotive and all the cars before him in a glistening arc. This was just how he had imagined it would be: "*Herr Doktor* Philipp Stein!" He said his name and title out loud in rhythm with the wheels' clacking over the tracks. Then he laughed and did it over again.

The train passed Donaueschingen and began its winding journey through the evergreen forest on either side. When the conductor walked down the aisle calling out the next stations, Philipp consulted his map. They passed by Hirschsprung's deep gorge, where a statue marked the spot a noble stag was said to have leapt across the chasm to escape a hunter on horseback.

Philipp knew "Hirschsprung" for another reason: Harald Hirschsprung, the Danish pediatrician, who had first described symptoms of acute blockage of the large intestine in infants, a condition now known by his name, "Hirschsprung disease." How wonderful it would be to discover, perhaps even cure a unique disease, to have one's efforts memorialized in its name! He rehearsed in his mind all the ailments and diseases that bore the name of the physician who first described them.

Every now and then, on the edges of sloping pastures, stood huge Black Forest farmhouses built atop their barns. Clear brooks cascaded alongside the tracks, one splashing Philipp's window as they passed. Unexpected tunnels swallowed the train in darkness, only to break opening just as unexpectedly with a light that seemed brighter than before. Finally, they neared Freiburg. The train slowed as it pulled into the station, revealing the celebrated view of the city and its Gothic cathedral tower against the forested hills that encircled it to the east.

From a distance the cathedral tower seemed to be a starched, crocheted cone of coarse yarn, rather than a carved latticework of creamy red-brown sandstone. Freiburg's medieval city walls and gate towers, its narrow streets, and half-timbered houses and shops were a welcome counterweight to post-war confusion. He did not look to the west, where he would have seen the city's slaughterhouse. If he had arrived in the middle of the night, he would have heard the sounds of the animals. Their smell was more noticeable at night, too, pervading the air in a way that seemed both ancient and familiar.

The last thing on Philipp's mind, however, was an ominous vision of the future. He wanted to meet Hoche and his fellow residents. He wanted to get to work. The difficult times were behind him and, for that matter, behind Germany, he thought. After four years of turmoil, the currency had been stabilized. The government seemed to be in control of fanatics on the right and the left. Employment was up. Begging and thievery were beginning to subside. He looked forward to playing his part in building a better, stronger *Vaterland*.

He had hoped that he would be met by someone from the medical school, perhaps another resident or an orderly from the hospital. When no one appeared, he found a porter, got his trunk on a pushcart, and checked it at the freight counter. The porter then carried his two large suitcases to the curbside and a taxi. He had written ahead for lodging at the *Neue Pension zum Schwarzwald*, near the university and its hospital.

"No visitors in your room. No smoking in your room. No drinking in your room. You surely understand the reasons for these rules," said the landlord, *Herr* Lenkel, politely but firmly, his wife standing at his side, nodding.

Philipp registered for a week and paid in advance, telling the Lenkels that he might be staying longer, if he couldn't find a suitable apartment to rent. His room was clean and sparsely furnished. He asked for hot water. When the chambermaid brought it, he quickly washed, shaved and changed his shirt. By then it was nearly five in the afternoon, but he thought that he would report to the university hospital that he had arrived.

The hospital was just a few minutes' walk away. He found his way to Professor Hoche's office. In answer to his knocking on the door, the professor himself shouted, "It's open. Come in."

Philipp was eager to meet him. Hoche's medical reputation, especially his courage in addressing complex social and ethical problems were the reason he applied for this *Praktikum*. On his train trip from Munich, he kept rehearsing his side of their initial conversation. Should he say, 'You have no idea, *Herr Professor Doktor* Hoche, how much of a privilege it is for me to meet you? No, too fawning,' he decided. Or, crisply, standing at attention, with a great show of self-discipline, 'Your obedient and devoted student, *Herr Professor Doktor* Hoche, reporting for my assignment, sir,' much as he had reported to his superior officer in the war?' 'No, too stiff and likely to be thought insincere. Perhaps simply, *Herr Professor Doktor* Hoche, I thank you for the opportunity to work with you. I shall endeavor to repay you for the confidence you have placed in me. Yes, something like that,' Philipp thought, but not quite as long-winded. He settled on '*Herr Professor Doktor* Hoche, I am privileged to report to work for you,' and rehearsed the line over and over.

Now, face to face with the eminent professor, unexpected beads of perspiration began to form on his brow. All he could say, his voice a bit strained, was, "I am Stein, *Doktor* Philipp Stein, from Munich. *Guten Tag, Herr Professor Doktor* Hoche."

Hoche smiled an easy smile. "*Dokto*r Hoche is enough. I was a doctor before I was a professor. *Guten Tag, Herr Doktor* Stein. Welcome to *Albert-Ludwigs-Universität*, welcome to Freiburg-im-Breisgau. You will start tomorrow morning, 6:30 sharp, with me on rounds in the veteran's ward. In Herdern, north of here. We'll meet there. Ask the porter downstairs how to find it. You'll need a bicycle. Tell him I said to loan you one. You'll find the ward interesting, I am sure. We can arrange your work schedule then. Any questions? No?"

Philipp barely had time to open his mouth before Hoche continued, "Fine. Until tomorrow. Oh yes, you'll have your midday meal with us afterwards at my home. A little custom I like to practice with new residents. And you'll meet my assistant. So, *Auf Wiedersehen, Doktor* Stein!" Hoche's rapid speech pre-empted any statement Philipp might have wanted to make. Dismissed just as if he had been addressed by a military officer, he turned briskly and left as quickly as he had come. He was being put into service promptly. Well, he thought, that's exactly what he wanted. And Hoche seemed to live up to his reputation for relative casualness in comparison to others of his standing.

After talking with the porter and borrowing an old bicycle, Philipp decided he would explore the city. He sat for a while in an outdoor café on the market square next to the cathedral, with a beer and some cheese, wurst and bread, and looked over the local newspaper. News of Munich was minimal, save for a front-page item about the impending trial of First Quarter Master General Ludendorff and a paramilitary group led by a corporal named Adolf Hitler. The two men headed a group of brown-shirted anti-communists who wanted to start a "German revolution." They had shot up a beer hall, then were wounded and captured by the police when they tried to march on city hall. He was surprised to see how much attention that exploit was receiving here, on the other side of Germany. He thought it was a Munich bagatelle, an odd blend of Ludendorff's ultra-nationalist bombast and a ludicrous cabaret satire. From the photograph in the paper, Philipp couldn't imagine how anyone could take Hitler seriously. A funny looking little man. He reminded him of an organ grinder's monkey—chattering and seeking attention. He turned to the section on Freiburg's cultural affairs. An operetta based on Strauss' *Wiener Blut* was opening in a week. Perhaps he would go.

Philipp soon felt tired. He decided to return to the *Pension*, unpack, finish the book he had begun on the train, and go to bed early. On arriving back at the *Pension*, he accepted *Frau* Lenkel's offer of dumpling soup left over from the midday meal. Although he was not hungry, he had promised his mother he would take care of himself.

When he went upstairs to his room, he got absorbed in his book, Jakob Wassermann's *Caspar Hauser*. His parents had given it to him as a going-away present. His father had inscribed it: "For Our Own Innocent! With Love, Your Parents." Besides an iron-framed bed, his room had a writing table and chair, a dresser and a small briquette stove. The chair was not comfortable enough to accommodate relaxed reading, so he stretched himself out on the bed, with the eiderdown puffed up around him. As he read, he sympathized with good Caspar, the simple soul whose innocence amused and angered those who came in contact with him. He dozed off, awoke with a start when the book fell to the floor, got undressed, crawled back in bed, slept soundly through the night, and awoke at dawn.

It was a long bicycle ride to the fringe of the city and the university's psychiatric clinic. When the porter told him he was the last to arrive, he hurried to find Hoche and the others in the ward. After giving Philipp a brief glare, Hoche introduced him to the two other residents—"*Herr Doktor* Pelcher, Heidelberg, and *Herr Doktor* Schetzeler, Breslau"—watched with an amused look as they exchanged the obligatory handshakes, heel clicks and head nods, and then strode off with the three young men trailing behind.

They stopped at random, while Hoche described what he saw with studied detachment. "Notice, gentlemen, this man's yellowed eyes, his sallow complexion, his brittle nails." As he spoke, he reached behind the patient's head and turned it toward the assistants, touched the sagging skin on his cheeks and jaws, and held up the man's hand. "What do you make of all this, *Herr Doktor* Pelcher?" Hoche asked without looking at the thin, bespectacled resident standing behind him.

"Damaged liver, obviously. Perhaps the aftermath of gas." Pelcher's high-pitched, nervous voice hung like gauze over their heads. Philipp's mind flashed back to the gassed men he had seen in the field hospital near Nancy.

The patient's head stayed where Hoche had moved it. His hand hung in the air. His eyes looked vacantly through the men assembled at his bedside. His gaze seemed fixed on a star at the other edge of the universe.

Hoche spoke. "This man is a piece of clay, a crumbling piece of clay. His consciousness fled him long ago, somewhere on the battlefield. He has not survived the war, although he breathes and we occasionally see him move or open his mouth as if to say something. He is living, but is not alive. His last act of will was to attempt suicide a few months ago. We have sedated him ever since." Hoche described the man much as he would describe a dried and hollowed gourd. "Yes, alcohol. And gas. Both. Each would have been enough to warp him. Now he is broken. Who can fix him? Not me. Not a surgeon. No one alive. And God doesn't seem interested in fixing him, either. He's been here, in and out, for nearly five years. Permanently since March last year. Permanently. What Shakespeare would have called a 'walking shadow.' From *Macbeth*."

Hoche started to turn toward the next bed. Then he put his hand on Philipp's shoulder. "This 'walking shadow,' what would you do for, or should I say, with him, *Herr Doktor* Stein? Tell us, please."

Philipp bent over and looked into the patient's eyes. Then he stood up and looked into Hoche's. The contrast was profound. The man's eyes were clouded, opaque, and dull, like bits of sand-washed glass at the seashore. The doctor's were clear, bright, intense, behind thick glasses that made them look oversized, relentless, the eyes of a purposeful man seeking practical, reasonable, logical answers to his questions. The patient's eyes asked no questions, registered no thoughts. Philipp knew the answer Hoche expected.

"His life seems 'not worth living… a useless eater,' to use your terms, *Herr Doktor*. He is consuming resources we should be investing in others who have a better chance of recovery and finding a meaningful existence again. As you say, he is not truly alive. Sad. Tragic. If we could be certain that there was no remedy for his condition, I suppose I would have to agree with your argument, *Herr Doktor*, that a painless death would be better than this form of living. I hope…"

Hoche interrupted him. "I am glad you see that, *Herr Doktor* Stein. *Ja!*" he sighed. "This man, this shadow of a man, I should say, might as well be dead. But here he is, breathing, eating, being cared for. I see no chance for his recovery. And we are not permitted by our laws at present to do what should be done." Hoche came closer to the man's bedside, bent over him and looked into his face. "Had you been wounded with a grenade or a piece of shrapnel, a comrade would have put you out of your misery. That would have spared you all this. We must find the will to make that possible now." As Hoche turned toward the residents, Philipp saw the veteran's eyes flash briefly in fear.

The four men proceeded along the ward's center aisle, stopping whenever Hoche came upon a patient whose condition he wanted to discuss. Schetzeler hung on the professor's every word, making a great flourish of writing in a leather-bound notebook. Pelcher fidgeted and looked up at the ceiling. Philipp kept looking back over his shoulder, unable to block out his memories of the wounded soldiers in the field hospital in France. Nurses, the black wooden crucifixes on the chains around their necks swaying forward as they curtsied, cast their eyes down as the group passed. As they reached the other end of the ward,

Hoche gathered the residents around him and described his collaboration with Karl Binding, a prominent retired professor of law, in their controversial little book of a few years earlier. All the residents nodded. Schetzeler wrote furiously.

"Lawyer Binding and I argue," Hoche said, "as you all know, that mercy killing is justifiable and ethical, and not just because we want to put the patient out of his misery. We have a moral responsibility to healthy citizens, to the *Volk,* to preserve our precious, limited resources for the future. Especially now, weakened as we have been by losses in the war, we must nourish the strong and healthy among us. To do otherwise is sentimental, false pity. And it threatens the future, the very survival of the *Vaterland.*"

The group then began walking back down the aisle. Philipp felt as though he was in a warehouse. At each bedside, Hoche gave a short history of the man's condition, asking the residents questions and challenging their responses, drawing them out into general discussions of this or that symptom or treatment. When they came to the bed of the jaundiced man where they had started, Philipp saw that he had pulled the sheet up over his head.

At eleven Hoche dismissed them. "Here's my card with my home address. Until midday, then. *Auf Wiedersehen, meine Herren!*" The three residents went their separate ways for the next hour. Philipp stopped and sat a while by a fountain on the bicycle path back to Freiburg.

He was careful to be on time at Hoche's home. All three arrived and stood together, waiting for someone to open the door. In addition to having a similar appearance—their shoes, their haircuts, the chains of their pocket watches hanging just so—they had several traits in common: ambition; high energy; an appreciation that approached reverence for Hoche; and confidence in the benefits that would come to them as a result of their work with him. They shared a determination to succeed, to become important. They also believed in the ability of the human mind to scientifically investigate and solve all problems in human health. They could have been medical students and physicians anywhere in the westernized world.

Frau Hoche, a lively, bright-eyed woman, welcomed them warmly and showed them to seats in the parlor. A young woman was already seated there, reading a book. She glanced briefly at each of the three and stood up. Frau Hoche was about to introduce them when her husband came in from his study.

"Gentlemen," he said, "excuse me for not greeting you myself at the door. My wife and I welcome you to our home. I have the pleasure of introducing you to my assistant, *Frau Doktor* Seligmann."

Philip stood behind the other two residents waiting to be introduced. He saw that the *Frau Doktor* wanted to shake hands and not just nod her head in greeting. 'A modern woman,' he thought. He was surprised by the firmness of her grip. Hoche gestured for them to be seated again. After a few minutes of conversation about the lovely weather and the abundant roses by the front door, a maid announced that the meal was ready. Everyone followed her into the dining room.

They began to eat their soup in silence. Philipp looked up to see everyone else looking up at the same time and smiled. He was about to say something complimentary about the soup when Hoche asked abruptly, "So, what about death? Tell me your ideas, gentlemen. You and I will listen, *Frau Doktor* Seligmann, to hear what wisdom our new associates have learned in their studies."

"Alfred, can't this wait until after our meal?" *Frau* Hoche said, knitting her brow as she looked down the table at her husband. "Must we talk about death?" Philipp saw her face melt into a wry smile that gave him the impression that her husband's question and her comments were part of the day's ritual for the new residents. Hoche smiled briefly in return, and made no effort to retract his question.

The three young men all concentrated on their bowls of soup. Schetzeler was slurping his audibly, while Philipp and Pelcher were noticeably being careful not to clink the bowls with their spoons. *Frau Doktor* Seligmann slyly smiled and winked at *Frau* Hoche. She winked back.

"Come gentlemen, surely you have thought about death. I suspect you have seen hundreds by now, in the war. *Herr Doktor* Stein?"

"Yes," Philipp said, putting down his spoon. "I have seen many men dying, and many more dead. A field hospital, near Nancy. Far too many. Still, I know that death is the natural consequence of life. Life is a death sentence." When Hoche laughed out loud, the other residents joined in. Philipp continued, "We all die. I want to know why. I want to prevent death. I suppose it is my enemy. Our enemy."

"Fine." Hoche looked at Philipp. "And I am sure you know that you must understand your enemy before you can conquer him," he said, matter-of-factly, as though he was repeating a maxim out of von Clausewitz' treatise *On War.* "As you say, death is natural. And since it is natural, it is not to be feared. Do you agree?" he asked, not so much of Philipp as of the entire group. But Philipp answered.

"I don't look forward to my own death. Nor to anyone else's, for that matter. We fear death with reason. And not just because of the pain involved...."

Hoche interrupted. "What pain? Most deaths, in the last instant, are painless." He looked at his assistant, who was nodding in agreement. "There is more pain involved in going to the dentist than in dying on the guillotine," he said. "An entirely painless death, I assure you. The criminal's consciousness disappears instantly upon the severance of the arteries in his neck. The blood pressure in the brain falls so swiftly he doesn't know what happened to him. The same effect occurs in hangings. Also in drowning, once the brain is deprived of oxygen. And with a bullet to the brain or the heart, likewise. While death may be slower, it is the same with gas poisoning, too. That is to say, in peacetime, not the gas attacks of the last war. I concede, those are a different matter."

"But we fear death, even instantaneous death, *Herr Doktor,*" Pelcher said across the table. "And with good reason, I think." Despite his squeaky voice, Philipp thought that he was less nervous than he had been in the ward.

"No, what you fear, *Herr Doktor* Pelcher, is the process of suffocation. The process of dying. Even animals show this reaction. True, we might fear death because of our consciousness of life and death in the abstract. But, death as such is nothing special, especially if it is handled properly."

With his last sentence, Hoche tilted his bowl to catch the last spoonful of soup.

"You seem to be saying that death is good," Philipp said.

"Why not, *Herr Doktor* Stein? Why not? Some deaths are very good. And I don't just mean the deaths of heroes or altruists. Death is normal, natural, even desirable, given limited resources and the need for the species to remain vigorous. We aren't going to live forever. You said so yourself. And we can learn so much about living from dying. It is the condition which provides controls for our experimental thinking about human health and disease."

Frau Hoche, noticing that her husband had finished his soup, motioned to the maid to clear the table and bring in the next course. Hoche then leaned back in his chair. "Now, when is death good? When we can learn from it." The young doctors all looked at him as though he were revealing a holy commandment after having personally spoken with the Deity. *Frau Doktor* Seligmann was about to speak, but a glance from Hoche told her that he wanted to address his own questions.

"In Heidelberg, before the war," he said, "in the Children's Hospital, a nine year old girl was dying of a puzzling brain infection. She had lost consciousness. Her pulse was weak. We knew she would die in a matter of days, if not hours. Medical science demanded we determine the cause of her illness, and we prepared to do an autopsy at the earliest possible instance. But her father had told us that he wanted to take the child home to die, which of course was his right. I knew that if we released her, the delayed autopsy would be less satisfactory than one before any necrosis set in. The father would be arriving in a few hours. Should I give the child an injection of morphine before he came to claim her? It wouldn't have to be a large dose, given her weakened state. Then we could do our autopsy before the father arrived. What would you do, *Herr Doktor* Schetzeler?"

Schetzeler, a portly man with stringy hair that hung over his forehead, was chewing on a roll and chose that moment to begin coughing.

"Your thoughts, *Herr Doktor* Pelcher?" Hoche and the others turned to look at him.

Pelcher rolled his eyes and gulped. "Well, I suppose I would have consulted with other physicians." Seligmann smiled and sent another wink to *Frau* Hoche.

"Not necessary in this case, *Herr Doktor*," Hoche said. "You are the responsible physician. You want to know what's killing her. Do something."

Pelcher gulped again. "Well, yes. I would have given her the injection, then commenced the autopsy." He had small beads of perspiration on his forehead.

"And the father? Would you have told him the truth? That his daughter died of morphine, rather than of her brain disease?"

"I would have told him that she died," Pelcher said, sounding more confident. "If he assumed it was because of her illness, I would not have corrected him. On the death certificate, of course, I would have to write, "Infection, or rather, inflammation of the brain." And that would be true, to an extent. The girl died because her brain was infected, inflamed. That was the condition that robbed her of her health and necessitated intervention. The morphine could be explained, if anyone wanted to know, by the child's pain."

"Bravo!" Seligmann said.

Schetzeler nodded, but said nothing. Philipp was surprised and impressed by Pelcher's decisiveness, too, but wondered to himself if the morphine might not have impacted the girl's brain and skewed the results of the autopsy. He wanted to raise this point, but before he could, Hoche said, "Yes. Good, *Herr Doktor* Pelcher. I agree with my good assistant. Bravo! But you might be interested to know that I did not do that. And now, looking back, I think I should have. The nurse was away at her midday meal. I sat alone by the child's bed with a hypodermic syringe all prepared. Should I? Should I not? In the end, I didn't. The benefits did not appear that certain. Now, I think differently. Of course, each case is different, gentlemen. Each case is different. There is no absolute rule." He paused. "The only rule we always must consider," and here he looked directly at Philipp, "is to do whatever we can to learn what we want to know. Whatever we can." Hoche smiled a quick, stiff smile. It was gone from his face almost as fast as it appeared. "Still, as my beloved Shakespeare says,

'Our doubts are traitors
And make us lose the good we oft might win
By fearing to attempt.'

There is much in Shakespeare we should heed. A wonderful observer of human affairs. Someday I shall write about Shakespeare's usefulness to us in psychiatry."

"I have read Shakespeare in English," Schetzeler said with obvious self-satisfaction. "He's better in German." He was about to continue when the maid brought in the main course, a tureen of stew. *Frau* Hoche ladled it out onto each man's plate. A bowl of noodles was passed around the table. Without warning, *Doktor* Hoche asked, "Where do you stand politically, *Herr Doktor* Stein?"

Philipp hesitated. Was this a test? Why did he ask him in particular? Did Hoche have a strong political position? How important was it to agree with him? And why was *Frau Doktor* Seligmann smiling? He hadn't heard anything in particular about Hoche's politics. He guessed that, like the politics of most physicians and professors of medicine, they were right of center, but not necessarily anti-democratic: voting was a right for those who were responsible, educated, industrious, and a questionable privilege for everyone else. Hoche and his peers believed in the clarity of social distinctions, what they saw as a natural order that confirmed and rewarded their importance to society. Philipp shared their belief. After a few moments' hesitation, he said. "I don't think much about politics. Maybe I should, considering the conditions we are in, *Herr Doktor* Hoche. But I haven't given it much time. My studies...."

"Yes. Of course. Fine." Hoche said. "We can save that conversation for another time."

Philipp noticed that Seligmann began to frown and busied herself with her stew and noodles. When they all had finished eating, *Frau* Hoche signaled the maid to clear the table. A basket of apples was passed around. Everyone took one and complimented *Frau* Hoche on the meal.

"Better than the university's *mensa*," Schetzeler said, to everyone's laughter.

Philipp felt obliged to continue the conversation about politics. "I have followed some of the debate between the socialists and the conservatives and..."

"You lean to the conservatives, do you?" Hoche asked. Seligmann looked intently at him.

"Well, no."

"The socialists then?"

"Not entirely. A group calling itself 'the League of Socialist Physicians' held meetings in Berlin during the semester I studied there. I went to a couple, but I did not join. Later, I saw some materials they mailed to a fellow student in Munich. I like some of their arguments. But..."

"But what?" Seligmann asked.

"I am a physician before I am a socialist. I think they have it backwards. My calling is to be a physician. Not a socialist."

"Just so, *Herr Doktor* Stein," Hoche said. "Just So. Good. And there the matter rests." He looked at Seligmann, who was frowning.

"It all depends, doesn't it?" she said firmly, gesturing with the little, ivory-handled fruit knife. "Socialism is necessary in societies where the state has been tyrannical, where some have abused their privileges at the expense of the masses. To *not* be a socialist in such a society is to betray the principles that animate us as physicians." She neatly cut a wedge of apple and began to eat it. Philipp had the feeling she had said all this to Hoche before.

"And where do you suppose this 'society' is, *Frau Doktor?*" Hoche asked.

"It can be anywhere,' she said. "Wherever economic and social conditions warrant. In Berlin, I'm told, the poverty is quite severe and health care is at best uneven. Public health is a necessity. Given what we know about diseases like cholera, tuberculosis, diphtheria, and many more, a comprehensive health care system is vital for every citizen, whatever their place in society. Socialism makes sense because it flows from the same spirit of compassion that has led us to become physicians."

Philipp nodded, "I must agree. The problem is knowing when conditions demand radical political action. It's dangerous to change things too quickly."

Seligmann shot him a bemused, impatient look. "Tell that to the mother whose child is dying of cholera because of polluted water, or tuberculosis because the air is filled with smoke from the factories."

"So, I see that we'll have some interesting discussions." Hoche interjected, eager to maintain harmony among his team of assistants. "I trust we shall solve this problem. And all the others that confront us." He raised his glass, smiling and nodding to everyone at the table.

The others followed. Fearing that his earlier coughing spell had cost him his chance to impress Hoche, Schetzeler said, "It seems to me, that we are entering a new, international era. A new time of international understanding and cooperation. Someday we shall see the old terms *liberal* and *conservative* melt away. They should have been blasted away by the war. Now we must concentrate on social problems, on economic disequilibria, on political tension, and so on. Practical solutions are at hand, I believe, for poverty, for unemployment, just as we are finding practical solutions for mental illness, for instance. Factionalism is counter-productive because…"

"So, *Herr Doktor* Schetzeler, you would welcome the Bolsheviks into this international era? You think they can be trusted?" Hoche asked.

"I think they will be responsible," Schetzeler answered, "especially now that Lenin is dead. They need to cooperate with the West. At least for a while. Eventually, they will either become our ally or we will have to conquer them. We conquered the Slavs before. And we'll do it again. But we need strong leaders now. That was the lesson of the war."

"I don't trust the Bolsheviks, *Herr Doktor* Schetzeler." Hoche said. "They have come to power with ruthlessness. I can't trust that. And I don't know why you would."

"Yes, I see," Schetzeler blurted out. "Why yes, *Herr Doktor Professor* Hoche. I do agree. It goes without saying, the Bolsheviks are not to be trusted, because of their ruthlessness and their…"

Hoche interrupted him. "Yes. Well and good, ladies and gentlemen." He appeared both disdainful and amused, looking at Schetzeler much as an experienced oarsman might have looked at a man trying to row a boat for the first time. "Political action in moderation, my young colleagues. In moderation. That's how we will gain progress. We must do what is logical. What is reasonable. What science teaches us. We must not tolerate nonsense." As everyone nodded, Hoche looked around the table, pleased. Philipp saw the uneasy smile on Schetzeler's face and told himself to be wary of him.

"Yes, we must be on our guard against nonsense," Hoche continued. "Nonsense like *Herr Doktor* Freud's in Vienna, for example. Our actions on behalf of our mentally disturbed patients must be based on solid evidence. Not on some pseudo-science about dreams and preposterous childhood desires. We don't have to exorcise any imaginary demons. Reality is hard enough to understand."

Philipp had read some of Freud's work and wanted to reply, but before he could, Schetzeler said, "I've read Freud. He's.."

Hoche interrupted him. "And now, my young colleagues, I like a bit of quiet for myself after the meal. My wife insists on it." He smiled at her. "So, excuse me please, I want to have my daily consultation with my friend, Shakespeare, before I go back to work. We will see each other again at 3 o'clock sharp, to set up working schedules. There is a small room adjacent to my office."

They all rose and began thanking their host and hostess with crisp bows and handshakes one by one. When his turn came, Schetzeler clicked his heels. Philipp and the others smiled when they noticed that he was wearing black patent-leather shoes.

Pelcher jumped on his bike and took off. Schetzeler bent over to put something like stockings over his shoes. "I like to keep them shiny," he said to Philip. "This wet weather is hard on the leather." They hadn't gone a hundred feet when they had to swerve out of the way as Seligmann came up behind them, ringing her bicycle bell. As she rode past, she said, "*Achtung*, my boys! *Frau Doktor* coming through!"

"A modern woman, to be sure!" Philipp said.

"Who let all these women into our profession?" Schetzeler said, maneuvering his bike back onto the path. "She's headstrong.. Another headstrong Jewess. A dangerous combination. Why do they think they can be doctors? She's pretty enough, I must say."

Philipp said he had to keep an appointment, and began pedaling as fast as he could toward the university. It wasn't the last time he wondered how they would be able to work together.

The three residents soon settled into a routine. Seligmann set up their schedule: overlapping ten hour shifts in the clinic around the clock, six days a week, with everyone off on Wednesday afternoons for a three-hour seminar meeting with Hoche; on rotating Sundays, six more hours of clinic; emergency cases and extra duties whenever necessary. Philipp found bicycling back and forth to the clinic tedious, especially in the rain, when the gravel path became muddy, and at night in the dark. Often he slept in the clinic on one of the straw-filled sacks in a small anteroom by the foyer. He was given responsibility for a third of the patients and saw them all on each of his shifts. That meant daily conversations with shadows of men. That meant morphine. Restraints. Occasionally a discharge, but more often admissions, especially re-admissions. Most patients were passive. A few were violent, at least until they were subdued and medicated into a stupor. An average of two suicide attempts per week. All the patients were veterans. Most were his age. He also did his share of consultations with anyone who walked in looking for psychiatric services. Grieving parents, mostly mothers. Anyone who had symptoms of mental disorders—hysteria, depression, suicidal thoughts.

Hoche was a good mentor, Philipp knew, and he was grateful. While Luise Seligmann interested him for more than her medical skills, he did his best not to let her know it. He had little to do with the other residents. Pelcher wanted to talk only about the patients, one day raging about their lack of gratitude, another weeping over their plight. Philipp told Seligmann, who in turn told Hoche, that Pelcher was unstable, but as far as he knew nothing was done. As for Schetzeler, Philipp avoided him as much as possible because of his increasingly crude remarks about Seligmann, about the patients, about Jews, even about Hoche. Pelcher and Schetzeler soon became constant companions, feeding each other's emotional needs, as Seligmann put it, in order to endure their responsibilities. Philipp was the odd man out. That suited him just fine. Let them talk all they want, he told himself. All of them were overwhelmed by the intensity of their work. There was so little they could do for their patients.

Philipp's greatest refuge from his frustrations was an old fountain each day on his ride to and from the clinic. He stopped there whenever he could and sat for a few minutes on a stone bench cut into the fountain's base, closing his eyes, listening to the sounds of the water dripping and the gurgling of the pigeons that perched on the cast-iron spigots.

Some two months after he arrived in Freiburg, he saw Luise Seligmann sitting at the fountain.

"I was hoping you would come," she said. "I've seen you sitting here before."

"May I join you, *Frau Doktor?*" he asked.

"That's why I'm here. To sit and talk with you. I like the way you work. Your thoughtfulness with the patients. You really seem to care for them."

"Don't you? From watching you, I think you do, too. You're good with them. Kreisler, for example. I saw you reading to him yesterday."

"Yes, of course I care," she said. "Poor Kreisler. Blinded by gas and now wasting away. I care for him. For all of them. How can we not care? I have to control how much I care. Not be overwhelmed by helplessness. I force myself to look through them. Caring for them too much leads to disaster. Pelcher cares too much, I fear. That's a dangerous thing for a doctor. And Schetzeler. Well, he'll overcome his insecurities sooner or later, and become a good technician. But I think you are different, *Herr Doktor* Stein. You don't look at these men as pathetic creatures. Or look through them in order to avoid seeing their pain. That interests me. That's why I want to talk with you."

He was taken aback by her directness. All he could say was, "We've got twenty minutes before we have to be at the clinic. What do you want to talk about? I assume it's not Schetzeler's patent-leather shoes."

She laughed. "No. Not his shoes. Nothing particular." She paused a moment. "Do you have a sweetheart back in Bavaria?"

It was his turn to laugh. She *was* direct. "No. No sweetheart in Bavaria or anywhere else. But now I get to ask you a question. "Are you married?" He looked at the ring on her finger and then feared for a moment that she might be a widow.

"No," she laughed, "not married. I knew you would ask. I wear this to keep a proper distance between me and the patients. And everyone calls a professional woman '*Frau*' nowadays anyway. I have to smile whenever Hoche introduces me as *Frau Doktor*. Why it can't just be *Doktor* Seligmann, I don't know. Someday, perhaps. Any more questions?" She was smiling. Philipp liked the way her eyes flashed and the sound of her voice, her energy. "But before I ask you another," she continued, "I'll tell you more about myself. My family's Jewish. Much like yours, I imagine. Not likely that you'll see any of us in a synagogue."

She laughed a quick laugh, reached over into the fountain and let a few drops of water trickle over her fingers. "I'm from Hamburg," she continued. "Studied there, then Cologne and Heidelberg, then here. My older brother and my twin brother were killed in the last year of the war. Both in the navy. My father died of a heart attack shortly after we got the news about Gerhard, my twin. Mother died in the influenza epidemic three months after that. Five years ago this month. My father was a broker. My elder brother, Heinrich, was just starting university, law, when the war began. Gerhard and I were in *secunda* then, already planning to be doctors. My father and brothers were good to me—and for me. They didn't protect me so much as they challenged me to compete with them—sailing, swimming, chess, violin, you know. My mother was a strong woman, even through their deaths. I looked up to all of them. The war was supposed to separate the weak from the strong. Instead, it's taken the strong and left us the broken and the weak. I'm the last of my family." She looked at Philipp.

"And now I'm here," she continued, "as Hoche's assistant. He's taken a special liking to me since a psychology seminar, before I passed my state's exam a year ago. I did a paper on hypnosis that he liked, disputing

Freud's nonsense on dreams. Stayed on after my residency as his assistant. He and his wife have been very good to me. Sorry, that's more than
you probably wanted to know."

Philipp smiled. "No, not at all. Now it's your turn to ask me."

"Oh, I know all about you. I read your application to Hoche, your
vita and dissertation, and, of course, your daily reports in the clinic."

"Then I'm an open book to you?"

"None of us are open books, *Herr Doktor*! You should know from
your psychology studies." He saw that she was teasing. "But I try to be
open," she said after a pause, "or at least ask myself why I am doing what
I am doing."

"So why are you doing this? I mean, why are you sitting here, talking
with me?" It was his turn to be direct. He hoped he had not overdone it.

"Well, I think we should be friends as well as colleagues," she said.
"We have a lot in common. Our racial heritage, our professional interests, among other things."

"Good," he said, smiling. "I'd like that. But we should be going. Let's
talk again, *Frau Doktor*, maybe later today, after duty."

"No more *Frau Doktor*, please. At least when we are outside the
clinic. It's Luise. And yes, this evening, let's meet. I know a place. Good
wine. Or do you Bavarians only drink beer?" She laughed as she got
on her bicycle. He had trouble keeping up with her on the ride to the
clinic. She's certainly a new woman, he thought. Wonderful eyes. And
yes, exotic looking, too. He already knew that he loved the sound of her
laughter.

After that, they met often. Long bike rides, once across the Rhine
toward Colmar, when a thunderstorm forced them to turn back. Hikes
through Gunterstal and up Schauinsland, where they picnicked and
enjoyed the view of the Black Forest. They often sat by the fountain.
Their fountain, as they called it. They talked about their patients, about
medicine, about their families, their ambitions and hopes. Philipp ached
for every moment they could spend together. He had never been seriously involved with a woman before. He had told himself he would postpone all that until after he had gone back to Munich to begin his practice.

Despite the cheerlessness and futility of the clinic, he was happy. He felt comfortable in Freiburg. *It's a small city with few of the problems and many of the benefits of a large one,* he wrote to his parents. *Its charm is its quaintness, a welcome distraction from the factory-like hospital ward. I am content, immersed in my work.* He mentioned nothing about Luise until his father wrote, asking if he had any friends and hinting that he should be thinking of "settling down." *I work with a remarkable young woman,* he wrote back, *and we've become good friends. I'll tell you more when I come home.* No point in building up their hopes, he thought.

His favorite place in Freiburg was the market square by the cathedral at sunrise. Luise would sometimes join him and they would walk among the peasants setting up their stalls for the day's market. The farmers brought the smell and colors of the countryside with them: their purple-topped turnips, dark red beets, long red-orange carrots, braided onions, lacy dill weed, smooth, brown-skinned mushrooms. Tomatoes, pickling cucumbers, baskets of eggs, potatoes. Everything heaped on mats or shallow boxes on the cobblestones. Beside them, tethered goats, chickens and ducks in coops, and an occasional suckling pig in a crate. Best of all were the ruddy-cheeked, old peasant women. "Just look in this duck's mouth," one jolly, toothless crone with a bright blue kerchief, exclaimed to them. "The cleanest, plumpest duck in the Black Forest. A true feast." Philipp felt like he was back in Pohlendorf.

Luise and he often bought buns and wedges of cheese or tomatoes for their breakfast, which they ate while sitting on a bench. As the mist steamed off the tiled rooftops and the housewives and maids began to outnumber the peasants, they would go inside the cathedral and watch sunlight fill it up with shimmering colors as it poured through the stained glass windows. The incense from the early morning Mass lingered in the air and mixed with the earthy smell of the farmers who had come inside for the service.

He was not religious. He could not even recall being reverent. As a child, he and his family rarely attended Pohlendorf's tiny synagogue. When he occasionally accompanied Johann to the Lutheran church service, he went home feeling more entertained, especially by the music, than uplifted. Religion, he believed, was something he just did not need, much as a person on a warm day does not need a coat. But in Freiburg's cathedral, he began to understand what it must be like to be part of the orderly mystery of a faith. The windows, the ornate altar, the ritual, every facet of the experience fascinated him.

"Yes, I do like it here," Luise answered, when he asked her, "but I don't know why. I don't have much feeling for religion. My family would be shocked."

"That you're in a Catholic church?"

"That I'm in any church. Or synagogue, for that matter. They gave up synagogues two or three generations ago. Some on my mother's side became Christians. I mean believing Christians. Not just for the convenience of it. But most of the family just walked away from any religion. No, they'd be shocked that I was in any church whatsoever. They thought of me as a rebel, opposed to all this."

"Are you?"

"Yes, basically I am opposed to whatever has kept us from becoming whatever we want to become. The church certainly did that for most of its believers. I learned enough history in *Gymnasium* to know that. But maybe I shouldn't be so quick to blame the belief as the believers. I don't know if that's true for Jews. Probably not, given our inclinations to study and strive."

"What do you believe in then?"

"What do I believe in? Myself. Medicine. Science. The future. A better world. No more husks of human beings, living useless lives in psychiatric wards. I believe in social engineering to solve our problems. Don't you believe in all these, too? Or are you a secret Catholic?"

Philipp laughed. "No, I am not. And I believe in everything you said. I am just a bit uneasy by the certainty of our beliefs as doctors. I believe in medicine as a process, but less in the practitioners. As you said about belief and the believers. Christians have been just as certain in their beliefs. And look at what's happened because of those certainties."

Out of the blue, she said, "I like being with you. I am growing very fond of you, Philipp." She reached for his hand and held it as they walked back together into the market square.

CHAPTER SIX

The Throat of the Monster

It is not as though I didn't have eyes to see what was happening. I looked right into the throat of the monster. But I refused to imagine what we all would become if we let it devour us. I don't mean the man, Hitler. I mean the anger, the hatred, the contempt for others that dwelled in him, in me, in most of us. That was our doom.

As my mother told me, I had set a trap for myself and did not know it. And in that trap I was snared. Snared by my own ambitions. By my grand dreams and delusions. By my foolishness. Like most of us, I was a fool. A fool for Hitler.

He wondered about foolishness—his own and others'—a great deal in those so-called "Zero Hour!" days after the end of World War II, when all across Germany everything had to begin again from nothing. He saw its consequences in the city's ruin around him. He saw it in the "Doctors' Trial," turning upside down everything that he once believed in. In the dock sat, to use his mother's phrase, "the high-and-mighties," now somber, dejected, defeated. Those whom they reviled as weak and worthless before the war now sat in judgment. He had sensed that vast foolishness years before. But now he saw that it was more than absurd. It was evil.

'My God! We were fools,' Johann almost said aloud one afternoon during the testimony of a woman who showed the scars on her calves where sections of her muscles had been severed in a medical experiment. He turned his head quickly toward the two photographers near him in the corner of the courtroom. Had they heard him? If they had, they did not show it. Looking toward the row of seats in the gallery where Helga had been sitting, he was relieved to see she was not there.

Two American military nurses helped the woman down from the witness stand. The prosecutor next called a defendant to testify about the woman's scars. The defendant professed complete ignorance, although a document read into the record showed he was personally in charge of such experiments and had performed them himself, 'How can he claim that he knew nothing?' Johann thought. 'The honorable thing would be to admit it and then explain to the court why he believed the procedure was necessary. But to profess ignorance?'

He remembered the speech by the jewelry store in Munich. 'Did this dishonor, this evil horror begin there? And if it did, could it have been stopped, while it was still small? Could I have known what would happen?' He remembered being extremely tired in those days, but in a different way than he was tired now. Tired from his studies. Tired from his frustrations at the policlinic. From his worries about his parents and his *Vaterland*. Tired, but not like now, weighed down by the burden of all his choices and their consequences.

*****

Johann had finished his residency and was working in a different policlinic near the *Magdeburgerstraße* in a rundown part of Munich. He had hoped for a more prestigious position. A better neighborhood and a better class of people. But Helga and he had married a few months before their son, Paul-Adolf, was born, and he had to take what he could get. 'I'll get good experience,' he told himself. 'And it's the right thing to do, being in the trenches rather than far away from the front,' remembering how much he used to complain about the high-ranking officers who stayed as far as they could from the actual fighting.

The policlinic offered general medical services and emergency care to patients who could not afford to pay for private physicians. He was on duty ten hours a day, six days a week, plus two out of every three Sundays. Sundays were usually busy patching up wounds and bruises from Saturday night brawls, on top of the usual array of human ailments. He preferred dealing with private, paying patients. They at least tended to comply with his advice. Without them, he and Helga would have had a difficult time giving his mother something each month toward rent and providing food for themselves and their son. There was never any money to put aside. But he told himself he was not working for the money. He believed this constant duty and sacrifice was expected of him. But gradually, he began to feel the same self-pity he had admonished in his father.

His private patients were a "better sort" than the ones he saw at the clinic. They welcomed him into their homes, offered him tea, paid him in cash or with favors, and showed him respect. Clinic patients were surly, ignorant, suspicious, untrusting, frightened. They were poor, trapped in lives that kept them in harm's way. What could he do about their long-term nutritional problems, except say, "Eat better"? An emaciated day laborer probably would eat better if he could. The same thing when he said, "Drink less." The forty-seven year old prostitute he saw that morning probably needed alcohol or something like it more than most people. She was dying of advanced syphilis. He was treating her sixteen-year old daughter (or was it her granddaughter?) for the onset of the disease. 'A generation of syphilitics. How did we let it get this bad, when we know so much about pathology? Syphilis. Gonorrhea. Lord only knows what's next. Curing one disease seems to set up people for the next. Tuberculosis is worst of all, especially in children. And not a bit of pleasure involved in getting it.' Compared to those he saw at the policlinic, his private patients had more inconsequential problems. About the only thing they had in common with his clinic patients was that they also drank too much.

Johann and Helga were lucky to be able to live in his parents' apartment. Just after they married, within the space of a few months, his father died of a stroke, his sister went to live in an apartment across town with "her crazy friends," and his brother emigrated to America. It made sense for them to move in with his mother. They could not afford such a large apartment on their own. They got a larger bed for Johann's bedroom and rearranged his brother's bedroom for baby Paul-Adolf; a screen in the parlor sectioned off a sort of waiting room for private patients, and his sister's bedroom served as an examination room. It was hardly the comfortable life that he believed a doctor should provide his family. But when his mother offered to take care of Paul-Adolf, so Helga could go back to work—she was quite willing to do so—he said, "Absolutely not!"

Only after his father's death did Johann realize how much they had become alike since the end of the war—sullen, angry, bitter, disappointed. He knew that his parents had sacrificed for him and exhausted their savings. He thought that one day he would be able to help them, repay them, and give them a comfortable old age. He had told them that when he started his practice, they would never have to worry about money again. Now his father was gone and he and Helga could not afford an apartment of their own.

'This should not be happening to a graduate of a university, to a physician,' he brooded. His life seemed like a drunken carnival mummer's stagger down a cobblestone street: determined to be exuberant and in control of himself, yet always tripping over the curbstone. After a long day at the policlinic, he saw how easy it would be to take refuge in a bottle. Day after day, he saw shallow, selfish, bullies and their bruised women and skinny offspring. He saw unemployed men fathering more children on their unemployed wives and other women. Prostitutes and the young girls and boys destined to be prostitutes. Drunks, pimps, addicts, alcoholics, derelicts, degenerates, and the deranged. That he could do so little to change the conditions around him made him angry.

After a year of this, he was losing sight of the future he promised himself. He worked in a ramshackle policlinic in Munich's roughest, poorest district, sitting at a small desk in a dingy examination room, a converted closet, really, that also served as his office, looking out a small, dirty window at the freight yards. He heard the muffled noises from patients in the waiting room and the movement of the other doctors and nurses up and down the corridor. He smelled the carbolic acid, the alcohol, the cold, slightly acrid smell that drifted out of the examination rooms, the whiff of feces that drifted down the corridor from the toilet.

Had it been worse when he had first come to this policlinic? Or had he just gotten used to it? The doctors and nurses were not strangers any more. They had developed a kind of collegial informality within the predictable pecking order: the clinic director, Sprenger; the senior physician; another physician, Bock, who had a glass eye from the war; Johann; the resident physician, Steublein; and finally, the nurses, *Schwester* Forster and Schwester Arens, and the newest staff member, *Schwester* Mannesmann. He watched them all grow numb to what they dealt with. He saw them become half-hearted in what they tried to do for their patients. How else could they get through the day? Their banter about patients or the state's health insurance bureaucracy, or the weather or, rarely, politics were like so many shrugs, so many concessions to the inevitable helplessness they all felt. He tried to avoid their idle conversations. He wanted to do his job. But he slowly saw that he, too, was dragging himself through the day.

The days began the same: staff meeting at 7 a.m. sharp. *Doktor* Sprenger invariably told them to be careful about dispensing medicine. "We have a monthly quota, people. It must last, you know." Then he mumbled his other predictable words about doing good work for public health. "The *Volk*, the nation requires our professional expertise and authority. We are like military officers who must keep order and cleanliness as our highest priority. We have our nation's destiny in our hands."

"Yes, yes," they all nodded, smiled quick, flat smiles at each other, and began seeing the day's patients. By 7:30 a.m., the waiting room had filled up and a line had formed out the front door. At 10 a.m., the staff met again in Sprenger's office to catch their breath. Bock invariably would hum some marching song, offer to take out his eye, and chuckle to himself while the nurses looked disgusted. Johann usually excused himself to sit in his cramped office/examination room and have a cup of tea along with the bread and cheese or piece of fruit that Helga sent with him. He tried not to pay attention to the giggles of *Doktor* Steublein and *Schwester* Mannesmann in the office next to his.

Looking out his window, he watched four boxcars being uncoupled from their locomotive. Some men dressed in blue overalls—they looked like blue ants from this distance—jumped out of the way, as the engine, free of its load, puffed black smoke, pulled ahead and moved away onto a siding. Then a small, dark, muscular-looking locomotive began to back toward the cars. They lurched as it coupled with them. He imagined the sound of the impact. The work engine barely slowed down, pushing the cars backward, behind a long storage shed, out of his sight. Its smoke rose over the roof of the shed, billowing darkest orange in the sunlight.

As the smoke grew denser and blocked the sun, a red-brown haze spread over the yard toward the policlinic. His life was like one of those boxcars, pushed and pulled without its own volition. Two days before, he had told Helga about how little he felt in control and how much others—he would not have identified them, just "others"—seemed to be manipulating everything to his disadvantage. Instead of the sympathy, indeed the pity he secretly hoped for, she scolded him. She had come back to it again just that morning.

Paul-Adolf was in his high chair, sucking on a bread crust. "What an excuse! Blame someone else!" she said. "It's much easier that way! And you never have to confront your own limitations!"

"You don't understand!"

"I understand well enough. You don't like things the way they are. Fine, neither do I. You don't see how they can be changed! Fine, I agree, it'll be difficult to change things. But that doesn't mean they won't ever change. That you have no responsibility for trying. And if you cannot change them, at least you'll know that you tried."

"Be quiet. My mother will hear us."

They had been talking about their limited income and how much they hoped to find a more modern apartment. If they ever were going to do that, Helga told him, she had to go back to work so they could save. Their mothers could take care of the children. He told her again he would not allow it. No wife of his would work. Paul-Adolf needed her at home. They had been through it, over and over again.

His parents' apartment was shabby. He was ashamed of it. He had trouble saying it was his and Helga's apartment, although he was officially registered as the "head of household" with the local police after his father died. He was ashamed of the neighborhood, too. Once dignified, after the war it had become a warren for the poor and the disappointed. His neighbors hurried past each other with sparse greetings, ashamed of their poverty.

Helga needed a new coat, but claimed she was fond of her old one because it fit so well. Their old icebox leaked, but she told herself that they all do. Johann said he was glad they lived with his mother, since she needed their support. He tried to think of how much worse his policlinic patients lived. But he could not quite convince himself to be grateful. He berated himself each day for not being able to support his family as well as he wanted to. They would not be able to move to a more respectable neighborhood any time soon.

Helga tried every day to soften his distress with her happy moods. On their Sunday afternoon walks in the park, Paul-Adolf looked smart in his neatly pressed and starched little outfit. In warm, late afternoons, they sometimes sat together on the back stairs, Paul-Adolf between them. Johann would tickle him until he squealed and laughed his deep, throaty laugh. Then Helga would laugh her higher-pitched melodic laugh. Johann's deeper laughter surrounded theirs. It was like a simple folk song. When the wind blew, the air smelled fresh. Helga's blond hair had the highlights of their son's even blonder curls. With them, or just thinking about them eased Johann's worries. Walking home and thinking about them, he would find himself whistling a tune and then be startled into smiling at himself. But those times grew rarer as he began putting in so many hours at the clinic and in his practice. When Helga told him she was pregnant again, he worried how he was going to support another child.

His income from the policlinic was fixed by the state's health insurance fee schedule. It was barely adequate. He had a bit left over each month for his mother, to add to her pittance of a widow's pension. His private patients had to be billed—Helga saw to that—and they were often late in their payments; sometimes they brought eggs or potatoes. "Better than nothing," Helga would say.

"More doctors are graduating every day. Too many. The state wants to break us by flooding the profession. That way they can cut the fees even more," he grumbled.

"That's why I say, be glad for the eggs and potatoes," she would answer and try to coax a smile out of him.

Being a physician was supposed to be a noble profession. He served people with his intelligence and his good will. In return, he deserved a good income. Not a fabulous one. But enough to have a house with a garden for his family, decent clothes, nice furniture, a meal out now and then in a good restaurant. Eventually, an automobile, a vacation somewhere with his family. What he wanted above all, was not the money but the respect that money brought. The respect a doctor deserved. Instead, he found himself working long hours for a meager salary. Five days a week, and another half day on Saturday, to say nothing of two half-Sundays each month for emergency cases at the clinic. Always pushing papers back and forth across his desk, filling out forms for every diagnosis, procedure and prescription. He could not see any end to it.

The newspapers reported that the general economic situation was improving. The currency crisis, the unemployment, Belgian and French troops occupying the coalmines in the Ruhr—all the terrifying problems of the past two years—had evaporated. There was a building boom in Munich and elsewhere in Germany, too. There were fewer loiterers and beggars on the streets. He could see a bit of a recovery at the policlinic, in his patients' clothing, if not in their general health. But he had no confidence that it would last. As his father had said, if their money could be worthless once, it could be worthless again. "Nothing lasts," had been his father's dying words.

His mother's mind seemed clearer than it was a few years ago, but her jaundice, evidence of her liver disease, was recurring. Although he told her not to worry, he feared she was dying.

He was grateful that her spirits were high, although she must have seen her yellowing skin every time she looked in a mirror. She tried to make him believe she was healthy. She sang in the kitchen, she showed him the sweater she was knitting for Paul-Adolf, or smiled over a letter from his brother in America. She bustled back and forth as usual. She teased him about his unpolished shoes and the clumsy knot in his necktie.

"Some doctor you are, wearing shoes like those. And your necktie looks like you never untie it, just slip it on and off over your head. No wonder you don't have lines around the block for private office hours. Now sit down. We'll eat in the kitchen. Helga and little Paul are over at her mother's for the day. I have made your favorite—*Fleischsuppe mit Knödel*." She ladled out a full bowl of the dark, thick soup and dumplings for him and took a smaller portion for herself.

"So, Mama. You'd go to a doctor based upon how well he dresses. Who cares about what he knows?" This was a frequent dialogue between them, almost word for word. He smiled each time she started it. And she started it, not because she was distressed by his shoes or his tie, although she was certain they revealed a minor flaw in his character. She worried about him. He had become dour, strained. Had come back changed. The war, of course, had changed everything, including her beloved Johann, her first-born.

"Mama, I want you to try another medicine."

"No. It will just upset my stomach. Like the last one."

"Yes, it may. But it may help. Your color is poor, Mama."

"So. I won't live another fifty years. We both know that. I don't want to anyway."

"Please, Mama." He stirred his soup.

She tried to change the subject. "Johann, who is your doctor? If you are sick, who would you see?"

"I could see one of the physicians at the clinic. The clinic director, *Doktor* Sprenger, I suppose. Or Steublein. He's good, too. But I am not sick, Mama. Why?"

"I just wondered. That's all. Your color is not so great either, you know. And besides...." She trailed off, not wishing to upset him.

"Besides what?"

"Nothing."

"Besides what, Mama?"

"It's just that I worry about you. You always look tired. You act tired. You used to be so energetic. And you used to have real joy in concentrating on something. Even when you were tired, you didn't act tired."

"Nonsense. I'm fine. Really."

She could not contain herself. "I wonder, Johann. You seem to be, how should I say it? Angry? No, not so much angry as frustrated. Yes, that's it. Frustrated."

"Where did you learn such a big word, Mama?' he asked with a smile. 'But yes, it's true. I am tired. I put in a lot of time at the clinic and then at home, too, in the practice."

"You are frustrated. I can see it."

He had not heard her talk this sharply, this pointedly, for as long as he could remember.

"I know you, Johann. You think I am simple, but I know you. You are troubled. I don't know what's troubling you, but something is. And it's probably because you have always wanted to be independent, to be in control of things, to be first and best and tallest and smartest. You want to be just like you were when we all went on walks on Sunday afternoons, in Pohlendorf. Always running ahead. Always pretending you were an explorer. Or a drillmaster. Chasing your brother and sister along the path. Repeating whatever your father told them, in an even sterner voice. And you can't bring those times back. You can't."

He just looked at her.

120

"I'll tell you a story. I've told it to you before, I know. But maybe you'll understand it better now."

It was as though he was a little boy again. She talked and he just listened.

"A spider wants to travel. To see the world. It runs away from its mother and father. It loves them, but it wants to be free of them. It doesn't know where it is going. It doesn't know what it wants to do. It just wants to go. But it is still a spider. No matter how far it travels, no matter how different it wants to be. It was born a spider. It will die a spider. It must do what spiders do. It must spin a web. It must stay in its web. It cannot roam. The web is where it belongs. Where it must stay." She took a sip of her tea. He looked puzzled.

"*Ach*, Mama. Don't get yourself..."

"Wait," she said. "The story is not finished. Living in the web, the spider eats. It controls its destiny, more than if it would pick up and wander. That can be good. But living in the web brings its consequences, too. It must prey on others. It must admit to being dependent upon its web. In the end, a spider can only be a spider. Do you see?

"Yes, Mama, I see," he said.

"What do you see, Johann?"

"That you love to tell stories."

"But what does this story tell you?"

"That I am a spider? I suppose you mean that I am like a spider. And..."

"*Ja*. You are a doctor. A doctor is like a spider. You must have your web. You cannot escape it. In a way, it traps you. Just as a spider is trapped. Just as it traps its prey. The web entangles everyone. Especially the doctors."

"What do you mean, Mama?"

"I mean that the spider has to be what it is. So it must have a web. You are a doctor. So you must do what doctors do. The spider's web is beautiful. The web even works well to catch the spider his dinner. But the web is dangerous. It is even dangerous for the spider, don't you see? The spider lives at the expense of others, maybe even some who should not have been trapped in the web. That brings them pain. And the spider, even though it can't help what it does—it has to eat—can end up doing harm, even when it thinks it is doing good. It's just doing what spiders do. Now do you see?"

He shuffled his feet. "I want to do good. I want to help people get well. You know that."

"Of course I do, my little Johann. My *Hansl*. Of course. But maybe you're frustrated by not being able to do as much good as you want. And that can be dangerous, given the powers you have. Maybe more dangerous than you or I can imagine. I've heard what happens in hospitals. They've got you and can do what they want to you."

"Oh, Mama. How do you work yourself up into these knots? Your ideas about doctors and medicine are from the last century. I know what I am doing. I know what I want to do. My only problem is that I can't do it as fast as I want to. But I will do it. You'll see. You'll see."

"Please be careful, Johann. Enjoy what you have. You know what Papa said. 'Nothing lasts.'" She began to weep. She had not talked to him like that since he was a child.

He looked away while she wiped her eyes with her napkin.

"I'll be going now, Mama." He touched her cheek and she smiled. "I must go back to the policlinic. Please tell Helga I'll be home later than usual. Thank you, Mama. It was good to have our midday meal together, just the two of us for a change." He hugged her, surprised by how small she was in his arms. As he left, he heard her washing the dishes in the sink. He could not be sure, but he thought she was singing.

That night he dreamt of spiders. Spiders in caves stretching their webs over each passageway, snaring every living thing that came along. Each spider had a tiny face, the face of a medical student or a professor or of the two physicians who worked with him at the clinic. Each trailed a thread on which patients had been bound with loops around their waists. As the spiders danced up and down around their webs, the patients were jerked along behind them, like sausages, or slaves all knotted together. He was a spider, too, with a thread like the others, dragging patients behind him. But he was also being dragged along by other spiders, to whose webs he was tied.

At the policlinic the next morning, with his nightmare still fresh in his mind, he asked for a private conference with *Doktor* Sprenger. Sprenger, nearly thirty years his senior, had earned his medical degree before the war. He served as a field doctor all four years on the southern front, specializing in amputations. He was proud of his record and recited it at every opportunity: "Sixteen in a day, five days in a row! At least ten each day were above the knee. At least three were multiple. Forty percent survival after three days. I knew what I was doing!" The unspoken part of Sprenger's litany was his bitterness with his destiny since then. Johann knew he was an alcoholic. By noon, he could smell it on Sprenger's breath. No question now of him doing any surgery. Once he had passed out at his desk. The nurse and Johann decided instead to let him sleep it off, rather than risk his anger at knowing they had found him drunk. She said that Sprenger's only son was killed in the war, that his wife was one of the first to die in the influenza epidemic. He thought that Sprenger, despite his drinking, was a good doctor, trying to make the best of a bad situation. He went to him hoping to get some advice, or at least encouragement. Of late, the clinic director seemed more resolute, almost cheerful.

"Good morning, *Herr Doktor* Sprenger." He quickly went over in his mind what he planned to say.

Sprenger nodded and motioned toward a chair. After a pause, Johann clenched his fists. "I think you should know, *Herr Director*, that I am distressed by our situation here in the clinic. I don't believe we are doing enough to stop all this disease and suffering. I always thought…"

Sprenger interrupted him. "I'll tell you this, *Herr Doktor* Brenner. Things will have to change for us to get justice in the world. Drastic change. And not with this government we have now, if you can call it that. Weaklings. Cowards. We need a leader. We have never needed a leader more than now." He grew red in the face and began to sputter.

Johann had not come to discuss politics, but he could not stop him. Sprenger went on, "We cannot expect the world to respect us if we don't show them that we must be reckoned with. Germany, our Germany is drifting. We doctors must be respected."

"*Herr Doktor Direktor*, I ..."

Sprenger wasn't finished. "None of us true patriots are respected, Brenner. None of us can stomach what is going on today. But there is hope! Yes, we have a leader among us! Now! Here in Munich!" Sprenger was speaking so loudly now that everyone in the clinic could hear him. "Here," he continued, standing up and pushing his desk chair back with a screeching sound, "here is the work of the man we need!" He pointed with a flourish to a copy of *Mein Kampf* on his desk. The book faced forward, like an advertisement.

Until then, he had seen only medical texts in Sprenger's office. Like most Germans, Johann already knew something about the book's author. Newspapers had given front-page coverage to Hitler's attempt to overthrow the state less than two years before. He remembered the incident all the more because it occurred the night before he and Helga got married. If Hitler and the others had succeeded, the government would have collapsed and their hastily planned civil ceremony in the municipal registry office would not have taken place. Hitler's trial was in the news for weeks.

"*Herr* Hitler's book has just been published," Sprenger said. "There is powerful truth on every page, I can tell you." Then he shouted out the title while he looked up at the ceiling: "*My Four and One Half Years of Struggle.... Mein Kampf....*" Johann thought for a moment the clinic director was talking about his own life.

"Read it, Brenner. Borrow it and read it. You will gain from it. We all will."

'This isn't what I've come for,' Johann thought, but he decided the best way to get out of the conversation was to take the book. "I'll bring it back tomorrow," he said.

"No. Not tomorrow. Take your time. Read it. You must read it."

He started it that evening, intending only to skim it. He found himself sucked into a giant waterfall. He had heard that visitors to Niagara Falls, leaning over the railing at its edge, felt pulled into it by some unseen, overpowering hand. The book was like that. It drew him into its vortex of assertions and promises. It drowned him with historical observations and philosophical claims. Its sentences flooded into his thoughts, swirling through them so completely that he could not tell which were his own and which were Hitler's. Though he probably had read no more than a hundred of its nearly seven hundred pages when he returned it, those pages made an impact on him.

Johann worshipped certainty and authority. And Hitler was so certain, so confident that he knew the answer to all of Germany's problems. He had devoted himself, he wrote, to Germany and would do nothing to harm the *Vaterland*. Johann thought of the oath he had sworn to serve his patients, to first do them no harm, and then to cure them by all means at his disposal. Hitler sounded a doctor. A doctor of a people. A doctor for the *Volk*.

Johann felt unable to dissect Hitler's categorical statements, to think of opposing arguments, to consider the implications of what he was reading. He had never been taught to think critically, to ask why and how an author might be trying to grab his mind and shape his convictions. His whole generation had assumed that if a statement appeared on the printed page, it must be true. Swept along by the book's long sentences, its unqualified statements, its assumptions and confident assertions, his only response to Hitler's claims was "*Ja!* Yes!"

Mein Kampf's sheer weight was intimidating enough. But what overpowered him most was Hitler's evocation of his primal fears. Yes, he told himself, we Germans should take responsibility for our own affairs! No foreigner, no outsider, no enemy of our *Volk* must be permitted to have power over us. Germany was not guilty of causing the World War. We only were guilty of letting our enemies trick us into an unjust peace. What patriotic German could disagree with this? He struck his fist on the table as he skipped through the pages, landing on ideas and phrases that seemed as monumental and true as the Alps. Reading *Mein Kampf*, he forgot that he was a man who praised science and scorned unquestioning faith. If foreigners, outsiders and enemies are in our way—as they always have been—we must overcome them. In any way we can. It is a question of survival. That's how this world works: the fittest survive, the rest perish. Exactly! Again he banged the table. Helga looked up, startled.

"Johann, Paul-Adolf is asleep. Please."

He barely heard her. His mind was racing. Hitler's arguments confirmed his own beliefs and hopes. He saw that he could no longer avoid taking responsibility for what he saw in the lives of his patients; for what Helga and he were enduring in their struggle to achieve some material success; for what was happening to his *Vaterland*. Everything was inseparable. Everything now made sense. Helga is right, he thought, I should not just complain. I should act. Act. *ACT!* When he went to bed on Sunday evening, he had decided to go see Hitler himself.

It was not as hard as he imagined it would be. Sprenger told him the address. Hitler's headquarters were in a shabby office building not far out of his way on his walk home. He was there before he knew it. He expected to be dazzled by a complex protocol that would demand he show proper credentials and the required obeisance, like a supplicant before a throne, as he bowed and scraped his way toward the divinely chosen leader of all Germans. Indeed, he hoped this would be the case. It would add weight to the conversation he would have later that night with Helga:

'Oh, by the way, I saw Adolf Hitler today, the man who will be the savior of Germany. Yes, I really saw him, and talked with him, too. He was most kind to receive me, of course. We had a good conversation. I think he was impressed with me and wants to me to join him in the struggle for our *Vaterland*.'

Then he would smile, walk over to her and draw her near to him. She would look up at him as she used to, back when they were first stealing minutes out of their day to be with each other. She would say, 'I'm so pleased. So proud. Now you are doing something for Germany, for the three of us. Most importantly, for yourself. You have taken responsibility at last!'

He closed the street door behind him. The smell of stale urine followed him up the stairs. He needed to hold on to the banister to help him pull his stiff leg from one stair up to the next. Paint was peeling off the walls. At the top of the landing, down a hallway to the right, he saw a man in a uniform standing stiffly in front of a glass-paned door. On it was painted in black letters outlined in gold, "National Socialist German Worker's Party. Adolf Hitler, *Führer*"—centered under an eye-level, thick-armed swastika. The guard was expressionless, wooden, dumb looking. His ludicrously short black necktie was pinned to his starched brown shirt with a small, silvery swastika. A shiny-handled pistol bulged from a worn holster hanging on his black patent-leather belt. Black polish could not hide the scrapes on the toes of his run-down boots.

The guard asked him in a coarse Bavarian accent to identify himself.

"I am Brenner, Johann, Doctor of Medicine, Munich," he said firmly. "I hope to see *Herr* Adolf Hitler, please." He reached for his identification papers but before he could take them out of his breast pocket, the guard knocked twice sharply on the door, opened it, and announced, "The doctor is here."

Johann stepped into a small, clean room with large windows at the rear. In front of the center window was a modest desk. On either side of the room were other desks, and at each one, head down, sat a man looking at papers or writing. A typewriter somewhere clacked out an insistent rhythm. If he hadn't known what the sign on the door had said, he would have imagined he was in any business office. The men at the desks looked just like the bureaucrats in government offices around the city. Men in shirtsleeves with dark neckties, their coats neatly on hangers against the wall. The faint odor of pomade and mildew. At each desk, a blotter; a metal stand that held a dozen or more rubber stamps at the ready; a letter opener; a block of writing paper; a typewriter. Without turning around, he could picture the standard clock on the wall. 'These are the headquarters of Germany's salvation? Impossible!'

As he stood there, waiting for someone to acknowledge him, he studied the room. On the walls were framed photographs of Hitler: in his World War I uniform; in a trench coat, speaking, his right arm raised in a fist; in business suit, speaking with both arms raised over his head; a close-up, staring purposefully into the distance; another, staring back into the viewer's eyes. Black and white posters with bold red lettering advertised *Mein Kampf* and the party—"Deutschland's salvation!" Several framed certificates hung on the wall to his left, too far away to read. In the corner, were what he thought were boxes of *Mein Kampf*. Loose copies were stacked on the floor nearby.

After a few moments, he concluded that the man seated at the central desk, with his head down, writing furiously, was Hitler. He took a step or two in that direction. Then the man to his right looked up, stood up noisily, opened a side door with the words, "The doctor is here, *mein Führer,*"and motioned him to go through.

He entered. Directly opposite, at a large desk in front of a bright window, sat the man he knew from the photographs. The late afternoon sun outlined Hitler's head and shoulders in orange. Before he could introduce himself, Hitler said, almost in a whisper, "You are not my doctor. Who are you? Who let you in here?"

"I am Brenner, Johann. Doctor of Medicine. Johann Brenner. I want to speak with you, if you can spare me a moment, please, just a moment."

"I need a doctor, Brenner. What kind of doctor are you?"

"I practice at the policlinic near the *Magdeburgerstraße*. General medicine. I was certified in general medicine in 1923, more than two years ago now. You called a doctor?"

"I have persistent head-aches. My throat is dry and hurts. Six days, no, a full week now. I don't want to take medicine. Aspirin doesn't help me anyway. I expected my personal doctor."

"I see. Perhaps you would like me to examine you?" Johann regretted this almost as soon as he said it. Examining another doctor's patient was a serious breach of professional etiquette. But he did not have the courage to withdraw his request.

He watched Hitler look him over, watched his hands clench and unclench. When Hitler stood up and stepped away from his desk, Johann was surprised how short he was. Even more, he was surprised Hitler's voice was so soft, so difficult to hear. Perhaps it was because of the dryness of his throat. He looked feverish, too. Puffiness around his eyes.

Redness around his nose. His lips seemed parched. A pitcher of water and an empty glass were within arm's reach on the desk.

"All right. Examine me then. But quickly. And take care. My skin is sensitive. I don't like to be touched. Now hurry. I am expected across town. I am already late. I cannot be too late."

Johann then realized he had left his doctor's bag at the policlinic. He didn't think he would need it at the Nazi Party offices. "Please step over here, *Herr* Hitler."

Johann stood with his back to the window. He moved so his shadow did not fall on Hitler's face, which looked flushed, accentuated by the reddening sky outside. "Open your mouth wide, please. Say 'Aaaaah….'" He glimpsed swollen tonsils but couldn't see further into his enflamed throat. Hitler's tongue quivered. "Close please."

The whites of Hitler's eyes were watery and bloodshot, contrasting peculiarly with the pale blue irises. His pupils contracted from the window's light, making his eyes even bluer. Johann gently pulled down first one, then the other of his lower eyelids. He felt a slight chill as Hitler stared at him, not blinking. "Now turn around, please," he said and began palpating the base of the fleshy, soft neck. He could hear Hitler taking short, noisy breaths—the quiet snorting sound reminded him of a tubercular patient he had seen that morning. Standing behind him and reaching over his shoulders, he probed gently with his forefingers along his throat, under his ears and jawbone. As he suspected, the lymph glands were swollen, and the carotid pulse accelerated; the skin was clammy, yet dry and pasty feeling at the same time. The stubble on Hitler's closely shaven throat was barely noticeable, but here and there, a single hair stood a bit higher than the rest, barb-like and odd, given the fastidiousness that seemed so important to the man. Later, Johann wondered if Hitler shaved himself, or if one of his aides were trusted to put a straight razor so close to the *Führer*'s jugular each morning. That was all he could do for a makeshift examination, since he did not have a thermometer, his stethoscope or even a tongue depressor.

"You have felt like this for nearly a week?" he asked.

"*Ja*. I don't sleep well."

Hitler turned to face him again. Johann sensed that he had used up all the time allotted him to stand so near. He stepped back to the other side of the desk.

"So, what do you think, *Herr Doktor*? What is your name again?"

"Brenner, *mein Herr*. My name is Brenner, Johann. You have a low-grade infection, most likely a common upper respiratory infection, although I cannot be sure from such a short examination. It seems to be a simple cold. It should pass soon, in a day or two, I would say, considering you have not felt well for a week now. If it persists another week, you should be tested for tuberculosis. Meanwhile, you must drink liquids, as much as possible. No alcohol, of course. Hot teas. Tea is better than coffee. It would not hurt to drink chamomile tea. It will help you sleep. Peppermint tea is all right, but chamomile is better. Herbal tea is preferable in any case. If aspirin doesn't work, don't take it. And sleep is important, I don't have to tell you. Do you want a prescription for a sleeping tablet? I will write one."

"Fine, *Herr Doktor* Brenner. I don't drink alcohol anyway, so that's no problem for me. Yes, a sleeping tablet. Or a powder, preferably. Something natural. It must be natural. I don't like artificial medicines. Aspirin upsets my stomach. Leave the prescription with Schreiber in the outer-office, please. Thank you. *Guten Tag*." Hitler sat down and continued reading some papers. He didn't look at Johann again, but merely raised his arm and motioned him toward the door.

Before he had finished writing the prescription at the desk of the man he presumed was Schreiber, Hitler emerged from his office. Everyone abruptly stood up and raised their hands in a stiff salute. Without thinking, Johann did the same. Hitler said, "Get the good doctor's address."

An aide handed Hitler his trench coat, and followed him out the door.

When Johann left a few moments later, the long stairwell was already empty. Only then, as he was going down the stairs, did he realize that he had said nothing to Hitler about why he had come. 'How stupid! When will I have another chance like that? I could have at least purchased a book. Perhaps an autographed one. Yes, that would have been the thing to do. Ask for an autographed book. I could have returned the next day and picked it up. And then spoken with him.'

Looking through the doorway at the bottom of the stairs, he saw that the red sunset's colors drenched the street, still wet from a brief afternoon rain. Silhouetted passers-by cast lurching shadows up the stairs, moving left to right, right to left. Looking down at the staccato light and dark, Johann felt himself grow dizzy. He could still feel Hitler's pulse, still see his eyes. He wished for his cane, though just a few days before he had felt proud that he had not used it for five full years.

He walked home, forcing himself to go more briskly than usual. At this pace, his stiff leg gave him a swerving, undulating gait that made him look drunk. Climbing the stairs to their apartment, Johann called out to Helga before he reached the door. He was eager to tell her that he had decided to become a man of action. That he had seen the *Führer* himself.

CHAPTER SEVEN
A Cruel Gospel

You warned me about the Nazis, Helga. About how they blamed others for every problem we had. How they were willing to make others weak in order to make themselves strong. For a while, I heeded your warning. It was easier to see through their lies when times were good. It was harder when I struggled to believe in myself.

Phillip saw through them, too. But in his case, I thought he was only trying to discredit the Nazis because they blamed the Jews for all that was wrong in the world. I even thought that I was stronger than Philipp. That he was a dreamer, but I was a practical man. Despite his talents, I thought he was somehow ordinary, weak. At the time, to be honest, I thought his kind had always been weak, that weakness was a cause of corruption. I have learned to my shame how very wrong I was.

The early evening sky was still light. When the trial adjourned for the day, Johann walked toward the old city. The small square where his *Volksbank* had been was now a dreary space defined by rubble. A few young girls and old women still were silently sorting the debris. The old man, however, was missing.

'Perhaps he is ill today, or tired,' Johann thought. 'Perhaps he is just tired of it all."

Many new people were arriving in Nuremberg from the east. What never ceased to startle him were the women with photographs of their husbands, brothers, parents, their children, and their questions: "Have you seen…?" "Do you know this…?" "Did you pass through…? That's where I was separated from my…. Where I last saw my…." Their tears were barely dry on their cheeks before new ones appeared.

Was the whole world lost? He thought of all those with whom he had lost contact. He thought of his neighbors. Of patients. Of colleagues from before the war. Of Schumann and Clauberg. Of Mengele. He thought back to Auschwitz and the last time he saw Philipp.

When he returned to the Palace of Justice, Philipp stayed in his mind. If Johann was beginning to ask himself how his own life had taken the course it had, he was only slightly less curious about his childhood friend's, whose fate was so interwoven with his—and so different.

*****

"What shall I call you, boy?"

"Blibberblubber Klibberklubber Schnipperschnupper…," the child shouted.

"Georg! Now, tell the good *Herr Doktor* your name," the boy's mother prompted.

"He didn't ask me my name, Mama. He asked what he should call me. You can tell him my name. I don't want to."

"As you see, *Herr Doktor*, Georg can be difficult. Sometimes I wonder what he is thinking. He cannot get along with other children. He's so small for his age. As I told the other doctor, neighborhood boys throw stones at him. Just last week, he came home bleeding and crying. Look, here, on the back of his head." The woman turned Georg around so Philipp could see a place where, under the boy's dense, black, crinkled hair there was a large scab.

"I *am* a butterfly," Georg announced, whirling around.

"Tell me why you are a butterfly, Georg." Philipp bent over so he could look directly into the boy's green eyes.

"Well, I am not a butterfly yet. Right now, I am a worm. A special worm. Someday I will turn into a butterfly. Then everyone will see how beautiful and strong I am."

"That's the story I have told him, *Herr Doktor*. Georg is, well, as you see, Georg is ... not fully German. My fiancé was killed in the war, at Verdun. We were going to be married as soon as he came home on leave. He never came home. I lived with my mother in the Ruhr Valley then, near Essen. After the armistice, the French sent in troops. Moroccans. I was young. I met one in the market place. We got to know each other. He was handsome. He had a beautiful smile. Beautiful teeth. And such smooth, brown coffee skin. He said he would marry me."

The boy began to sing. Philipp smiled at him, and he smiled back.

"I never saw Georg's father again. Georg was born seven months later. He was terribly small. And I had no milk. Or not enough. We had nothing. My father and sister died in the influenza plague, just after the war ended. My mother and I tried to feed Georg as best we could. We moved down here, to Günterstal, where my mother came from. But her family is all dead, too." She began to cry.

"And the butterfly?" Philipp asked.

"I told Georg he was like a little worm when he was born. So hairy. Look at his kinky hair. And his skin. Dark. Not as dark as the man who fathered him. But dark enough. I told him he would not always be so ugly, like a worm. He'd grow up to be a big, strong butterfly. All this talk now in the newspapers about the "*Rhineland* bastards." The children can't help it, you know. They say that there are thousands like Georg."

"I am a worm. But I will be a butterfly. Let's go, Mama. Back on the street car."

"Georg," Philipp said, as he put his hands on the boy's small shoulders, "your Mama brought you here to the hospital because she wants us to help you grow up and be strong. We want to help you, too. Here, look at this. I have a little wooden man on my desk. You play with it on the floor while I talk some more with your mother."

135

He handed the mannequin to the boy. Georg began to move its arms and legs back and forth on their hinges. He turned its head around and around. He began to sing again, a soft, little melody.

Georg's mother sighed. "Please understand, *Herr Doktor*, I cannot take care of Georg any more. My mother died. A month ago now. She would have him during the day when I was at work at the factory. He's too small; well actually, he's too unruly to be at school. I know he's different. Not just physically, I mean. He will not speak for days on end. He just sings. Like now, but often much louder. He can sing any song he has heard, even if he heard it just once. We went to Mass at Easter in the cathedral and heard the chorus. On the way home, he sang long parts of what we heard. Not the words, of course. La la la. But perfect melody. Perfect. It frightens me. He needs someone to take care of him. I don't know what to do with him."

"*Frau* Grimmel, we cannot keep him in the hospital just because he is different. I don't find anything seriously wrong with Georg. From his records, neither did the other doctors who examined him." Philipp stopped himself from saying that the boy was seriously underweight. The woman probably had little enough food for herself. "His file shows you have been here often. Haven't you any other family? Or a helpful neighbor, perhaps? You live in Günterstal, perhaps the nuns at the cloister there can help?"

"I don't live in Günterstal now. When my mother died, I moved nearer the factory. Besides, I don't want to give Georg up. The nuns wanted me to give him up. But he's not an orphan. He just needs a doctor. I know it. A mother knows."

"Well, what do you think is wrong with him?"

"He's not normal. He's in his own world. He cannot make friends. He cannot play with others. It doesn't help, of course, that he looks so different with his green eyes and dark skin and that hair. He may never fit in. I think something is wrong with his brain. Perhaps you can fix his brain somehow. Not an operation. Some pills, perhaps. Please do something, *Herr Doktor*."

"Let me talk with my supervisor, *Frau* Grimmel. I will write you a letter and tell you what we can do. It will take awhile. A month, perhaps."

"Thank you so much, *Herr Doktor*. Thank you. Good by. Come Georg. Now give the nice doctor back his little man. We are going now."

Georg stopped singing. "It's mine. The little man is mine. He gave him to me. I want him." When his mother tried to pull it out of the boy's hands, one of its legs broke off. Georg then threw it at the floor, breaking the other leg, and began to scream. With apologies to Philipp mixed with shouts at the child, *Frau* Grimmel picked up her son and hurried out the door. Philipp heard the boy's howls echo down the hallway. He picked up the pieces of the mannequin and set them on his desk. After pacing back and forth a bit, he started writing a memo to *Doktor* Hoche, with a copy to Luise, describing the case in detail, and asked for a meeting to discuss the case.

Later that afternoon, he received Hoche's response, written at the bottom of his memo. "Send the boy to Emmendingen. He has a chronic mental illness. It's a good place. Fresh air. We're too crowded here. Sending him now will make it easier on him and on his mother." He went down the hall to Hoche's office. Luise was there.

"The boy's barely seven, *Herr Doktor Hoche*," he said. "He's not a 'walking shadow.' He's a child. He needs to be with his mother. She needs help with him, I grant you. But how can an institution for the mentally ill be appropriate for a little boy? What the mother needs is some safe place to put him while she's working. She has no family." He hoped that Luise would agree with him. She looked at Hoche and said nothing.

"Just think a minute, *Herr Doktor* Stein," Hoche said, leaning back in his chair. "From what you have told me, the mother feels burdened by the boy. And he is a burden, both mentally and practically for her. He reminds her of her dalliance with a Moroccan. You say that she has no one else to help her. She is poor. So she fills the boy with fairy tales. A butterfly! Imagine! That's certainly her wish for him—and, it seems to me, for herself. I can understand that, given her prospects. But from what you wrote in your memo, the boy will more likely change into a hoodlum. He shows classic signs of anti-social behavior. So he sings. Will the mother get him singing lessons? No, he will grow up to be a criminal. A useless eater. And most likely father other useless eaters. He was spoiled at birth, or by conditions since then. Whatever the case, he'll be well treated at Emmendingen. It's a modern facility." Hoche leaned forward and assumed a resolute pose, with his elbows on his desk, as though he had thought this through long before. Luise still said nothing. Philipp looked at her.

After a minute's silence, she said, "I agree with *Herr Doktor* Hoche. Emmendingen is the best solution." Philipp gritted his teeth.

When Hoche saw that Philipp was not persuaded, he continued, speaking slower than before, "Consider this, *Herr Doktor* Stein. The boy's mother is not helping him. He already is a cost to our society. Without him, at least she could work without distraction. She's not so old yet. She might marry and have healthy, productive children. This child is a loss. Yes, it is sad, but no less true." Out of the corner of his eye, Philipp saw Luise nodding in agreement.

Hoche continued, "A loss to her and to Germany. Another curse from the accursed war. There may be other children in Emmendingen. And the mother could visit him on holidays. Thirty minutes by train. Who knows, she might even find work in the town. That's the most reasonable, the most effective solution to a bad problem."

"That seems so dispassionate, *Herr Doktor Hoche*." Again he hoped Luise would support him. He turned to her. She saw the hope in his eyes but was silent.

Hoche was leaning back again. "Dispassionate? Dispassionate? Please! I've mentioned to you before, Stein, you must get over this emotional weakness. You are a doctor. We need to think progressively. We have to protect what is healthy. We cannot afford sentimentality. 'Lives not worthy of life' are precisely that. Unworthy lives. Lives not worth living. It might not be fair, but it's reality. The weak must make way for the strong. We have a responsibility to the strong, first and foremost." Hoche stood up. His eyes looked right through Philipp as though it was barely worth his time explaining to him these fundamental facts of life. "I thought you were more realistic, Stein. There is not enough for everyone in the world. Not enough food. Not enough room to live. And not enough health care. Giving too much of our resources to one person, especially to someone who has such limited potential, is a crime against our *Volk*. Short and simple, *Herr Doktor*, anything else for the boy besides institutionalizing him is bad medicine."

"How do you know what Georg's potential is, *Herr Professor*? How do you know that the boy will become a criminal?" Philipp's defiance surprised even himself. For the briefest moment, Luise was astonished.

"His potential? Simple," Hoche answered, smiling and looking at Luise. "I know because I know human nature, my dear young colleagues. Only the rarest of the rare rise above their origins. This boy will be trouble as long as he lives. We should send him to Emmendingen. They will at least keep him under control. He can find his potential there," Hoche gestured toward the door. "Maybe they even have a choir he can join," he said softly, smiling a paternal smile, sat down again, drummed his fingers on his desk and began shuffling some papers. Luise said she needed to go back to the ward and left.

Philipp knew that saying anything more was futile. He knew, too, that his anger was sharpened because Luise had not supported him. That, as much as the boy's situation, was unbearable. He wanted her entirely, not just her body, but her heart and mind. At the clinic and in the wards, over the past few weeks she often had been curt with him. When he asked her why, she had said it was so no one would think that she was being partial. He said he understood, but he could not deny that he was stung. Now, in Hoche's office, he felt she had let him down. He would not have admitted to anyone that her authority over him made him feel more and more uncomfortable. But it did. Worst of all, he thought she was flirting with Schetzeler. Had she courted him to win his willingness to work with her? Was she handling Schetzeler the same way now? He knew he had to ask. That made things even worse.

"Schetzeler needs confidence," she had said, sitting by their fountain one evening. "He can be better than he is."

"I don't disagree with you there. But does that mean you have to encourage him so often?"

"He's entitled to encouragement, to praise when it's deserved. You all are. You're all going to be good doctors. My job is to help you. That's all I am doing. Why? Are you jealous?"

"No, I am not jealous," he had heard himself say.

"Don't lie to me, Philipp. There's no cause for jealousy. And about Schetzeler of all people!"

"I saw you yesterday with him in the hallway. Laughing. It didn't look like you were talking about medicine."

She had shrugged. Then she began laughing, uncontrollably. That was the last thing he had wanted her to do.

"Maybe we should not be together so much," he blurted out. "Maybe you're right. The others should not think that you are being partial to me—or any of us. Maybe we should make a little pause." He had not planned to say any of this.

She was quiet in an instant. "A pause? Now? I don't..."

And before she could finish, he had said, "Yes, we're both working too hard. We've gotten too close for a purely professional relationship. Hoche is counting on you. I think we should focus more on what we do with our patients. The outpatient clinic is growing every day. I'm behind in my reading." As soon as he had said all this, he wanted to take it back.

Now she was quiet for a long time. He remembered hearing the fountain gurgling behind them. "All right, Philipp. A pause, then. Yes, a pause, *Herr Doktor* Stein. As you wish." She had said, then touched his cheek, got up, got on her bicycle and rode off. He had just sat there, not knowing quite what had happened.

He had tried to believe that she would come back. That she would circle the block and come back. But he knew she wouldn't. He had tried to go on with his routine and not think about being with her. But he couldn't. He knew that Hoche noticed how somber he was, how he was less engaged in their seminar discussions. She must have noticed, too. He spoke as little as possible with her, and when he did, it was always matter-of-fact. He resented that she seemed unchanged, still intense, still fully committed to her work. He began to linger more often at their fountain, but despite his hopes, she never appeared. He thought of going to her apartment, of telling her he was wrong. Of saying that he hoped they could be together again. But he didn't.

When she announced that she was going to take a week off to go to Hamburg for family business, he thought she looked pale and told her so.

"It's nothing. I need a few days off, that's all," she had said briskly, and walked away.

When she returned, he asked her if everything was all right. She only gave him one of her shrugs. While he missed her and wanted her, he could not forget her betrayal about the Moroccan child. He felt angry. Angry and betrayed. Hoche meant well, he knew, but his attitude about the boy was alarming. Would he have wanted his own child to be treated that way? Would Luise have wanted that for hers? Hoche's book, *The Permission to Destroy Life Unworthy of Life,* once had seemed so reasonable. So calm and logical. But couldn't he see, couldn't she see, what that meant for innocent children? For anyone whose life had taken an unfortunate turn? For anyone who was vulnerable to disdain or hatred? He still sought certainty in medical science. He still believed that German doctors would be the ones to achieve it. But he could not accept the implications of Hoche's decision about Georg. Its consequences were too far reaching. He would have to resign from his *Praktikum.* But he put it off as long as he could.

He tried to distract himself from thinking about Hoche and Luise, about the clinic and the forlorn patients there, and especially about little Georg. One Saturday morning he walked among the peasants arranging their wares in the marketplace by the cathedral. Walking along the north wall of the church, behind three peasants' stalls smelling of fresh herbs, he noticed a pair of outlines deeply carved in the red sandstone, just above eye level: a fat oval shape, pointed at each end; and next to it, a larger incised circle. Further to the right, an iron bar was anchored in the wall.

Behind him, a cheery voice asked, "What do you suppose those are for?" Philipp turned to see a tall young woman standing behind him. She had addressed her question to him.

"Standards for the market, I think," he said. "The oval is probably a one-pound loaf of bread. The circle, a two-pounder. See those loaves over there, just about the same size. The iron bar is a standard length for cloth, an ell most likely. The Church established the rules, or rather, I suppose they would have said, God did, and the Church enforced them. If you disputed the peasant or the merchant, you could come here for support." He turned to look at her.

She nodded. "Thanks for the history lesson. It is a wonderful church. So small and so complex. I am going to climb up the bell tower as soon as they open it."

"I wanted to last week, but it was raining."

"Come now," she said. "The view should be grand."

Philipp introduced himself. Another modern woman, he thought, from her firm handshake. He assumed she was a new student here at the university, but she was still in fresh in *Gymnasium* and lived in Augsburg, despite her north German accent. She had wandered away from her class in Freiburg on a school trip. Her classmates were already lining up to climb the spiral staircase in the tower.

"You should not climb something unless you have walked around it first," she said. "I think you need to be like the builders were. They put the foundation down first, then the walls, and then they built the tower. This will give me a better feeling for their accomplishment."

He was taken by her fresh, clean beauty, and even more, by her enthusiasm and delight. He wanted to know more about her. He guessed she was eighteen or nineteen. Her fine, light brown hair was short and curled, fashionable. It suited her. Her blue eyes were quite large, and strikingly bright.

She told him that she was originally from Osnabrück. Her family had moved to Augsburg at the end of the war. Her northern dialect was definitely noticeable, but as she talked, he began to hear some Bavarian patterns. She held her "r's" long enough to make them sound throaty. She softened some of the "s's". Her voice was light, airy, musical. She told him her name was Naumann. Christine Naumann.

"We are on a school trip all week," she said.

"Welcome to Freiburg-im-Breisgau, *Fräulein* Naumann."

"*Danke schön*. You're not from Freiburg. You're a Bavarian. I hear it easily enough."

He laughed. They walked around the cathedral to the main portal and the entrance to the tower. They continued talking while ascending the spiral staircase. He saw her ankles flashing below her long skirt and heard her voice echoing sweetly off the red sandstone walls. Her father had been in the war, but escaped injury. Her elder brother had been in the war, too: wounded, but recovered. He began university in Göttingen, but then left to go to sea, she said. She missed him. She wasn't going to go the university, although her teachers told her she should. "What's the point? I can find a husband in Augsburg if I want to," she said, and then, louder, "If I want to..." and laughed. She said she liked to read. She liked to go for bicycle rides and for walks. Climbing the stairway seemed to cause her no problems at all. He puffed behind her while she practically raced ahead of him, answering his questions in such detail he was disarmed by her honesty and openness. Once she stopped and waited for him to catch up to her.

"Don't you get much exercise?" she asked.

"I suppose I don't, considering how out of breath I am."

"You should take long walks. Or bicycle." She almost said, "We could ..." But she bit her tongue. Before they reached the platform, he asked her permission to write to her.

"Yes," she said, without hesitating and told him her address before he could take out any paper and pencil to write it down. As he fumbled in his pocket, she said, "Remember it," and laughed again. Then, as they came to the top of the stairs, she ran over to her classmates, blending into a group of girls who giggled and gave him sidelong glances. She said no more to him, but looked at him whenever she could. He stole looks at her, too. When she saw him looking at her, she smiled. He had to leave for the clinic and his 10 a.m. shift. That evening, he wrote her a letter. She replied immediately. He wrote her often over the next few weeks, always receiving an answer within days. He never mentioned his concerns about his patients. Instead, he wrote about what he saw in the market place. About a flock of starlings banking and wheeling through the sunset. About the shadows cast by the moon on one of his early morning bike rides to the clinic. He hoped to see her again.

The first time he mentioned something related to his work at the clinic, he merely said he had decided to leave Freiburg because he had a "difference of opinion with his professor and his assistant about the most appropriate treatment for an unstable child." He told her that he envisioned setting up a psychiatric clinic somewhere for children, coupled with daycare if their families needed it. Before he could do that, he would have to accumulate some savings and find a well-to-do partner, a patron or an investor. But first he would have to transfer to a hospital or policlinic and finish his residency. Eventually he'd have an opportunity for some income from a private practice on the side. "Why not in Augsburg?" he wrote. Two days later, he received a letter from Christine with only one sentence: "Come to Augsburg!"

He found the addresses of hospitals and policlinics in Augsburg and wrote to several to them. He wrote a brief letter to *Frau* Grimmel telling her to make an appointment with Hoche for a decision about Georg's treatment. If the boy were going to be sent to Emmendingen, Hoche would have to be the one to tell her.

Within a week, he received a positive reply from two Augsburg policlinics. He accepted the one with the most flexible hours, saying he would arrive within six weeks. Hoche raised no objections to his resignation and congratulated him for acting on his convictions. "I see we are not of one mind about important matters. Too bad, *Herr Doktor* Stein. Still, I wish you well."

When he saw Luise, she only said, "*Lebewohl!*" 'Live well!'

He had hoped she would beg him not to leave. He wanted to embrace her. Instead, she offered her hand.

"Our paths may cross again," she said as she turned away from him. He watched her go down the corridor. Was he merely a creature on a path that interested her for a while?

Nearly eight months after he arrived in Freiburg, he awaited the midnight train that would take him to Augsburg. An unusually cold wind blew from the west over the slaughterhouse toward the platform where he stood. Given Freiburg's size, its municipal slaughterhouse was remarkably small. When arriving passenger trains slowed down, swaying as they were shunted onto the sidings toward the station, a traveler who looked out toward the west, away from the old city and its cathedral spire, might not have noticed the long, low building. The overgrown train yard fencing nearly hid its gently sloping red-tile roof and narrow, opaque windows. Surrounded by a nondescript stucco and board wall, the slaughterhouse was wedged between factories, warehouses, and an apartment building for derelicts.

Even if a train did stop on the nearest siding, the hissing and grinding sounds of the brakes masked any snorting, sighing or bellowing from the cattle or calves. Any frantic squealing from the hogs. Any bleating from wide-eyed sheep. Passengers arriving by day on a train that stopped at a platform alongside these tracks ordinarily turned quickly away from this noise, thinking it was an eerie echo of the train's own sound. Just signs of the times, they thought. Train stations and slaughterhouses. Steel and flesh. But at night, sounds and smells were more fearful. Within the shadows, nothing could be trusted.

Tonight the smell of warm blood came to Philipp's nostrils. For an instant, he thought he was back at the field hospital in France. The night sky had an ominous texture. Low clouds unevenly reflected the light from the city's gas street lamps—the phosphor-green and gray clouds that hung over exploded shells when illuminated by flares. The pungent oil and steaming railroad ties still wet from the afternoon's rain reminded him of how they cleaned the bed frame each time a soldier died of his wounds.

A train appeared, coming from the south. The platform began to tremble. The engine's bulk blocked his sight of anything else. It slowed.

Cattle cars moved past, one by one. The smells and sounds were crushing. He grew dizzy. Then more and more boxcars. Finally, the caboose. Silence. He opened his eyes and looked down the track. Nothing but night and a thickening fog.

Minutes passed. He saw his train coming from the south, growing larger. Too fast, he thought. Much too fast. A hot wind swirled up around him. Is it stopping? What if the engineer were mad and did not stop the train? What if there were no engineer? The train would suck him underneath its wheels, dragging him and the slaughterhouse all across Germany, blood gushing out of the cars and turning into lurid, gory-smelling steam as it dripped on the hot tracks beneath, a path of blood everywhere it went. He staggered backwards, away from the edge of the platform. He felt the blast of air. Smelled the hot flood of the engine. Heard the screech of metal on metal.

When he opened his eyes, the train had come to a stop before him. He steadied himself, took a deep breath, and, prompted by the conductor's call, climbed aboard and found a seat. Everything would be all right, he told himself. He was going to see Christine.

CHAPTER EIGHT
Other Strengths

I knew that Philipp's strength came, at least in part, from Christine. Just as I drew strength from you. But he had other strengths that I lacked, despite your hope that I would find them in myself. The strength to examine my preconceptions, my prejudices, for example. The strength to admit that I might be wrong. Most important of all would be my lack of compassion. It hurts me to admit this, Helga, but I have come to see that my lack of compassion was my greatest weakness. How strange! I once thought that having compassion was a weakness. To my shame, I turned against those who had it. And I did not challenge those who lacked it.

When the trial was not in session, Johann took early morning walks. He was beginning to feel the need to be more useful. He would have volunteered at the hospital, but he had been well known there. Staying away from places where there were large numbers of people was uppermost in his mind. Still, he kept returning to the ruin of the *Volksbank*. He often saw the old man pulling bricks off the pile of rubble and felt awkward just watching, when he could help.

"*Guten Morgen!*" he shouted one day.

The old man seemed not to notice. Perhaps he was deaf.

"*Guten Morgen!*" he shouted, louder this time.

"Same to you" came the reply.

"Hard work, this." Johann walked to the edge of the rubble.

"*Ja.*"

"I'll help a bit."

"If you want."

Johann picked up a brick and carried it to the stack. Then another. When he saw that his pace was quicker than the old man's, he slowed down. When he was at the rubble pile, the old man was at the stack, meeting each other half way, twice each trip. Back and forth. A routine.

After a while, the old man introduced himself. "*Grüss Gott!* I'm Meier. Baker, retired. Are you from here?"

"*Grüss Gott, Herr* Meier," Johann said. "Name's Westermann. Working in the courthouse," Johann said, gesturing in that direction with his cane. He was about to say 'janitor' but before he could, Meier asked again, "Are you from here?"

"No, from near Dresden. I'm a born Saxon," Johann said, his new identity papers shaping his answer.

"You don't sound like a Saxon."

Johann ignored the comment and shrugged. "Hard work for someone your age," he mumbled.

"Speak up. I don't hear too well now. Bombs."

"Hard work. Don't you have an overcoat? It's cold."

"No need for a coat. The work warms me up," Meier said. "Seventy-five. Born 1871. As old as Germany. Soon I'll be seventy-six. Sometimes I feel much older."

"Congratulations."

"Birthday's still two months away. But *Danke schön!*" Meier said over his shoulder, walking toward the rubble. When he picked up his pace a bit, breathing loudly, Johann cautioned him to slow down and did so himself, pointing with his cane to his stiff leg. "First war," he said, moving toward the pile.

Meier stood in his way and looked him up and down. "Don't I know you? You look familiar. What did you say you did for a living?"

Johann tensed. Meier looked familiar to him, too. His ruddy face, his graying, bushy sideburns, his drooping, still red-blond moustache—all quite familiar, but a face from another era. "Janitor. Palace of Justice," he gestured again with his cane.

Nearby church bells began to ring. A man in an American Army parade uniform and a woman in a wedding gown come out of the church followed by a handful of cheering well-wishers. They threaded their way through the rubble toward a waiting jeep. It was a strange contrast: life and laughter amidst destruction and chaos. The women sorting rubble on the other side of the square stopped to watch, but none smiled and all soon returned to their tasks. Johann and Meier watched the newly-weds drive away in a jeep while the wedding guests cheered. As he bent over to pick up another brick, Johann remembered to the last marriage celebration he had attended, Philipp and Christine's. Helga and he were official witnesses at Augsburg's municipal office registry, along with a portly, bewhiskered, red-faced man and his wife. They sat across from each other in the restaurant afterwards. Meier was Christine's uncle.

*****

Philipp moved to Augsburg without difficulty and rented a small, cheap garret apartment. It was clean, in a neighborhood with many gardens, and a short walk to the policlinic. He liked the chief physician and his two colleagues, all Augsburgers, and the rhythm of the clinic. When he completed his residency requirements, he would be fully licensed and could think of a bigger apartment and private patients. Augsburg was bigger than Freiburg, more like Munich. Not only more interesting, but also more like home. He was happy with the move. He had fallen in love with Christine.

Her family lived a good half-hour walk from his apartment. He went there often for a Sunday meal. Within a few weeks, he knew the way in his sleep. He noticed that he did not think about Luise or Hoche or his patients in Freiburg for days on end. He wrote his parents that he was *"well and happy"* in his work. *"There's another reason, too. I hope you will meet her soon."* He told them about Christine and their plans to visit Munich in three weeks on his mother's birthday.

So he was stunned when he received a letter from the Augsburg Medical Society's Ethical Review Board, requesting him to appear for *"a hearing on charges raised by Herr Reinhard Scharff, M.D., Augsburg."* His accuser's name was written in large block letters in the appropriate blank, *"Name of Complainant."* At the bottom of the sheet were the illegible signatures of the directors of the Board. The hearing was scheduled for his mother's birthday.

He learned that the *Doktor* Scharff in question was the same Scharff who had refused to greet him at his first general rounds at the Augsburg hospital. They had not met since then. What grounds could he have for a complaint? He wondered if the chief physician in the policlinic knew anything about it, but decided not to speak with him unless it was necessary. When he asked his two colleagues if they knew Scharff, both men groaned. Blum, the older of the two, from Frankfurt, had been practicing in Augsburg at the clinic and privately for eight years. Conzelmann, although not much older than Philipp, was in his third year at the policlinic.

"Schaaarrfff!" Blum said, puffing out his cheeks. "He's an old farter, a real burden. More of a barber than a doctor. The war did not do enough to remove these antiquated bastards."

Conzelmann chimed in. "Scharff's from the old school, arrogant, not up-to-date in his techniques or knowledge."

Blum nodded. "Not only that. He's both crude and vindictive. If he ever was an effective doctor, it was long ago."

Scharff was an old Augsburger from generations of physicians. He practiced out of his family's home, Blum said, a block away from Philipp's apartment. Scharff was a spiteful, arrogant crank, venting most of his anger on newcomers, especially on Jews. Conzelmann thought Scharff was in Augsburg's branch of the *SA*, the Nazis' paramilitary organization. Every day on his way to and from the clinic, Philipp crossed the street to avoid a knot of noisy, brown-shirted "Storm Troopers." He wondered out loud why a doctor could possibly want to belong to such a group. Blum and Conzelmann shook their heads and shrugged.

Later, Blum called Philipp aside and said, "We can't be too careful, you know. There are Scharffs under every rock. Even here in Augsburg, where the Jewish community was not afraid to build a new synagogue at the end of the war. Or maybe *especially* here—because of the new synagogue. Seen it?"

"I've walked past, but not gone inside."

"Go inside. It's stunning. The domed ceiling is like heaven itself. Cost a fortune to build. They say it is the largest synagogue in all of Germany. And, of course, our good German brothers are envious. They say that profits from the war built it. Go see it, before they burn it down."

"Burn it down? Are you serious?"

"I wouldn't be surprised," Blum said. "Anything can happen. There are good people here. But they don't seem to know what to do about the bad people."

"Do you go to synagogue often?"

"No," Blum said. "Haven't gone since my *Bar Mitzvah*. Doesn't matter. We're foreigners no matter how long we've lived in Germany. You know that already. Go see the synagogue. And keep your eyes open. All the time."

"But I already don't get enough sleep!"

They both laughed and went back to their patients. All Philipp could recall about his accuser was Scharff's bulbous, purple nose and thinking, rosaecea or drink, or both. He had no idea about his accusations. He told himself to be calm until he had more facts, but that was difficult. Because he did not want to tell Christine, she found him unusually tense and quiet. He tried to change the subject when she asked him what was bothering him. She persisted.

Finally, he said, "We'll have to postpone our trip to my parents." When she asked 'Why?' he simply responded, "Professional duties here. We'll go another time, I promise."

The three weeks passed slowly. He was angry with himself for feeling anxious, but he could not help it. He arrived early and sat in a row of chairs against the room's back wall. Scharff was nowhere to be seen. When his case was announced, he took a seat at a small table near the front, facing the three doctors on the Ethical Review Board. Scharff came in at that moment, puffing and wheezing, and sat next to him. When the white haired, squinty-eyed chairman of the Board read the formal charges, Philipp was more amused than angered. Scharff claimed that he would lose patients and suffer professional harm if Philipp opened a private practice in his residence, since they lived so close to each other.

Scharff was then invited to speak. He stood up, leered at Philipp and gestured stiffly toward him. "This *Herr Dok...tor Stein*," he said in a gravelly, mocking voice, had already begun to "lure his patients away from him." He paused for effect, then shouted. "Outrageous *Pfutscher*! Yes, he's a quack! An interloping bastard! An uninvited, unwelcome foreigner. My family has practiced here..."

The chairman interrupted him. "Calm down, please *Herr Doktor Scharff*. We know you and your family have a distinguished record of service. Now give us some evidence of your charge," he said dryly.

Scharff puffed up at the reference to his family. Taking a deep breath, he told of the recent "flagrant" case of a house painter whose "family," he said, his voice rising again, "had been cared for with professional acumen by my family for nearly two generations. This *Pfutscher* will contaminate our noble Augsburg traditions!" He pointed at Philipp and sat down with a flourish. The three members of the Board busily wrote their notes.

Philipp was told to stand and address the charges. After a quick glance at Scharff, he calmly said that he had no intention of opening a practice at his residence, indeed that his landlord and lease agreement prohibited it. Further, he thought it was not possible to have a practice in his apartment, since he could hardly expect patients to walk up four flights of stairs to see a doctor who had only two small rooms under the attic. About the house painter, he said the man had fallen off a scaffold early on a Saturday morning while he was working on the building next to his. A downstairs neighbor called him to the scene of the accident. He had temporarily splinted the man's leg and waited with him for the ambulance. He had no idea of his name, had not sent him a bill or processed any insurance claim, and definitely had no intention of conscripting him as a patient. He sat down while the board members wrote more notes.

Scharff stood up immediately and, glowing red in the face, hotly disputed Philipp's testimony, repeating his complaints about "incompetent, conniving and cheating foreigners," and about "unfair competition and the corruption of the profession." For good measure, he concluded, "Socialized medicine is a Bolshevik plot to destroy German medical science." He was panting for breath and wheezing. The chairman motioned for him to sit down.

Although Scharff made no specific mention of Jews, Philipp understood him well enough. The board members conferred briefly in whispers. After a few minutes, he was told to stand again and solemnly warned by the chairman that he could not open a private practice without their prior approval: "We are required to ensure the best interests of the medical community and the citizenry of Augsburg," the chairman said. He excused Philipp's treatment of the painter, saying only that he should have alerted *Herr Doktor* Scharff immediately about the injury after the patient was transported to the hospital. The other two members shuffled the papers in front of them.

A disappointed Scharff glowered and stood up so abruptly that he tipped his chair over. "Outrageous!" he shouted, "Simply Outrageous!" He clicked his heels, made a perfunctory formal bow to the Board, and left the room with a loud slam of the door. Philipp, not wanting to encounter him in the hallway, sat down at the back of the chamber and stayed through the next case.

It concerned a young physician who was charged with unprofessional conduct for placing an advertisement in the newspaper for his practice. "True," he admitted, looking at his accuser, a bewhiskered physician with folded arms and a defiant look. "I have done that. But I have to, esteemed colleagues. There is so much competition here. Jews, you know. More every day." The chairman again conferred briefly with his colleagues. When they all nodded, he issued a warning about the advertisement, followed by another short lecture on professional conduct that ended with the same words he had spoken to Philipp. The accuser and the accused left the room together, both looking disappointed. Philipp, stung by the comment about Jews, wondered if he should stand and address the Board, but decided not to. All this would pass, he thought. It's just disappointment about the war. And the economy. They have to find someone to blame.

When he told Christine about his case, he imitated Scharff's voice and mannerisms. "Called me a *Pfutscher*! A quack! And a foreigner! Imagine!" He began to laugh. But she was more concerned than he thought she should be, particularly because he believed the matter was over and seemed in retrospect so absurd.

"I know about *Herr Doktor* Scharff," she said. "My father used to go to him. I think my grandfather went to him, too. My father says that Scharff is a bitter, vicious man. That he wants to fight the war again. Just before you came to Augsburg, his picture was in the newspaper, in a uniform with other men under a swastika flag. They were upset about something. Versailles, I suppose."

Philipp let out a groan.

"Now I remember," Christine continued. "The article in the paper said Scharff had given a speech saying we would not lose the next war, when—not if, but *when*—men like him were in charge. I laughed, but my father said such men were dangerous, not to be taken lightly."

"Well, he is not the first Scharff I've met, nor the last, I suppose."

"What I don't like is his angry tone. Who would want another war? How monstrous."

"Yes. Monstrous. But I imagine plenty want another war. 'Do it right this time,' they say. 'Germany should not have lost.' I agree. Germany should not have lost. But I am not ready to try it over again. More than just Germans lost the war. Everyone lost. English, French, Russians, Italians, even Americans. Sooner or later, the Scharffs of the world will die out, like the dinosaurs. Violence just makes more violence."

"What does the Medical Society's Ethical Review Board do?" she asked.

"Usually, they just oversee petty professional conflicts between doctors. Has a doctor advertised? Does this doctor steal that doctor's patients? Does this doctor charge less that that doctor? They ought to be called an Etiquette Review Board. What they should do is handle cases where a doctor has taken advantage of a female patient. Or where someone has refused to treat a patient who cannot pay. Or where a doctor has compromised himself through unprofessional conduct. Drinking, for example. Now that would deal with important, ethical questions. But most of the time the Board worries about the wrong things. Much like our politicians."

"I hope it's over, as you say." She turned their conversation toward what they might do Saturday evening. "I would love to see *'The Cabinet of Dr. Caligari'* again," Christine said, and began to imitate a maniacal sleepwalker. Philipp matched her grimaces and wide eyes. They both laughed. "And we could have a picnic on Sunday, if the weather stays warm." By the time they parted, Scharff's accusations had been forgotten.

Three months later, Philipp asked Christine to marry him. When she said 'yes,' the first letter he wrote after the one to his parents was to Johann.

*****

Johann had not seen Philipp since he left Munich for Freiburg. Letters between the two came in bursts, with long pauses in between. Sometimes one or the other would raise a medical topic, with a reference to a patient's ailment or an article in a medical journal, but most were about their families. Johann was surprised to hear that Philipp thought of leaving Freiburg and wrote back asking for details. But several months passed before Philipp's next letter, telling him about his move, about Christine, and inviting him and Helga to be official witnesses at their marriage ceremony.

"Let's go, Johann," Helga said. "It's been almost a year since your mother died. You've not taken any time off since then. By the time of the wedding, I won't be wearing mourning. I can sew myself a new dress."

"All right," he said, "we'll go. I'm curious to see how Philipp is doing. I wish he could have been a witness at our wedding. I'll write him this evening. And you can begin thinking about your new dress."

They took the train to Augsburg. Although Johann praised his used automobile to the skies when he described it to his colleagues, he didn't trust it on a long trip. He yearned for a brief escape, to be free of his patients and his doubts. If he could have spoken his thoughts, he would have said he was tired. But he could not shake his fear that his career was already at its peak.

He telephoned Philipp from the hotel's front desk.

"Good, you've arrived. Everything all right? A good train? Paul-Adolf and little Greta safely looked after? Room in order?"

Johann broke into a smile. Philipp had not changed. Effervescent. Concerned. Outgoing in a way Johann knew he could never be. Philipp's voice reminded him of Pohlendorf. A lost landscape. His only link to it, his childhood friend.

"Everything's in order," Johann said. "When do we see you and Christine? We're eager to meet the bride-to-be. I have some things to tell her before she marries you, you know." Philipp laughed.

"You're too late, as usual," came the reply. "I won't see her again until tomorrow, at the marriage registry office. She wants to 'stay hidden' tonight. One of her aunts insists that it is bad luck if I see her on the night before we marry. A silly tradition, really. Anyway, I thought you two, my parents and I would meet later this evening for a glass of wine or two—or beer if you prefer. They're eager to see you again. We'll go to a *Weinstube* near our apartment. I'll pick you up at 7, or should we make it earlier?"

"Seven's fine. Until then."

Johann and Helga unpacked, hung up the clothes they planned to wear the next day, and changed into the clothes they brought for that evening. He had a new jacket. She had sewn herself a new dress. They went out on the balcony to see the view. The Basilica of St. Ulrich and Afra was a few blocks away and beyond that, rising above the trees, they saw the church steeple at the centuries' old residential quarter for the city's poor, the *Fuggerei*. Traffic noise filtered up from the square. A lovely old fountain that they had seen from the taxi was hidden from view. He remembered a school visit to Augsburg when he was fourteen or fifteen. Philipp and he had tried to escape from the class, but *Pfarrer* Bosch had made them walk at the front of the group as they toured St. Ulrich and Afra. He remembered the Roman ruins in the church's courtyard. "Emperor Augustus' own city, boys! Named for him! Just imagine! The first Roman Emperor!" Bosch had enthused. "Now let's go see where Martin Luther dared to defy Emperor Charles the Fifth!"

"Augsburg is more modern than Nuremberg," Johann said. "Are you sorry, Helga, that we didn't move here?"

"No, I like Nuremberg. It's comfortable, pretty, especially at Christmastime. I like our apartment. I'd miss my family's home in Munich wherever we lived. But Nuremberg is fine."

"I prefer it to Augsburg," he said. "I like Nuremberg's compactness. And its traditions. There is too much money here. And too many doctors, I hear. Life seems too fast, compared with Nuremberg. Best would have been Pohlendorf, but that's impossible now."

Helga looked at him, surprised he had such thoughts. "I knew you liked Nuremberg for your professional opportunities. But I didn't know you paid much attention to anything else there."

"You know I like Nuremberg, and not only for my profession. It has a past. A German heritage. It's like an anchor. No, more like a foundation. Indestructible. On such a foundation Germany can build its future."

"Augsburg has a glorious past, too, going back to the Romans. And Luther and the rest. Anyway, what's indestructible nowadays? We're lucky the war happened beyond our borders. You repeat what the Nazis say." She knew she had said enough when Johann stepped back and glared at her.

"Listen to me. The Nazis are important. They know that for us to survive, we must have pride in ourselves. They wouldn't have tolerated our humiliation at Versailles. Criminals signed that treaty. Just as they say, 'November criminals!' Now we bear the murderous reparations payments. Germany will be bankrupt into our grandchildren's lives. The Nazis can teach us to have pride again."

She could not hold her tongue. "I think they have too much pride. Arrogance, I would call it."

"Please, Helga. You don't understand these things. Men need to take action. We need to believe in ourselves. Especially now." He looked out over the square, his hands firmly on the balcony railing.

"Fine," she said, trying to keep her voice even. "Fine. But at what cost? I see a lot of misplaced pride in all the uniforms and slogans. I hear a lot of shouting. The Communists do the same. Each side thinks the others are devils. Someone will have to pay."

"Leave all that, Helga." he said, turned away and shrugged.

She didn't know what to make of his interest in politics. One day he would go on and on about how the nation would be transformed under the guidance of Adolf Hitler. He would cheer when a truck of Nazi faithful went by, its horn blasting. But the next day he would merely shake his head when Helga asked him what all these political rallies were supposed to accomplish. He would attend Party meetings for several weeks, then stop abruptly, cringing when he read a newspaper account of the Nazis' participation in a street fight that was little more than a drunken brawl, and grumbling about some statement by a Party member that he found outrageous. Despite his many proclamations to do so, he had not joined the Party. Of late he seemed to think better of it, worrying that it might adversely affect his career.

She was glad that he had not joined, although what she said on the balcony was the closest she had ever come to telling him her views. The Nazis seemed to her a bunch of young, immature bullies playing schoolyard games. But if he had joined them, she would have felt some relief. The worst aspect of Johann's indecisiveness for her was its unpredictability. His favorite comment had become, "Things cannot go on like this. This is wrong. Something must be done." And then he did nothing. She once thought him imaginative and determined. Had she misjudged him? Was he always this indecisive? Or was he becoming a different man than the one she had married.

Helga knew that the day-to-day activities of the Nazis interested him little. She was sure they often embarrassed him. The hooligans and rowdies, the drinking and shouting. She even thought that the Jew-baiting distressed him. He had told her that such passions could becloud the Party leaders' judgment. Part of him was still the dreamer she knew, but it was as if his dreams had become more unrealistic, more fantastic. They took place on a landscape so far away that he could not describe it to her.

"I hope the children are all right," she said, deliberately changing the topic, and went inside. The sun had set and the air seemed chilly.

"Let's go for a walk before Philipp comes," he said.

Afterwards, they sat on a bench outside the *Gasthaus* and waited without talking much. Both were glad they had brought their light wool coats. Johann said, "It's too cold for June." Helga only nodded.

Philipp drove up to the curbside punctually at seven o'clock. After the two friends shook hands warmly and Philipp made a comical display of kissing Helga's hand which caused them all to laugh, Johann could not restrain himself from asking about Philipp's new automobile: "When did you buy it? How does it handle? How fast can it go?" He desperately wanted a new car, but Helga and he agreed they couldn't afford it. First, they had to pay off his father's and mother's funeral debts and make sure that his private practice was stable. Another year, maybe eighteen months. The used one would have to do until then.

"Too many questions, my friend!" Philipp said. "First, let's get to the *Weinstube*. It's on the west side, near my apartment. My parents will meet us there. I can't bring myself to say 'home.' Home is still Munich. No, home is really Pohlendorf."

Johann sighed, "Yes! Pohlendorf," and turned to look at Helga in the back seat.

"But that's so long ago," Philipp continued. "It is good my parents moved here. I am just glad to be getting out of my tiny apartment. Christine and I have found a larger place around the corner. We get it in a month. We'll live upstairs, over the practice I'm opening in a ground floor storefront. It will do. Far enough away from any other doctor's so I am not a threat," Philipp said, laughing.

"Threat?" Johann asked.

"Absurd, really. Shortly after I came here, I was told I was encroaching on another doctor's practice. As though we have too many doctors."

"Some say we do. At least in the big cities. A crisis for the profession. Many medical journals editorialize about it." Johann said, about to name them.

Philipp cut him off. "If there's any crisis for the profession, it's that we don't have enough good doctors up-to-date with the latest methods." He signaled that he was turning left.

"Yes," Johann said, now distracted by the bustling street-scene and the many new automobiles. "Look at that new Mercedes. And there's another." The two men began to discuss motorcars, while Helga sat quietly.

The *Weinstube* was quaint and cozy, with stuccoed walls, heavy velvet curtains and old oak tables. A small bunch of flowers in a pottery mug decorated each table. Philipp's father rose to meet them. Johann saw at once that he had aged. Hunched and much thinner, his hair had turned from dark and curly to white and wispy. But *Herr* Stein's broad, happy smile and the way his eyes sparkled had not changed. And Philipp's mother was still plump, with smooth, glowing skin and her dark hair coiled in long braids around her head like a Bavarian peasant woman. She smiled a bright, gold-toothed smile at her son's childhood friend.

"Good to see you both looking so well, *Herr* and *Frau* Stein! You remember my wife, Helga. We congratulate you on your son's marriage."

"Thank you, Johann. Thank you both," Philipp's father said. "Pleased to see you again, *Frau* Brenner. How I wish your parents, Johann, could be here to celebrate with us. Our condolences again on your loss. Sad. So sad." Philipp's mother nodded.

After a suitable pause, Herr Stein continued, "Johann! Dear Johann! It's been too long." "I only have this one son to marry off, and after that, when will we see you?" He looked at Helga. "Philipp told us that Paul-Adolf has a little sister now. A son and now a daughter. She must be very pretty. Just like her mother." Helga blushed and smiled.

"Greta is indeed beautiful, *Herr* Stein." Johann said, beaming. "She's a happy baby. Eighteen months old tomorrow and on solid foods. Cow's milk. She's growing before our eyes. And Paul-Adolf…"

"… must be nearly four years old now," Philipp's father interjected. "Imagine! Two children! You hear, Philipp. Two children already." They all burst into laughter. When they sat down, Philipp ordered wine, and they chatted about the days before the war in Pohlendorf. About their moves since then. About the weather that spring. About how the strawberries seemed redder, plumper, and more expensive that year than any they could remember.

Johann looked long at Philipp's mother and thought of his own. The two women had often discussed making jellies or canning fruits and vegetables, back in Pohlendorf. His mother was happy then. The whole family was happy. He could see his mother, picking peas in their garden. See her admiring their espaliered pear tree and counting its pears. See her scooping handfuls of grain for the chickens from the baggy pocket in her apron. Hear her clucking to them and see her smiling when they came scurrying toward her. She was synonymous with Pohlendorf in his mind. Simple. Happy. Safe. He still missed her. Immersing himself in his work did not help.

The waiter brought the wine and glasses. Philipp's father did the honors and filled his wife's and Helga's glasses.

"Now you, Johann, and then Philip and me."

He came out of his reverie with a start, expecting to see his parents sitting there with them, as they often had, in celebration of one or another's birthday, in Pohlendorf's best *Weinstube*. "*Ja, bitte*," he said. "*Danke, Herr Stein*."

When Philipp's father finished pouring, Johann raised his glass. "A toast to the groom's dear parents—and the beginning of our family's friendship in heavenly Pohlendorf!" he said. Everyone clinked glasses and took a sip, smiling and nodding approval. The wine was cool and tangy.

"To better years to come!" Philipp's father said, raising his glass. More nods and smiles.

Johann looked at his friend. "So, Philipp, where did you meet Christine? Knowing you, she's probably a movie star."

Philipp laughed. "She was born in North Germany," he said, "but her family moved to Augsburg after the war. Her uncle and his family also live here. You'll meet them tomorrow. All good people. Christine is a bookkeeper. Just licensed. Very pretty, naturally. She could be in the movies."

Philipp's father winked and laughed, "No plain women allowed in our family! *Verboten!*" More laughter.

Philipp continued, "We met by accident when I was on my assistantship with Professor Hoche in Freiburg. She was there on a *Gymnasium* trip. We wrote each other. We saw each other again when I came through Augsburg on my way to visit my folks. We've known each other for over three years now. You'll see, we're a good match. She's quiet, like Mama. Not as good a cook, of course. I'll suffer in that respect." Now it was Philipp's mother's turn to blush and beam. He continued, "It took a while for her parents to accept me. They're Catholic. But everything is fine now."

"Why wouldn't her parents accept you? A promising young doctor, with an automobile, no less!" Johann said, hiding his envy.

"You can guess why. To be blunt. I'm Jewish."

"And so? You may have been born Jewish, but what difference is that now? You don't go to synagogue. Besides, you don't act Jewish. I don't think of you as Jewish," Johann said. Helga tensed. The entire room seemed stopped in time.

Philipp stiffened and held his glass in the air for a moment before raising it to his mouth and taking a sip. "No, I don't go to synagogue. I don't think of myself as Jewish," he said, trying to keep his voice from quivering. Then louder, "Yes, I think of myself as German. During the war, my whole family certainly thought we were German. My Uncle Max was killed by a French soldier. He certainly thought my uncle was a German. I served as best I could. My father and mother gave to the war effort. Made sacrifices. But that doesn't matter now. What happened nearly ten years ago hangs like a curse in the air. No matter that Jews had nothing to do with the outcome of the war, and little to do with the

Peace Treaty, if that's what it can be called. No, Johann, I am seen as Jewish and always will be."

Philipp took another sip of wine. "Just read the papers. Just listen to the horrifying speeches here in the park every Sunday afternoon. Anyone, no matter how slightly related to a Jew, is a Jew. And damned for it. Damned for all time. Whatever is wrong with our *Vaterland*—and there is plenty wrong—is the Jews' fault. A vicious logic." Philipp looked down into his glass. He spoke slowly. "Christine's family is all right. They mean no harm, but for them, and for you, too, perhaps, Johann, I am a Jew, and will always be a stranger, an outsider in Germany. Some of us are tolerated better than others. I seem safe enough. And Christine's parents can't help giving her what she wants. She's the apple of her father's eye. I'm glad he has spoiled her a bit. It makes it harder for him to refuse her wishes now."

Philipp paused again to empty his glass. "But Johann, I have to ask—even though I am not eager to hear your answer—what do you mean, 'act Jewish'?"

It was Johann's turn to stiffen. He tightened his grip on his wine glass. "*Ach*, you know. The usual description of Jews. Money grubbing. Deceptive. Clannish. As you said, an outsider. *Jewish*," he said, his voice trailing off. "Not you, as I said. I mean no offense, Philipp."

Johann did not realize what he was saying. If Philipp had asked him then and there, "Where did you learn all this? Who taught you this?" he would have been hard pressed to give an answer. He would have been the first to admit that Philipp was not what typical Germans imagined when they thought about Jews. Philipp was his closest friend. At the same time, he had a vague belief that a Jew could not be a true friend of anyone but another Jew. In Pohlendorf, however, the few Jewish families mingled freely with everyone. There was no such distinction there, no separation or tension worth mentioning. No one complained that he and Philipp were friends, or that their families often spent time together. The contradiction confused and disturbed him.

His ideas came "just from hearing people." But which people? From Nazi Party speeches and Hitler's book? Not really. When he read or heard similar accusations by anyone, they sounded flat, unconvincing, false. Anyway, he had never finished reading *Mein Kampf*. No, they came from before he ever heard about the Nazis. From his father? From his teachers? Perhaps. But his ideas seemed older. Like paths through dark woods. So old no one could remember exactly how they got there. 'The Jews' for him were an abstraction, a force of nature, like gravity, nightfall, stiff winds, winter. Something that had to be taken into account. Seeing *them* as a constant, immutable presence helped him explain the world. In this, he was like millions of others at the time, and not only in Germany.

He knew this explanation was illogical. He hardly knew any Jews. Aside from Philipp and his family, there was one other Jewish family in Pohlendorf with whom he had much contact: the Semmelbergs, with their general store and its *pfennig* candy, and they had always treated him and the other children kindly. From the lists he had processed in the war, he knew of injured Jewish soldiers. In his university days, there were several students he imagined were Jewish, but he had nothing to do with any of them. He knew few other medical students beside Philipp. Once he began practicing, he had frequent contact with the druggist, Kerner, who lived near his parents' apartment. His mother liked the local greengrocer, Goldberg, too, and chided his father for complaining about both as cheats. Johann knew nothing that corroborated this and agreed with her, often telling his father so. In Nuremberg, he bought a Munich newspaper now and then from "Old Man" Eisenberg, the blind, bearded, Jewish man in the kiosk in Nuremberg's train station. He liked the way the man always smiled and wished him a sunny day. He occasionally had brief conversations at the hospital with one or another of Nuremberg's Jewish doctors. But to date, he had never been to the city's Jewish quarter. No, the Jews Johann knew were not *the Jews* of the Volk's imagination.

The conversation was making the others uncomfortable. Helga finished her wine. Philipp's mother began turning her ring over and over on her finger. Philipp's father kept clearing his throat, but said nothing.

"Why do I think we have had this conversation before?" Philipp began. "Don't tell me, Johann, that you can't see how ridiculous such stereotypes are. If they ever were true—and I sincerely doubt it—those times passed long ago. Anyone who believes them now is blind to modern times. Jews may have once had to be defensive and secretive, in order to survive. Look at the pogroms and prejudice, the miseries they endured. If I thought I would have to run for my life at any moment, I would store up jewels and gold under the mattress, not trust my neighbors, and worry whether my friends really were my friends. But times have changed, my dear old friend. That's why all this public nonsense about 'the Jews this!' and 'the Jews that!' is so absurd. Pathetic. We live in a Germany where we all have an equal chance. A great future. The *Kaiser* has gone. Our King Ludwig had to go, too. Germany doesn't need an emperor. Bavaria doesn't need a king. And even those times were good for Jews. Better than anywhere else in Europe. But now we have a democracy, thank God. Long live the *Deutsche Reich*!" Philipp raised his glass in a toast, and the others did likewise, eager to smooth out the conversation's edge. Johann drank what was left in his glass in one swallow.

If all that Philipp was saying were true, Johann knew that he was investing a great deal of energy and wasting a lot of time worrying about the *Vaterland*. If Philipp and the others, Jews or not, on the left wing, were to be trusted, then all the ravings of Hitler and the Nazis were just that, ravings. And worse yet—if Philipp was what he said he was, if Jews were loyal, thoughtful citizens of Germany—then National Socialism was a diabolical plot to undo a healthy, growing, productive state, destroy some of its most productive citizens, and deliver power over to selfish, arrogant lunatics.

Johann had thought this a few times before. The Munich street speech of 1921 had been powerful at the time. But over the next several months, as the emotions it awakened had subsided, Johann felt like he was a river returning to its banks after a spring flood. Mud and debris had been washed up that shamed him and made him anxious and afraid. At the same time, hearing that speech and feeling the enthusiasm of that crowd was exhilarating. It gave him a purpose, a sense of urgency.

He had to choose. How were others able to make such certain choices? That crowd of men in Munich had made a choice. Philipp had made a choice. Why couldn't he? It bothered him that Philipp sat there so matter-of-factly, so obviously rational, so apparently good-natured. And so incontrovertible. He knew he would have to sort out this matter of "Jews in Germany" someday, since so much of the Nazis' argument hinged upon it. But right then, it confused him.

Philipp's father put his hands on the table. "Good people, we live in a state of laws. A *Rechtsstaat*. We Jews have done nothing wrong. I speak for myself, of course, but also, I believe, for the vast majority of German Jews. There are always some rotten fish. A stinking herring here and there." Philipp's father made a gesture of smelling something foul. Helga laughed out loud.

"But," he continued, "the Jews in Germany have done nothing wrong. Why would we? We have a good life here. No, we have done nothing wrong. If we had, we would have been punished. We would deserve to be punished. But here we are, happy to be together. Celebrating. Why get so upset, my boys? What's there to upset you before such a happy, happy day?" Philipp sighed. Johann took a deep breath. When Philipp's father changed the subject back again to the old neighborhood in Pohlendorf, both men were more than willing to join in.

The civil marriage ceremony just before noon the next day was short. Christine and Philipp held hands, formally agreed to marry each other, signed where the registrar told them to sign, and kissed. Johann, Helga and Christine's uncle and aunt signed as the required four witnesses. The bride and groom's parents and their guests sat waiting in an anteroom. When the couple and the witnesses appeared, everyone applauded. Led by Philipp and Christine, the group descended the city hall steps and walked to a large restaurant on the square, like schoolchildren, babbling and laughing in the bright June sunshine. Onlookers smiled and waved. When a trolley car clanged its bell, everyone cheered.

Johann and Christine sat across the table from the Meiers'. *Herr* Meier, a red-faced, portly, balding man who looked to be in his midfifties, sported fluffy, graying side-burns and a huge moustache. Johann thought how much he looked like a flushed Chancellor Otto von Bismarck. The tableside chitchat was predictable, what one would have heard at a wedding anywhere in Germany—the lovely June day, the beautiful bride, her wedding outfit, the handsome groom, his lucky family, the meal, the wine. Christine's uncle seemed to enjoy the wine more for its quantity than its quality. While the waiters were clearing the table of the main course dishes, the bride and the groom as well as guests got up and mingled, talking and laughing. Johann took the opportunity to go to the men's room. When he came out, Meier, standing in the foyer, gestured to him.

"Do you smoke? I'm going outside for my cigar. My wife can't tolerate me smoking indoors. Come outside for a bit. We can talk."

"No, I don't smoke," Johann answered. "But I could use some fresh air. Big meals at midday always make me sleepy."

"Come outside. I need some fresh air, too. Too much wine too early in the day."

The two stood against the restaurant wall, near the front door. The noontime's warm sunshine seemed like high summer. Meier took out a fat cigar, clipped it, and lit it with a flourish. "Swedish Match brand. *Willem II* for our dear old Kaiser. Wonder what he would say to that. It's pretty good. I saved it for today. Hand rolled," he said, talking quickly. "I've got two more. One for the groom. Sure you don't want the other?" He began to reach again into his vest pocket.

"No, thank you very much," Johann said, careful to stand so the smoke blew away from him.

Christine's uncle inhaled deeply, faced the sun, closed his eyes, and exhaled. A bluish cloud of smoke curled away. "It's very good. Are you sure?" he said, again reaching toward his inside coat pocket. Johann shook his head. Meier inhaled again, exhaled slowly and, lowering his voice while turning to face Johann, asked, "So, *Herr Doktor*, what do you think about the situation in our *Vaterland*?"

Johann stepped back a bit. "Well, I believe that times are improving, *Herr* Meier. Life in Germany is returning to its predictable pace."

"Then you think we are out of the woods."

"I believe things will get better. We will find a powerful leader to help us find our way. God perhaps has already sent him to us. Adolf Hitler is very promising, I think. His book impresses me. He's a shrewd man. I am interested in knowing more about him. I like his confidence. His enthusiasm for the future."

"You like the Nazis?" Meier asked, stepping closer to Johann, who backed away until he was against the wall. A fly buzzed around his head.

"Yes, with reservations, of course. They're better than the communists and the socialists. Better than the Center Party. I want action."

"The communists and socialists promise action."

"Their action is destructive," Johann said. "Destructive of our German values."

"That's what all the nationalists say," Meier said.

"It's true. Look what's happened in Russia. All the traditions overturned. Stalin is power crazy."

"I look at it differently. I see Russia catching up with us. You can't stop a people wanting to live comfortably. But they are so far behind they need a powerful ruler. Besides, that's in their tradition."

"You seem to know a great deal about current affairs, *Herr* Meier."

"My union's little newspaper is good. The socialists represent our interests pretty well."

"Not for me. Not for us doctors. Maybe in backward Russia, but not here in the *Vaterland*."

Anyway, Hitler's a socialist, but he's a *national* socialist! That's putting the nation first. Socialism without nationalism is absurd. Before we can take care of the poor in other countries, we should take care of our own," Johann said.

Meier took another long puff on his cigar. "I'm a baker in a factory. I see workers every day, underpaid workers. Men making barely enough to support their family. Destined to remain poor. What do you know about being poor?"

"I see the poor every day, too, *Herr* Meier. And I have to deal with bureaucrats that treat me like a lowly factory worker and get in the way

of my helping the poor. The state health insurance plan is enough socialism for me, thank you."

"I forgot, you're a doctor," Meier said, with barely disguised disdain.
"Why should doctors get rich off people who are poor and sick?"

"We doctors are not getting rich, I assure you." Johann felt himself
bristling. "If anything, we are underpaid for our skills." He was eager to
go back inside. He wasn't comfortable talking with a baker about matters he thought bakers couldn't understand. "Let me just say," he said,
walking toward the restaurant's doorway, "I like what Hitler stands for.
If not him, someone like him. A strong leader. We need to believe in
ourselves again."

"Hitler is a dangerous man." Meier rubbed off the glowing tip of his
cigar on the restaurant wall.

Johann stopped abruptly. "What makes you say that? He's got
answers. He knows Versailles was an outrage." Meier nodded and tried
to say something, but Johann kept talking, "Hitler definitely understands
that our *Volk* does not deserve this shame. Our socialists would just hand
us over to the Russians." His words from his mouth like stones.

Helga appeared at the door and motioned them inside. "Johann,
they're beginning the toasts."

"Yes," he said.

Johann planned to offer his toast after Philipp's father's. Before he
could stand up, Christine's uncle thumped the table with his hand. "A
toast. A toast to the bride! To the beautiful bride." Everyone turned to
him as he rose.

"Dear Christine. Dear, dear Christine. My pretty little niece, Christine." A bit of laughter escaped from those who imagined the wine was
talking. "I've known you all your life, of course, as your uncle, which I
am now, still, too." Louder laughter. "And I have always been proud of
you. Which I am now, still, too." Still more laughter, as the guests began
to think they were going to learn a family secret about Meier. "You have
always been a sweet, innocent, and beautiful child, and will always be
so to me, and to my dear wife, too. A fine cousin to our son." Everyone
smiled, some applauded. Christine's aunt was fearing the worst. Their

son loudly whispered, "*Vati*, sit down now, please." Meier pretended not to hear. He began to laugh, then stopped. Everyone thought he was done. He started to sit down, then he stood up again, holding his glass in front of him.

After a few moments silence, he continued. "Now you are soon not going to be so innocent. A married woman. Wife of a doctor. A doctor's wife. Yes. Yes. A doctor's wife. A Jewish doctor's wife. Isn't that right? A Jewish doctor's wife." His words came slower, louder. "Be careful, Christine. I fear you have chosen a dangerous future." Puzzled looks. "You can always come to us for help," Meier continued. "Always. And you may have to. Who knows what we may do with our Jews? Who knows what we should do with our Jews? Well, some of us think we know, don't we?" he said, looking at Johann. The aunt gave her husband a scowl that he could not misinterpret. "Strong leaders may be needed in our future," he said in a deep voice, "but we must beware of strong policies. Policies that are only strong because they take advantage of the weak. And we must beware of those who would use our anger against ourselves." Many guests began to applaud, thinking Meier was finished. He wasn't.

"I only want to say, Christine," he said, facing the bride and groom, "we wish you and your new husband well in our beloved Germany. May you and it prosper, with all due respect and honor. To your health! For the future, a happy one for us all! For *Deutschland*!" He raised his glass so abruptly that the wine spilled out and over his wrist, dripping down his sleeve and onto his plate.

The others drank too. But Maier had more to say. He turned and stared at Johann. With the air of a man who knows that others will mock him, but without the slightest concern for their mockery, he put his now empty glass down on the table. Raising his right arm stiffly, Meier leaned over the table and shouted, "*Heil Hitler! Heil* your little, mustachioed *Führer, mein Herr Doktor! Ja,* please, do heal your *Führer*, for the sake of a healthy Deutschland!"

Johann gasped. Philipp stood up abruptly. His father shouted something. The other members of the Stein family jerked their heads to look at Meier. When he sat down, there was a hush.

'Outrageous!' Johann thought. 'Why did I talk with this fool? Everyone's come to celebrate this marriage and give it their blessing. Philipp is a good fellow. His bride is radiantly happy. They have every appearance of being destined for one another. This drunken uncle, this oaf is spoiling the day.'

He had wanted to be carefree for a day or two. He regretted what he had said the night before at the *Weinstube* and had hoped he could apologize to Philipp and his parents in private. 'What did I say to the uncle, anyway?' he asked himself. 'And why would the oaf drag me into this? This is not a beer hall or a street corner. This is not the place for political salutes and slogans.' He was mortified. 'This mudslinging is outrageous. How typical of the left-wing rabble. No manners. No sense of decorum.'

Then he thought, maybe that was why he had been seated across from Meier. 'Did Philipp know I had thought of joining the Nazis a year ago? Did he know I did not join? Maybe Christine's uncle thought I was a Nazi and was baiting me? More likely, the man is just a blowhard. Yes, and a socialist or communist on top of that.' Johann felt sweat break out on his forehead and upper lip. 'This was another of Philipp's jokes: seat me near a communist crank and watch the fireworks. But at the celebration of his marriage? This business about the Jews is too extreme. It intoxicates people.'

Johann felt himself grow dizzy and closed his eyes. He couldn't bear to look at Helga. He could feel her icy mortification. Gradually, conversation resumed. The small group of musicians began playing a waltz. Many of the guests rose to dance. When he opened his eyes again, Christine's uncle's seat was empty, as were those of *Frau* Meier and their son. The salute, the talk about the Jews had stained everything. He felt people looking at him. All except Philipp and Christine, who now stood with their backs to him, talking with Philipp's parents.

Johann and Helga left the restaurant a short while later. When they wished Philipp and Christine a long and happy life together, he could sense the eagerness that Philipp hoped they would just go. What could he say now? They walked back to their hotel in silence.

Later that evening, lying in bed, he decided he had been right not to join the Party. He must be cautious. He was a doctor, not a man of politics. He wanted clarity. Certainty. Truth. He now was of a mind to leave politics to others, to hotheads and drunken oafs: 'Let them dirty their hands and waste their time. If Hitler or anyone else ever persuaded the German people to join up in his cause as one, then I would join, too, wholeheartedly. That would be good, to be a member of an entire nation, united in will and purpose.' He drifted off to sleep. Helga lay next to him, her eyes wide open.

CHAPTER NINE
To Gain the Future

I have learned something over the past few days that I should have known long ago: how pathetic it is when people blame others for their own poor decisions. We humans have a habit—a sickness, actually—of doing that. I have not been immune to it.

Everyone now tells how Hitler tricked us into doing his will. At the trial earlier this week, one of the defendants tried to argue that he was only doing what he was told: he was just following Hitler's orders. As though Hitler had him in chains, unable to escape. Hitler may have been a great demon! But we Germans should have had will enough of our own to resist him. To tell the truth, we did not want to. I was willing, so many of us were willing, to do what we thought we had to do to gain the future we believed we deserved.

Although I managed to escape the Nazi trap for a while—thanks to you, Helga, more than to any great wisdom on my part—eventually I was blinded by my selfishness. I let my own angers and fears ensnare me and become my master. The demon was not Hitler. It was me.

Eight days had passed since Johann had begun his letter to Helga. 'I gave myself twenty-one days. Only eleven are left,' he thought.

'Will she read it? Will she understand?' His fears assembled themselves in the shadows, whether his eyes were open or closed.

Sundays were the hardest. The Palace of Justice was quiet, except for some of the attorneys looking through documents. The American businessmen who had rented space in the building looked through him as though he wasn't there. He would have gone out to work on a rubble pile, if only to distract himself, but no one did that on Sunday. He did not dare go anywhere near his old neighborhood or the hospital. 'Did Meier know who he was? Even if the old man remembered him, what would that prove?' It was all so complicated. He yearned to go back in time To Pohlendorf. Free of all the shadows.

If he thought about Pohlendorf, he thought about Philipp. Their lives crossed over each other, back and forth, like the serpents around the caduceus' staff. Braided together until the end. He began to see that he would understand himself only when he understood what, if anything, made him different from his childhood friend.

The Nuremberg he loved—its great brown-gray walls; its timbered houses, steep jumbled roofs and dark, glinting, cobblestoned alleys; its balconies overflowing with blooms; its brightness in late spring; its sum-mers that stretched into October; its sense of itself as permanent and proud—all that was destroyed. It once had given him a sense of purpose and importance. Of pride. Other German cities were too big, too com-mercial, with too many foreigners, too many dialects. All not home.

Pohlendorf was home. But Pohlendorf and his childhood were for-ever lost. So he had chosen Nuremberg. But did the city he imagined exist? Or was it a dream? A fairy tale world of princes and castles? He remembered imagining himself as a doctor in 15th century Nuremberg, ministering to the Duke, having a role in city affairs, becoming a city councilor, with Helga and he having a special place in the town's proces-sions and in the church. Imagining the towns-people taking their hats off to them and to their children. He might have been Albrecht Dürer's physician. 'Oh, to see those delicate, gifted hands,' he thought, 'those piercing eyes, in such noble, inspired service to mankind!' They would have lived near the *Heilig Geist Spital*, beneath the imperial castle. Would

have taken Sunday walks with his family along the banks of the Pegnitz and enjoyed idyllic picnics in the Steigerwald. The Duchess on horseback, riding by, would stop and greet them, would tell them how beautiful their children were and how happy she was to see them.

When they moved to Nuremberg, he felt certain that his future lay here in the old imperial city. He thought himself destined to be a part of Nuremberg because he felt he had been a part of it forever, that his roots reached back into Germany's past. Back before the wars and the swarming beehive of modern life. He thought that if he devoted himself to his profession, he would help Nuremberg flourish anew as it had five hundred years before. Its glorious heritage and its energy would become a beacon for Germany's rebirth. He would be known for his dignity, his honor, his service. Now he was empty. A ruined thing, like Nuremberg. Lying on his bunk in the basement, he realized that his fantasy had helped chase him into Hitler's arms.

And what about Pohlendorf? Did it exist the way he remembered it? Was something wrong there, too? Its idyllic harmony and friendliness were snuffed out with the war. Gone in just a few years. How real could it have been? His father's business had failed. Others, too. Like other small towns from a bygone age, it was smothered by changes beyond anyone's control. Was he, were all those who were lured between the wars into thinking that places like Pohlendorf and Nuremberg would never die, not to blame for such delusions? And for the choices that he, that so many others made that were based on these delusions. Could they not have foreseen the consequences of their choices?

What never changed? Or, if it did change, should not have? Among the most painful changes of his life was his friendship with Philipp. How had Philipp handled those times?

*****

Philipp and Christine moved from Augsburg to Berlin in 1928, little more than a year after they were married. Philipp believed it would be a better place for him to build a practice and eventually open his own clinic.

"More people means a greater need for doctors. It's as simple as that. Let's try it for awhile," he said to her. "I didn't like Berlin before, right after the war, mostly because I was so lonely. That won't be true now. We can always come back to Augsburg."

She wanted to live in a larger city, too. But if he had said he wanted to move to the North Pole, she would have agreed.

In Berlin, he sometimes complained about the frenzy and the noise. She was surprised by how much she missed her parents. Still, the metropolis energized them. The city itself seemed alive, defying other living things to catch up with it. Electric lights everywhere. Trains coming and going day and night. Tourists gawking on the boulevards and thronging to the sideshows in the alleys. Black-caftaned Eastern European Jews arriving by the thousands. Syrians and Egyptians haggling with German housewives over kitchen pots and carpets. The Chinese neighborhood mushrooming into the Japanese neighborhood, which crowded against a Turkish and then a Greek quarter. Stately urban villas and massive concrete housing blocks facing each other on either side of the canals that drained the city's swamps. Skyscrapers taking root. Motorcars circling monuments and fountains at countless intersections. Subways and overhead railways spilling across the city like an unraveling ball of string. Zeppelins and airplanes so commonplace that only children looked up to watch them. It made them giddy.

They loved the city's dazzle. Its ornately gilded movie houses, complete with organs and orchestras, with lines of people waiting to enter, even for the morning and afternoon showings. Its nighttime cabarets, bars, brothels, and casinos, all flashing electric lights, drew patrons like moths. They could hear symphonies from every era, see classical ballet or modern dance, choose between Shakespeare, Schiller, Schnitzler and bawdy bedroom farces. They laughed as the ridiculous went arm in arm with the sublime in every art form imaginable. They followed jazz players, singers and exotic dancers from America. They tried exotic foods. They knew that all around them were fantasies that satisfied the most extravagant desires. If Berlin had become a magnet for Europe's long-ings and lusts, if homosexuals found freedoms that they only dreamed of in the more staid capitals of the continent, they were not bothered.

Philipp knew that he had seen Berlin at its worst just after the war. Now it was again a place of marvels, a boiling cauldron of ideas and innovations. The city had a hothouse atmosphere. For anyone who had a need to flaunt, or dared to be different, it was a paradise. "Live and let live" and a shrug was the typical response of the rich and soon-to-be-rich. But most of his patients and their families could ill afford any of these "freedoms."

Not all Berliners or Germans visiting the city were accepting of the city's variety. And Philipp agreed that the city's temptations could contaminate its youth. But he could only support the socialists' gradual approach to the problem. Their confidence in reason, their emphasis on social engineering made sense to him. By contrast, he saw the Nazis fiercely protesting the degeneracy they imagined in every alley and in every modern art gallery, and he heard the Communists shrilly decrying the gap between rich and poor.

"Both Nazis and communists yearn for a way back to a world before all this change," he said. "Both long for the violence they believe will usher in paradise. Both are willing to shed innocent blood for their dreams. And both would plunge us into nightmares."

"They have to believe in something," Christine answered. "It's their religion."

"A religion shouldn't be based on violence."

"From what I know of religions, all of them are, one way or another."

"When did you learn so much about religions?"

Christine just looked at him. "I know you married me for my looks. But I'm not dumb."

He laughed. "I know that. I just am surprised to hear you say something about religion." Philipp wanted to tease her by saying something about her looks, but he thought better of it.

"I grew out of religion before I met you," she said, pouring him a cup of coffee. "I read about world religions while I was in *Gymnasium.*

Religion's fine for those who need it. For children. For tribes living under a volcano. And for the dying. And every religion has its god who protects them while they kill their enemies. Religion is an excuse for violence."

"Well, the Marxists certainly have their holy book. And their expectation of violence. And the Nazis have their Messiah. You're right."

"Let it be known, my husband thinks I am right!" She raised her cup in a salute. Then they both laughed.

"You should not have married me," he said, looking into her eyes.

"Why?"

"You should have gone to university. Become an art historian or whatever you wanted to be. You could have had a career."

"We've talked about that before. I can have a career if I want, as a bookkeeper. And after I met you, I didn't want to go to university. I wanted to marry you."

"And I just said you're not dumb!" He touched her cheek and sighed. "I don't understand why so many Germans are so unhappy with the way things are. We have so much to be thankful for. The war is over. People are working. We are making progress with diseases. I don't..."

"But you complain, too," she said. "About your patients' living conditions. About the children."

"True. I complain. I'm impatient. Especially when I see the children."

Philipp was aware that he moved toward the left politically as he treated more and more young girls and boys with venereal diseases. He could excuse their parent's sexual frenzies, even their choice to become prostitutes if they wished, but children ought not to be forced into such choices. He blamed their poverty and squalor. He was willing to accept the city's blatant sexuality as a temporary alternative to progress toward economic justice for all Germans. A fever that had to work its course. But his patience was limited when he examined twelve-year-olds who bore the bruises of sexual exploitation. Perhaps someday this social ailment would be cured and overcome. Meanwhile, he treated the children as best he could.

What frightened him most was the eagerness of the extremists to spill blood for their beliefs. He read the pamphlets handed him on the street and picked up newspapers from benches. He paused to catch the drift of speakers in the parks and near the train stations. He read the accounts of clashes between street gangs of Nazis and Communists. He saw the open trucks with brown-shirted *SA* men making their rounds, their loudspeakers roaring hatred of Jews and communists. In Wedding, near his policlinic, and, he knew, in Kreutzfeld, Lichterfeld and the other working class districts, the communists had barrels and bricks ready for instant barricades. Everywhere he went in the city, the *Litfass Säulen*, ubiquitous concrete columns that displayed advertisements, theater bills, concerts and the like, were plastered with political posters and slogans. Banners hung from electric lines across streets. Parades, demonstrations, and the fights that followed were regular weekend occasions.

"Is there no one who defends the present?" he would ask, only to see Christine's blank face and know what she was thinking. That he was not doing anything either.

Sustaining his optimism was hard. Every article in the medical journals he read pointed toward a crisis. Researchers feuded with each other in ideological wars. The professional outlook for younger physicians was dim, given their burgeoning numbers. The financial picture for all physicians, young and old, was deteriorating, because of the rising cost of living and the meager fees from the state's insurance plans. And his daily work was a constant struggle. Everywhere a crisis. But he refused to be discouraged.

During a break at the policlinic, he picked up an issue of a medical journal that focused on psychiatric care. It had an article by *Frau Doktor Professor* Luise Seligmann, *Medizinische Fakultät, Universität Heidelberg*: "*Sustaining and enhancing the sexual drive of veterans with genital wounds: a psycho-therapeutic technique.*" So, she had become a professor of medicine, just as she said she would. He remembered having discussed the article's argument with her—veterans suffering from some forms of paralysis and even mutilation from war wounds could be assisted in overcoming inhibitions related to their sexual activities with hypnosis and counseling. He recognized some of the subjects in her study as patients in Hoche's clinic.

She had often talked about the men in the wards, especially after making love in her apartment. How sorry she felt for them. How they deserved at least such pleasures. That those who were denied them would have difficulty overcoming their depression and coping with their other physical ailments. She argued that sexual passion and satisfaction could be harnessed as a wonderful medicine. Her article was well done, he thought, modest in its assertions, concrete and convincing. Not many other physicians, let alone female physicians, would have had the courage to tackle this problem. He mailed her a note of congratulations on his way home that afternoon, and thought, not for the first time, how different his life would have been had they stayed together.

But Philipp's professional life was satisfying. He and a half-dozen other physicians worked in a policlinic in Wedding, Berlin's notoriously rough working class district. He enjoyed the challenge: poor patients with a whole palette of symptoms and syndromes that tested his skills and ingenuity. Alcoholism and prostitution were rampant. Patients with chronic venereal diseases were constant throughout the year. Tuberculosis cases rose and fell with the seasons. Cases of depression seemed to increase in the autumn. Suicides peaked in early spring. Psychic ailments seemed to be affected by the weather as well as by physical health and economic security. Everything was intertwined.

He knew that ancient medicine and folk wisdom both described how the seasons and the environment influenced physical and mental disorders. He knew, too, that some modern medical researchers were studying these correlations. What he saw in his patients confirmed what was being described with increasing clarity in the medical journals: early childhood experiences, especially nutrition, parenting, and education, had a significant long-term impact on an individual's mental health. He had already begun to make notes for an article.

At the same time, he was finding the current emphasis on racial explanations for mental health, personality traits, indeed for all social behavior, superficial and unrewarding. He knew he was going against the current beliefs. But that line of reasoning was far too simplistic. How many of those twelve-year-old prostitutes could avoid his or her fate in the streets? Who of their parents could find happiness outside of a bottle? Racial categories, he was coming to see, were generally irrelevant to his patients' world and their behavior in it. Saying someone was of this or that "race" was not helpful. More important, he believed, was an individual's general physical health, intelligence, and temperament, all of which were shaped by external forces quite beyond his or her control. Where others wanted to argue such things were determined by race and biology alone, he held them to be just as strongly influenced by social and economic factors.

Philipp wanted to help his patients to the best of his ability, one by one, toward a healthier, more productive, happier life. That meant more than just giving them the right medicines. It meant helping them find hope in the future. He gave the children toys and books and sometimes gave their parents money for clothes and shoes. He smiled and helped them smile, soothed their fears and gave them reasons to hope. He thought of his patients as plants that needed special care.

He often talked with Christine about how they would raise their children. How they would feed them, clothe them, teach them about their responsibilities toward others, especially those less fortunate than they were. How they would teach them that the world's beauty was made for everyone to enjoy.

"Yes," she would say, "but not until we can provide for them."

"Of course," he'd answer. "Of course." But whenever he thought they were ready, she said, "not yet." He tried not to be disappointed or impatient. They had a favorite, shady bench in the park near the zoo where they would sit on Saturday or Sunday afternoons, depending on his schedule at the policlinic. The city's hum just beyond the park blended with the sound of the wind in the trees. As the train passed on the elevated tracks nearby, Berlin seemed to combine the best of both worlds—nature and metropolis. On such days, he never thought of Luise.

Christine also loved Berlin. Her only complaint was the subway. "Why go underground when we can walk or take a trolley or even a cab? I feel like a mole or an earthworm down there, Lippi! Even if it is faster, I would rather walk today," she said, as they stayed on the sunny side of their street until it joined *Friedrichstraße*.

"Fine, we can walk. Just like our ancient ancestors." He grinned and let his shoulders droop down, bent his knees and began to swing his arms with his knuckles just above the pavement, scampering ahead of her.

"Oh Lord, I have an ape for a husband!" He heard her call behind him and glanced back as she turned to go the other way. He reversed his direction, too, and monkey-walked quickly up alongside her, grinning, grunting and hooting.

"You are an ape! A real ape!"

"And you love me because I am so natural. Admit it!"

Christine abruptly stopped and laughed her fullest laugh. "I do love you, my Lippi-ape. I do!"

They drifted arm in arm along the sidewalk. In the window of an art gallery, they saw themselves reflected in the glass, and simultaneously stuck their tongues out at each other. More laughter. More hooting from Philipp.

"You ape!" Christine repeated. "Behold, *Herr Doktor* Lippi Ape!' she shouted, loud enough for others to hear. Passers-by either smiled or frowned at their exuberance. None could pretend not to notice.

Then Philipp took his antics to another level. Seeing the kiosk behind them reflected in the pawnshop window, he monkey-walked backwards, stopping directly in front of a waist-high campaign poster for Hitler. Philipp bent over, his butt a few inches away from the *Führer*'s nose, and did his monkey-dance, arms swinging, hooting, and laughing. Christine laughed even louder than before.

Almost immediately, a short, balding man with his belt too tight under a bulging belly, started yelling at Philipp. "You degenerate! You stinking asshole! Who do you think you are?" A small crowd quickly formed.

Philipp straightened up. He was taller than his accuser by nearly a foot. The cursing did not stop. "There ought to be a place for you and your ilk! A prison. Worse. You defile this country! You are a crazy man! Asshole!"

Philipp at first tried to smile. Christine tried to pull him away. He would not budge.

"So, you think this is bad," Philipp said in his normal voice. "Wait until the day when you can't do this, my good man! This Hitler of yours would make us all into his puppets. No thank you. He means no one well but himself. *Führer*! Hah!"

"You know nothing!" the other shouted back. "You are as dumb as an ape. Go on, ape. I spit upon you. I spit upon all enemies of Germany. The communists, the Jews..."

Philipp bristled, "Look, you ...

Christine pulled harder on Philipp's arm. "Come, we'll be late. Come, Lippi!"

"This little lump thinks Germany will be better off with Hitler. Same old crap. Same old, stinking, vicious crap. Where will it end?"

"I'm calling a policeman," the man shouted. "You must answer for your degeneracy on the public street!" He began hopping up and down, trying to look over the heads in the crowd. Much laughter. More cursing.

"We're going!" Christine said in her loudest voice. "We're going!"

Philipp turned, saw how upset she was, and decided to walk away. They made their way through the spectators, some booing, some laughing. The man waved his fists and began to orate to the crowd: "So, ladies and gentlemen. We see here what we have to deal with. Poor Germany. In the hands of apes. Democrats. Communists. All of them, Jewish apes." At this, a few men in the crowd began to boo loudly. Others tried to shout them down. The speaker continued his harangue. Slowly, the crowd dissolved.

Half a block later, Philipp apologized to Christine. "Sorry for that nonsense. I carried it too far, perhaps. I despise those types. So eager to hate. Hitler has all too many like that in his pocket. They'll find him a hard master. But he's what they want."

"You said once you liked some of his ideas," Christine reminded him.

"Sure. Versailles. Challenging all this corruption. Better health care. Respect for Germany. More authority for physicians. How can anyone be against that? But there's so much more in his bag of tricks."

"Oh, Philipp! Everything should be as easy as you want it to be. We have to take a lot of bitter medicine now. You of all people should know that."

He looked away. They continued walking in silence toward the *Potsdamer Platz*, where they were meeting Benjamin Gerschenkron and his wife at *Kempinski Haus Vaterland,* Berlin's newest attraction. Gerschenkron was senior physician in the policlinic. The two men had quickly become friends.

"You'll like him," Philipp told Christine. "And from what he has told me about his wife, Martha, we should feel comfortable with her, too. He's easy to talk with, you know. And she should be no different."

Benjamin Gerschenkron was fifteen years older than Philipp and perhaps for that reason somewhat less lively and spontaneous, but only to a degree. His unusually high speaking voice made him at first somewhat taciturn. But his intellect and his wit quickly became obvious. His most memorable physical feature was a ragged scar across his left cheek. "Just a war wound," he would tell everyone, "not a student escapade. No fraternity duels for me." Tall, with sandy brown hair turning gray at the temples, Benjamin Gerschenkron looked as distinguished as a motion picture actor.

Benjamin and Philipp had discovered they had much in common in their expectations of the importance of psychiatry, especially in the wake of the war's stresses. Both foresaw long-term mental instabilities and resulting social consequences. They welcomed the opportunity to become pioneers in the development of new medical techniques, and were especially interested in children and child development. They talked about bringing poor children out of the city to the countryside or to the North Sea, where their health would be restored by a wholesome diet, outdoor games, fresh air and sunshine. Benjamin spoke enthusiastically about the day when brain surgeries would cure depression, anxiety, even criminal tendencies. Philipp imagined new, powerful medications, anti-depressants and mood altering drugs, even those that would stimulate moral behavior. Each man held doubts about the other's expectations, but they agreed with each other more than they disagreed, and respected each other's professional judgment. Meeting socially, they hoped for a deeper friendship between themselves and their wives.

The Gerschenkrons were from Breslau, Philipp told Christine, and had moved to Berlin shortly after the war. Benjamin was the third physician in his family. His father was a respected family doctor in Breslau's Jewish neighborhood. His uncle was an eye doctor with a wide reputation for expertise, as well as for his mastery of the violin and knowledge of music history. Among his uncle's patients were some of North Germany's most prominent musicians. Benjamin played the piano and had promise as a musician himself, but had decided as a young man that he would concentrate on medicine. Unlike Philipp, he maintained at least some of his Jewish traditions. He saw only emergency patients on Saturdays, taking extra Sunday duties at the policlinic instead. He announced the dates of the upcoming major Jewish holidays long in advance in staff meetings, and offered to work on Christian ones. Given his command of Yiddish, he often found himself treating patients who spoke that language.

Philipp hoped that Christine would like Benjamin as much as he did, and that their wives would become friends, too. Where the two women differed was in their religion. Martha, according to Benjamin, was as Jewish as a modern woman could be. Christine was modern, but hardly Jewish—or anything, for that matter. Her Catholic upbringing was a repository of awkward memories she turned in to amusing stories. Philipp was not surprised that she had never offered to convert to Judaism, given his own weak connection to his religious heritage. Still, Benjamin's proud description of Martha's conversion made him wonder if Christine's minimal interest in his faith signified a weak commitment to him.

Martha had converted to Judaism shortly before she married. Her schoolteacher father and her "modern" mother had raised no particular objections to their daughter's decision, especially after they met

Benjamin. "Any apprehensions vanished when they saw my good looks!" Benjamin had said. Philipp had snickered, and then both men had laughed out loud.

They arrived at *Kempinski Haus Vaterland* just after the Gerschenkrons, who were waiting near the front door. The newly opened *Kempinski* catapulted the city even further into the twentieth century. Its sparkling electric lights transformed the night. Berliners and tourists alike could not resist it. Christine had read a newspaper review of its many attractions: a palatial movie house and accompanying orchestra, plus several smaller theater stages, arcades, and many cafés, and restaurants that offered the flavor of different regions of Germany and much of Europe. An electric sun "set" over a mock Alpine scene in the *Löwenbräu* beer garden while waitresses hurried back and forth in their Bavarian *dirndls* with *steins* full of foaming beer. A thunderstorm brewed over a *Rhineland* café as guests selected from the best Mosel wines. Gypsies with red silk bandanas played *czardas* on their violins and strolled from table to table as patrons sipped sweet white wine on the Hungarian steppes. Waltzes delighted the guests in the *gemütlich* Viennese garden. A Spanish dancer twirled to flamenco guitarists in a bodega. The Kempinski's grand marble staircase, fit for a prince's palace, led to five stories of distraction and amusement, all under a high domed roof, right in the heart of Berlin on the *Potsdamer Platz*. "They even have a "Wild West Bar," with real cowboys and an American jazz band," Christine had told Philipp.

He had been looking forward to this Sunday afternoon for over a month, ever since Benjamin had suggested it. As the two couples ascended the marble staircase together and entered the spectacle of the building, Philipp and Christine forgot about the incident at the kiosk.

The Gerschenkrons insisted they go first to the Bavarian beer garden—"to revisit your roots, Philipp!" Guided by the sound of a zither and an ensemble playing traditional Bavarian tavern songs, they found a table. Many guests were already well into their beer. Behind a wrought-iron grille two stories high, a painting of the Bavarian Alps was lit by electric lights to a rosy, sunset glow. Adding to the effect, cigarette smoke drifting to the ceiling was whirled around by electric fans and colored the air with the fading, fake sunset. It was marvelous.

Beer flavored with lemon and cider helped their conversation flow. Remarks about the weather gave way to descriptions of their childhoods and their experiences during the war. Talking about their likes and dislikes in Berlin, the four soon knew they would become friends. The music, the conversation, the sunset on the Alps all relaxed them. When Christine told Benjamin and Martha about Philipp's antics earlier in the day, he had only to hoot and pretend to pick a louse from her hair for them to laugh so hard that they had to wipe away the tears.

"So you showed Hitler..." Benjamin began.

"My 'best side!'" Philipp interjected. Laughter rippled around the table.

"No," Benjamin said. "You showed him the only side he's worthy of seeing. The man revolts me. And the idiots that appear to worship him are even worse. He's a puppet master, as you say, but why on earth are there so many willing puppets? You'd think we Germans would be smarter than that. We had the last *Kaiser* to show us what happens when an unbalanced man has too much power. More evidence that people prefer being led than to thinking for themselves."

"But we do need a leader. A very strong leader." Philipp said in a loud voice, in order to be heard above the inebriated shouting at a nearby table.

Christine tried to hush him, to no avail.

"Please, Christine. We live in a democracy. That means I can talk as loud as I like. About anything I like. Besides, who's paying attention to me?" He continued, although quieter than before. "Anyway, the *Kaiser*, our dear *Kaiser Wilhelm der Letzte,* now living the good life in Holland, may have had some good intentions, but was blinded by his own authority. Now we need a leader who not only sees the problems we face but also sees himself. A man who can choose advisors who will contradict him, advisors who will temper his judgment with theirs. A leader who is long on wisdom and short on arrogance."

Benjamin tried to interrupt, "Is there such a..."

"Let me finish," Philipp continued. "This leader will be a homeo-pathic solution to Germany's ailments."

Benjamin guffawed.

"No, listen. I don't approve of homeopaths, either. But here's my point. Just as a homeopath prescribes a tiny portion of the very contami-nant—even if it is a poison—that he claims has made his gullible patient ill, just so, I say, we need a tiny dose of a dictator to cure us of our long-ing for a strong leader. The cause is the cure, as the homeopaths say. That would open the door for a democracy that people would believe in. Not this toothless state born in Weimar, with everyone on the right and the left trying to tear it down."

"And you'd be willing to let Hitler have this role?" Benjamin asked.

"Believe me, he is so ludicrous, so absurdly unqualified to lead any country, our *Vaterland* would be cured of wanting such a leader in under a month. Hitler is certainly not long on wisdom and short on arrogance. But he would do. The only thing that worries me is that in even a month, he could do some nasty mischief. They say he likes Karl May's cowboy stories and America's wild-west justice. Just what we need. A Chancel-lor from Texas."

Benjamin, Philipp and Christine all laughed, but Martha said noth-ing. That the conversation had turned to politics was not as surpris-ing to Philipp and Benjamin as it was to their wives. The two men had aired their political views before, although often in a shorthand fashion, briefly commenting on an item in the newspaper or laughing at a joke at the policlinic. Both women, however, despite their independent-mind-edness, were wary of appearing interested in political affairs. Both were glad to be able to vote. Both supported legislation that gave rights to women that their grandmothers could never have imagined. But it was hard for them to overcome the feeling that women should not be con-cerned with worldly matters.

Christine sighed. "Philipp says we should be grateful for what we have. I think he's right. I heard on the radio that the Nazis are not doing well in the by-elections. As the world gets better, no one will have time for Hitler's little games."

"I hope you are right. I fear him, though," Martha said, almost in a whisper. "Even more than I fear him—actually, he makes me laugh more than anything else—I fear the forces this little man will unleash. Whatever he wants, the German *Volk* will do. The *Volk* is not wise. Germans don't know what's in their best interest. They aren't being taught in school how to see through the Nazis' nonsense."

"Oh come, Martha. Don't be so dramatic," Benjamin said.

"I am not being dramatic. I wish this were that simple, Benjamin. You don't go into the shops each day and hear what I hear. I have seen the anger in these people. Hitler feeds it. And feeds on it. I cannot imagine that your patients are silent on the subject. Are you willing to ignore this hysteria? The masses have a great need—perhaps it is an understandable need—to hate someone or something. So many Germans feel cheated. Are you blind to that?"

"I am not blind," Benjamin said. "I know what you mean. But I have nothing to fear. This is a country of laws. Of established and guaranteed rights. I can imagine crises, of course, in which these laws might be challenged. The Constitution even allows for emergencies. But what harm can occur when there are so many controls? A sinister politician here and there—or a crazy one, for that matter. That's the price of democracy. But the constitution protects us from tyranny. We are already better off, since the current economic policies have taken hold. International statesmen are seeing the wisdom of peace. It's good for business. Things will get even better. Then the Hitlers and the Ludendorffs, the anti-Semites and the war mongers, and the wild-eyed communists and the revolutionaries will be talking to empty halls."

Philipp slapped the table. "Yes. Exactly. Well said, colleague. We still have a future here. And we doctors have a large part to play. More than ever."

"I hope you are right," Martha said. "We build our lives on this hope. But is it realistic. Or is it like this place? All flashing lights. Phony scenery. Fake. A mask meant to fool us into having a good time while the world rots." She put down her glass. "I do know though that if Hitler comes to power, we won't be safe here. And I don't mean just us Jews.

I mean the doctors. The teachers. Butchers. Bakers. Ministers. House-wives. Children. Everyone. The Nazis lust for war. The communists hope for it. They all believe war and revolution are the way to heaven on earth. How stupid! Everywhere, left and right, there's too much will-ingness to shout, to damn, to frighten the other side into fighting and drawing blood. What's to stop the next war from happening on German soil? Many greedy Germans would welcome the chance to get hold of their neighbor's property or make a profit from the war. The French want revenge, want to crush us. The Belgians would cheer. Lord knows who else." Her last words were drowned out by the Bavarian troop on the stage, singing louder than before, and the people at the tables joining in the familiar melody.

Martha continued, "So, I hope you're right, that just a little taste of Hitler would cure us of that nonsense. But I for one would not stay in such a country. I would leave."

"And where would you go?" Benjamin asked, surprised by his wife's outspokenness.

"That's the problem. Where *would* I go? Or should I say, 'we'?" She looked at him and paused before continuing. "Who would take us? Maybe Switzerland. Maybe America. Mexico or South America. Or South Africa. Or Sweden." She shrugged her shoulders. "I don't know. But I know we would have to leave."

"Nonsense." Benjamin looked at each one of them and then turned back to Martha. "Do you think there's no anti-Semitism in those places? And besides, we've done nothing wrong. Why give these hateful little thugs the satisfaction of chasing us away?"

"That's my thought, too," Philipp said. "So, before we leave 'good old Germany' for some unknown destination, I suggest we have another glass."

Violin music from the adjoining room competed with the Bavarian folksongs that began at one table and then swelled in volume as others picked them up. On stage, the troop of men in *Lederhosen* slapped their knees and clogs while blond, braided women with brightly colored *dirn-dls* twirled and clapped their hands in an infectious rhythm. The Alps were a bit too red, but it was not a bad imitation, Philipp thought.

In the *Kempinski Haus Vaterland,* people could escape from the present. Could pretend that Germany had already used up its share of calamities. Could pretend that the future would be one long *Volksfest* with bratwurst and beer. They could laugh and sing as though on holiday. The good humor of the waiters and waitresses, the drink, the infectious singing, the smoky haze blurred all edges, let everyone relax and believe everything would be fine again. In fact, everything in the *Vaterland*, they longed to believe, would be finer than it ever was.

Later, after the foursome had sampled the atmosphere in the Spanish *bodega* and looked in on the "Wild West Bar," they said their goodbyes. On the street, before they took different paths across the *Potsdamer Platz*, Benjamin and Martha invited Philipp and Christine to come to dinner at their apartment.

"I want to talk business, Philipp, mind you, but no need for it to be without some pleasure. Martha is an excellent cook. We might have her specialty, *Rouladen mit Knödel*."

"*Ja*," Martha said, "Please do come."

The Steins agreed. "*Auf Wiedersehen*, then." It was near midnight when they parted.

Philipp and Christine took a taxi back to their neighborhood in Berlin-Brandenburg. When they got in, Philipp paid the driver an extra *Reichsmark* to take them a bit out of their way, through an intersection governed by Berlin's first traffic signal, under the clock tower on *Potsdamer Platz*. They watched as the light changed to red and then back again to green and laughed when it did. The cab snaked along the Spree, the city's lights dancing off the river. Philipp told the driver to pull over so they could walk the last few blocks to their apartment, just to enjoy the evening air.

"What kind of business does Benjamin want to discuss, do you suppose?" Christine asked.

"I think he wants to open a private clinic for children and wants me to become his partner."

"But we cannot afford that."

"Yes, I know. And he must know we are still a few years away from any such situation. But let's see what he proposes. Maybe he has another idea. I think his wife inherited some money recently. Did you like them?"

"Oh, yes. He has such friendly, kind eyes. And I especially like Martha. She is solid. She says what she thinks. I find her a bit pessimistic. But I think she is very intelligent and observant. I can imagine becoming friends with her. With both of them. They both seem trustworthy."

"Good. That would be important when he and I practice together."

"You make it sound as though you will agree to whatever he suggests."

"Yes," he said. "Yes. You'll see. I have a good feeling about this. We both want to treat children from the working classes. There's a great need. He'll focus on physical ailments. I'll take on mental problems. Of course each of us also will cover for the other. I trust him. And I believe he trusts me. Martha's nursing background will be useful. And you can work as our receptionist and bookkeeper, keeping everything in order. It'll be perfect! More satisfying work for you than in the curtain factory, for starters."

"Philipp, you stagger me. Talk about counting your chickens. I suppose you've already given this clinic of ours a name?"

"No. But by tomorrow morning, I will have come up with something."

They both laughed and held hands the rest of the way down the street to their apartment building.

CHAPTER TEN

𝔚e 𝔥abe 𝔏ost so 𝔐uch

Hitler by himself was not powerful enough to cause our ruin. We Germans did it ourselves. This truth makes me ashamed. And afraid. Oh, Helga! We have lost so much. So much. And for what?

I began my own descent into this abyss at the end of 1929. That's when I began to slide down an icy slope. So many of my hopes had collapsed. Soon after Greta took ill, I remember telling you how I saw the growing economic chaos as an echo of my despair and powerlessness. Given the state of the world around us, perhaps it is no wonder that I was losing confidence in myself, in my profession, in Germany's future. I felt like a spider whose web had been torn apart, with no other recourse but to spin another.

The Doctors' Trial began by focusing on a variety of experiments about which Johann knew little: the deliberate exposure of concentration camp inmates to freezing temperatures, to malaria, and to immersion in seawater. The testimony about sterilizations came on the day Helga recognized him in the courtroom. Over the next few days, the prosecution introduced evidence of the Nazi effort to collect Jewish skeletons for anatomical research. Next was evidence about the experiments that deliberately induced jaundice and tuberculosis, and about the application of sulfanilamide and other drugs to concentration camp prisoners whose living bone and muscle had been deliberately exposed to blood infections.

The trial was scheduled to adjourn before Christmas and resume in early January, with a week of testimony about more experiments on deliberately contaminated blood and wounds, and on the effects of mustard gas and other biological warfare agents. Several more days would focus on the euthanasia program. The prosecution planned to conclude its portion of the trial with evidence about the "Nazi criminal organization" that facilitated all these experiments.

Johann dreaded especially the testimony on euthanasia. The vast enterprise of Nazi medicine was being stretched out like a corpse on an autopsy table. The stench nearly overpowered him. He feared that he could not endure it. That he would not be able to tell Helga what he had done. And if he didn't tell her, that he would lose her forever.

*****

After almost six years of marriage, Helga had settled into the daily routine of a *Hausfrau*. Waking up before six, she washed, combed her hair and put on her housecoat. Next she tended the briquette stove in the parlor—with luck it had not gone out over night—and started a fire in the kitchen's wood stove. While water was boiling for coffee, she laid out Johann's clothes for the day, and then returned to the kitchen to put breakfast on the table—milk for the children, usually bread with jelly, and on Sundays, some slices of ham or *wurst* and cheese. If all went well, the coffee finished brewing just as Johann appeared at six thirty. He left for his rounds at the hospital before seven, and then spent the rest of the morning at the policlinic.

Paul-Adolf, just past his fifth birthday, would usually wake up before his father left, but stay in bed until he and his sister received their ritual good-bye kisses. Little Greta, not quite three, would not cry or fuss much until she heard her parents talking, so they usually whispered through their quick breakfast. After Johann left, Helga helped Paul-Adolf wash and dress himself and gave him his bread and milk. Greta got a fresh diaper and began to nurse while Paul-Adolf was eating. Then Helga did the breakfast dishes. Afterwards, she played briefly with the children. Once they were occupied, she would open the bedroom window to air the room out, hang the feather bed over the windowsill and lay back the bedding to the foot of the bed. Then she would make a list of things she needed to buy. 'If only the icebox were bigger, I wouldn't have to shop so often. I could keep more butter, eggs, and milk,' she thought almost every day. Usually, she would take the children on her errands to the shops. If for some reason she saved shopping for the afternoon, she began washing, ironing, dusting, cleaning and mending her way through the morning.

By eleven, she had begun cooking the midday meal. Some days Johann returned home, some days he ate at the hospital or the clinic. When he returned home to eat, he usually read a newspaper and looked through the mail while she finished cooking and setting the table. After the children were cleaned up, the four of them sat down to eat. Greta had learned to handle a spoon and amused herself with mashed potatoes or peas. Paul-Adolf ate whatever was put in front of him. If the children behaved and were quiet, as they were expected to be, Helga and Johann would have a bit of a conversation, usually about the weather or the morning's mail, especially if it included news of their families back in Munich. They almost never talked about politics or the news of the day.

After Johann finished eating, the children would both sit on their father's lap for a little song or a story, while Helga cleaned up in the kitchen. He left by one-thirty, usually going back to the policlinic, but sometimes to the hospital. She would continue her chores. Ideally, Paul-Adolf played by himself—toy soldiers under the dining room table—while Greta napped. In the mid-afternoon, if the weather permitted, as it did on this bright October day, she liked to put on one of her three nicer dresses and her coat, which helped hide the fact that she only had three, and take the children to the park. There she often would meet *Frau* Klemmer, whose children were about the same age as Paul-Adolf and Greta.

Frau Klemmer's husband was a lawyer. She and Helga had much in common: devoted, but professionally absorbed, ambitious husbands; children who had become the center of their attention; a household budget that denied them some of the fashionable clothes they both admired; and a vague feeling of distress about being in Nuremberg, because it was "just not home." Since Greta's birth, Helga missed her family and Munich more than she ever dared to tell Johann. *Frau* Klemmer, who was from Hamburg and six years older than Helga, also missed her native city, and all of Northern Germany. Unlike Helga, she made her husband well aware of her homesickness.

Frau Klemmer liked Helga, despite her disdain for her rough, south German dialect. And she was not entirely comfortable with Helga's comparatively casual supervision of her children's play. Helga's lack of style irritated her. No one in Nuremberg had style, she thought, another reason to miss Hamburg.

Helga, for her part, had little trouble understanding *Frau* Klemmer's clipped north German speech. She liked *Frau* Klemmer, although she often was dismayed by her long silences and her commanding tone when she spoke to the children. Helga decided that someday, she'd have to invite the Klemmers to their apartment. But first they needed a new carpet. She did not know *Frau* Klemmer's husband, but it couldn't hurt to have Johann get to know a lawyer. Maybe they would become friends. Johann had so few friends.

The two women sat on their usual bench. The sunshine brightened the golden leaves in the trees overhead. A light wind muffled the occasional sound of traffic beyond the park. They watched the boys assemble a fortress from grass blades, leaves, twigs and pebbles that they gathered from the path's edges. *Frau* Klemmer held her daughter on her lap while Greta napped in her baby buggy, carefully placed so that the sun would not shine directly on her face.

"Your little Greta looks so fine today. She is sleeping so sweetly."

"Yes. Yesterday she was colicky again, and I don't think she slept so well last night. She had a good nap right after our mid-day meal and now she's asleep again. She looks a bit flushed, I think. My husband says this colic will pass, as she gets older. I worry too much, he says. But she's not nearly as healthy looking as her brother was when he was her age. She's gaining weight so slowly. I don't dare feed her too much, because of her colic."

"My little Monika won't stop nursing," *Frau* Klemmer said. "She's got the sharpest little teeth now, you know. I'm ready to leave off this breast-feeding routine, especially at night. My husband agrees, but somehow I can't quite bring it off. How old was Paul-Adolf when he was weaned? My Horst was just past two, maybe two and two months. A little younger than Monika is now. He didn't have such sharp teeth!"

"Paul-Adolf was about two and a half. Not quite Greta's age. Yes, their teeth can be sharp."

"I wish I had not begun to breast-feed at all," *Frau* Klemmer said.

Helga looked over at Greta in her baby buggy. The child's breathing was so loud that both women could hear her. Helga feared she was getting cold and got up to adjust her blanket.

"Have you seen Meyerberg's store window this week?" Helga asked when she sat down again. "They have a beautiful new sofa and arm chair, rust brown with lighter stripes. It looks so comfortable. Of course, they display it so well, with a lamp, elegant china cabinet, and pictures on the wall. The whole room's in the window. There's even a mannequin sitting on the sofa. Very modern. In our apartment, the old walls and the floor would make that furniture look so out of place. We'd have to paint and get new carpets, too. I'd rather move first. Meyerberg's carries quality furniture, of course, but so expensive."

"No, I've not seen it. My Richard and I were going to go for a walk in the town yesterday evening, but he came home late again, and didn't want to go out. Maybe this weekend, Sunday afternoon. Our couch and chair are new, just before Monika was born. And I find Meyerberg's much too expensive. They make too big a profit, I am sure. Anyway, it's a washing machine and a new ice box that I really would like."

"Oh yes, I hope for that too, some day. Johann says to be patient. His practice is doing well." She hoped Frau Klemmer would not notice the hesitation in her voice. "Perhaps next year we can get a larger icebox. We bought a used one when we moved to Nuremberg. It leaks if I am not careful. But Johann says that things have gotten much better overall."

"My Richard's practice is going very well now. He would agree with your husband. Everything seems to have gotten so much better. We are planning to get a new automobile next year. And we might take a two-week vacation into Switzerland. He's talking about moving. Back to Hamburg. He wants to be a judge. Better chances in the north. I don't know why he thought we should move here."

Helga began thinking about a vacation to Switzerland. She knew Johann would not agree to any long vacation. At the most, a weekend near the lakes east of Munich. While their finances had improved dramatically over the past four years, they were still forced to cut corners. The payments Johann received each month from the state's medical insurance system were never enough to allow them to save as much as they hoped. Johann often moaned, "They want a professional medical doctor and pay for a day laborer!" He hoped to buy a reliable used automobile in the spring. "Let someone else have problems with it over the winter," he would say. They both knew they would not be able to afford the one he wanted unless there was something wrong with it.

Everywhere Helga and Johann looked, others seemed to be prospering and getting ahead faster than they were. Although their income had increased—thanks to his private patients—the cost of everything had risen, too. Helga noticed this in her groceries. When she told Johann that they should make a contract to get all their winter's coal at the current price, he was not interested. "Why should I speculate? Leave that to those who dirty their hands with such business!" She told him their rent would probably go up in the coming year. "We'll see," he replied, without looking up from his newspaper.

Helga hesitated to talk with him of her concerns about their finances. He would say, "Let me worry about that." Besides, he seemed troubled of late. She was concerned about his sleeplessness and what she felt was his increasing distance from her and the children. He looked so tired. She knew he was disappointed in his work at the policlinic. She hoped that getting an automobile would resolve some of that and was saving every way she could in the household. She would surprise him at Christmas, by telling him how much she had saved through the year.

Little Paul-Adolf and Horst had run out of patience trying to shield their leafy fortress from a scattering wind, and came over to their mothers shouting and pushing each other. It was time to go.

"*Auf Wiedersehen, Frau* Klemmer. Say '*auf Wiedersehen*' to Horst, Paul-Adolf." Horst meanwhile had run down the path.

"*Auf Wiedersehen, Frau Doktor* Brenner. Wave good-by to Paul-Adolf, Horst," Frau Klemmer shouted at her son.

The two women had known each other for over a year, yet never called each other by their first names. It would not occur to them to do so. Still, their acquaintance had evolved towards a kind of friendship. Their conversations never touched politics or religion, what *Frau* Klemmer's husband called, "the heavy questions of the day." While they had opinions on these matters, they never voiced them. That was their husbands' domain. The two women were used to suppressing their thoughts. Both believed it was improper for women to express independent ideas. Independent women were irresponsible, misguided, discontented—to be pitied or scorned. Everything they knew about the way the world worked reinforced their views. Helga occasionally edged toward expressing her disdain for political extremists, right or left. She suspected *Frau* Klemmer of leaning toward the right. But the conversation usually revolved around their children and remained there.

By late afternoon, Helga would return to their apartment, give Paul-Adolf a snack, nurse Greta ('yes, her teeth *were* sharp!') and then coax both children into some quiet activity. She changed into an older housedress, or put on a newer one that she had made, with a smock over it. If she were caught up with her mending, she might read a woman's magazine or a penny-novel. She preferred stories set in an earlier century: nobility, village girls, mistaken identity, sentimental, but still believable, with happy endings. The book she was reading, borrowed from *Frau* Klemmer, was entitled "The Castle on the Crag."

By the time Johann returned home, usually after six, the children were playing, and Helga, who had resumed her chores, was ready for some relief. She was grateful for the extra income from his private patients, but disappointed for the loss of a quiet evening with him when he had to make a house call. She knew he needed the contacts to advance his practice. And they needed the money. If he did stay home, and there were no patients in the little waiting room they had fixed up in the parlor, then they would play with the children or read them stories. If the weather permitted—so much of their lives depended on the weather— they would all go downstairs for a short walk together around the park. After they returned and the children were in bed, Johann would read, while Helga would knit or embroider. The radio would play quietly, perhaps an operetta, never jazz. By ten o'clock, another day was done.

Johann would go to bed first, usually by announcing, "I suggest we retire!" in a sing-songy way that amused him more than it did her. Helga would follow, after setting the table for the morning, checking the children, the stove, the windows and the door locks. This was her realm, and she prided herself on maintaining it all. If he had the world of his profession, here she was in charge. She needed this feeling of control, much as he needed to feel he was in control of his professional destiny.

Lately, he felt he wasn't in control of his professional destiny. To be a university physician or a prestigious surgeon was out of his reach. But to be renowned as a heroic family doctor, a general practitioner for the masses, now that was a different matter. He thought he could be such a doctor. And that was what he believed was needed to serve the *Volk*. Everywhere he looked, he saw Germans who, as he said to Helga, were "running around their own shadows, not knowing what is good or healthful." He saw it every day at the policlinic and in the hospital. He saw it in his private patients, though they had more money and their lives more resembled his. He would cure them! That was his hope.

But something was wrong. The surface looked solid, but he feared there was rot and ruin underneath. The summer's financial upswing was welcome but seemed unreal. People were living like there was no tomorrow. Even Nuremberg had a frantic, frenzied pace. Nothing like Berlin's or Munich's`, from what he read, but still disquieting. The daily newspapers told harrowing stories of crime, corruption and violence. He wondered who was in charge and where Germany was going.

Given his dissatisfaction with his professional world, he tried to escape to the refuge of his home and family. But he could not convince himself that he had Helga's and the children's admiration. And if his family did revere him—well, that was as it should be, normal. It was a different matter for the outside world. Lying awake in the night, he began to fear that he would never become the physician he wanted to be, never become a hero for the *Volk*. At the very best, his career in Nuremberg would earn him local influence and prominence. He wanted more. A few years earlier, at thirty-two, he had been confident of his future. Now, the future seemed meager.

He was gaining ground in his private practice. He knew many who would envy him his profession, his beautiful wife, his two children. But the daily struggle to get ahead was wearing him down. The state's health insurance system paid so little. Doctors paid as though they were piece-workers in an assembly plant! Galling! He saw no end to the constant filling out of forms, of reporting and summarizing the reports, and then reporting again—paperwork instead of medicine, down to accounting for every minute and every pill, every unexpected rise in a patient's fever. Everything and everyone was under suspicion, doctors as well as patients. In the middle of the night, he would mumble "Outrageous!" over and over, until he fell asleep again.

He saw himself as a small tooth in a huge, cogged wheel. An unimportant and insignificant bit of machinery locked in a monstrous, impersonal engine. He could not escape it. And he could not change the engine's direction or speed it up or slow it down. It was carrying him along a path of its own, at a pace of its own. He felt trapped.

On the same October afternoon that Helga and Frau Klemmer sat on the park bench, Johann, after having examined a jaundiced widow and her fifteen-year-old, half-witted daughter, both reeking of alcohol and both complaining of sore throats, opened the window in his office in the policlinic. He needed air. Throughout the day, he had seen wretched human beings in various states of decay. Were these the *Volk* he hoped to heal? He was a worker at an assembly line, sweating and short of breath, trying to keep up with a conveyor belt that sent specimens of uncared-for flesh, one after the other, endlessly streaming by him.

The policlinics where he had worked, first in Munich and now in Nuremberg, instead of restoring the health of the ailing, were a revolving door for decay. In and out, day after day, the destitute, the desperate, and the degenerate. A faceless parade of the hopeless, of diseased body parts and foul smells. Patients that he thought he had cured last year or last week reappeared, with the same complaints. Those he saw that morning were interchangeable with those he treated five years before. He no longer felt the need to look into their faces. He had seen them all before.

Instead of faces, he saw an ulcerous mouth, an enflamed eye, an infected ear. He heard a wheeze, observed a slow reflex, palpated a bruised ribcage. He felt contusions and probed goiters. He lanced boils. He saw body parts, not the whole human being. A dreary parade of ailing flesh and bones, all marching by him without end.

He had learned this detachment in medical school. To elevate medicine into the realm of science, patients had to become numbers. Depersonalized aggregates of carefully constructed groups with statistically measurable variables. The human body was a collection of parts subject to the physical forces of the universe. His professors had told him that, for the sake of medical progress, for the gains we must achieve in human health, we must forsake the distractions of compassion and sentimental concerns for the individual patient. The patient was only a composite of tissues of various elements and properties. The liver or the lymph gland or the femur was but cells and fluids, of a certain chemical composition when healthy. The effective modern doctor must decide how—or if—the unhealthy component could be restored to its proper balance and function. He must learn when to administer a tablet, an injection, an ointment. Or wield a scalpel and excise the diseased part. Focus only on the unhealthy tissue, organ, fluid or bone. Isolate the specific from the general. Measure everything. Objectify and quantify. Achieve the necessary clarity and certainty through precise, dispassionate observation. This was the necessary path of true medical science in the twentieth century. Optimistic. Empirical. Rigorous. Efficient. Detached. Self-righteous. Modern. It meshed perfectly with Johann's temperament. He and German doctors like him, would apply their discipline's hard-won knowledge and reap its fruits. Then all Germans, all mankind would hail them as heroes.

But where were those fruits? Where were the tributes to his heroism? Only the same complaints came through the policlinic's doors. He felt he was drowning in a flood of human flesh. The bodies of countless men, women and children had congealed in his mind to a single patient. A giantess, a grotesque parody of a human being. She towered above him, her huge gray face an ashen moon. Her bulging eyes were rimmed with viscous ooze. Stooping down for him to examine her open mouth, he felt smothered by her sour, hot breath. Her voice was loud and grating. Her stringy, snarled hair hung down around her face and over her shoulders. Strands of it seemed to reach out and cling to him like a gray parasitical plant. Her breasts hung over her ribs like empty coal-sacks. Bones protruded improbably from her ulcerous, bloated body. The specter haunted him, over and over again.

The vision always ended the same. He desperately pushed the woman away, fearing she would topple over on him like a rotted tree. As she fell backwards, she shattered into shards of bones. Her skull rolled away, with its eyes staring at him. He tried to scream, but her scream was louder and drowned his out. He began to perspire. He felt himself growing dizzy to the point of vomiting. Coming out of these episodes—it seemed to Johann that they lasted for an hour, but in fact they passed within a minute or less—he felt drained, the specter's scream reverberating in his head.

His wondered about what he had been taught: 'What if the professors' lectures and the thick medical textbooks have created a fiction about human health? What if they are wrong in supposing that the standard is fresh-faced, bright-eyed, vigorous youth? What if the opposite is true? What if the patients I see every day—the tubercular, the syphilitic, the bent, broken, and anxious men and women, the children in pain—what if they are the norm? What if rosy-cheeked children and clean, clear-eyed, wholesome-looking adults are a myth, an impossible ideal, never to exist in this world except as briefly as a cloud?'

Johann could not stop himself from seeing his patients' dull, limited, frustrating lives as a burden. They slid toward their graves while looking for something to relieve their boredom and give them hope. 'The grave is everyone's end no matter what I do,' he thought. 'My problem is finding my proper role in this inevitable process. Why shouldn't I welcome, perhaps hasten a patient's death? Especially the death of a patient who is living with suffering, hopeless and helpless, shunned by those around him!'

He knew his obligation, his ethical responsibility, so solemnly defined by that ancient oath he had taken when he finished medical school: "First, do no harm." 'Hippocrates had good intentions,' he thought. 'So have doctors ever since. But doesn't the decision about what is harmful or not to the patient depend upon the patient's ability to lead a useful, meaningful life in a society? And doesn't society have a voice in the matter? Most importantly, doesn't society have an obligation to protect itself from a patient's egocentric desire to live at all costs? What gives the patient the right to be so selfish?' Maybe the oath should be different: "Do no harm to a patient if you do no harm to society." And then, the logical corollary: "If you must, harm the patient, in order not to harm society."'

With each visit to terminally ill patients at the hospital, he asked himself, 'Why are we keeping these patients alive? So they can continue to suffer? So those who love them can suffer with them? Their care deprives others with more hope for recovery and a productive life.' Hoche and Binding's little book had made that case. He and Philipp had agreed with their argument.

He thought of the discussions they had had in medical school. Johann envied Philipp anew his chance to work at Hoche's clinic. If only he had been accepted by Lenz for a fellowship. If he and Helga hadn't had to get married. He had had to take the first residency he could, at the policlinic in Munich. Feeling cheated by the drudgery of his daily routine and frustrated by his inability to cure his patients, he began to justify his desire to cure society of them. 'My dying patient is a parasite that must be destroyed, in order for its host to survive.' Hundreds, if not thousands, of people thought the same way.

At first, he resisted. 'Be positive,' he said to himself, 'Be positive! My duty is to my patients. Regardless of their condition, I must do what I can, as much as I can, to cure their illness, to relieve their pain, to do good! To do good.' He said this over and over to himself, as though repetition would convince him of its logic and calm his mind. But he could not escape the idea that in order to help the most seriously ill patients avoid senseless suffering and for the good of the *Volk*, he should encourage the natural process of their dying. 'Then,' he thought, 'I not doing harm. I am doing good. By helping my patients to a "good" death, I am doing something good for them. And for the *Volk*.'

Still, such logic bothered his conscience. What kind of "good" was it, when parents wailed at their child's death? Or when children cried for their dead parents? When lovers longed for their dead beloveds? Who of them saw "good" in death? At the most, some would admit relief that their child's "suffering was over," or that a parent's or an aged loved one "had lived a full life" and it was good that they were no longer suffering.

He had thought this sort of thing would become clear to him after he completed his medical studies and become an independent physician. In his memory, medical school was a necessary path through a dark and threatening forest. It was worth the stress and the struggle, because, once completed, the dedicated physician would enjoy sunny vistas and well-deserved blessings. But working in the policlinics, he saw little sunshine and received few blessings. He soon realized that medical school was far removed from the real world of daily medical practice. And he had other distractions: his responsibilities to Helga and their children; Germany's political tensions; and the economic uncertainties of the time. In his twenties, he had thought that he would be able to reason out any problems. He had not anticipated this confrontation with his own sense of inadequacy. Finding no answers to his questions made him desperate. His anxiety prevented him from recognizing that he yearned for certainty more than he did for truth.

Johann carried his distress with him day and night. Late one October night in 1929, he fell again into a troubled sleep. He dreamt of trains, trains rushing down tracks and into endless tunnels, tunnels filling with smoke, the passengers coughing uncontrollably.

The coughing was real. It was coming from little Greta. It woke Helga and Johann at the same time, but she was out of bed first. When he came in, tying his bathrobe around him, their daughter was sitting up in her mother's arms on the edge of the bed. She was coughing a dry, hacking cough, surprisingly loud for such a little girl. Johann felt her head. Fever, to be sure. "Open your eyes, *Gretchen*. *Vati* wants to look into your pretty eyes." She refused. "No, too much light. Too bright."

"*Vati* won't hurt you, Greta, just open your eyes."

Paul-Adolf woke up and Helga went to him in his bed on the other side of the room.

"What do you feel, Greta?" Johann asked. Where does it hurt?" She put her hand to her throat and chest and, for good measure, her stomach.

He took her temperature and listened through his stethoscope to her chest and back. He felt her little body heave under his hands. The child was sweaty, pale, fragile-looking—remarkably so, since she had seemed fine when she went to bed.

Helga looked worried. She had a premonition that their daughter's coughing was not just a cold. Greta seemed changed, different, as though something foreign and vicious had come into her body and was gaining control.

"What is it, Johann? She looks so poor."

"Perhaps influenza. We should be careful. Some honey in warm water for her cough for now. In the morning, I'll go down to the druggist's and get some stronger syrup. Let's try to reduce her fever," Johann said. He put a cloth soaked in alcohol on her forehead. "It's probably too late, but to keep Paul-Adolf from getting it, we should move him into our room. She's calming down now, see. Probably she had a bad dream with her coughing."

In the morning, Greta still was coughing—a cough that made Helga wince each time she heard it. Johann went to the hospital, as usual, but came home early for the midday meal. The child's cough loosened and she brought up heavy, yellowish sputum. Her eyes were blood-shot. Her fever was 102°. Then the dry, cracked coughing returned and intensified. Johann left later than usual for the policlinic. He told Helga to keep Greta warm, to give her liquids and the syrup, and to keep the bedroom darkened. He feared mumps.

After three more days, Johann suspected poliomyelitis. There were other cases in the city. He gave Greta mild sedatives that worked for a short while, but was afraid to increase the dose. She cried a pathetic, incessant cry. One heard it everywhere in the apartment. She flailed her arms and kicked her legs up and down with shrieking and gasping that would have made anyone think she was being tortured. In the afternoons, she quieted down somewhat, but at dusk she would scream or shriek anew. Johann and Helga feared that Paul-Adolf would fall ill and arranged for Helga's sister to take him to his grandmother's in Munich.

Greta never called for her mother, only her father. Johann was beside himself. There was little he could do. He knew polio would take its course. Most children recovered without any physical harm. Some developed paralysis of varying degrees or the disease afflicted their lungs, which never again were fully healthy. He remembered one of his medical school professors saying that a medal and a fortune awaited whoever could invent a mobile breathing device to replace the massive "iron lungs" that were these victims' only recourse.

Should they move Greta to the hospital? That meant the overcrowded children's ward, with its pungent smell. Who knew what else she would contract there? Besides, Johann knew that putting their daughter in the hospital would be terrifying for her, as well as for all of them. So they kept her at home.

After ten days, the child improved. She smiled and did not cry as often. Her cough subsided. Her lungs seemed clearer, and her breathing normal. But Johann knew that she would never have a normal life. Both her legs and her left arm were affected by the disease. Johann showed Helga how to massage Greta's limbs to stimulate circulation. They kept warm compresses on them. They rubbed them down with warmed cats' skins, as Helga's mother recommended. Johann could not believe he had consented to such a medieval remedy. But he would try anything.

On the evening of the day that the *Nuremberger Nachrichten* reported the stock market crash in North America, Johann told Helga he believed their daughter would never walk normally again. Greta lay asleep on the bed, unaware of her father's prediction.

"We must hope for a miracle," Helga said and started to sob.

Johann looked away. His faith in miracles had been crushed by the outcome of the war. He only muttered, "Miracles. Yes, we must hope."

Helga looked at him as he had never seen her look at him before. The tears on her cheeks drained the life out of her eyes. Flat, cold, they faded to gray. He imagined that she accused him of not curing their daughter. He accused himself.

Johann left for the policlinic right after breakfast. He did not hear what Helga was saying to him as he hurried down the stairs. "No, I don't have time to see Greta. I'm late," he shouted from bottom of the stairway. He could not bear to see his daughter, his beautiful, innocent little Greta. Her helplessness cursed him and confirmed his own.

CHAPTER ELEVEN
The Right Thing

I tried so hard, Helga, to do the right thing. For our children. For us. Greta's condition was a test, I now see. And you were better than I in dealing with it. Better than I, the doctor. I wanted to help. In some cases, I believe I did. But I could not accept my weaknesses and needed more than ever to believe in my strengths. Things were changing so fast. And not for the better.

Johann remembered his desperation at not being able to help Greta. How trapped he felt as the Great Depression hurtled down on all of them like an Alpine avalanche. At the same time, he had paid a house call on an old, dying Jewish woman whose grateful husband had thanked him for his kindness. How had Philipp had fared, he wondered, during that time when everything seemed to be falling apart?

*****

Johann's private practice was growing, despite the hard times. But his patients could not always pay in cash. Widow Beugner, who owned the little bakery at the corner, brought him loaves of bread; *Herr*

Regensburger brought writing paper and envelopes from his stationary store; the old farmer, Schwarz, promised 100 pounds of potatoes at the end of the season; and so on. What else could these people do? They all wanted medical attention. And they were not that well served by the policlinics. They wanted more personal attention. Tuesday, Thursday and Friday afternoons, beginning at four o'clock, three or four patients would sit in the small "waiting room" he and Helga had set up on one side of their apartment's front parlor. Some had appointments. Others just walked in. Johann masked his grumbling when he saw them, but invariably fumed after they left. Helga served as a receptionist and helped in the evenings with the paperwork.

After Greta became ill, Helga didn't go to the park. She was surprised to learn from the grocer that the Klemmers had moved back to Hamburg. Johann never met them. He was too busy or too tired to consent to invitations from others; after a while, none came. They had few friends. Their only social outing was once a month, when he and Helga went to a Saturday afternoon matinee at the cinema; *Frau* Bitzer, their hunchbacked, downstairs neighbor, sat with the children.

Greta's poliomyelitis had stabilized, but she was unable to walk. The child's sunny disposition was tried by the constant pain. It did not help that Paul-Adolf had taken to mocking his sister as "the little cripple." Helga did her best to soothe and distract her. Johann, for his part, read everything he could about the illness. But he could not bear to be with his daughter for any length of time. His distress led him to increase his working hours at the policlinic and in private practice.

Coming back from the policlinic one September afternoon, Johann noticed a familiar looking old man sitting in the "waiting room" with the two private patients he was expecting. He couldn't remember where he had met him.

"Who has been here longest, gentlemen? I will see you now."

The old man rose from his seat. Now Johann was remembered. As he closed the curtain to the waiting room behind them, he asked, "Aren't you *Herr* Semmelberg, the shopkeeper from Pohlendorf, near Munich? I remember buying penny candy in your store."

"Yes, I am Semmelberg. Unless you remember my father. Some say I look more and more like him, the older I get. I remember you too, *Herr Doktor*, as a boy. You were an energetic youngster, and always polite. You never were rude to me or my wife. Some of the boys were little demons, you know. Some stole. But you were always respectful. You and the little Stern boy. We never saw one of you without the other. That was over twenty years ago. Pohlendorf was a good place." He sighed.

Johann nodded. "I miss it, too."

"Well, times have changed and we must change with them. We gave up the shop and retired six years ago to live near our daughter, Ellen, here in Nuremberg. She worked as a nurse in the hospital. Maybe you know her. She was just ten when the war began. A sweet little girl. The light of our life. Then last year Ellen moves away to Berlin with a no-good and we barely hear from her. That's life, Rivka says. You remember my wife, Rivka?" The old man, wheezing slightly, looked intently into Johann's eyes.

Johann nodded.

"We always thought you would become something someday. Such a nice boy you were, and bright. But I never knew what until last week, when an old neighbor from Pohlendorf wrote and told us you're a doctor, and that you practice, right here in Nuremberg. Small world. Excuse me, I am talking too much, like Rivka says."

"It's good to see you again, *Herr* Semmelberg. Are you ill? You look strong and healthy"

"Me, thank God, I am fine, old but fine. Rivka, my wife, she is not. She needs help. She will not go to the polyclinic. Or to the hospital. She doesn't want a doctor. But she is ill."

"What's the matter with her?"

"She's very heavy, very heavy. Fat. Very fat. Poor Rivka. She breathes so hard. She has pains in her legs, her arms, her chest. She looks bad. Yellow. She says she is dying and wants to die in peace. I am so worried about her, *Herr Doktor*. You must help her, please. Please come and see her. Give her some medicine, something. Please."

"I remember *Frau* Semmelberg. Where do you live?"

"*Grübengasse* 17, upstairs, over Bergen's, the cheese and dairy shop."

Johann wrote the address down. "In the quarter? Yes. I'll come by before dark, *Herr* Semmelberg. I have two more patients here, and then another house call to make, on the *Kirchenweg*, not far from your neighborhood. I'll come to you as soon as I finish there."

The other two patients were relatively routine—a case of stomach cramps, and a case of stiffness in the joints, probably arthritis. Johann completed their files, told Helga he was going to make two house calls, and left.

Going down the stairs, he noticed his shabby shoes. They had been re-soled three times now, and the heels replaced at least twice. The left shoe was especially worn, thanks to his limp. Because he walked to and from the policlinic and to most of his house calls, he was not surprised. The expense of a new pair, though, was worrisome.

Down on the street, he was greeted by passers-by. Johann knew most, but not all of them. Some had been his patients. Some were acquaintances from the neighborhood. Occasionally a city official or a member of a political party would tip his hat: "Good evening, *Herr* Doctor." Someone would stop and tell him that his aunt was better or that her son's cough was not, or that the month's rain had brought on gout. He invariably was polite, dignified.

"Give my regards to your aunt, please," or "Bring the boy around to see me tomorrow in the afternoon," or "Yes, the weather can bring on gout. More likely, it's rich food. Aspirin can help," he would say, with a smile, touching his hat. Some who greeted him did not know him personally. His suit and tie, his doctor's bag, made his presence something to be acknowledged. "I am a doctor. Respect is due me." Most of those who greeted him recognized him as one of their "betters," a man above them on the ladder of German society. Even the communists showed him a certain deference.

He absorbed this attention with outward good will and great internal pride. For him, it was one of the pleasant aspects of his profession—to be seen and acknowledged as a physician, a man of substance, in service to his fellow men. The acknowledgement was a sign of social order.

He had read that begging in Germany's larger cities was increasing. In Nuremberg, there was talk of people having to sell things to raise cash. Near the train station, now and then, a crippled war veteran asked for money, probably to buy another beer or *schnapps*. But there was harmony here in Nuremberg, despite the economic crisis. Another reason to be glad he lived there.

He found the Semmelbergs' apartment in Nuremberg's Jewish quarter. Although he infrequently went to this part of the city, he was fascinated by it. "Jews tended to see their own doctors," he once told Helga, who wanted him to have more Jewish patients because Jews, she said, "paid their bills on time, and in cash." The Jewish neighborhood seemed more authentic and, he had to admit, in an odd way, more like the Germany he longed for than did the newer parts of the city. Its streets were too narrow for automobiles. On either side of the street, the stumpy buildings, among the city's oldest, seemed to lean on each other, closing off direct sunlight except at midday. The walls were a blend of brick reds, old greens, fading yellows and glowing ochres. Electricity lines looped and sagged overhead. Shop signs hung jumbled one over the other. The air smelled faintly of decay, roasted almonds and burned raisins, bitter and sweet at the same time. He would have told an inquirer that the neighborhood offended his sensibilities. But in fact he relished its smells and energies, from a lost world—not the newer, more mechanical world that attracted and frightened him.

This teeming segment of Nuremberg and his childhood in Pohlendorf shared an underlying wholeness and vitality that nourished and shaped them both. But Johann was afraid of appreciating the deeper identity of these two worlds—their energy, their sense of history, their intense pride, their rigid codes and rules, their love of their own kind and their apprehension at the outsider. To do so would blur the differences between himself and these people. He was determined to believe in their "otherness." It was necessary, in order to believe what he wanted to believe about himself.

Johann believed as much in Germany's natural superiority as he believed in the benefits of modern medicine. For him, the two concepts were simply different sides of the same coin. He thought in terms of health, vitality, self-control and independence of action. Economic health and political independence required strong national leadership. He feared foreign oppression and communist dogma—to his mind both a kind of invasive cancer or festering gangrene. Ultimately, he feared, such decay would contaminate all of Europe. This meant the end of decency, creativity, law and order, of civilization. Everything worth saving was doomed without vigorous, unswerving national leadership in Germany. This alone would maintain the *Volk*'s vitality, the survival of Europe, and everything worthwhile in the world. Civilization's *colored* enemies— the "Reds" in Russia, the "yellows" in Asia, the "blacks" in Africa, and the mongrelizing, chameleon Jews everywhere—must be controlled and contained. If they could not be conquered, then like a cancer, they had to be surgically isolated and cut out for the sake of humankind. Drastic times called for drastic measures. That was his remedy for the "crisis" he felt overtaking him and his Germany. And yet here he was, envying the vitality of Nuremberg's Jewish quarter.

Turning the corner of *Kaufmannsstraße* onto *Grübengaße,* Johann slowed as he passed a grocery, with its casks of dilled and garlic pickles beside the door. The warm, pungent smell enveloped him, a sweet smell that comes just when something is turning sour. Instantly, he was flooded with memories of himself, ten years old, on a hot sunny afternoon, sitting on the stump of an ancient larch tree, between his parents' and a neighbor's house, eating a pickle.

Cages of live chickens were set outside the next doorway, a butcher's shop. Three women, all dressed in black, with kerchiefs around their heads, crowded around the cages. One tucked a bird under her arm and gripped its feet while she stretched out its wings and looked to see how much yellowish fat showed through the thinly feathered, bluish-pink skin. Johann found himself pausing to watch the examination. Through the shop window, he saw dead birds hanging upside down from hooks alongside quarters of beef and chains of red-brown *wurst*. Sawdust from the floor had spilled out on to the sidewalk, with footprints tracking it in either direction.

As he walked on, the men and women who passed him looked like men and women anywhere else in Nuremberg at this time of day—going home, bundles under their arms. From the open apartment windows above the shops came bubbling stew of pianos, violins, conversations, and babies crying. When he looked into the open courtyards, he saw the clothes and bedding hung out on lines, boys playing marbles, lazy dogs, wary cats. And here was Bergens', where wheels of cheese were stacked four high on a platform by the door and lumps of butter glistened on shaved ice in a display case in the window. Inside, the black and white tiles on the floor and walls gleamed. Children with liter cans of milk or carefully wrapped paper bundles of eggs left the store and scattered up and down the street.

The courtyard entrance just beyond Bergen's and the stairway up to the Semmelbergs' apartment were dusty but not uninviting. Some flower pots on the steps and more on the first landing distracted him as he climbed the stairs. He knocked at the door, not thinking much about what he might have to do.

Herr Semmelberg greeted him, apologized for the apartment's disorder, and took him immediately into the bedroom, which was so much darker than the courtyard that Johann had trouble at first seeing where he was. As his eyes adjusted to the light, he saw *Frau* Semmelberg was not the woman he remembered. The *Frau* Semmelberg of Johann's childhood had been rosy, lively, plump, healthy-looking in every way. Now she was grotesquely obese, lying on a sagging bed. Her hair—he remembered coal black hair—was a gray and white matted cobweb that clung to her neck and shoulders. Her face had a yellowish, chalky cast. She looked away from him as he entered the room. Johann forced himself to smile as he leaned over her bed.

"Rivka, here he is, I told you," Semmelberg said, "remember little Johann Brenner, that sweet little boy? Now he's a big doctor. An important doctor. See. He's come to visit us. He's come to see you, Rivka. Say "hello" to *Herr Doktor* Brenner, Rivka."

Johann responded to her silence with "Good to see you again, *Frau* Semmelberg. How are you feeling?" No response. Johann tried to not notice the room's heavy air. The sticky smell of honey-scented candles burning on a little table at the foot of the bed only made him imagine the underlying pain all the more.

After a while, the old woman groaned. The sound was like a heavy chair being dragged across the floor. She tried to turn her head even further away. Her husband looked at the doctor with despair. Johann opened his bag.

"Let me take your pulse, *Frau* Semmelberg. Turn over toward me, please."

She slowly complied. She still looked away from him, toward the ceiling, then closing her eyes, began quietly to cry.

Johann took her wrist and began to count her pulse while looking at his pocket-watch. Her heartbeat was rapid and weak. He then gently placed his stethoscope's chestpiece and listened to her heart—so faint—and her lungs—quite congested. Next he turned her head toward him and pulled up first one, then the other of her eyelids. The whites of her eyes were unmistakably yellow, her pupils glazed and dull. When he asked her to open her mouth, she did so like a puppet. Strands of saliva netted her teeth and tongue. Finally, he tried to measure her blood pressure, but her arm was too heavy to allow an accurate reading. He guessed that it was dangerously low. But he had seen enough. "Thank you, *Frau* Semmelberg. Rest now. Rest."

"I want to die," she muttered, or something that sounded like that. Her husband squeezed her hand.

Johann said, "Let's go into the other room for a moment, *Herr* Semmelberg."

They sat in silence for a moment on bright yellow chairs at a green wooden table. Semmmelberg stood up to open the window. The curtains blew into the room, fluttering around his head and shoulders like a gauzy cloud. The room smelled of sour milk. The old man sat down again. His hands were clenched together. He looked like he was going to cry.

"Your wife is very ill, *Herr* Semmelberg. You don't need me to tell you that, of course. Has she eaten anything? Does she have bowel movements or pass water? Does she get out of bed? Has any doctor seen her?"

Silence. Finally, the old man said, his lips trembling, "No. Nothing." After another silence, in a kind of chanting tone, "She just lays there, *Herr Doktor*. At least three days now, nothing. Not eating. Not drinking, except a sip of water now and then. Three days. Maybe longer. She's been sick for months. Since March at least. She's given up, *Herr Doktor*. She's given up." Tears welled in his eyes and began to spill down his cheeks.

"I suspect progressive liver disease. And a weakened heart. And maybe now an obstructed bowel. Perhaps other internal organs—kidneys, for example—are failing, too. I can't say exactly without tests. She should be in a hospital for a series of tests. But..." Johann paused, lowering his voice, "I must tell you, *Herr* Semmelberg...she is dying. That's clear. I am so sorry. Where is your daughter? Berlin? Maybe you should telegraph her. Can you do that?"

Semmelberg seemed to slump in his chair, tears spilling off his face and down onto his shirt. His hands trembled the moment he unclenched his fists. Hearing Johann say what he had long known seemed to crush him. For a long while, he said nothing. Then he forced himself to sit up straighter than before.

"Yes, I will telegraph Ellen."

"*Herr* Semmelberg, I will give your wife something to help her sleep better."

"I don't want her to sleep. You don't understand. I want her to be well. Make her well. You are a doctor. A good doctor. A nice boy. Make her well. Please. Please."

"I can help her, but I cannot make her well. You must understand, *Herr* Semmelberg. She needs to sleep."

"'Sleep,' you say. You mean, 'die.' Yes. Die. I know. What's the difference now? You want to help her, but you are telling me that you can't make her well. I know. So then..." His voice trailed off to a murmur. "So then, help her die, *Herr Doktor*. Please." Semmelberg looked Johann straight in the eyes. "Yes, I want you to help her to die. My Rivka's suffering. She's lost her will. She was always such a proud woman. So proud. So clean. So worried about not being clean."

Johann tried to say something, but Semmelberg continued. "You saw her, *Herr Doktor*. You saw. She's suffering. And ashamed. That's not right for my Rivka. She deserves better than that. She's been a good wife. A good mother. She even forgives our daughter for moving away with that no-good. She should not have to have this suffering. You heard her. She wants to die. Give her some pills then to make her sleep, as you say. Give us the pills. I will help her. I will help my Rivka." His lips kept moving, but no sounds came out.

Johann just looked at him. After a minute or two, he asked, "Did she ever tell you what she...."

The old man interrupted, knowing what the question was. "Yes. We talked about this many times, Rivka and me. We promised each other we would do what had to be done. I won't break my word to her. No. I won't. Just give me the pills, please. I will pay. Of course, I will pay. And thank you for coming here. Thank you. You are very kind. So very kind. You know what I am feeling. What Rivka must be feeling. I thank you, *Herr Doktor* Brenner. She would thank you, if she could. I know it. We talked often about it. She would do the same for me. My beloved Rivka..." He stood up and wiped his eyes. Then he firmly shook Johann's hand, unfolded a new ten-*Reichsmark* note from his pocket and put it on the table, and went back to his wife's bedside.

Johann left ten ten pills in a folded piece of paper on the table, next to *Herr* Semmelberg's money. He had no intention of taking it. He slowly walked down the stairs to the courtyard and out onto the street, past the butcher's and the chicken coops, past the grocer's and the pickle barrel. The sounds and smells in the street had not changed. It was twilight. The branches of the square were silhouetted against a clear, pale blue sky. The traffic at the corner was the same. The newspaper still bore the same headline. The newspaper boy still wore the same green cap. What had changed? A pitifully ill, old woman was dying. An old, sorrowful man was powerless to do anything about it. He, Johann, had given them a way to end her suffering. No thunderbolts fell from the sky. No divine signs of disapproval. No police swooping down on him to cart him off to jail. Nothing. Just the pills on the table where there were none before.

And soon, Johann thought, the poor old woman would be out of her misery, and the poor old man would be relieved of some of his.

When he got home, Helga was busy with Greta. Paul-Adolf was playing with some blocks and marbles and wanted to show his father a raceway and a tunnel he had built. Johann watched him send a marble along its course. Then he picked him up. Together, they found the *torte* on the kitchen table that Helga had made. Green, plump, yellow-veined gooseberries and smaller red currants, like beads, spiraled out from the center toward the edge. Each shone through the glistening jelly that Helga had poured over them. The whole *torte* sparkled like a jewel. Instead of waiting, Johann cut two small wedges, gave one to his son, and ate the other swiftly there in the kitchen, not even sitting down.

Johann cut two more small wedges and took them to Helga and Greta. Helga gave him a scolding look that he knew she didn't really mean. Greta smiled up at him and tried to reach for the torte. He held her head up while she ate. The currents colored her lips red. He sat by her bed until Helga called him to supper.

The visit to the Semmelbergs mingled with Johann's thoughts about his family, his day at the policlinic and his other private patients. Pleased with his day's work, as he sat down he said, "Tomorrow, I will buy myself a new pair of shoes."

$$*****$$

Philipp had privileges in Berlin's most respected university hospital, the *Charité*. This gave him some contact with the latest thinking of Germany's pre-eminent physicians and medical researchers, whose grand rounds lectures and discussions he attended whenever he could. He was still as confident as ever that medical science was the path toward a better world. In this he was like Johann.

Philipp closely followed the social hygiene movement in the professional journals. He wrote some short commentaries, never published, about the relationship between working class mental health and the lamentable sanitation in Berlin's slums. If Grotjahn, the now-famous founder of the social hygiene school, recalled Philipp's interest in a residency with him nearly ten years before, he gave no sign. Once, Grotjahn, in a grand rounds' panel discussion, congratulated him on a comment about the mental health implications of child prostitution in the city. Philipp couldn't wait to tell Christine.

Shortly after that, he submitted an article to Grotjahn's journal, in which he argued that medical research would someday show that most physical ailments came from, or were exacerbated by, mental illness that in turn was caused by unhealthy social and economic situations. He was crestfallen when his article was rejected without explanation.

"Grotjahn seems more interested in racial explanations than ever," Philipp said, when Christine asked him why he looked so dejected after opening the letter from the journal's editor.

"Is he a Nazi?"

"I don't think so. But their influence overrides so much nowadays, I don't think that matters. He's an activist nearing the end of a very important career in public health. He invented the discipline of social hygiene for all intents and purposes."

"He still might be a Nazi. Are you so hurt? Does the article matter that much? You're doing important work. Take comfort in that. Your patients respect you and need you."

"I promised myself more than that."

"I know. But that's all that you can control right now." It wasn't the first time since they moved to Berlin that she tried to calm him and give him encouragement.

"I suppose it's easier for you," he said. "Your ambitions were not as high as mine." He knew she would be angry with him as soon as he finished the sentence.

"Philipp, how can you say that? I've told you how I wanted to go to university. Why else did I struggle through *Gymnasium*? I wanted to study art history. To travel and work in Italy. Maybe do archaeology. You know all that. We married instead." She could feel the tension rising.

"Yes, you've told me many times. But do we travel? Do you go to museums and galleries? I know, you say you won't go without me. But it either doesn't interest me, or I am at the clinic. Call Martha Gerschenkron. She'll go with you. Or if she can't, go alone."

"You'd sing a different tune if I did. Your jealousy would rise up and bite you on the neck. You'd have a wound there that you'd deny with all your might, with all your charm and sweetness. But you'd be jealous beyond belief!"

"Stop it," he said, keeping his voice as level as he could. "Test me. Go, why don't you. There's a lecture this Saturday morning at the *Altes Museum* on Roman statuary. I saw the announcement on a *Litfass Säule* earlier today. I even thought we could go together, but I am on duty at the policlinic. You go."

"I can't. I have to work. At least you don't want me to go to the synagogue."

"What?"

"At least you are not pressuring me to convert and go to the synagogue on Saturday morning."

"Will you stop it? We've finished that topic. I just thought that since Martha Gershenkron converted to Judaism, you might be interested in talking with her about it."

"I'm not interested."

"Fine."

"Why should I be interested, when you never go to the synagogue?" she said. "You never do anything that shows you want to participate in Jewish traditions. You even disparage the orthodox Jews in the city."

"Leave all this, please. I don't know what's gotten into you lately."

"You're the doctor. You should be able to figure it out. And if you can't, here's a hint. We're walking on eggshells. You're angry about not getting ahead. And I'm tired of hearing you complain. The world we love is falling to bits. I read the newspapers, Philipp. I listen to the radio. I hear what they say in the shops and at work. No wonder we're on edge. Everyone knows things will get a lot worse before they get better. A while back you told me that every fifth word in your medical journals was 'crisis' or 'race' or something else that combined the two. Well, that sense of crisis is not limited to your profession. Everything is in crisis.

And everybody sees race. Which means hatred. I'm worried for you. For both of us." She tried to calm herself, to make her voice softer. "All you can do is what you are doing, Lippi. That's all I can do, too. We have made our choices. I chose you. You, me. You, your profession. I am happy with that. Happy with you! Most of the time, despite your stupid jealousy. Now, enough."

He stopped himself from saying any more. He knew she was right. He should take her advice and focus on his work at the policlinic. His mind drifted to the patients he had been seeing. Working-class children with stomach disorders and persistent coughs. What was the connection between their symptoms and their living conditions? In most cases, the state's compensation plan did not cover them beyond an initial diagnosis and one follow-up. Since the parents rarely could afford to pay for any extended treatment, he ended up waiving his fees for a series of visits and gave them medicines for free. When he could, he tried to spend more time with them, even visited them in their cramped apartments. He wished he could take some of them home with him. He had stopped wishing that he and Christine had children. Leave that, he told himself. It's not to be, as Benjamin Gerschenkron had said about their not having children. Maybe it's for the best. What's the point bringing a child into the world ruled by those who hate Jews? His thoughts trailed off to a blankness that left him dizzy.

Although he was challenged by his work in the policlinic, he was not inside the circles where important decisions about public health or the treatment of mental illnesses in children were being made. He began to suspect that he never would be. His hopes to open a private clinic with Benjamin Gerschenkron were still that, just hopes. The two continued to talk, vowing that they would start up as soon as the economic picture brightened and Germany's politics calmed down. But both knew that was not too likely in the future.

"You know the old joke, Benjamin, about why it's good to lay down in the gutter?"

"No. Why?"

"Because there's only one way you can go from the gutter. Up!"

"That's not funny, Philipp. Given the way the world is going, the gutter might not be the low point."

"You're reading too many newspapers. I gave them up months ago: bad for my health."

"A dangerous strategy, especially now," Benjamin said.

"Maybe. But if you are right about the future, I might as well enjoy myself as much as I can now."

"Let's hope I'm wrong. Meanwhile, let's get together Sunday evening. Maybe a film."

"Good. Christine and I want to go to the cinema."

When Christine found a job as a bookkeeper in a curtain factory, she considered herself lucky. When *Herr* Meininger, the portly, self-centered son-in-law of the company's founder, occasionally said something that made her uncomfortable on his rounds of inspection, she never told Philipp. Her co-workers, subjected to his same crude attentions, thought the boss's wife was to be pitied. Any real problems they would bring to the old head bookkeeper, a quiet, solitary man who looked down whenever anyone spoke with him. In any case, she would never tell Philipp.

Meanwhile, there were distractions enough to keep them amused. They had fallen in love with Berlin's spirit. It was like living on the side of a volcano. Some would find it precarious and threatening, but they found it exhilarating. The city had become the center of a new planet, separate from old Germany, stodgy, hidebound, and stiff. They felt its indescribable surging and pulsing power, even if the economic outlook was grim.

They walked often in the evenings around *Potsdamer Platz* and along the *Kurfürstendamm*, with its electric lights reflecting off the storefronts' aluminum and glass and the passing, noisy automobiles. Sometimes a zeppelin hovered with an audible hum overhead. More than once Philipp said, "I feel like we are in a movie. This city is a modern feature film, complete with sound. It's hard to know what is real anymore." Christine would squeeze his hand in agreement.

When Benjamin telephoned that Saturday to say that Martha was not feeling well, they went to the cinema by themselves. They decided on a double feature in Berlin's chic Charlottenburg district. The first film was a silly comedy, the second, a new Soviet film, *Turksib*, about the construction of the Soviet railway between Turkestan and Siberia. Complete with orchestrated music and synchronized machine noises, the film had been banned elsewhere in Germany as pro-Soviet propaganda. The controversy it generated in the press guaranteed a large audience.

The story was simple and heroic. Soviet engineers staked out a route for a railway across vast deserts, to the dismay and astonishment of the peoples whose lands they crossed. Workers, industrious and self-sacrificing, swarmed to the task. The soundtrack seethed with enthusiasm: pounding pistons, churning wheels, locomotives roaring like lions. The film celebrated engineering and machines above human beings. Its confidence in machinery was infectious. This, it shouted, was the way of the future. Society could be engineered just like a railway. Progress by decree. Philipp was sure that if there had been no sound, he would have heard the heartbeats of everyone in the audience.

When shouting first filled the theater, they both thought it came from the raucous soundtrack. But around them people were standing up and waving their arms. A group of men who had been sitting near the wall, far to the right, rose sharply to their feet as if in a military drill and began throwing bottles and rocks at the screen. The lights came on, revealing that they had unfurled a Nazi banner. Another group of men began climbing over the seats and shouting as they made their way toward the Nazis, who now turned to fight them off. Both gangs had knives and clubs. Screams from the other patrons made the scene even more frightening. From outside came the sound of approaching police sirens.

Philipp and Christine escaped through a side exit. They found themselves in an alley and made their way past heaps of rubbish toward a street lamp where the alley joined a back street. The sound of the riot inside was instantly muffled by the sounds of the city's normal noise. Breathless, they found a café across the street from the cinema house and watched the riot's aftermath through the window by their table. A dozen men emerged from the cinema hoisting their Nazi banner, torn but held high. The police let them go. They marched, singing loudly, down the street. Their banner floated above the heads of the crowd. The police herded a group of other men, some bleeding, still clutching their red banner, into vans and drove off, sirens wailing.

A minute or two later, it was as if nothing had happened. The electric lights in shop windows and signs shone brightly. The electric trolley car made blue-white, crackling sparks overhead each time it passed under a splice in the line. Pedestrians strolled along the sidewalks. An occasional horse-drawn wagon went by amid the motor cars. It all seemed as though they were still watching a film.

The next morning, Philipp looked for some account of the incident in the newspaper. Instead, he found a story about a near-riot at another film, the American-made *All Quiet on the Western Front*, based on Erich Maria Remarque's anti-war novel. The book had been serialized in the *Vossische Zeitung*. Philipp had remarked several times about its painfully clear description of how madness was induced by trench warfare. The film version, having already won several of Hollywood's Academy Awards, was controversial even before it opened, thanks to the attention given it by reviewers in the extremist press. The Communists found it pathetically sentimental and *bourgeois*. The Nazis found it offensive—cowardly, decadent and anti-German.

Philipp paraphrased the relatively bland newspaper account to Christine. "One hundred and fifty Nazis, led by Josef Goebbels, the Nazi Party's chief organizer in Berlin, attended the film at the *Mozartsaal* on the *Nollendorfplatz*. They sat in the balcony and soon after the film began, threw stink bombs down into the audience below. Simultaneously, other Nazis released dozens of white mice in the orchestra pit. The women in the audience jumped up on their seats and started shrieking. The Nazis then ran up and down the aisles shouting "*Juden 'raus!*"—"Jews get out!"—and slapped anyone they thought was Jewish. Goebbels cunningly had pre-arranged the entire spectacle and pledged to shut the film down." He paused. "We went to the wrong circus." After another moment's silence, he added, "I am going to have to do something."

"What can you do about such *Dummheit?*" Christine asked.

"Yes, such stupidity! I might have to join with the socialists after all. The League of Socialist Physicians. These Nazis are really beasts. Or maybe I should not insult beasts."

"Socialists? Do you want to have us all become like the ants we saw in the film?"

"Of course not," Philipp said. "That film was an exaggeration. The work of a desperate regime, trying to prove it controls the future. It's like Hitler. Both the Soviets and the Nazis are exaggerations. The one would shoot us forward like a rocket ship. The other would jerk us backward into the Stone Age. I'm a moderate. You know that. But if I have to take a stand, it'll be with the socialists. The socialists at least are passionate about the things that interest me—broader opportunity, more education, and especially the breaking down of privilege and corruption. They're not perfect. I used to think they were fools. But I don't see them preaching the viciousness that I hear from the Nazis or advocating the necessity of violence I hear from the Communists. I think the socialists have their eye on the future health and well-being of all human beings. They'll take things more slowly and reasonably in the right direction. Above all, they're not just a movement for a few party leaders and the brutes that support them, like the Nazis."

"Well, I agree there. The Nazis are sordid. My boss is an example."

"Meininger? He's a Nazi?"

"Yes. I think so. Oh, he's nothing to worry about. I just avoid him and go to the old bookkeeper or the office manager. Meininger is greasy and self-serving. The Nazis don't have any prize in him, believe me. They deserve each other."

"Did you tell him you were married to a Jew?"

"No, why should I?"

"Don't tell him. You'll lose your job."

"Oh, Philipp. You worry too much."

"Benjamin and I've discussed the League of Socialist Physicians. I have some of their literature. I once thought they had it backwards, that one should be a doctor before being a socialist. Now I am beginning to think otherwise. They have a regular group here. I think I'll go to one of their meetings."

"I wonder how all this is going to end."

"I fear it will get worse before it gets better. I suppose I must do something."

"If you think so," she said. "Yes! These times call out for action!" They both smiled as she gave voice to the slogans on the political posters pasted on the city's kiosks.

*****

Philipp arrived at the hall the League had rented for its meeting just as it was about to begin. About sixty doctors, mostly men, filled the room. Benjamin had left the day before for a holiday. He took a seat near the back. When five people took their chairs on a little podium, he was stunned to see that Luise Seligmann was one of them. She was thinner. Her dark hair had a streak of gray. Her face seemed narrower, her eyes deeper. 'Eight years and no word from her,' he thought. 'She knows I'm in Berlin. Why didn't she contact me? Why no answer to my note congratulating her on her article?' He wondered whether he should speak to her at the end of the meeting.

He recognized *Frau Doktor* Frankenthal, their district's representative to the Prussian parliament and an outspoken advocate for women's rights, who called the meeting to order and introduced the speakers. He tried to pay attention to what was being said, but found it all predictable. The Nazis were a threat. Physicians had been turned into bureaucrats. What he had been thinking and saying for years. One speaker, from Frankfurt, railed against the consequences of the constitution's prohibition of abortion: cruel and dangerous procedures for impoverished women. Philipp saw that first hand almost daily in the policlinic. Another, from Hamburg, described the epidemic of syphilis among the city's prostitutes and how it was impacting their children. He saw that in Berlin, too—children with peg-shaped teeth, going blind and stiff before they became teenagers. Horrors. But what was the League going to do about all this? He wanted to hear a practical strategy to reverse these crises, not bitter complaints, nor petty politics. What good did it do to attack the communists, when the Nazis were the immediate enemy? And all the while, he could not take his eyes off Luise.

She was last to speak and the best. She denounced the growing militarism. The harm it created for the masses. The profits it made for the plutocrats. "Should doctors serve such a cause? Should we support and protect this corruption? No!" she shouted, echoed by a chorus of "no's" from the audience. "We must do more than just denounce violence. We must refuse to serve it in any way." Cheers drowned her out. When the cheering stopped, she said, in a much quieter, calmer voice, "We must not participate in the coming war, unless it is on the side of the working classes." Louder cheers than before erupted, but Philipp's was not among them. Was that the plan? Wait for the war? And forsake the wounded, unless they were workers? How could a doctor be so partisan? What good could come of that? He didn't listen to much of what she said after that.

As Luise finished speaking, she looked at him, and then sat down amidst more cheers. The meeting was over. When he stood up to leave, he saw Luise coming toward him. Before he could speak, she said, "Good to see you here, Philipp."

"I am surprised to see you," he said.

Others passed them in the aisle, making her step closer toward him. "You must not have come to the last meeting, when they announced the agenda."

"No, this is my first meeting. I see you're quite active in the League. I had no idea. But I suppose I should have. I still remember what you said when we first met at Hoche's home."

"I try to be involved. We have a group of regulars around Heidelberg. It's difficult. But no different than anywhere else. Lots of right-wing zealots, rabid students, and as many Nazis as cobblestones. And the opposition of the communists doesn't help. You'd think every devoted physician in the *Vaterland* would be outraged about what's going on. Who knows what has to happen before they wake up." She had not lost any of her intensity.

"I liked your recent article," he said. "I've read all your publications. Crisp. Persuasive." The noise in the hall was so loud now he could barely hear what he was saying.

"Thank you. Have you published?" she asked in a louder voice.

He looked away, toward the banner over the front of the room. "Let's go outside. It's too noisy here."

"All right. First, I need to tell *Frau Doktor* Frankenthal and the others. I'll meet you outside. Give me ten minutes or so."

The November evening air was crisp. Groups of doctors milled around, smoking and talking. He would have joined in, but he didn't want to miss her. After nearly twenty minutes, she appeared in the doorway, looking for him.

"I know a *Weinstube* nearby," he said. "Maybe you'd like a glass of wine."

"I can't stay long. I promised I'd go back. A meeting of the local board." As they began walking, she asked, "How are you, Philipp? What you are doing now?"

He told her about his work at the policlinic, his thoughts about the children he saw, his fading hopes to publish an article in Grotjahn's journal. All the while, he looked down at the pavement rather than at her. He remembered walking alongside her in the hills around Freiburg. The stairway up to her apartment. How she pronounced his name. Her voice had seemed brighter then.

They found seats at a small table. She took a cigarette case out of her purse.

"You smoke now?"

"One of my many sins," she said, striking a match.

"I never would have thought you'd smoke."

"Why? I know, the research says it's harmful. Can lead to cancer. Perhaps. The Nazis tell us not to smoke. Maybe I do it just for that reason."

He laughed. "You haven't changed."

"Gray hair. Wiser. Less eager to please. I've changed."

"I don't remember you as someone eager to please," he said.

"I'm glad. But I was. Hoche, for example. I liked him. That clouded my judgment. He was very kind to me. His wife even more so. But I let him influence my thinking too much. You were right to leave."

"There have been times when I'm not so sure."

"Why?" she asked. "Because you've changed your mind about sending young children to institutions?"

"No, not that. Sometimes, I know, an institution's best, given the child's prognosis and the parents' ability to deal with it. But that child and his mother needed something else. No, I mean, my career. I might have gone on like you to a university position."

"It's not always that wonderful. You have to put up with a lot. Arrogance. Politics. Maybe more for me, as a woman. But Heidelberg leans to the Nazis. I suspect all the universities do. And anti-Semitism. It's not always on the surface. Sometimes I wish it were. Then I'd know where I stand. I've been lucky. I get to see interesting patients. A few good students. Still, it's a lonely life."

He looked closely at her. Her eyes still flashed when she spoke. But he saw that there was a look of disappointment about her. The lighting in the *Weinstube* made a haze from her cigarette' smoke and tinged her face a yellow gray.

"So," she said, "are you really married, or do you just wear a ring to keep things in order?" She was smiling now. He noticed then that she was not wearing a wedding ring.

"Yes, I am married. Some seven years ago."

"And..."

"And she's good. Pretty and good. A very good woman, my Christine. I'm very lucky."

"Congratulations. Children?"

"Thank you. No children yet. I have hopes, but no. I want them more than she does. Christine's anxious about bringing children into the world. We'll see."

"I can understand her. But you'll be a good father." She took a long drag on her cigarette, stubbed it out, and raised her glass about to take another sip of wine. "Do you remember Pelcher?"

"Pelcher? The resident who was so nervous all the time?"

"Yes, him. Poor man began drinking heavily. To the point of missing his rotations. Hoche was beside himself. First you left. Then Pelcher shows up drunk more often than sober. Hoche tried to remove him. But before he could, Pelcher, to put it professionally, went crazy. We learned afterwards that he saw and maybe did some terrible things in the war. Schetzeler and I found him after his midnight shift under a patient's bed. Screaming hysterically. He broke away from us and attacked the patient. Tried to strangle him. Shouting, 'The *Boche*! The *Boche!*' Terrifying! Had to sedate him myself. We finally got a jacket on him, but he kept raving. Never really came out of it. His father came to get him."

"And Schnitzler?"

"You mean Schetzeler? The one you were so jealous about? I can tell you a story about him, the asshole. After you and Pelcher were gone, the *Schwein* thought he owned the place. I tried to get him to follow my instructions, but he wouldn't have any of it. Told me I was not fit to be a doctor, just fit to have babies. Hoche threatened to send him packing when he said it once during seminar, but Schetzeler knew we still needed him in the clinic, with you and Pelcher missing. Shortly after that the bastard came after me, thinking I couldn't resist his charms. Grabbed me from behind in the supply room. I scratched his face something fierce. Bloody, deep scratches. He screamed and ran out. Dressed the wound himself, for fear of telling the nurse on duty what happened."

"I never liked him."

"Oh, and then there's the story about his shoes. Remember? Patent-leather. Shiny. The nurses told me he would come up behind them and put his foot down in a way that he could see up their skirts in the reflection. They despised him and did everything they could to stay away from him. And you thought *I* liked him! How jealous you were! Jealous of a pudgy ass with a squeaky voice, stubby fingers and patent-leather shoes!"

He laughed. "So, what happened to him?"

"When Hoche saw him later that morning, he asked him about the bandages on his face. He had the nerve to say a patient did it. Hoche ordered an extra sedative and isolation for the patient, until I found out and told him what really happened. Hoche dismissed him on the spot. Never saw him again. A few months later, someone told me he went to Breslau. Or was it Königsberg? Into gynecology. Him, a gynecologist! Imagine! We had to bring in five third-year candidates from the university to help in the wards. I put an announcement in the journals for new residents. It was rougher than usual for a while."

"I saw the announcement, but I didn't know what had happened and didn't feel I could ask. Hoche was good to me when I left, you know. He helped me transfer my residency to the policlinic in Augsburg, but it was still awkward. Schetzeler made a remark about you the first day we met. Called you a headstrong Jewess. Wondered why they let women become doctors. I didn't like him from then on. But I still think you paid too much attention to him."

"Don't start that up again. That's long behind us, Philipp. That and anything else between us. Now we have work to do." She stubbed her cigarette out in the ashtray and looked intensely at him for a few moments. "I can't resist telling you something," she said softly. "I was pregnant with your child. I had an abortion. In Hamburg. I went away for a week, remember? It was shortly after you disagreed with Hoche about sending the mixed-race boy to Emmendingen."

He sat there, frozen, not knowing what to say. He would never know what to say for the rest of his life. Finally, he asked, "Why are you telling me this now?"

"I wanted to tell you before, many times. But we had quarreled. And you were so jealous. So stupidly, insanely jealous. I was so angry with you. And then you decided to leave. Well, I didn't want to have a child alone. And I didn't want the child to chain you to me out of a sense of duty. That's not enough reason to bring a child into the world."

He sat there in silence for what seemed several minutes. "My child?"

"Yes. Ours."

"You should have told me."

She stared at the ashtray.

More silence, until he finally said, "I'm sorry, Luise."

"I'm sorry, too. It's done now. Maybe I shouldn't have told you."

"It's done. But I loved you. We could have been together. We would still be together. With a child. Our child. You *should* have told me. You should have." He trailed off, thinking how much he wanted to be a father. He looked at her, hoping that she would look at him. Instead, she fumbled in her purse for another cigarette, lit it, and inhaled deeply.

She turned to blow the smoke away. "We've made different lives for ourselves. We've made choices," she said, "Choices that can't be undone." She punched the cigarette into the ashtray. It broke in half, its smoke hovering around her hand.

That word again, he thought. Choices. For all their differences, he saw again how much she and Christine were alike. "You're married," he heard her say. He was barely listening. "You say she's good, Philipp. I am very happy for you. If it matters to you, I'm not unhappy in my work. And I believe in the League. There's so much to be done. I am doing what I can."

"Yes," he said, still dazed by what she told him.

"The League is good," she said. "Not strong enough yet to stop us from rushing over the cliff. But the latest elections give me hope. The Nazis have lost some strength. If only the communists weren't so determined to feud with us. But people are waking up. We might escape the whirlwind yet."

He was barely listening to her. "Whirlwind? Yes. Whirlwind," he said.

"If Hitler comes to power, I am leaving," she said firmly. "I've already made up my mind. Palestine. A new beginning."

He clenched his fist. "I won't leave. This is my country. Not Hitler's."

"It's my country, too. But when he takes over, it will not be our country." She drank what was left in her glass and abruptly stood up. "Come with me. I'll introduce you to the others. We need more help here."

"I'm not a revolutionary. I don't want a revolution. I'm a doctor."

"We don't either. We want to work within the law. But if that's not possible, we have to be prepared."

"A doctor doesn't seek violence. Violence of any kind. 'Do no harm!' Remember?"

"An ancient oath, for another time. Violence may be needed now to avoid a greater violence. But I need to go back to the others. They're waiting. Frankenthal is excellent. You should meet her. Please think about joining us."

"Not if you're planning to do something violent."

"Don't worry. I'm not going to burn down the *Reichstag* or something like that. More likely I'll chain myself to the front door."

He laughed a little, but the look in her eyes said that she meant it. Before he could respond she stood up and said a quick "'*Wiedersehen!*" They shook hands. He watched her put on her coat and stride toward the door, sensing that he would never see her again. Her broken cigarette in the ashtray continued to smolder.

CHAPTER TWELVE
Jt was Easier that Way

*Then came 1933. That fateful year. I can admit it now, Helga, I was fright-
ened by the chaos all around us. At the same time, I still was hopeful. If the Nazis
showed their vicious edge, I tried to look beyond that. Didn't we all?*

*Everyone agreed, the Vaterland needed to get its health back. Even if the
medicine was bitter. At first, I was among the masses willing to stand back and let
Hitler and his Party do their work. If I awoke every morning and went to sleep
every night consumed by my powerlessness in the face of Greta's illness, I at least
needed to believe someone could heal the Volk of our dissension, our loss of self-
respect, our vulnerability to foreign forces and to degrading behavior. Hitler's victory gave me, gave all true Germans, hope. "True" Germans I find myself writing.
I must correct myself. I was so convinced I knew who was a "true" German, a "true"
Jew, a "true" communist. I saw things so sharply, so clearly. It was easier that way.*

Johann continually reassured himself that any of his patients—he
had encountered none, despite his certainty that he would—could
have no knowledge of his activities as a physician in a Nazi uniform. And
any former Nazi colleague would seek the same anonymity that he did.

As long as his false identity was not challenged, he should be safe. Then came his chance meeting with *Doktor* Reinhard Graeber, the senior physician in the Nuremberg policlinic where he had practiced before the war.

He was thinking about the past few days' testimony—the freezing, malaria and seawater experiments. The exhibits of photographs were grotesque. The witnesses' testimony was painful and shocking. He felt like he was being drawn into a whirlpool that he could not escape, sucked closer and closer to revealing his own role in what he now saw as the sordid and evil world of Nazi medicine. After the judge adjourned the trial for the day, he went outside for a walk.

He did not notice a drunk staggering toward him. They collided and fell to the ground. The drunkard, struggling to his feet, shouted "You asshole!" Johann got up slowly. That voice! The unmistakable, gravelly voice of *Herr Doktor* Graeber, his superior in the policlinic.

"Oaf! Stinking *Schweinhund*! I will have you arrested, you…" Graeber stopped abruptly as he recognized his former colleague. "Oh, it's you, is it? I know you. Brenner! *Herr Doktor* Brenner. How fine! How perfectly fine! Here on the ruined street in our ruined city, just like all the rest of us." Graeber began to snort and jab at Johann's chest, shouting even louder. "Here, everybody, here is *Herr Doktor* Brenner. My colleague! We were supposed to become heroes! Do you hear, heroes! We are noble doctors. We greet you in the name of our *Vaterland*! We…" Spittle began to form at the corners of Graeber's mouth. Passers-by gathered around the two men. Two American military policemen stopped their jeep to see what was happening.

"I don't know what you are talking about. I don't know you," Johann stammered.

"No, *Herr Doktor*? I think we *do* know each other. Yes, I am sure of it. You are Brenner, *Herr Doktor* Josef, no… *Johann* Brenner. And I am your superior, remember, Graeber. *Doktor* Graeber, *SA*, a loyal German, now as before. I am not ashamed. We are good Nazis! You and I. And most of these good people here, too, I'll bet! You and you and you," he shouted, pointing at the onlookers, "you were all Nazis, weren't you?"

Many quickly walked away. Graeber shouted after them, "Cowards! Admit it! We tried to do what had to be done! We are the heroes! I am not ashamed!" His voice failed him at this point. His booming shout came out as a squeaky falsetto. He was weaving back and forth, his eyes bulging, veins standing out on his forehead. Saliva drooled from the corner of his mouth.

"He's drunk. He's crazy," Johann said, tapping his temple and rolling his eyes in a sign language that he hoped the MPs would understand. One MP gestured for Johann's and Graeber's identification papers in broken German. "*Mach schnell! Mach schnell!* Quick! Quick!" Johann fumbled in his overcoat and complied. Graeber did not. Instead, he shouted in German, "This man was a Nazi, too!" and tried to poke Johann in the chest again. "I know him. We practiced medicine together. We were Nazis together!" Then he staggered and raised his hand. "*Heil Hitler!*" The MP quickly grabbed Graeber's arm, twisting it behind his back. "You are under arrest!" Graeber cried out in pain. The other MP let Johann's papers fall to the ground. Graeber was forced into the jeep and driven off in a cloud of dust, as he shouted, "*Auf Wiedersehen, Herr Doktor* Brenner!"

"War does terrible things to a person," one old woman in the crowd said, "We all must pay for it! Everyone one of us." She started to cry as she walked away. Johann just stood there, gasping for breath. After a moment, he retrieved his papers. He decided to go back at once to the Palace of Justice. It was safer there.

He thought about Graeber for the rest of the day. How unpleasant and crude the man was. He remembered a day in the policlinic, shortly after Hitler came to power. His daughter's illness, the fire that destroyed Germany's parliament building, and Graeber's coarseness were inseparable in his mind. Underneath all that were his doubts about himself.

*****

When Johann came home each day, Helga always tried to paint Greta's condition in the best light. "She slept soundly at least an hour this afternoon," she would tell him when their daughter exhausted herself with coughing and fallen into a deep sleep for fifty minutes. They both saw that Greta was getting weaker. He knew that Helga was not telling him everything.

His exasperation led him to fire off a series of questions like a policeman interrogating a criminal.

"How frequently was she coughing?" he barked. Before Helga could answer, he shot back, "Dry, hacking coughs? Or loose? Any sputum? Her temperature? Did you take her temperature? Did she thrash around when she was asleep? Did you notice her eyeballs moving under her eyelids? Was her breath shallow?"

Helga waited him out in silence. He would take up the mail or the newspaper, or stand with his back to her and stare out the window at the plum tree in the courtyard. Finally, on a gray afternoon in early March, she grabbed him by the arms, looked into his eyes, and steadied herself. "She's awake now, Johann. Go in to see her, please." He probably had not noticed but this was the first time in weeks that Helga had dared to look directly at him as she spoke about their daughter. She did not want him to see the mixture of anger and pain in her eyes, fearing it would drive him even further away. But it was deeper than that. Sensing him in his fitful sleep each night drained her spirits. Ever since Greta's illness it was as though they had been walking on parallel paths separated by a dense grove of trees. Just when she and their daughter needed him the most, he had withdrawn from them.

"Go in and see her, Johann. Please. Before we eat supper. Your newspaper and the mail can wait. Go in and see her. She needs you."

"I will. Later. This evening, after I have seen two patients. *Herr und Frau* Hammacher are scheduled."

"No. You must go now, Johann. Please go in and see her now. She wants to tell you something." Her tone was so firm that he knew he could not avoid doing what she asked.

He found Greta lying semi-curled up in her bed. The feather-filled coverlet barely revealed any living body underneath. Helga had combed and braided her hair—it was longer than he remembered—and put a little blue barrette over each braid. It made her look older, but also thinner and frailer. Her blue eyes still sparkled, just as he remembered before her illness. He had tried to keep his memories of her intact by avoiding her, which he had done as much as possible.

"So, my little Greta. Here's *Vati* to say 'Good evening to you!' *Mutti* said I should come in to see you. I thought you would still be taking your nap."

"No, *Vati*." Her voice was raspy and deep.

"Shall I open the curtains? It's not so bright outside now."

"No, *Vati*."

"Tomorrow morning you'll see the plum tree outside your window. Its leaves are coming out of their buds. Spring is coming."

"The light hurts my eyes, *Vati*."

Johann wanted to leave. It hurt him to see her like this. Helga and he had spoken about their sense of helplessness. But what Helga did not seem to realize was that he felt this twice over, both as a father and as a physician.

He forced himself to stay. "*Mutti* says that you want to tell me something."

"*Vati,* do you know the 'Tinies'?" Greta asked.

"What are the 'Tinies'?"

"Well, not 'what?' but 'who?' The 'Tinies' are my friends. They come to visit me each day. And sometimes I dream about them, too. They are my little, little friends."

"I see. Are they here now?"

"Oh, no. Not yet, at least. They don't know you, *Vati*. They are very shy, you know. They will come later, after I tell them it's all right."

"I see. They're your very own special friends."

"Yes. And they sing to me and tell me stories and watch out that no ogres and trolls and wolves come, and they do other good things for me, too. You'd like them."

Johann was only mildly interested, but enough to make him sit down on his daughter's bed. It depressed him to see her. The medical journals had discouraged him, there was so little positive in them. After he had

239

read all the articles on polio that he could, he just pushed it out of his mind.

"You see, *Vati,*" she said, "the Tinies are little people, lovely little people. Each one has a name, of course, but they are so small they have very little names, so little you cannot possibly say them. Each name sounds like a little sniff or puff or whoosh. I've given them names, but these aren't their real names. But because they like me, they come when I call them by the names I've given them." She was about to tell him more but began coughing.

He smiled and handed her the glass of water by her bedside. She took a sip. When she stopped coughing, he said, "What are some of the names you have given the Tinies, Greta?"

"Well, *Vati,* my favorite Tiny is *Herr* Johann Winzig. Just like you, *Vati,* 'Johann!' Greta smiled and handed back the empty glass. "And he really is '*winzig*,' you know, '*tiny!*' He could sit on my fingernail. This little fingernail." She moved her right hand feebly. "His wife, of course, is *Frau* Helga Winzig—Helga, just like *Mutti!*—and she's even smaller. Smaller than my little fingernail! They have a son, Paul-Adolf Winzig." Greta giggled. "And they have a baby, too, a little girl..."

"Greta!" Johann guessed.

"Yes, Greta, like me. But their baby is so small I can't even see it yet, *Vati!* I think she's sick, too. They'll show her to me when she gets bigger and feels better, they tell me. There are lots of other Tinies, but those three are my favorites."

Johann laughed. "Why do you like *Herr* and *Frau* Winzig best?"

"Well, they help all the other Tinies. *Herr* Winzig is a doctor, like you, and *Frau* Winzig knits beautiful dresses and likes to sing, just like *Mutti.* They are always doing nice things for the other Tinies. And for me, too. They warn me when the wolf is near. And they sing to me. They're my friends."

"But they're so small, Greta. How much can they do if they are so small?"

"Oh, they do a lot. Being small is not a problem for them. They are as big as they are, and no bigger. But no smaller, either. They are just right. Being small is not bad, is it, *Vati?*"

"I suppose not. Being small might be all right, if others don't decide to hurt you or take advantage of you."

"See, that's the nice part. The Tinies don't hurt anybody. They only like to help. I like them just because they are so good. Why should their size be important? They're my friends."

Johann drew a deep breath. "Well, my little beauty, my little Greta, *Vati* has to go now. I will talk with you again later this evening, I promise. We haven't talked as much as we should have lately. And I want to meet the Tinies someday, too."

"Yes, *Vati*. You'll like them."

Johann gave his daughter a kiss on her forehead and quickly left the room. He went over to where Helga was standing at the sink and hugged her from behind.

"Thank you," he said. "Thank you."

When Paul-Adolf came to the supper table, he was still excited from his school day. "Our teacher, *Herr* Bayer told us all about Adolf Hitler, our new Chancellor!" he said. "We have his picture now on the classroom wall."

"You have a picture of *Herr* Bayer on your classroom wall?" Helga teased.

"No, silly! Of Adolf Hitler, of course!"

"And what does *Herr* Bayer tell you about Adolf Hitler?" she asked.

"What adventures he had as a boy. How brave he was as a soldier. Why he is Germany's Chancellor now. How he will save us from our enemies. How he is the friend of every German schoolboy and schoolgirl. Lots more things."

"Johann, do you hear this? The boy is not quite ten and he is being prepared to be a Nazi."

"Leave it for now, Helga. The teacher is trying to build patriotic pride in the boy. We had the same thing when we were children. The Kaiser's picture was on all my classroom walls. On yours too, I would think." Helga nodded, but her brow was furrowed. Paul-Adolf was a bright boy, eager to please his teachers and grateful for their praise. His only trait of late that made Johann and Helga anxious was his lack of sympathy for Greta since her illness. Whenever Helga paid attention to her, Paul-Adolf resented it. "With time," Johann tried to reassure her, "he will soften. You can bet he'll defend her if any of his friends ridicule her." Helga nodded, but her expression was doubtful.

After supper, Paul-Adolf answered the knock at the front door. A man and a woman came into in the waiting room. "The *Frau* asks how long you will be."

"That will be *Frau* Hammacher and her husband. Yes, I'm going." With a pat on his son's head, Johann began talking to the waiting patients before he reached the doorway. "Good evening. Who'll be first?" For the rest of the evening, he gave no more thought to his children or the state of the world, save to repeat in his mind the phrase from supper, "…over time…."

The next morning, a thunderstorm and downpour unusual for Nuremberg in March persuaded him to take the streetcar to the policlinic. Waiting for it, he saw the headlines on the newspapers at the kiosk: "*Reichstag* destroyed by fire!" The front-page story in the *Völkischer Beobachter,* the Nazi Party newspaper, stated that the fire was a communist plot. The perpetrator was a half-witted Dutch criminal, a card-carrying communist, caught at the scene. Other communists were arrested, too.

Johann would not have been surprised if the newspaper had stated that this Dutchman, van der Lubbe, was a Jew: "'Just as pain follows injury, chaos follows Jews!' Wasn't that the old saying?' His father often had said it. So had his teachers. An age-old declaration from the pulpit, in classrooms and lecture halls, in the press and the marketplace. And not just in Germany, but in the entire Western world, for nearly two thousand years. No matter that Jews had been welcomed back in Germany since the early 1800s after their centuries' long exile. No matter that they had legal protections and opportunities denied them elsewhere in Europe. No matter that they had made sacrifices in the war. That they were benefactors of hospitals and schools. That they appreciated and loved the *Vaterland*. No matter that Philipp and he had sworn to be blood brothers. As Johann's father had said, "… chaos follows Jews!" He carried the fear deep inside him, unaware of its presence. Now it erupted like a boil. 'Jews cannot be trusted. Scoundrels and traitors. Van der Lubbe was probably paid by Jews to set the fire.'

A fire in the nation's parliament building, where so much of Germany's destiny was launched. Such boldness! Frightening! He could barely grasp it. Germany's enemies—civilization's enemies! devils!—were everywhere. There was no other possible explanation. According to the *Beobachter*, there was but one way for Germany, for civilization itself, to escape destruction: Adolf Hitler! He alone would not allow any harm to befall the *Vaterland* and lead it to its deserved destiny. How fortunate for humankind that he was now Chancellor of Germany! What else needed to be said?

The newspaper article helped to clarify Johann's view of the world and the way it worked. If the Nazis were in a position of authority at last, thanks to Hitler's position as Chancellor, then it was just in time. But if the Communists, in their desperation, were fomenting revolution now and trying to take power, what other maliciousness might be expected? Even greater economic chaos? The worldwide Great Depression had played right into their hands. And now they would stop hard-working Germans, would stop the *Vaterland* from overcoming the Depression. Until they had their revolution. Then barbarism! The end of order! Anarchy and chaos!

The newspaper reminded its readers that a cunning cluster of Jews had planned and started the Great Depression. All the bankers and stockbrokers, all the fat capitalists, all the useless rich were Jews. In league with the Jew communists. The Jew was the enemy, whichever way one looked. Eternally greedy, insatiable Jews had unleashed this latest crisis on the world to gain even more wealth, and let everyone else sink into destitution. The Jews' age-old goals were the destruction of everything beautiful and the acquisition of wealth at the expense of the hard working, law-abiding citizen. Whether a capitalist or a Bolshevik, it didn't matter. Not a *pfennig*'s worth of difference between them! In the end, the Jew prospers from others' ruination. This explained all the world's problems and pointed the way toward their solution. Johann—and countless other Germans—sought an explanation like this, just as a drowning man, grabs at anything he can. Any other way of looking at the matter was too unsettling. It would have meant questioning assumptions, finding valid evidence, rejecting hasty conclusions. It would have meant countering the Nazis' accusations. Instead, he found refuge in believing what he heard and read, even if that was absurd. That was more reassuring, more comforting than painful, time-consuming reasoning could ever be. So Johann bowed to Hitler.

He had been leaning in this direction for several years, but had caught himself from succumbing until now. His friendship with Philipp; his recognition that his father had little grounds to be so opposed to the Jews; his recent experience with *Herr* Semmelberg, and most important of all, Helga's straightforward way of looking at things: all of these forestalled his sliding down into the abyss. But now none of that mattered. He must join the Party. As he folded the newspaper, the streetcar swaying on its tracks as it approached *Wodanplatz*, he muttered to himself that March morning: 'We must be grateful that Hitler has appeared. He has been sent to save our *Volk* and our *Vaterland*.'

If he joined the Nazis, it would not be for his own gain, he told himself. It was for Germany's survival, for what the Nazis would do for the world. If everything pointed toward "The Jew" as a cunning parasite, as Hitler and the Nazi Party declared, then whatever was necessary had to be done to rid Germany and the world of their pestilence. And if Germany *fell*—in his mind the word took on the same solemn tone that he would have used for a comrade who fell in battle—then what could one expect for a happy future, for progress, for civilization, for life itself?

The streetcar screeched to a halt. A scene from the battlefield flashed through his mind. He felt nauseous. He told himself that it must come from his perception of the daunting challenges ahead. That the only way to overcome it was to accept his duty, to do as good Germans everywhere were doing, in order to save the world from evil. At the same time, his intuition and his idealism told him that doing "whatever was necessary" would take them all into uncharted, perilous territory. He was frightened.

He tried to calm himself by reminding himself of what he knew for certain: 'Our destiny is perfection. Our faith and our courage make us invincible. As surely as the sun rises, good must triumph. It will triumph over every evil. That is our destiny. Germany will heal the world. Will rid the world of evil.' His thoughts swept him on to the question: 'But then why is the world in such a sorry state?' His answer? 'Every good German has been betrayed with the betrayal of our army at the end of the war. Every good German has been saddled with the outrageous claims and demands of the treasonous treaty signed at Versailles. Every good German is now paying for the weaknesses of our misbegotten government. Worst of all, every good German is being contaminated by the excesses and the degeneracy of this godless age.'

He slumped down in his seat as the streetcar lurched forward. 'And who betrayed us? Weak-willed parliamentarians. Selfish unions. Social Democrats with their internationalism. Communists in the pay of Russia. And everywhere, in all these dark corners, Jews. Jews can never be trusted. Jews can never be good Germans.' He balled his fist, his mind drawing up images from he didn't know where. 'The *Volk* is diseased. It has been infected by parasites. It is undergoing necrosis. It is like a diabetic who, having neglected his infected toe, must now have his foot amputated to stop the gangrene that has set in. Only by destroying the parasite will the *Volk* be cured. If the parasite is not destroyed, the *Volk* will die.' Round and round his mind went. It all seemed so logical, given his starting point. And with each loop of the argument came the reassuring conclusions, all based on the hopeful assumptions that soothed him and strengthened his resolve. There was only one problem—and Johann was not ready to think about it. The destruction of the "parasite" meant doing harm.

'What other choice do I have but to join the Party?' he thought, not realizing that he had been predisposed to answer the question long before he considered it. Leaving Germany had never occurred to him. Joining the socialists was treason, as far as he understood what they wanted: a radical transformation of the world into a vague internationalist blending and mixing, dragging everything down to a common, base level. If there was to be any form of socialism, with its praiseworthy goal of protecting and enhancing every member of society, he had told Helga, let it be within and for the *Volk*. Yes, a socialism within and for a nation—Hitler's National Socialism!

And how could any German physician, as a scientist, support the most extreme of all the socialists, the blood-soaked, godless communists, with their denial of any distinctions among peoples? He could only answer that such a renegade failed to see the fundamental differences in human society and in civilizations. It was absurd to forsake German civilization for some vague illusion of a world living in a "pseudo-peace" built on the ruins of all that was beautiful, noble and strong. Christianity, science, law, art, music—all these and more were doomed, he was certain, if the communists, if the Jews, achieved their goals.

Johann lamented his earlier vacillations. He so wanted to be a man of action. He felt a secret shame that he was not. It nagged at him when he lay awake in the middle of the night. He worried that he was a coward, that he was not a real man. He prayed for the strength to do something important with his life.

Now the time had come. 'The *Reichstag* fire is the beginning of a worldwide conflict. Helga and I, Germans all across the *Vaterland*, even Germans outside Germany, are called upon to make many sacrifices for our children, for a better, purer world.'

He noticed that the storm clouds overhead had passed. The sky had cleared with such suddenness, such ferocity, as if a massive hand had swept stale crumbs off a table. He looked up, over the rooftops, to see a penetrating blueness that awakened a memory of his childhood. He felt himself pulled upward, as though he were being sucked off his feet, twirling like a leaf in the wind. It was a dizzying, terrifying and yet exhilarating feeling all at the same time. The sky's blue brilliance seemed to accentuate the purity of his thoughts. He took this for a sign.

Then, as though no clear sky, no certainty, could exist without some doubt to becloud it, he realized that he would have to tell Helga of his plan. He had come to this juncture before. Whenever their conversations had reached this point, she would say no more. That was the only way she knew to get him to stop his rant. At first, his exuberance tricked him into believing that her silence meant that she understood and accepted his argument. But he soon saw that was not true. He knew she had a different vision of duty than he did. That she even had a different vision of Germany, to say nothing of Jews. That her hatred of war was absolute. And her hatred of politics was not far behind.

"Leave all that political game to the politicians, why don't you?" she would say. "When the politicians die in war, rather than sip fine wine in their villas, when they send their sons to fight in the trenches rather than climb mountains and sail their yachts around the world, then I might begin to believe they are interested in the likes of us. But not until then, Johann. Not for a long time. Why don't you see that?" Her firm voice hung in the air.

"Sons of generals, of admirals, of politicians have been killed in battle," he would respond, trying to stay calm. "You know that. You just don't understand these matters."

When she said nothing more, her silence would wither his enthusiasm. He kept asking himself, "What could she really know about the way the world worked, about the way progress had to be earned through sacrifice and devotion to one's goals? She was a woman. A good and beautiful German woman, but a woman just the same." That alone was enough in his eyes to discredit her judgment about practical matters outside the sphere of their home. Despite her intelligence and her practicality, he could never admit that he needed Helga's counsel about public events, any more than he could doubt for any length of time his own ability to do whatever he thought had to be done. He could not disentangle these knots of confusion, these contradictions. He had given up trying.

And so, he kept coming back to it. The Nazi Party stood for the action he believed was essential for Germany's salvation. If he had not yet joined, his reason, in one word, would have been "Helga." 'Until now,' he thought, as the streetcar neared his stop. 'As soon as I get home this evening I will tell her that I am going to join the Party.'

First, he wanted to speak with *Doktor* Reinhardt Graeber, his superior at the policlinic, a specialist in internal medicine. He didn't like

247

Graeber. But Graeber was a Nazi and that was what mattered now. He had been hounding Johann for nearly three years to come with him to a meeting of the local "Brown Shirts." He never saw him without his silver swastika lapel pin on his white coat. Graeber would know, he thought, how a German physician should best approach the Party and offer his services. To hear him tell it, he was a Nazi from the very beginning of the movement, even before Hitler went on trial for trying to overthrow the government.

Before Hitler was appointed chancellor, Johann once told Graeber that becoming a Nazi was unprofessional. Graeber had just snorted. "On the contrary, *Herr Doktor* Brenner," he said in his gravelly voice, "becoming a Nazi is the best way we doctors can get the respect we deserve. Who else is going to push all these goddamned monkey Jews back where they belong? And I don't mean just the drooling Jews we see climbing up into the affairs of state, in banking, in the arts, in business. I mean the goddamned Jews who are doctors, competing with us for our livelihood, for the privilege of treating German men and women and children, for the sanctity of our profession. The shit-eating, goddamned monkey Jews! Fuck them all! You and every good doctor must join us now! If you don't, well, I know whose side you're on."

Johann despised vulgarity. When he saw it in his patients, he tried to be tolerant, even forgiving, and at the same time, congratulating himself that he had superior breeding and was more dignified. When he heard crude language from his colleagues, he was outraged. After all, they had an education and a calling. Hearing Graeber's incessant obscenities was revolting. He cursed himself for not speaking his mind, but what could he say? He gave his usual feeble nod as Graeber unleashed his familiar tirade.

"Hitler will use us physicians well, I can promise you, *Herr Doktor* Brenner!" the chief physician continued, loud enough for everyone in the policlinic to hear. "We have great work to do. Great work! The most important work of all, to my mind." He stood so close that Johann could taste the smoke of his morning cigar. When he attempted to step back toward the wall, Graeber moved toward him until there was no escape.

"We must purify the race," he hissed, jabbing his finger into Johann's chest with each word. "Physicians will be the heroes of the *Vaterland*—heroes in every sense of the word—*mein lieber Herr!*" Then, with the usual spittle forming at the corners of his mouth, he shouted even louder than before "You want to be a hero, don't you? You aren't a coward, are you?" Here Graeber grinned broadly, showing the row of gold-capped teeth that startled Johann every time he saw them. What the chief physician probably intended as laughter came out half as guttural cackle, half as a sucking sound. When he pushed himself closer, Johann thought he was going to faint.

At the peak of his laughter, Graeber began coughing and hacking. Johann ducked to the side and escaped into his own office. Feeling obliged to answer Graeber's accusation as he left, he said, "Of course not!"

When Hitler was appointed Chancellor in January, Graeber had given Johann a cigar and invited him to have a beer in the nearby tavern. Johann had excused himself then by saying that he had private patients that evening. Was he a coward? Was Graeber right?

On that March morning, though, before he could speak with Graeber about the terrifying news from Berlin and his newfound resolve to join the Party, he was swallowed up by what became a typical, hectic day at the policlinic. The waiting room was full when he arrived, with a line forming down on the street. In quick succession, he saw an injured arm; a nosebleed that wouldn't stop; an infant with diarrhea and its panicky mother; inflamed tonsils; another injured arm; two patients with hacking coughs; gout; and three complaints of rheumatism, at least one of which was probably shirking work and seeking a formal medical excuse to cover up for it. Johann made a mental note to check the files for earlier instances of such behavior. No sooner had he dispatched one patient than the next one was in his examination room. He would have to wait to speak with Graeber at noon. Or at the end of the day's work.

The chief physician went out for his midday meal. Johann would have joined him if he had been asked. Instead, he ate some apples and read journals in his office. He could hear the mumblings of the patients who stayed in the waiting room, rather than go home to eat, for fear of losing their place in line. The afternoon began when he examined a relatively young farmer who complained of difficulty swallowing. The man's tongue was blackened and ulcerous. Johann suspected cancer, especially when the man told him how much and how long he had been smoking. In the adjacent examination room, he could hear Graeber talking loudly with a woman who had brought in her ailing son. A moment later, Graeber was shouting and cursing. A nurse gave a shriek. A door slammed. More shouting in the hallway. "Damned swine! Damned dirty, little swine! Let the damned Jew-doctors take care of their own! We Germans should not have to waste our time with the likes of these lumps of shit! Asshole Jews!"

Johann told the farmer to wait for him. In the hallway, he saw Graeber striding away, toward the policlinic's closet library and the doctor's lavatory just beyond. By the time he caught up with him, Graeber had bolted into the lavatory and slammed the door. Johann turned to go back down the hall and his patient, only to find the nurse prodding mother and son down the hallway toward him. He stepped aside to let them all pass. The boy was crying. By that time, Graeber emerged again, still fuming and swearing, while he tried to fasten his swastika lapel-pin on a fresh white smock. He overtook the woman and the boy, who was trailing behind his mother, and grabbed the child by the back of his neck.

"You little monster! You did that deliberately! I should have expected it. What else should I have expected from a little Jewboy! A dirty, little swine!" The boy cried out in pain and terror. Graeber was oblivious. He towered over the mother, pinned her to the wall, and shouted, "How dare you bring this little devil in here? How dare you! Your kind will stop at nothing to overturn our good work and contaminate our good nature! Get out! I want nothing to do with you and yours! Get out!"

The mother just gasped and began to tremble, whether from anger or from fear, it was impossible to know. She hurried back into the waiting room, grabbed her son's and her own coat from the hooks on the wall, and left without saying a word. Johann saw the startled looks of the other patients.

"What happened?" he asked.

Graeber was red faced and smelled of beer. White specks of spittle dotted his shaggy moustache. "He vomited all over me. The little swine! He did it on purpose, I am sure of it! I was depressing his tongue, examining his inflamed tonsils—I suspected diphtheria. These vermin don't know how to avoid it and infect all the rest of us with their diseases. The little monster began to gag. I pulled out the depressor. The boy then leered at me. His eyes flashed red, I swear it. He reared back and the next thing I knew, he vomited so quickly I could not get out of the way. Stinking swine! All over me, the stinking Jew-boy swine!" Graeber grew more and more agitated. "I should have poked his eyes out! I should have given him a hypo that would have numbed him on the spot!"

Johann was appalled. It was just a little boy, a frightened little boy. Not much older than Paul-Adolf. These things happened. He knew how a gag reflex often precipitated projectile vomiting, especially in a feverish or excited child whose tonsils were enflamed. Diphtheria would make it even more likely. He had known all this since his first year in medical school.

Graeber should have known, too. 'What kind of a doctor was he anyway?' Johann thought. 'Was this the kind of doctor who would save the nation? Was this the man whose judgment and reason could be trusted?' Just last week, Graeber had pinned Johann to the wall with his incessant finger-jabbing, insisting again in one of his in rants that the Nazis were Germany's only hope. These outbursts in all their vulgarity made Johann hesitate, to doubt the prudence of following anyone like that. 'If such a physician were given free rein,' he told himself, 'the Lord only knew what might happen in the *Vaterland*.'

He took Graeber's ugly display with the Jewish boy and mother to be another omen. The boy and his mother were not destroying Germany. They were harmless. Not every Jew was a devil. Graeber was wrong in treating them so crudely. If joining the Nazis was the choice he would someday have to make, it could wait for now. He would let things take their course awhile longer. The Nazis were certainly in control. According to the newspaper, Hitler would use all the powers he had been granted by the parliament to secure the nation from its enemies, just as little Paul-Adolf's teacher had told his pupils. Well, he thought, that was important. Germany needed order. The order that could only come with authority. An order that rests on morality and decency. Then, after order was restored, Germany could realize its hopes. Rebuild itself. Achieve its destiny. He asked himself, 'How long after all would it take for Hitler to do whatever he was planning to do?' And he provided his own answer: 'A few months, at most. Either his strategy works, and there'll be no need to get involved. Or it does not, and by then some other solution will arise. In any event, the crisis cannot last.' So he decided, despite what he had planned to do that morning, that he would wait a while longer to join the Party.

He took a deep breath. When he went back to his examination room, the ashen-faced young farmer was looking out the window. "Such a blue sky now. Soon we'll be planting." The man's speech was slurred by his ulcerous tongue but Johann understood him.

"Yes, it should be a fine spring. Spring will be good for all of us. We all look forward to better times." He was relieved not to have to answer any questions about the incident. He gave the farmer a prescription for an opium paste that he could rub on his tongue, referred him to a surgeon at the hospital and wished him good luck with his crops. Other patients filled up the rest of the afternoon, with no sign of Graeber. He had left the clinic early.

When Johann got home that evening, he said nothing about Graeber's outburst to Helga or about his plan to join the Party. He sat for a while with Greta, then looked on as Paul-Adolf did his arithmetic homework. After supper, he saw the three private patients in his waiting room, read a medical journal and a newspaper, and went to bed earlier than usual.

The next day, despite the threat of rain, Johann walked to the policlinic. Before he could take off his overcoat, Graeber called him into his office. Johann stood in front of his desk. "You know, dear *Herr Doktor* Brenner, that we all are working under terrible conditions. Just the same, we try to do whatever we can. Our lives as *Deutsche* physicians"—

he stressed the last two words by saying them slowly, pursing his lips with each syllable and smiling broadly when he finished—"are full of responsibility at every moment. As we all know, the goddamned Jews are our misfortune." Here his voiced dropped to a rasping whisper. He stood up and came around his desk. Johann tried to step back but could not, given the size of the room.

"Yes, *Herr Doktor* Brenner, we German doctors must at all costs preserve our energies for our contribution to our *Vaterland*. Therefore," he paused, took a deep breath and put both his hand on Johann's shoulders, "therefore, my dear man, my dear colleague, I trust with certainty that I am not going to hear any more about that trivial event of yesterday." His voice trailed off, its tone rising ever so slightly, implying that it was Johann's unavoidable responsibility to answer in the affirmative. That any other answer would have been unpatriotic.

"You said that you were provoked, *Herr Doktor*. You lost your temper for a short while. These are tense times. Difficult. We must all keep trying to do whatever we can to deal with the circumstances at hand." Johann's voice trailed off, too, as he looked away from Graeber toward the floor. That was the most he dared say, despite his disgust. Then he added, "I do hope the mother will bring the child back for another examination. If he did have something worse than infected tonsils, we could have many more cases, a real crisis."

Graeber grew fidgety and wanted the conversation to end. "Sure, sure. No need to concern ourselves now. Diphtheria will show itself soon enough, at the rate we are going. We have a room full of patients waiting. She won't dare to complain anyway. Times have changed at last for our Jews. There are more than enough Jew-doctors to worry about that insolent brat and his ugly mother. Let's get to work. I'm glad you understand, Brenner."

What Johann understood most was that Graeber wanted no notations on his record. He also knew that Graeber had little to fear. The man was hoping to become a member of the Physicians' Ethical Review Board in Nuremberg; he prided himself on his contacts with both the mayor and with the Nazi Party. Johann worried that if he made a complaint, it might someday haunt him. On the other hand, if a complaint were lodged by the mother—not that she would, Johann thought, despite the provocation—Graeber would just say that she was "just another demanding Jewess with filthy children."

No matter how offensive he found Graeber's behavior, he knew he could not do anything about it. 'There's a lesson in this for me,' he thought. 'If I do join, I'll have to watch out for the likes of Graeber. There must be other, nobler physicians in the Party. Working with them,' he told himself, 'we will do great things for our *Volk* and our *Vaterland*. After all, these are difficult times, with much good work for everyone to do.'

CHAPTER THIRTEEN
In this Direction

Some will say that Greta's death did this to me, that it made me do terrible things. I even tried to say that to myself, for a while. Yes, I felt our daughter's suffering and I suffered, too, but my suffering was much different, much less than hers—and yours. Most of all, I felt sorry for myself, so powerless to do anything for her, so unable to accept this about myself. Instead, I sought to find power where I could, in order to believe in myself again. That may account for my joining the Party when I did and for my work with the Nazi Physicians' League in the Rhineland. But it does not excuse it. I was headed in this direction before Greta took ill, before we married, perhaps. I wanted to be a doctor. I wanted this power.

Johann thought about the children. About Greta and Karl Adolf. About the little boy with Graeber in the policlinic. The boys and girls in Koblenz. The girl in the policlinic after *Kristallnacht*. The children he saw on the ramp at Auschwitz. And especially about that harmless boy at Grafeneck. So many children. All of them now, harmed and lost.

*****

When Greta had to be taken to the hospital for the third time to clear her lungs, Johann did not suspect she would die there. He knew his daughter was not improving. She needed to be able to sit up, to take deeper breaths, to move around. Instead, she lay in her bed for months, unable to stand unless Helga held her up. She barely spoke now, quiet except for her wheezing. Her eyes were dull, her skin, waxy. She could only swallow thin soup. Still, he did not think she would die.

They visited her every evening in the ward. Other children looked worse, they thought. In the hallway, the parents greeted each other with little nods and faint smiles. In the ward, parents stood at each child's bed, stroking their son or daughter's hair, showing a favorite doll or toy, urging the child to eat. When Helga and Johann looked out the ward's window—the curtains were often drawn during the day, but in the evening, they were pulled back—it was out of despair. They were unable to look at what had become of their Greta.

Two children died the day before she did. Their beds were taken by others. He wondered if they, too, had been diagnosed with poliomyelitis, or with diphtheria. He had read that there were many cases of both in the north. There was a rise in scarlet fever cases, too. Surely, the hospital would not have put diphtheria or scarlet fever cases in with children who had been diagnosed with polio. He did not even tell Helga of his suspicion, but vowed he would ask about it. But never dared, fearing it would be worse to know and not be able to do anything.

Greta died shortly before dawn, six days after she was admitted. A messenger came from the hospital while they were having breakfast. Paul-Adolf opened the door and took the envelope he was handed back to his father. Helga knew what it said even before Johann opened it. She began to cry. Johann got up from the table, told her to get her coat, and telephoned the policlinic to say he would be coming in late. They all left their apartment together. Paul-Adolf went to school. Helga and Johann went to the children's ward at the hospital for the last time.

Later in the morning, they sat in silence on a park bench. After awhile, Johann got up, and walked toward the streetcar. Helga walked back to their apartment, afraid to start crying for fear she would not be able to stop.

When Johann got home in the evening, he told Helga he had stopped by the newspaper office, to put in the death announcement. "We'll see it in the morning."

"And the funeral?"

"Thursday afternoon, as you said."

"Good. Paul-Adolf, you will miss school on Thursday in the afternoon."

"Yes, *Mutti*."

No more was said about Greta over the next few days, when condolence cards began to arrive in the mail. Helga's sister, Erika, telephoned from Karlsruhe to say that their mother was ill and they would not be able to come to the funeral. Johann wrote a letter to his brother in America and his sister in Austria and included a clipping of the death notice.

On Thursday, when Johann came home at midday from the policlinic, Paul-Adolf was already there. "The principal said I should leave early, after Geography. There is a card from him on the table. *Mutti* has read it already."

Johann picked it up and put it down without reading it. He did not explore the rest of the day's mail, with its black-edged envelopes dominating the little stack. He looked away from Paul-Adolf and said, "There was nothing we could do for her, you know."

"Yes, *Vati*."

"Nothing. She was taken from us. There was nothing I could do."

"Yes, *Vati*."

Johann went into the bathroom to wash his hands. For the first time since Greta died, he began to sob, but caught himself in time. When he came out, Helga and Paul-Adolf were sitting at the table, waiting for him.

"I am going to Munich for three weeks in May," he said, as he began to eat. "I am interested in a series of special "Continuing Education" sessions sponsored by the Nazi Physicians' League. They might be informative." Helga gave him a stare.

"I have not joined yet, Helga."

"But you want to."

Johann continued, "The head of the League, *Doktor* Gerhard Wagner, will be ..."

"Do you know him, *Vati?*"

"Don't interrupt, Paul-Adolf. As I was saying, *Doktor* Wagner will be there for some of the sessions. No, I have not met him yet. But I hope to. He is the highest-ranking physician in the *Reich*. It will be an honor to meet him. And others from the Ministry, too. If possible, I shall come home on the weekends. But I don't know yet if this will be allowed."

"Is he related to Richard Wagner, the composer, *Vati?*"

"No. At least I don't think so." Johann raised his eyebrows at the thought that that his son would know anything about Richard Wagner. "I don't even know if he likes opera. But he has done good work for all of us doctors in the state's health system. The system is clearer now, and more in our favor. The Nazis have done good things. I hope they will do more for us, for all of Germany."

"Yes, *Vati.*"

Helga said nothing as she moved pieces of stewed meat and noodles around her plate.

"When you are away, I will be, too, you know, *Vati*. All our neighborhood's Hitler Youth groups, including mine, are marching and camping in May for four days in the Frankenwald. We all take a special train to Weissenbrunn. I think, it's Weissenbrunn..."

"Paul-Adolf," Helga said softly.

"We are there for four days and three nights. In tents, *Vati!* And we'll have compasses. And campfires."

"Paul-Adolf, please..." Helga said.

"And I will have my new uniform by then. I have been saving, and you said you would help..."

"Paul-Adolf! Stop, now." Helga was near tears. "Can't this all wait until after the funeral. Can't we think about something else. About Greta! For God's sake! Your sister…"

"Yes, *Mutti*."

"The boy's just excited, that's all," Johann said. "You can't blame him for looking forward to his trip. He's nearly twelve years old. Soon he'll be moving up to the *Jungvolk*, no longer a *Pimpf*." He smiled at Paul-Adolf.

"We'll have races and games and go hiking. We'll learn about our *Führer*. And we'll take an oath on a blood banner."

Helga looked down at her plate.

"You know the oath already, Paul-Adolf?" Johann asked.

"Yes, *Vati*. 'In the presence of this blood banner, which represents our *Führer*, I swear…' What's a "blood banner," *Vati?*"

"A blood banner is…"

Helga got up abruptly and went into the bedroom. They could hear her sobbing, long after they stopped talking. Finally, Johann stood up, looked at the mail without really noticing what was what, put it down, picked up that month's issue of *Goal and Path*, the journal of the Nazi Physicians' League, and sat down in his chair. Without looking at his son, he said, "Paul-Adolf, help your mother clear the table and do the dishes. We still have time before we have to go to the cemetery."

It was a sunny afternoon, warm for April. Helga wore only black, including a dense black veil and black silk stockings. She had bought them in January, as Greta began to weaken. For days afterwards, she was ashamed of herself for losing hope. They walked the short distance from the cemetery chapel to the open grave. Helga's sharp-edged shadow on the gravel path became a kind of physical extension of herself. When the pastor spoke, his voice a low, rough growl, she only saw his mouth move.

Paul-Adolf had insisted on wearing his "Hitler Youth" shirt and kerchief, with a black band around his sleeve that he made from one of his mother's ribbons. He looked around in vain, hoping to see some of his friends. His group leader and three boys in his squad had promised to attend the funeral, but perhaps had been delayed at school.

Johann stood as tall and still as he could, his weight on his good leg. His black suitcoat hung limp from his shoulders, the lapels stretching wide on either side. His black felt hat, usually worn only in winter, sat forward on his head, casting a shadow over his face that made it look almost as gray as his necktie. Helga received no reply when she asked him why he had brought his cane, after he had not used it for several years.

The sweet smell of moist earth filled the space all around them. When they reached the gravesite, Johann seemed to be squinting against the sunlight. In fact, he was holding back tears. As Greta's coffin was lowered into the ground, he tightened his grip on Helga's hand. She did not tell him that it hurt. One of the nurses from the policlinic and a few neighbors stood near the graveside. Their downstairs neighbor, *Frau* Bitzer, cried bitterly. It was quickly over. The flowers were already limp in the sunshine.

They walked from the cemetery to a nearby café. *Frau* Bitzer and her daughter accepted an invitation to join them, as did a few of the other neighbors. They sat at separate little tables in groups of three or four, murmuring and looking from time to time around the room, with faint smiles and nods, as though they had all been on a voyage together and now did not need to say anything to evoke their memories of it. Helga and Johann had tea. Paul-Adolf had hot chocolate and a slice of hazelnut *torte*.

After a few sips of his hot chocolate, Paul-Adolf asked, "What is an oath, *Vati?*"

"You know what an oath is."

"Yes, a promise. A special kind of promise, I know that. But why is it special?"

"You must keep an oath all your life. More important than any promise. It's not like saying, 'I promise that I will wash my face and comb my hair.' Or, 'I promise that I will study for this or that test.' It's much more serious than that."

"So, when I swear our *Jungvolk* oath, you know, in the Hitler Youth, with my comrades…" The boy sat up tall and looked straight ahead of him and raised his voice, "I will swear to 'devote all my energies and my strength to the savior of our country...'"

Others in the café looked around. Paul-Adolf gulped a deep breath, and continued, "'AdolfHitler!'" making the two names into one. He took another quick breath. "'Iamwillingandreadytogiveupmylifeforhim, sohelpmeGod....'"The words melted into one long sound, from 'Hitler' to 'God.' "When I swear that, *Vati,* I must keep this promise as long as I live?"

"That's what makes it an oath. But you must not say it so quickly. It is not a game, this oath, Paul-Adolf. An oath is not a game."

"Have you ever sworn an oath?"

"Yes. In medical school at the university, after the war, I swore an oath to do whatever I had to do to be a good doctor. It's called the Hippocratic Oath. Hippocrates was a Greek doctor in ancient times."

"That's all?"

"Well, of course, when your mother and I married, we promised to be faithful and good to each other for the rest of our lives. And before the war, when I was a soldier, I swore an oath to the *Kaiser*. If I join the Nazi Party after I go to Munich, I will swear an oath to Adolf Hitler."

Johann could tell that Helga was uncomfortable, but he continued, "When I was a boy, a friend and I..."Then he looked down into his cup of tea. For a moment, he was lost in the thoughts of his unfinished sentence. "When I was a boy..." He said, more quietly this time, then stopped, again looked out the window toward the cemetery, stirred his tea, and poured a bit more into his cup from the small steel pot on the table. His hand was trembling. The sugar bowl on the table was nearly empty, and he glanced toward the waiter. "We'll talk more about this some other time, Paul-Adolf. Drink your hot chocolate."

Nothing more was said about oaths or anything else. Helga looked down into her empty cup. Johann kept stirring his tea. When Paul-Adolf finished his *torte*, he wished that he had ordered the chocolate cake with whipped cream instead.

*****

In May, Johann attended the conference in Munich. The lectures were predictable, boring. With that came a reassuring certainty, an insistent, convincing authority. No one expressed any doubts or concerns. If the diatribes against the Jews and racial contamination served as a reminder that there was still work to be done, no one doubted that German science would find solutions to every problem and show the way for the *Volk*'s health and happiness.

After the lectures, the assembled physicians and Party officials preferred to discuss their private interests and passions: fine food; wines; the past ski season; what to expect from the next year's Olympics in Berlin; the mild, warm spring; the newest automobiles, especially the Mercedes; motor-car racing; and the triumph of German thoroughbred horses. The same conversations could be heard that spring across the *Vaterland* over cocktails in luxury resorts and in the gardens of elegant suburban villas.

Johann listened more than he spoke, but felt welcome with whatever group he joined. 'What a change from just a few years ago,' he thought, when the outlook for the medical profession and for Germany was so filled with gloom. And now, directly or indirectly, we German physicians are responsible for this wonderful turn of events! Even if we don't design automobiles, breed horses, craft elegant wines, and win the medals in Berlin, at least we provide the medical care that supports these triumphs!' He ate and slept well. Away from Nuremberg and its disappointments, he relaxed. He felt appreciated, an equal among worthy individuals.

The lecture of an anthropology professor from Berlin's Kaiser Wilhelm Institute, especially interested Johann. Speaking about preventive medicine and eugenics, *Doktor* Wolfgang Abel argued that, in order to protect the vitality of the *Volk* from any contamination of its "life-giving blood, from which all strength and honor flowed," all foreign elements must be purged. "Yet," he said, raising his finger above his head, "in the *Rhineland*, at the end of the World War, the French, British, Belgians and Americans monstrously and deliberately infected our *Volk*'s life-blood. The unjust terms of the armistice let them station troops on German soil. And so they sent in dark-skinned men from their colonies, or, in the case of America, black men who had been slaves. The dangers to German civilization, to civilization itself, cannot be exaggerated!"

Johann joined his fellow doctors in loud agreement. Shouts of "Unacceptable!" "Outrageous!" "Criminal!" rose above the applause.

Abel continued in his clinical, dispassionate tone. "This unspeakable assault on the *Volk* inevitably meant rape, misery and suffering to Germany's women and to the nation's honor. Now, the misbegotten children—hundreds, if not thousands of children—of those black rapists are themselves ripening sexually. Could anyone doubt that they would likely"—here he dramatically corrected himself, his voice rising—"no, they would *certainly* further the mongrelization and corruption of German purity? Could anyone doubt that this needs to be stopped as soon as possible?"

More angry shouts and applause.

Abel then described the cure: a simple medical procedure would avert the *Volk*'s contamination and decay—sterilization! If it were not undertaken, civilization would succumb to savagery. "Sterilization is the only recourse," he argued, since no one else wanted these "*Rhineland* bastards," calling them what the Nazis and the right-wing press had for years.

Johann applauded loudly. He stood up to state his wholehearted support for such policy. His face was flushed, his voice quivered at first, but after he cleared his throat, he filled the room with his words: "This is a proper use of our skills, gentlemen. We are being called upon to serve our people in the most important way—to protect our *Volk*'s future from any contamination. This is good medicine." When he sat down to a general hum of assent from the audience, he was pleased with himself.

Later, he brought up the topic with his dinner companions. "Sterilization is for the good of the *Volk*. We must do it. Other nations, America, for one, are ahead of us on this. They have been doing such things for years to their blacks and imbeciles. If we delay, we only make the problem worse."

Between mouthfuls of soup, his companions nodded. No one challenged Abel's assumptions. Some seemed bored by the obviousness of the proposal. Johann persisted: "Even if these young bastards show German sentiments and declare their loyalty to the *Volk* and the Party—and I suppose that might be true for a clever few—they cannot be allowed to breed. If they want to show their loyalty, let them make this small sacrifice." More nods. "Sterilization is essential, if we are to survive," he said, gesturing with his spoon and surprising himself with his outspokenness.

"Pardon me, *Herr Doktor*," one of the men at the table said, looking at Johann. "Are you one of us? Are you a member of our Party? I do not see any indication of it: you are not in uniform; no insignia; no swastika pin in your lapel."

Johann faltered. "Well, no, not yet," he said. Then, louder, "When I get back to Nuremberg. I have already signed up for the swearing-in ceremony."

"Good then. Very good! *Heil Hitler!*"

All stood up and raised their hands in the salute. Johann, flushed with his self-satisfaction, raised his hand high. But there was no extended conversation on the matter. A waiter came over and removed their soup bowls. Another refilled their wine glasses. A third brought them their main course. The conversation turned to rock climbing in the Austrian Alps: "Mark my words, one of our boys will conquer the Eiger!" a doctor exclaimed. Johann concentrated on his *sauerbraten*.

The next day, he was approached by Abel himself. "Thank you for your support yesterday at my presentation, *Herr Doktor*."

"I am honored, *Herr Professor Doktor* Abel."

"Are you interested in a conversation later today about my topic? Quite private. Just a few physicians and a government official."

"Why yes! Of course!"

He sat down a few hours later with Abel and four others, one of whom introduced himself as an officer from the *Reich*'s Ministry of Health. Abel handed them each a copy of an article he had written earlier that year about "morphology and anthropology." Johann discreetly thumbed through it while the others were talking, pausing over a series of photographs of children, arranged in rows, filling the page. The caption said they were born to European and Moroccan parents and to European and VietNamese parents. Each child was shown in a full-face and a profile image. They might have been Greta and Paul-Adolf, but with darker eyes and skin, and thicker, darker hair. Johann found them innocent, even wholesome looking. A little girl, probably not much older in her photo than Greta when she died, had an open, trusting face. A curly-haired boy, about the same age as Paul-Adolf, wore a sailor's jersey with a striped collar draped backward over his small shoulders. He looked tired, not bestial. Another dark-skinned boy looked surprised. All of them appeared to be clean. Healthy. But none had blond hair or blue eyes or fair skin. Therefore, all were specimens of what Abel described as a lethal contamination.

"So, you are in agreement, then, that it is our responsibility, our duty, to take this step, gentlemen?"

Johann looked up from the pamphlet to see that the officer from the Ministry of Health was speaking now. Not sure what step was being referred to, he heard himself say, "Yes!" along with the others.

"Good, then please give me your addresses and signatures on this form. Soon, within a month, you will receive specific information about what we are asking you to do."

One of the men asked if it was legal. The officer snorted. "Of course. The mother of the child—or, if necessary, the mother's husband, who has adopted the child—yes, it has sometimes happened and the courts have had no recourse but to honor the procedure." He paused to look at Professor Abel, and continued, "The mother, as I say, or the adoptive father will have given permission. Our authorities will have seen to that. If not, the child's mother or the adoptive father, or both, would be sent for 're-education'" Seeing a question on Johann's face, he added, "To a concentration camp, to be blunt. They will have been warned that such a measure is likely, if there is any hesitation on their part. So, their ultimate consent to the procedure is certain. It will be quite legal. We have had our counsel check it out thoroughly."

Now Johann was listening closely. Abel looked bored. The officer thumbed through some notes before saying, "This task will require at least four, perhaps five days away from your normal responsibilities, gentlemen. In mid-June, most likely. No later than the last week of June. We will conduct the procedures in the *Rhineland*, probably in Wiesbaden or Ludwigshafen or Koblenz. The site or sites have not been determined yet. You will be compensated for your travel and accommodations, and receive payment in accord with the health insurance fees, of course." He paused, looked at each man sitting around the table, lowered his voice, and hunched forward. "I need not tell you, gentlemen, that this matter must remain in strictest confidence. Strictest confidence!" He paused again. "The foreign press would no doubt use it to stir up some nonsense. I will now inform my superiors of our decision. As we all agree, this is in the best interests of our *Volk*. Thank you."

They all nodded. There were no questions. When the officer rose to his feet, so did they, stretching their right arms upward: "*Heil Hitler!*"

*****

As soon as he returned to Nuremberg, Johann applied for membership in the Nazi Party without telling Helga. Three days later, he reported to the Party's headquarters in the city to take the oath. There were eight others: a young architect, a middle-aged engineer, another physician whom Johann had met but whose name he could not recall, and four others whom he did not know. Johann had listed Helga on the application form as the witness who would accompany him. At the swearing in ceremony, he lied and said she was ill.

Coincidentally, among the others' witnesses was Graeber, who had come to stand up for the architect, his brother's youngest son. Johann was startled to see his superior. The senior physician approached him with a smirk, reached out to touch the shiny lapel pin on his coat, and winked. Johann could tell that Graeber had been drinking. He avoided the socializing after the ceremony and left immediately, saying that he needed to go home to be with his wife.

Helga thought he had been making a house call. She noticed the lapel pin as soon as he came home, stared at him for a moment, and then turned away. He waited until they were in bed and had switched off the light to tell her what he had done. She still said nothing. After a while, he could tell that she had fallen asleep.

About two weeks later, Helga signed for a confidential letter from the *Reich*'s Ministry of Health. She knew better than to ask what it was about. She had given up asking him about his professional interests, and now about politics. Nor had she ever looked into his files. It was not that she was disinterested, or because she believed him when he told her that she should leave such matters to him. She merely was unwilling to challenge him anymore. Partly, she felt discouraged since Greta's illness and death. Partly, she knew she could not prevent him from doing what he wanted to do. At least, she told herself, he seemed more at ease, more content than he had been since their daughter had fallen ill.

He read the letter after dinner and put it in his briefcase without comment. It will be a good experience, he thought. He had liked what he saw of Koblenz during boot camp and welcomed the chance to explore it. June would be lovely in the *Rhineland*.

But his duties were demanding. On the first day, at a long table with another physician and a member of the Ministry of Health, he sat reviewing a stack of data sheets about children between the ages of fourteen and seventeen. Each child was "a descendent of the former colored Allied occupation forces" with "corresponding anthropological characteristics. Therefore," as the form put it, the child was "to be sterilized." Johann attested to the necessity of the action with his signature on each form, below those of another doctor and a Ministry representative's. The forms soon blurred together, his signature reduced to a few quick strokes of his pen.

Over the next three days, Johann was one of several teams of physicians performing the procedures: vasectomies for the boys; tubal ligations for the girls. He instructed the attending nurse to drape each child so that he would not see its face, nor it his. He turned to the wall as each one was wheeled in and out of the room. After the first few, it became routine. He preferred doing the boys, but he could not have said why. There were forty the first day.

In the evenings, the doctors gathered to drink the tangy-sweet Mosel Riesling and stroll along the Rhine. Johann stayed up late each night, sitting on a bench on the riverfront, watching the barges pass by. He was back in Nuremberg long before many of the children were deemed well enough to be discharged from the hospital.

*****

One day that same June, Philipp came home early from the policlinic. He heard Christine coming up the stairs and hurried to finish setting the table for their supper. She began talking even before she closed the door behind her.

"Walking to work this morning, I saw something that would have sickened you, too. In front of the *Volksschule*, a group of little girls, seven years old, eight at the most, pigtails, pretty dresses, sweet little girls. Marching in the street past their teachers. All of them, teachers and little girls alike, arms stiff and high, shouting *"Heil Hitler!"* All of them, saluting our dear *Führer*. All that was missing was the goose-step!"

He finished slicing the end of a loaf of bread and put it on the table. "I'm not surprised," he said. "The posters are everywhere: 'You belong to the *Führer!*' Posters for the Hitler Youth and the League of German Girls on every street corner. And we both know that teachers are in thick with the Nazis. That was so even before Hitler took power."

"Yes, but to see those sweet little girls with my own eyes. Marching like soldiers. Saluting."

"The boys, too," he said. "For every girl, there's a boy doing the same thing."

"I can't understand it. The teachers. Encouraging them! For what?"

"We know for what. For the fantasies of our *Führer*. For the glory of our *Vaterland*. For a greater Germany. Which means, for war." He put a plate of cheese and wurst next to the bread.

She washed her hands and sat down. "The Nazis believe they own those children. Their parents, even if they wanted to stop it, are powerless. That's why, Philipp."

"That's why what?"

"Why I don't want to have any children. Not as long as the Nazis hold power."

"But our child would not be like that."

"How can you be so sure? Since you refuse to leave Germany, our child will grow up here. The Nazis are in power. And our child will be half-Jewish. Please be realistic. Our child will be hated. Or it will hate us. Or both! I don't want to bring a child into such a world. We could have a little girl the same age as those I saw this morning. What would you do when she shouted '*Heil Hitler!*' or called you a 'dirty Jew'?"

"You're over-reacting." He smeared butter on a piece of bread and put it down on his plate. His bitterness at their long-standing argument rose in his throat. "You don't want to have children. You never wanted to have children. And now you have found this excuse."

"You don't understand," she said. "You've never understood. We live on a knife's edge here. It was bad enough before the Nazis were in power. You used to say so all the time. Now it's ten times worse. Do you want our child to suffer all this? We won't be able to protect it twenty-four hours a day."

"Yes, things are bad. And yes, I don't like it. But this will pass. You'll see. And then it will be too late for us to have children. Too late."

"We've gone over this before. Who's going to take care of the child? I have to work all day. You're at the policlinic. Our parents are dead. No one will take care of the child. Be realistic for a change."

"I don't want to talk about it," he said, pushing his chair back from the table. "I'll just say this. After your second miscarriage, you decided you couldn't get pregnant. And you haven't. Even though the doctor said there would be no problem. So that's where the matter ends. I've resigned myself to it, much as I don't like it."

"Now don't blame me. You have no right to blame me. You are up there in the clouds most of the time, and I am the one who has to deal with what's going on down here. Don't you dare complain to me about this. Don't!"

"I won't. It doesn't do any good. Let's just drop it." He reached for another slice of bread.

She tried to find a calmer voice. "We still can leave Germany, Philipp. So many are leaving now. Nothing will be the same, anyway, once everyone leaves."

"I've told you over and over. I will not leave. I have done nothing wrong. I love my country. I have nothing to feel guilty about. I just don't know what I should do. I only hope that our *Volk* will recognize this crazy-headed regime for what it is. It just has to."

"The *Volk* has too little experience in such things, Philipp. You've said so, yourself. That may be why we have Hitler in the first place. How do you expect the *Volk* to see the light without being blinded for awhile?"

"I really don't know. I just hope."

She tried to change the subject. "Do you have any private patients this evening?"

"I did, until *Frau* Pickelheim cancelled. I know they cancel because I am Jewish. And we used to be invited out more. Now, if we invite people here, they find all kinds of reasons to decline."

"I've invited the Bruggers three times now and they've called to say 'no' at the last minute each time. The last time I talked with Erika Brugger—at the flower market—she couldn't wait for me to finish a sentence before she said she had to go. Two secretaries I used to talk to at work now avoid me and have planted little swastika flags on their desks. The butcher is particularly strange."

"Strange? How?"

"He's more interested in staring at me than serving me." Before he could reply, she said, "We should leave, Philipp."

He just looked at her. "I meant to tell you. Benjamin and Martha Gerschenkron are leaving next month for Sweden. Other Jewish doctors I know, too." He paused and thought about the postcard from Luise that was delivered that morning: *'From prison to Palestine. Lebewohl! L.'* "But leaving is not the answer. Then the Nazis get what they want."

"So you say, Lippi. I hope you're right. I have a bad feeling about this, but we'll stay as long as it takes."

"It won't be easy," he said. "It won't be easy for anyone."

That evening he wrote in his journal: "*I must not lose hope. We shall need all the energy we have to overcome this disease. I believe its sheer monstrosity will be its own undoing—like a boil that erupts, as the body cleanses itself. It will be painful. But it should not take much longer.*"

*****

On the surface over the next few years, Berlin thrived. Its "something-for-everyone" openness had ended, but the sidewalks and shops were still full. The rich shopped for designer clothes and rare wines, ate in elegant restaurants, greeted each other from their box seats at the opera and the concert halls.

"Piano-movers are doing a big business now," Philipp said, putting down the morning newspaper.

"What do you mean?"

"Jews are leaving. They can't take their pianos. Or much else. A Bösendorfer grand is going for a tenth of what it's worth. Art, furniture, rare books, family heirlooms, all dirt cheap. Jewelry, whatever price they can get. Our dear, noble, honest Aryans are grabbing it all up. 'Aryanizing' it. For *pfennige*. Contemptible! We see these Aryans in the newsreels, sunning themselves at the Nordsee or playing tennis in their crisp white trousers and pleated skirts. Not a hair out of place, looking sleek and satisfied. Contemptible."

"Are you still so sure you don't want to leave?" she asked.

"You said you wouldn't ask again. And the answer is still 'no.' Never. Is there more coffee?"

She poured him a cup, kissed him and got her coat. "I'm going to the baker's."

He watched her walk toward the door, smiled when she turned to look at him, and went back to the newspaper. Employment was rising. Factories had full shifts. And the Nazis have given themselves credit for everything, he thought: the *Autobahn*, the *Volkswagen*, the abundance in the shops, lower crime, even the good weather! Our little Austrian has become a saint. Is no one thinking how we bought this prosperity? But the *Volk* is comfortable, so why think? He shook his head and remembered the newsreel narrator's comment about the new prosperity. "No one needs to know any more!" How will it all end?

Despite his fears, he could not deny that people seemed happier. The city's pace, always quick, was now quicker, as though life had to be lived in march tempo. The streets pulsed with the Nazis' self-confidence. Christine told him about the frequent parades she saw from her office window, how the crowds cheered, how the people scurried to pick up the candy thrown at their feet.

She tried to cheer him up, but was increasingly impatient with his constant discontent. "If you don't like things the way they are, well, do something. Talking about it won't make a difference."

He agreed and said he would. But nothing changed. She tried not to mention things that distressed him, but could not avoid telling him what she saw each day. When he sulked, he would not say anything for a day or two, leaving her to feel guilty because of his silence.

On a hot July Sunday, they took the streetcar for a picnic and swim at *Wannsee*. Laughter and snatches of gypsy violin music drifted over from the villas on either side of the small public beach. They arrived just as a young couple with twin girls ran down to the water, splashing each other with delight.

Philipp held his hand to shield his eyes from the sun. "We'll be rid of our uniformed monkeys by Christmas, I predict. Everyone will have seen through them by then."

"Forget about that now, please," she said. "Look at those little twins." Two sun-tanned girls, their pigtails dripping water down their backs, squealed with joy as their father picked them up, one under each arm, and pretended to toss them further off shore. Christine smiled and threw her head back and closed her eyes. The sun reflected off her high forehead and her hair.

He watched the children and smiled, too. After a long pause, he said, "You're right. I should just enjoy the day. There's nothing I can do. Things will take their course. The new owners of these villas eventually will have to give them back. The law...,"

"*Ja*," she said again, interrupting him, hoping to make him stop by agreeing with him. She lay back on their blanket and pretended to go to sleep, her hand in his.

He knew he had said enough. "Nothing I can do," he trailed off. "Nothing." He got up quietly and walked down to the water. It was surprisingly warm and made soft lapping sounds at his feet. Later they swam together. The twins were fighting over a ball and had begun to cry, oblivious to their father's threats to take them home if they didn't stop. After their picnic, it began to cloud over.

Philipp looked toward one of the villas where a party was underway. "Must be nice to live here, even in winter. Fresh air and a beautiful view for those who need it least."

In September, she knit him a sweater for his birthday. He wore it and nothing else to bed that night and they laughed longer than they had for a long time. Every weekend for the rest of the fall, even in the rain, they took long, silent walks in the woods. He did not complain for weeks. She wondered if he was taking some drug to calm himself. When an early snowstorm came in November, they joined a bunch of children in the park lobbing snowballs at each other. They made love that night for the first time in a month.

At Christmas time, they walked with the throngs through the out-door market set up in *Alexanderplatz*, the city's hub. Philipp stared at the electrified swastika mounted on the towering fir tree in the center of the square.

"I wonder what they'd say to that in Munich or Augsburg?"

"For all we know, they have the same," Christine replied.

They walked from booth to booth, looking at holiday ornaments and trinkets, enjoying the festive mood and each other's company. All around them, shoppers bustled about. Children delighted in the lights and hoped-for treasures. Clerks grinned like so many mechanical dolls and wished everyone *"Ein frohes Fest!"* Philipp bought a cluster of straw stars. "We can hang these in the window," he said, laughing. "In case a neighbor—or some Party hack—thinks we don't have the right holiday spirit." Christine forced a smile.

Christmas was a hard time for her, since they didn't decorate their apartment or celebrate the holiday. Although she had abandoned her religious beliefs before she married, she missed the magic of Christmas Eve, of singing carols with her family, of the candles on the tree, of her favorite ornaments sparkling. She missed her mother's cookies, especially the buttery *Ausstecherle* cut in the shape of stars, the smell of oranges being peeled, and her father's teasing about what present the Christ Child might bring. He tried to understand and help her through the season, but it was never quite right.

On their way back to their apartment, they noticed a knot of people at the corner of a busy intersection. High-ranking Nazis were collecting coins for "the needy."

"Let's not go over there," Christine said and kept on walking.

He began to cross over anyway. "Why not? I want to get a closer look at the saviors of the *Vaterland*." He waited for a car to turn the corner and then caught her hand as she stood beside him. They went to the back of the line. It moved quickly. When they got closer, Philipp nudged Christine and whispered, "Look at that. It's little Goebbels himself. The dwarf at Christmas time." She squeezed his hand tightly and shushed him.

The Propaganda Minister was smiling and bantering with the people in line. When the woman in front of them replied to something he said with a derisive cackle, his expression changed instantly. "What are you laughing at?" he asked, gesturing with his head to a nearby *Gestapo* thug who began walking alongside her. Philipp and Christine put a coin in the box, and Goebbels instantly flashed his smile again.

After they walked a few paces further, Philipp said, "We'll see this farce in the next newsreel."

Although it was winter, there was new construction everywhere. Every day on his walk to the policlinic, Philipp joined other Berliners gaping at the sites with pride and enthusiasm. He could not deny being impressed by the new, massive buildings, especially by their thick, solid walls. He marveled at how smoothly traffic flowed. How Berliners were coming and going with more purpose and order than he had seen for years.

In the spring, they admired how the parks and public gardens were groomed to postcard perfection. Charlottenburg glowed. They mimicked the poses of the newly erected statues of heroic, larger than life Nordic-featured men and women, their jaws set, their shoulders broad, faced the rising or setting sun. "The *Volk* has new gods now," he said, his voice tinged with bitterness.

Philipp knew that the city's revival was uneven. In the corners and shadows of this hothouse, he thought he heard angry whispers. I am not alone, he kept telling himself. Some of us are still dreaming of a different world. Occasionally, he heard a husky, sarcastic laugh coming out of a doorway, or a derisive comment shouted at the back of an alley and his spirits rose. He knew that beer must still be flowing in the city's working class districts, in Wedding and Kreuznach, wherever Berliners could escape from cramped, cold, fourth-floor flats. That raucous singing in the taverns Friday and Saturday nights sometimes gave way to fights and arrests with politics as the cause. Walking through a park, he watched cautious friends sitting on an isolated bench wait until he passed before they spoke. He marveled at an old woman berating a uniformed SS man who refused to answer her questions. These glimpses of dissent came briefly to him, small shafts of light in a dense forest. He clenched his fist and said "*Ja!*" under his breath.

Philipp understood why few could resist the regime's logic or see the cage that had been built around them. He knew that many 'non-Aryans' were willing to support the Nazis. He might have been one himself, if he hadn't felt their sting in his professional life and the barriers they created for him. Their diatribes against Jews were simply absurd. His belief in scientific racism had weakened, but intellectually made some sense. Eugenics' emphasis on public health, hygiene and nutrition still appealed to him. He even agreed that compulsory sterilizations were appropriate for the criminally insane, while voluntary sterilizations should be encouraged by the state for the mentally ill, alcoholics and the destitute.

"The Nazis have misused science, blurred its edges. Taken what they want and disparaged what they don't. Misuse and abuse is their philosophy," he was wont to think aloud in the safety of his apartment. It was a habit he tried in vain to break. He knew Christine was tired of hearing him declaim on the subject, but he could not stop himself.

"No question but that there are differences among our species. Not only observable differences, like skin color, hair texture, shape of the eye. But we can measure other differences, too," he would say, varying the way he phrased it but always coming to the same point. "And the state has a responsibility to protect its citizens from corrupting influences. The Nazis see this with cigarettes, for example."

She knew when to begin pretending that she was listening, nodding here and there while he went on.

"Hematologists certainly will find more distinguishing characteristics in blood as they develop more precise filters and techniques. Neuroscientists will find differences in the way our nervous systems work. Muscle tension, reflexes, you know. The evidence about cigarettes and cancer incontrovertible. Public health is crucial. Learning about the influence of the environment on biology, that's the road to...."

"Yes, maybe," she said, not paying much attention.

"So far, they are only concentrating on blood. Understandable. But blood is not the only thing that is important. In any case, none of the physical aspects of the body is of ultimate importance. That's where the Nazis have it all wrong. They underestimate the shaping effects of culture, of tradition and history. Not flesh, but what the old scientists called spirit. Spirit. Personality. Formed by culture. Not just blood. Raise a German baby in China and it'll grow up Chinese."

She nodded, but couldn't resist adding, "Well, its eyes and skin will..."

"Of course, they'll be German," he jumped in. "But the child will speak Chinese, eat with chopsticks, like food you and I would never eat. If it's a boy, his parents will have him grow a pigtail. A girl will do things a German girl, a modern girl, would never do. The child will be Chinese. The difference between that child and a racial Chinese is not important. In spirit the child will be Chinese."

"What does all this matter?" She would say. "The Nazis are in power."

Philipp could only give one answer: "But they're wrong."

"They are in power," she repeated, and the conversation usually stopped. He kept thinking during the silence. The most important thing now is blood. What the Nazis alone decide is "pure" or "impure" blood. Blood for them determines who's good and who's evil. Blood separates the virtuous from the corrupt. Whether it's so or not. It's what Hitler and Goebbels say that matters now. How stupid! How outrageous!

He kept himself occupied with a reading program he devised for himself. He tried to let the seasons focus his life. To find each one's delights, especially when he knew his mood was affecting Christine. On his walks in the fall, he studied how the trees lost their leaves and revealed their essential forms. In the winter, how each fresh snowfall hid the city's grime. He looked forward to spring's longer days and warm breezes, to the exotic flowers for sale on the street corners. He hoped that spring would make him happy, but knew that it made many of his patients anxious and irritable. He felt he was sinking into a despair that was longer than the season.

He had to do something. But what? He tried writing an article on the mental health of working-class children in a time of economic stress, but gave up after several false starts. The "Laws for the Protection of German Blood and Honor," decreed in 1935, distressed him in the abstract, but were of little consequence to him personally. His marriage to Christine, which predated the laws banning sexual relations between Aryans and Jews, meant that they were still legally married.

When Jews lost the right to vote, he could only laugh because there was no one he would have voted for anyway. And when all Jewish civil servants were placed on leave or forced to retire, he felt sorry for them, but had to agree that there were more than enough civil servants. Since he refused to apply for a passport, he was not distressed by the thought that Jews would soon not be allowed to get one. The Nazis will think of more nuisances, he knew, but he would deal with them when he had to. It won't be too long now, he kept telling himself, until the *Volk* comes to its senses and chases the Nazis back into the sewers from which they came.

He still saw more reason to hide and to hope than to flee or fight. He accommodated himself to the law that required him to bow and lift his hat whenever a uniformed Nazi strode by. 'I just won't wear a hat and I'll change direction when a monkey comes towards me.' Walking along *Unter den Linden* or *Kurfürstendamm*, he stayed close to the curb, in case someone told him to walk in the gutter. When that happened, he tugged on Christine's arm and they both stepped into the street, as though they were going to cross. If a park bench said, "No Jews," he chose not to sit down. 'I don't eat kosher, so why do I care if the Nazis ban kosher ritual. I don't read Jewish newspapers, so that's not a problem either.'

Still, all this irritated him. And still, he did nothing more than grumble. 'I am a German first, and then a Jew,' he told himself with each insult. 'Not the other way around.' To protect himself, he did not hide his disdain for Berlin's teeming population of newly arrived, Eastern European Jews. 'They are Jews without a country. But I am a German. This is my *Vaterland*.' He knew they deserved pity, having escaped the edge of a Slavic sword only to fall upon a sharper Nazi one, but they made him uncomfortable. He avoided going on house calls into the *Scheunenviertel* whenever he could, protesting that he didn't understand their Yiddish. Christine asked him how it could be that different from the Yiddish he knew, but his only answer was, "They don't follow my advice, only what they hear from their rabbi. Superstitious fools, all of them. They rub chicken fat on their chest to treat tuberculosis." When the Nazis cleared out *Grenadierstraße* after the *Reichstag* burned down, he had felt sympathetic for a while, but after a day or two he gave the Jews there no further thought. At one point he caught himself thinking, 'The Nazis should just send them back where they came from,' but then realized, if they actually did that, they would not be gentle in the process.

More than anything else, he was rankled by the decree that prohibited Jewish doctors from treating Aryans, and his dismissal from the
policlinic. 'How criminal,' he thought, 'here in my own country, surrounded by people no different from myself, someone has invented a
new label, "Aryan," that makes them pure and me filthy! Do these good
Aryans not want a good doctor, the best doctor they could possibly find?
Can they actually believe that I am somehow incompetent just because
of my ancestry? Imagine a non-Aryan mechanic, able to repair a classic
Mercedes, but the owner would rather let it rust!'

Some of his private patients telephoned and tried to apologize.

"You must understand, *Herr Doktor* Stein. I don't want to make any
trouble. My little Peter likes to come to you." Or, "My Dora tells me she
likes you. You have been good to the children. But my husband says it
is the law. We are going to see *Doktor* Zimmer from now on. Down the
street from you. Maybe you know him?"

"Of course," he would say. "Of course. I do understand. *Herr Doktor*
Zimmer is a fine doctor. Thank you for calling."

At least they telephoned. Most never said anything. From one week
to the next, no one came. Even his few private Jewish patients drifted
away, as they left Germany.

He knew he would have to find a position that brought in some
income. Even more important, he could not imagine himself without
a daily professional responsibility. That ate at him more than any of the
ludicrous inconveniences concocted by the regime. So, after some weeks
of seeing Christine off each morning and then drinking several cups of
coffee, listening to radio turned low, interrupted now and then by a ring
of the door-bell by someone hoping for emergency medical attention,
Philipp tried to stop feeling sorry for himself and sought out work. His
only choice was the Jewish Community Hospital, on the *Iranischestraße*
in Wedding, about an hour's walk from their apartment. After the Nazi
attacks on the *Scheunenviertel*, Wedding was the only relatively safe place
in a cauldron of intensifying despair for Berlin's remaining Jews.

Long before he applied for a position there, he had heard about
the hospital's director, Walter Lustig. In the logic of the regime, since

Jewish doctors could only treat Jewish patients, there had to be a Jewish hospital. Philipp had heard that Lustig, reportedly a convert to Christianity and with close connections to the medical division of the city's police force before the Nazis came to power, had the contacts to be the hospital's director. He was a published authority on hospital administration, if not now a practicing physician. Two doctoral degrees. That must have impressed at least some Nazis. How it happened that the hospital continued to function he could only wonder. But function it did. It even appeared serene: a large, solid group of buildings surrounded by a small garden, set back from the street, a kind of oasis among the tenement buildings and factories.

A week after he completed the application papers, he received a letter from Lustig inviting him to an interview.

Lustig stood up and stepped from behind his desk to greet him. Philipp was startled to see how short he was.

"Sit down, please, *Herr Doktor* Stein."

Philipp thought that the director's chair must have several cushions or be up on a platform, because now he had to look up at him. Lustig's desk was large, with stacks of papers on either side. A metal stand holding an array of rubber stamps and three inkpads—black, blue and red—perched near the edge. Books lined the shelves behind him.

"Your application is in order. Good background. Good career progress, given the circumstances." Here Lustig broke into a broad grin. "Left Freiburg for Augsburg, and then moved to Berlin, I see. Restless, were you?" Without waiting for an answer, he said, "I've never been to Augsburg. Lovely city, I am told."

"My wife grew up there."

"Ah. I see from your application that your wife's name is Christine."

"Yes."

Philipp wondered which way the conversation was going to turn. Lustig looked out the window, toward nothing in particular. Philipp expected to talk about his education, his experience, and specializations. He was prepared to make some concessions, depending on what Lustig offered, he would even have been willing to work as an assistant physician.

"Christine… eh? What kind of Jewish name is that?" the director asked, leaning forward on his elbows.

"It is not a Jewish name. She's not Jewish."

"Ah. I see. Not Jewish." Lustig now rocked back in his chair and looked up at the ceiling. Philipp thought he was suppressing a smile. "Not to worry, Stein. My wife is not Jewish either. My father used to tell me, 'It's just as easy to fall in love with a rich girl as a poor girl.' But I prefer to say, 'It's just as easy to fall in love with a *schickse* as a Jewish girl.' It always pays to know which way the wind is blowing. Yes?" And without looking at Philipp, he continued, "I'm glad you agree." He straightened Philipp's application papers.

Philipp said nothing. He wanted this position. He wanted to work. He did not want to leave Berlin, even if he had someplace to go.

"You have neglected to state your other name, *Herr Doktor* Stein!"

"Excuse me?"

"Your other name, you know. We will all soon be called 'Israel,' as far as the authorities are concerned. And our Jewish mothers and sisters and wives—our Jewish wives, that is—all will be named 'Sarah.' Mark my words, the Nazis will decree that, sooner or later."

Philipp again said nothing. Lustig smiled down at the papers before him.

"My parents were cleverer than yours, Stein." Lustig laughed again out loud.

"I beg your pardon."

"My parents were cleverer. They had me baptized when I was a baby. I'm not entirely safe, but safer than you. And I know important people. You were never baptized, I notice. Too bad! You will regret that someday."

Philipp thought of leaving and began to stand up. "With your permission, *Herr Doktor Doktor* Lustig."

"Sit down, Stein. I think we understand each other. We have to, don't we? We need each other now. I can use you. More patients, more desperate patients, given the times we live in. And you need me. You want to work. I need someone like you. For night duty, six nights a week. Two others—useful, good doctors, Jews, of course; one is aged and seems infirm of late, but we will not be letting him go—two others, as I say, and you will staff the emergency room, with rotations to the ward. Privileges in the canteen, of course. Two cups of coffee per night, included. Pay for your own gowns. A small fee for supplies. You'll have a locker with a key, if you wish. Starting next Monday evening. Want to think it over?" Lustig smiled again.

"No. I will start Monday."

"Good. My secretary will provide you with some details before you leave. You have made a good decision."

Philipp stood to leave, half-expecting Lustig to exclaim, *"Heil Hitler!"* Instead, the hospital director merely said, "I would like to meet your Christine sometime. Yes? They say the girls in Augsburg are very pretty." Philipp pretended to not hear him, said his *"Auf Wiedersehen!"* and closed the door behind him. The secretary gave him some papers with a curt smile. Walking home—Jews were no longer allowed to ride the streetcars or the subway trains—Philipp told himself that he would never introduce Christine to his new boss.

That evening, when she asked him how the interview went, he said only, "The head physician is, well...." He was at a loss for words. "Well, let's just say that his name is 'Lustig.'"

"He's joyful?"

"Not really. 'Happy with himself' is more like it. A bit sinister. He has two doctoral degrees. And so he wants to be addressed, *Herr Doktor Doktor!* Absurd!" He did not want to tell her too much of what he was thinking.

"Why 'sinister'?"

"Well, cunning, I suppose, would be it. He has a streak of something slippery, something selfish that irritates me. I am only glad I won't have to work with him each day. I am assigned to the night shift. Six nights per week. That means he and I won't see each other much. It also means I won't see you."

"And you are glad about that, aren't you?" She smiled, the same wide, glowing smile he remembered from their first meeting in Freiburg, in what seemed like a different world, so long ago.

"Yes, I've been skipping around here all day, shouting with glee!" He grabbed her by the waist and they laughed together.

"You scamp!" She held him close and buried her head on his chest. His laughter echoed in her ear and blended with hers.

CHAPTER FOURTEEN
𝔚e 𝔠annot 𝔊o 𝔅ack

*After the trial today, I walked past the train yard. An arriving freight train
was switched by mistake from one track directly onto a siding, thereby dooming
it to a head-on collision with a parked locomotive. I saw what was happening
and I shouted as loud as I could. No one could hear me. Later I heard that the
engineer on the moving train and a workman on the parked locomotive were
both killed. Two other men were injured. As I stood there, unable to do anything,
I thought of how someone from another planet might feel, watching us, watching
me, over the last twenty years or more. Watching us approach our calamity. Our
doom. And we not knowing what we had done, what we were doing to ourselves.
To others.*

*There was a moment when we all took the wrong track, when we could not
stop ourselves from chaos. When, I wonder. The World War? Versailles? The Great
Depression? January 1933, when Hitler was named Chancellor? The Declaration of martial law after the burning of the Reichstag? When Hindenburg died in
1934 and Hitler declared himself* Führer *for life and most of us cheered? Or was
it* Kristallnacht, *with broken glass from Jewish shops and homes and synagogues
in the streets all across Germany? Then came the decision to invade Poland. To
build more slave labor camps. To build Auschwitz.*

Was it one of these decisions, these deliberate, logical choices that made sense at the time—or was it something beyond time, something in us, in all human beings, from the very beginning of time? I don't know why we let ourselves be switched onto the track that led to this chaos. All I know is that we cannot go back now.

The trial was tedious. At times Johann thought it was more about legal procedures than the guilt or innocence of the defendants. The lawyers and their aides passed papers and photos back and forth among themselves and handed them up to the judges who passed them back. Prosecuting attorneys introduced official Nazi documents and depositions from witnesses as evidence. Defense attorneys challenged their accuracy or relevance. Judges heard arguments and sustained or denied objections. All this made little sense to him.

But on this Friday, he listened to a witness who had worked in the laboratory at Dachau describe some of the medical experiments there: searching for a cure for malaria by infecting over a thousand prisoners with the disease and then testing a variety of treatments on them (most of the prisoners died); simulating what would happen to pilots in distress by immersing prisoners in icy water or depriving them of oxygen in high-altitude chambers (again, a high death rate); or forcing prisoners to drink seawater and then measuring the effects (more fatalities). The witness told how women were brought from Ravensbrück to temporarily warm up some of the prisoners whose body temperatures had been lowered to dangerous levels by bedding down with them before the men were put back in the tanks, with thermometers up their anuses; how, when their temperature dropped a specific number of degrees, blood was drawn from arteries in their necks, even after they had passed out or died. Johann could only shake his head. Did he know this before? Had he blocked it out of his mind? What else might he have chosen to ignore or forget?

The defense attorneys tried to discredit the witness as a lifelong criminal who had been arrested by the Nazis ten years before for falsifying documents and fraud, which he admitted. But he stuck by his testimony, implicating *Doktor* Wolfram Sievers, who was accused of selecting specific prisoners to be killed so he could mount their skeletons in an anthropological display. Johann looked over at the prisoners' dock, where Sievers was anxiously stroking his goatee. 'What a sorry business,' Johann thought. 'What foolish science—if it could be called science. Dachau sounds no different than Auschwitz. We pulled each other around by our noses.'

When the day's proceedings adjourned, Johann took a walk to the train station to clear his thoughts. After seeing Helga in the church, he missed her more than ever. His restless sleep was interrupted nearly every night by a frightening dream: their apartment house had been bombed and Helga was trapped inside, screaming from the front window in the parlor, while he and Paul-Adolf marched up and down the street in their Nazi uniforms, oblivious to what was happening.

As he crossed a footbridge over the train yard he saw the two locomotives headed for each other. He pressed himself to the fence. Saw the men jumping off the freight train like fleas. The yard workers scrambling. Remembered shouting just before it happened, but his words hovered around his head, with no capacity to affect anything. What could he possibly say to Helga? Two weeks had passed since he began the letter. He had promised himself he would finish it in three. One more week now. He must finish if he was ever going to see her again.

*****

"This explains the sirens." Johann put the newspaper down next to his breakfast plate, and pushed back from the table, scraping his chair on the floor. Startled, Helga turned around from the sink where she was washing potatoes.

"I wish you wouldn't do that. Look at the linoleum. It's all scratched. What about the sirens? I heard them all night."

"All over Germany, Jewish shops and synagogues were destroyed."

"Here in Nuremberg?" Helga asked.

"In all German cities, it says. There's a separate article about Nurem-berg, too. Synagogues were burned to the ground. Jews were rounded up. Jewish shops were smashed and looted. Streets are filled with glass."

"Terrible." She wiped her hands on a towel and looked at the news-paper over his shoulder.

"Clean-up will take a long-time," he said. "And cost plenty. The Jews must be made to pay for it. Why should German insurance companies have to pay? In any case, it was predictable."

"But was it right?"

"Was it right? The assassination last week in our embassy in Paris. Was that right? A petty, Polish Jew with a gun, a self-anointed Jewish savior, strikes down a German diplomat. You know that was a foul act. We had to draw the line." Johann put the paper down.

"Listen to yourself, Johann! By burning down synagogues and beat-ing up Jews? Can you blame them? They've been pushed into a corner." She stepped around the table to look at him. "First the state deports thousands of Polish Jews, some of whom were born and lived for dec-ades in Germany for all I know—they'll be so welcome there, I can only imagine. Then our state—always mindful of the law and inspired by justice, of course…"—she raised her hand in a mock "*Heil Hitler!*"— "our noble state confiscates and condemns the Jews' property and their synagogues. And now, when a single Polish Jew for whatever reason kills a single German in Paris, all the Jews in Germany have to pay?"

He scowled and sputtered. "The murder of a diplomat is no trivial matter." He jabbed at the newspaper. "What do you know about…,"

She saw that he was angry and tried to change the subject. "You know," she said softly, "I thought the new synagogue on *Hans Sachs Platz* was a beautiful building. That big round window. The two domed towers. The huge dome over the center. I wish I had gone inside at least once before that wild man Streicher destroyed it. Decided it didn't fit the architec-ture on the square and destroyed it. In August, was it? A bitter taste of what was to come."

"*Ach*, Helga. Don't be so naïve. Don't you know where the money came from to build that synagogue?"

"So what? So our clever Jews made a fortune in the hops industry. You drink beer and seem to like it well enough. Tell me, Johann, who has been harmed by our Jews? The city has benefited and prospered since they were allowed in. You know they've given much back to Nuremberg—parks, art, music. And I think it was a beautiful building, the synagogue. *Hans Sachs Platz* looks strange now, sad really, with it missing. I know, it didn't quite match the older buildings there from the Middle Ages. It was too big. Still, I liked it. Our *Bürgermeister* Liebel—he makes me ill, with his gloating over Hitler—he and your *Herr* Streicher are hardly friends of beautiful architecture."

"Liebel is a politician, Helga. No more, no less. You don't understand politics. Yes, *Gauleiter* Streicher's newspaper can be shrill, even vulgar, I admit. *Der Stürmer* minces no words, that's certain. I don't read it. But as chief Nazi administrator for the city and the district, with his power delegated directly by our *Führer*, he has brought us national, even international importance."

Helga laughed a mocking, edgy laugh.

"Don't you laugh!" he said, his voice rising. "All Germany looks to us for the Party rallies. And the Christmas market. The music festivals. Nuremberg has become the essence of the *Vaterland*."

She turned back to the sink, began peeling the last potato, and said softly, "I think the whole city looks different now, less pure, less real, with the liberal Jews' big domed synagogue on the Peignitz gone. Thank your *Herr Gauleiter* Streicher for that. What about the other one, the orthodox synagogue on *Essenweinstraße*? Did it survive last night?"

He lowered his voice. "Still burning, no doubt. If you look out the front room window, you probably can see the smoke. You just don't understand, Helga. Leave these things to the Party."

Helga did not go to the window. She began peeling and cutting up carrots. "Disgusting, Johann. Truly disgusting." She thought she had spoken so softly that he had not heard her.

But he responded, "Omelets require broken eggs."

"And what omelet comes from this, tell me?" Helga could not resist raising her voice and turning to look at him.

"We must have law and order. We must have the authority to protect ourselves from our enemies, from thieves and traitors."

"So we have streets full of glass and looting. Good Germans, good people everywhere, will not stand for it, Johann. Mark my words. When did you begin to hate the Jews so much?"

"I don't hate the Jews at all. I like many of them. Philipp, for example. I just think we—and they—would be better off if we didn't live in the same country. Let them find another place. Whoever takes them in is welcome to them. Now, stop. No more about this. Paul-Adolf is coming."

Their son, however, knew more about *Kristallnacht* in Nuremberg than they. "Good morning, *Mutti*. Good morning, *Vati*. Let me see the newspaper, please, when you have finished, *Vati*." Paul-Adolf was flushed with excitement. "I want to know what happened after I came home. The torch-light parade was marvelous," he grinned. "We celebrated our *Führer*'s first blow for freedom, fifteen years ago, back in 1923, the year before I was born. We marched around, singing. You should have been there!" Helga could not get used to his deeper voice. "And they told us more about the murder of our diplomat in Paris—he died yesterday, you know! Some crazy Jew shot him. We shouted until we were hoarse. Then, when I was leaving," he said, "some boys told us a bunch of motor cars with *SA* leaders was arriving. We all knew that something big was going to happen. I wanted to stay, but I knew you wanted me home by then. They said *SA* troops were marching across the Peignitz and toward all parts of the city, but especially from *Adolf Hitler Platz* toward the north end and the Jewish villas. Uphill. Toward *Pierkheimerstraße*. 'Jews' Quarter!' I wanted to go with them. But I came home." He smiled a self-satisfied smile.

"Eat your breakfast, Paul-Adolf," Helga said.

The boy had not finished telling his story. "On my way home, Heinzl and I cut through the park. We saw Meyerberg's on fire! A crowd stood around. The firetrucks weren't there. We wanted to stop and watch but we both promised we would be home. What does it say in the paper, *Vati*?"

"Meyerberg's? What a shame," Helga said. "And I can't get used to calling it *Adolf-Hitler Platz*. I keep wanting to say, *Haupt Markt Platz*. You saw some of this, *Paulchen*?"

"Of course, *Mutti*. We all marched back to *Hitler Platz* as soon as we heard what was happening. We cheered and cheered. The *SA* were all fired up, too. We wanted to go with them. But our leader said we had to be home. It was near midnight. One *SA* squad roared off toward the north end. I saw the fire and then came home. What does the newspaper say, *Vati*?"

Johann handed him the paper. Helga and he watched as their son beamed at the account.

"So, *Vati*. You see. It's as I said. But all over Germany. Wonderful! I wish you hadn't made me promise to come home."

"Eat your breakfast, Paul-Adolf," Helga said, looking out the window at the plum tree in the courtyard. The night's wind had taken off the last of its leaves.

"Yes, eat," Johann said. "Put the newspaper down now." He tried to shift the topic of the conversation. "Tell me now, before I go to the policlinic, what happened in your Latin exam yesterday. You still having trouble?"

"No. It's all right now. Schultzie helps me and lets me look at his homework before class," Paul-Adolf said, looking out of the corner of his eye at the newspaper. "We're doing Cicero. But I liked Caesar better. Best was Tacitus. But it's all right. Old *Herr* Plommers puts us all to sleep, though."

"What's your standing now?"

"I think fourth in the class. Maybe third, depends on the test results from last week. Since Birnberger and Saperstein had to leave the school, I think maybe third. No one misses those two Jew stinkers, I tell you."

"Paul-Adolf!" Helga had almost given up trying to scold him.

"It's fine, Paul-Adolf. Your mother just wants you to be a kind person. So do I. But we all must be honest, too. And face facts. Our *Vaterland* needs a good, honest, factual look. It's taken a long time to get us here. But now, the government is doing something that will make things better. Meanwhile, your mother and I want to you keep working hard in your studies." Paul-Adolf's eyes drifted again toward the newspaper.

"Latin is important," Johann continued. "I didn't enjoy it. But I am glad I had to learn it. For medical school, first of all." He looked at the clock on the wall and drank down the rest of his coffee. "And now I must go. I am late. The policlinic will be full, you can bet. I'll eat the mid-day meal at the canteen." Helga looked at the potatoes she had already peeled. "Don't worry," Johann said, "they'll keep until tomorrow." As he put on his coat he shouted from the hallway, "I'll be late tonight, Helga. I am going to a Party meeting. Eat supper without me. I'll get something when I come home."

Despite Johann's comments about the political situation, Helga was pleased that he was willing to talk with Paul-Adolf about his school-work. It was another good sign that he was dwelling less on Greta's death. For many months, he had hardly talked to the boy, had barely talked to her, for that matter. She didn't know which was worse, his silent rage during the first phases of Greta's illness, or his depression with her death. Perhaps his membership in the Party and in the Nazi Physicians' League was doing him some good, she thought, despite her bitterness about his decision to join. If that's what it took to bring him around to being a decent father and restore some of the joy in his life, she was willing to live with that.

She had forced him to take a week's summer holiday at *Starnberger See* in August, but he was grateful to her for making him go, just as she knew he would be. He told her so when they returned. Watching Johann and Paul-Adolf rowing together on the lake had made her smile. If only there were not this damnable Nazi presence in everything, she thought, from the newspapers to the movies to the daily trips to the marketplace. The whole city seemed to have become an advertisement for the Nazis. It was bad enough that Paul-Adolf absorbed so much of it in school. She did not dare try to prevent him from taking part in the Hitler Youth. She knew that her son needed to be with his friends, even if they were, like him, caught up in the Party's fervors. And Johann needed something to believe in.

Johann walked quickly to the corner and boarded the streetcar just as it was leaving. It was one of Nuremberg's newest models, a sign of the city's growing prosperity. The conductor gave him a hearty "Good morning, *Herr Doktor!*" Johann found his usual seat and began to think about the turn of events over the past five years, since the Nazis had come to power. 'There is no question but that conditions have improved,' he told himself. 'More prosperity. More public satisfaction. More pride. He should have pointed that out to Helga. Hitler was a blessing for them all. It was Hitler, he should have told her, who brought Germany's self-respect back. Hitler hunted down the communists. Hitler secured the *Rhineland* from the French. Hitler offered the world the joy of the Olympics in Berlin. Hitler's leadership brought a welcome order to Austria. Just last month, with the blessing of England, France and Italy, he brought safety and security to the Sudeten Germans in Czechoslovakia.' Even if Helga had given her usual reply, "Hitler may be in charge, but that does not make him God," she would have had to agree with him.'

"Everyone now is better off. *Ja!*" Johann said out loud to no one in particular. An old woman, sitting across the aisle, turned to look at him, then quickly looked away through the window toward the clusters of people working to clean up the sidewalks. He followed her gaze.

'Of course, not *everyone* is better off,' he thought. 'Not the Jews or the communists. But they deserve what they get. This action will clear the air. Rumors about this or that fear or worry, rumors about a coming war, are inevitable. We Germans like to worry, even when there is so little to worry about.' He smiled when it occurred to him that he was no different than all the rest. 'The Jews, though, have good reason to worry. Perhaps they'll see the light and move. They can go anywhere they want to as long as it is outside of Germany. If the *SA* and its hooligans pushed them a bit too hard, at least the outcome would be for everyone's benefit. Why would the Jews want to stay here when they are so obviously unwanted in our *Vaterland*? That so many are leaving is a good sign. But those who are staying must have some big gains in mind. Why else would they stay?' He shook his head as he looked out the window.

Turning the corner, the streetcar swayed and the overhead electric line crackled as it slowed down for the stop at the *Hauptbahnhof*. The old woman stood up to leave. Johann helped her with her suitcase. "These lower floors in our newer streetcars are a blessing," she said to him and the conductor in a stiff Frankish dialect. "Just two stairs coming in, two stairs going out. Good for my old bones. Everything's so modern now." This struck Johann as just the right view of things in general. "*Ja!*" he said loudly, as the streetcar started up again.

He continued to reassure himself that he had nothing against Jews, generally, and that he could understand how they might be bitter of late. But after all, Germany is not their homeland. Certainly not Nuremberg. No Jew had been allowed to live in Nuremberg for some three hundred and fifty years, from the end of the fifteenth century to the middle of the nineteenth. 'Now there are thousands—all there by the grace of the city fathers, who, just as they had allowed them in, could well tell them they were no longer welcome. Mayor Liebel was no fool. He must know,' Johann thought, 'how the Jews were taking advantage of true Nurembergers. If the mayor worked hand-in-hand with the Nazis it was not only for political necessity or for his own advantage. It was because he knew the Nazis were doing what had to be done, one way or another.'

As the streetcar moved toward *Hallplatz*, he saw more people sweeping the sidewalks. At each stop, Johann heard the brittle crackling sound of glass being swept up, the noise of shovels scraping the pavement. He thought to himself, 'Omelets.'

At the policlinic, the waiting room was full, but no more than usual. A dozen people sat coughing and looking drawn, a sign of the approaching cold season. Two patients complained of stomach cramps. Another had wrapped up a badly swollen ankle. A mother held an infant that would not stop crying.

"Who's first?" Johann asked the receiving nurse as he took off his coat and hung it on the rack.

"In the back examination room, a woman with a twelve-year-old girl. I thought you would prefer to see her, rather than *Herr Doktor* Graeber. The woman was here even before I arrived at 6:30, waiting with her daughter on the steps. *Frau* Rosen. The daughter is Sophie. Sophie Rosen. Here's the file."

Johann looked at the nurse, expecting more explanation. When she gave none, he walked down the hall toward the examination room. Inside he found a disheveled woman in her thirties, crying while trying to comfort her daughter, who seemed barely conscious. As soon as he entered, the woman stammered through her tears, "She's dying! She's dying! Do something, *Herr Doktor*. She's dying."

"Calm yourself, please. What happened?"

"Last night, men broke into our apartment. They hit my husband and took him away. We tried to hide. The children ran into our bedroom. They caught Sophie…" She paused to take a deep breath. "My *Sophiechen!*" The woman began to cry loudly.

"They hit her?"

"They pushed her to the floor. Kicked her in the stomach. She coughed up blood for awhile. She can't talk. She's dying! Look at her. She's so pale. Her lips are blue. Do something, please, doctor."

"You are Jewish. You should have taken her to the Jewish policlinic."

"We went there. We did. Right away. After midnight. It was chaotic. *Schrecklich!* The Jewish policlinic is full. So many people there. We couldn't wait. I came here. We live nearby. Sophie needs help, please."

"You must take her back to the Jewish policlinic, *Frau* Rosen. They will help you. Please go now."

"But you are a doctor. She's dying."

"She just looks frightened to me."

"But the blood?"

"She may have been injured, yes. But they will examine her at the Jewish policlinic. Please go there now. I have to see other patients." Johann kept his voice level. He heard Graeber grumbling in the hallway.

"Please," the mother said. You are a doctor. She needs help. Please." She began crying louder and louder, gasping for breath.

Johann looked closely into the girl's eyes. "Does your head hurt?"

The child nodded.

"Open your mouth." He held her tongue down with a depresser. Then he stepped behind her and pressed on her ribs. "Does this hurt?"

She winced and began to cry.

"Yes," he said. I think she has a fractured rib, maybe two. The blood comes from a cut on her tongue. She must have bit her tongue. I don't think she's bleeding internally. Now, take her to the Jewish policlinic. That's all I can do here."

He turned to leave the room. Sophie's crying had subsided to a whimper. He looked away and said, "You should leave. You both must leave, *Frau* Rosen." He caught himself before he said "*Auf Wiedersehen!*" When he closed the door to the examination room behind himself, he saw Graeber, red-faced and shouting. The nurse had a surprised look on her face that passed in an instant.

*****

In Berlin, Philipp felt the fury of *Kristallnacht*. He was working as a replacement for another doctor that night at the Jewish policlinic in Wedding. It was his one night off from the Jewish Hospital. But he and Christine needed the extra income. At first, it was a relatively quiet shift. A small group of patients in the early evening: five from one family complaining of stomach pains; a man who had cut his forehead when he fell down his stairs in drunken despair about his wife's infidelity ("You are lucky you didn't break your neck!" Philipp told him); and then, around ten, a woman who thought she was going into labor, but wasn't.

After midnight no one expected many patients, especially since Berlin's Jewish community was shrinking each day as families emigrated. Philipp, an intern, and a nurse-in-training had gathered around the receptionist's desk, talking. Its light cast harsh, angular shadows all around them.

Aside from their chatting, the policlinic was quiet. From the end of the street they could hear muffled sounds of scraping and thudding. Then the lights went out. There was shouting, the sound of men marching, and the unmistakable sound of broken glass. Crash after crash, as though a mechanical monster was moving down the street, smashing shop windows. An orange, fiery light flared and swept back and forth across the policlinic's windows just before rocks smashed through them, shattering glass everywhere. Philipp remembered thinking that the noise was like a wild, mismatched orchestra, with each section working up a different piece of music.

He looked at the intern and the nurse-in-training, a girl still in her teens. "We're being attacked," he shouted, his mind flying back to the memory of artillery shells in the war. "The city has been invaded." He barely heard himself over sirens and crashing glass. A crowd began to stream by on the sidewalk. The three rushed outside and were sucked along with it, like bits of wood in a swollen river. All around them, people in their night clothes pushed and shoved. Babies cried. Mothers called out for their sons and daughters. Husbands and wives tried to hold on to each other. Yiddish, German, Polish, and Russian all tangled into a jumble of desperation. Trucks with loudspeakers roared up and down the street: "…Jews… Rats…Jews…*Juuuu-dennn*!…*Raaaaattt-tennn*!" The drawn-out, raspy syllables rose over the din. More glass shattered in the distance. Horns blared and searchlights shone wildly up and down the buildings' facades. Squads of *SA* men with sticks hopped off open trucks, beating anyone they could. The crowd seemed to be stampeding toward its own destruction.

Philipp, panting, jumped into a doorway. He had lost sight of the intern and never saw him again. The young nurse-in-training was being pushed helplessly down the street. Philipp caught glimpses of her starched cap bobbing in the crowd. There was blood on his sleeve, not his own, he soon discovered. His glasses dangled from one ear.

He made his way back to the clinic and tried to find the telephone to call Christine. The line was dead. She might as well have been on another planet. He thought of his time in the field hospital, during the war, and searched for candles, bandages, morphine, and a scalpel. Soon, he feared, all of Berlin's Jews would be staggering in through the front door.

The arrival of injured people helped him focus. Two of the first group of wounded were also Jewish physicians. Another two were nurses. After bandaging each other, they joined forces. Someone found a military-issue flashlight that could be cranked up and needed no batteries. The cabinet with dressings and tourniquets was propped open. People began to sort themselves out, the most severely injured lying on the floor, the less injured sitting and waiting. Someone began to sweep up the broken glass in the doorway. The smell of smoke drifted inside from the street.

Apparently, the Nazis were attacking Berlin's Jews and their property. He thought that Christine would probably be safe, since their neighborhood would not be a target. It was different in the other sections of the city where the Nazis were forcing Jews to congregate. He was not surprised when someone shouted that the synagogue was on fire and one of its three towers had collapsed. A few people rushed out into the street to see if they could save the sacred scrolls.

Philipp knew that there would be murders, rapes, and beatings. 'For those who survived, the deepest, most festering wounds of all,' he thought, 'would be the humiliations. A great many Germans were kind to Jews, or at least no less kind than they were to anyone else. Others, however—and not all of these were Nazis—did not regard Jews as their equals, no matter how long they had lived in Germany. It was like a body declaring war on one of its parts, Philipp thought. As though the muscles had declared war on the nerves, or the bones on the muscles. It was too vicious and frightening for him to understand. Could a part of a body be so hated, so useless, so meaningless to the other organs that they could wish its destruction? Or could a group of cells try to attack another group of cells, with the purpose of ridding the body of their supposedly harmful presence? Perhaps the targeted cells were in fact harmful. Then the body's efforts to protect itself were reasonable, even wholesome. But how could this be in this situation? What harm were these Germans, who happened to be Jews, to other Germans? And who asked these Germans, who happened to be Nazis and thought themselves therefore better Germans, to take these drastic measures?

He walked between two old women lying on the floor toward a young girl no more than ten who began to whimper as soon as he came near. He could see that the child's right hand was crushed. She held it, limp and bloody, in her left, pressing both to her chest, and trying to hide behind her mother. A drying swath of blood had creased her nightgown and stuck it to her body. Her mother, barefoot, her hair hanging loose and sweaty, looked ashen. She babbled to her daughter in Yiddish, over and over, "No worry. No worry. No worry. My little Sadie. My *Sadiechen*. No worry." The girl began to cry loudly.

Philipp tried to calm the child, but she would not let him look at her hand. Her mother began to plead, first with Philipp, then with the girl, then with Philipp, over and over. "Do something, *Herr Doktor*. Let go, Sadie. Do something. Let go, Sadie." She might have gone on like this for hours. He was not sure what he should do. He wanted to help. He also wanted to fly like a bird, far away to some quiet, safe place. He knew that there was no such place in Berlin or anywhere the Nazis were in power.

"Let me help you," he said to the little girl. "Your mother and I want to help you. When we need help, we must let others help us. We want to help you. And we all need to help each other. Now, especially now."

CHAPTER FIFTEEN
The Best Interests of the Volk

As a wounded veteran of the first war, I was exempt from serving in 1939. You were happy with that, but I felt the need to serve. My big chance came when I wrote SS Generalleutnant *Brandt and he invited me to Berlin. That led to my brief service at Grafeneck. I was so happy then to be doing something important, Helga. If my friendship with Philipp was over, if he and I had to part ways, as you warned me we would, it was because we disagreed about Germany's correct path. Victory in Poland and Brandt's assurances were all the proof I needed: I was right and Philipp was wrong. But it was more than that, of course.*

Brandt inspired me then with his idealism. Now, watching him in the trial, I see him differently. His imposing bearing, his self-confidence and authority, his dispassionate Korrektheit—*everything that I thought represented the purest form of* Vaterlandsliebe—*I now see as hollow arrogance. Idealism corrupted by indifference. The cause of our ruin. Germany's. His. Mine.*

Johann knew that little separated him from the defendants. They had had more authority than he, but he had done many of the same things. Their further crime was in encouraging those like him follow their example. Had he encouraged others by his example, too? Of one thing he was certain: the only significant difference between the defendants and himself was that they had been caught and he was still free.

*****

Reading about sterilization and eugenics had become an obsession for Johann since Greta's death. Shortly after the invasion of Poland, he wrote a long letter to the Director of the National Health Department of the Interior Ministry in Berlin about an idea that had first occurred to him after he returned from the sterilizations in the *Rhineland*. Two weeks later, a reply was waiting for him on top of a stack of mail when he came home at midday. He was surprised to receive so swift a response, despite his hope that the authorities would be impressed with his idea.

He congratulated himself as he opened the letter. It was just a matter of being able to think about things a little differently than everyone else. Then taking action. Why couldn't he have an important idea about something that everyone in the medical profession was discussing? He imagined himself at the forefront of medical research.

Johann was not interested in the debate about which method—surgical, chemical or radiological, or some combination of the three—was the most efficient and reliable way to achieve sterilization. That was mere technology. More important were the benefits of the procedure for the human race. What better example to demonstrate the importance of modern medicine? What other animal, after all, could exercise the foresight to control its own reproduction in such a positive fashion?

According to the statistics in his medical journals and in the popular press, an increasing number of "defective individuals" were reproducing. Experts all agreed that this would lead inexorably to an exponential increase of physical and mental defectives: imbeciles, freaks, sexual deviants, alcoholics, criminals, incorrigibles. The only certain way to promote the vitality of the human race was to sterilize every undesirable man and woman before they reproduced and weakened the species. This permanently eliminated all potential offspring afflicted with the flaws of their parents. A merciful solution in every respect. He did not doubt the urgency and the legitimacy of such efforts. Since sterilizations resolved potential psychological, physical and social problems, they were ethically justifiable. Future generations would reap the benefits of eradicating disabilities and costly, degenerative conditions and diseases. Professors in the best medical schools in Europe and North America had been making the case for decades. America had been leading the way since the 1920s. "Three generations of idiots are enough," as their Supreme Court Justice said!

But how many physicians, Johann wondered, had given any thought to sterilization in the context of understanding its positive impact on chronic health problems in an otherwise potentially healthy, productive individual? Could sterilization help stabilize a person with a weak heart or lungs, by re-directing or re-balancing one or more of the body's hormonal substances that precipitated or contributed to the weakness? In his letter to the Ministry he had cited all the medical studies he turned up that seemed to bear on his hypothesis. He also had described in general terms the design of a controlled experiment. And he had indicated how important it was that the sterilization procedure itself be as "normalized as possible," that is, relatively free of stress and anxiety, given the fact that the subjects have health issues that might be exacerbated by any trauma. It would be best if the subjects volunteered for sterilization. In fact, that would probably be the only way for the experiment to be scientifically valid. Subjects would be informed that sterilization would bring them no significant harm and might bring them relief from their debilitating symptoms.

The vasectomies and tubal ligations he had done on the children in the *Rhineland* had been easy enough. A local anesthetic, an experienced surgeon, clean dressings for a few days, hospitalization for a week to ten days, then some restrictions of motion and types of clothing for a bit longer. That was it. Physical complications in most instances were rare. Any emotional trauma would be minimized by focusing the patient's mind on the potential benefits of the procedure.

His idea seemed so obvious that it had to be correct. He was proud of himself for conceiving it. He hoped to participate in a research team. But he never expected to receive an invitation to present his ideas in person to the Ministry. Yet here was a letter, signed by none other than Karl Brandt, M.D., Professor of Medicine and personal physician to the *Führer*, one of the *Reich*'s most important medical administrators. "I am pleased to inform you that your letter has received our official interest." Brandt proposed that they meet in two weeks in Munich. His illegible signature, neatly spaced mid-way under the exclamation, *"Heil Hitler!"* and a typed-out spelling of his name—with spaces between each capital letter: B R A N D T—gave Johann a chill. He read the letter over again, focusing on the words "official interest." This might mean an academic appointment or at least affiliation with a university hospital.

Without even looking up to see if Helga was in the room, he said, "I must have a new uniform shirt. I will wear my dress uniform. Yes, only a tailored uniform shirt would be suitable. And my coat and trousers must be pressed. Helga, did you hear me? I need a new shirt."

"What are you talking about?"

"I am going to see *Herr Doktor* Brandt, Hitler's personal physician. He's coming to Munich in two weeks. He wants to talk with me about ..., about some medical ideas I have."

"You need a new shirt for that?"

"Yes, of course. Buy me a shirt tomorrow, please. When you go shopping in the morning. *Schneider* Bender around the corner has a good reputation for shirts. But go to another tailor, if you think Bender isn't good enough."

Helga could only laugh out loud. "Since when have you been worried about your shirts, or whether or not your trousers have a crease? I found them last week on the floor of the closet!" She gave Johann a look that made him smile.

"I just want to be sure that *Herr Professor Doktor* Brandt pays attention to my ideas. It is important to look presentable, especially to the men in the movement."

"Movement! Movement! *Ach*, Johann. I wish I never heard the word. What we're talking about here is a politics, no more, no less, dear husband."

He had grown used to her sarcasm. He considered it a manifestation of her anger at Greta's death, a sign of what his mother used to call "nerves."

She waited for him to say something, but when he didn't, she went on, "Your *Herr Professor Doktor* Karl Brandt is a man who has joined a system in which he thinks he can gain something for himself. Oh, he may say he is working for our noble *Vaterland*, that he is devoted to the future of the *Volk*. I can imagine that he may have talked himself into believing that. But I assure you, he is no more selfless than you or I or anyone else."

She thought he was not listening. But he was. After a long silence, he said, "Why are you trying to puncture my hopes? Why do you express such cynicism, Helga? Give me an answer, please. Would you have me just stand back and let the world go by?"

She felt trapped. She wanted him to do something, anything that would bring him out of his depression, but now that he was, she thought what he was doing was wrong. She tried to put her arms around him, but he pulled away. "In this world, Johann, with Hitler and the mess that has piled up all around us over the past few years, it might be better to have nothing to do with 'your movement.' True, I don't know if you or anyone can stand back. It seems impossible to escape the Party. Wherever we turn, the Party is painted in front of our faces. The *Führer* is worshipped as a Messiah. I just thank God the war in Poland has ended without any calamity for us. It is amazing, truly amazing. I can't quite believe it is over so quickly. Soon enough, Paul-Adolf is going to be in active service. He is already too excited about warring. And for this we can thank 'your movement.'"

"Helga, it's not 'my' movement, as I have tried to tell you for God knows how long."

"All right then, not '*your*' movement. But '*the*' movement is no miracle from on high. We are lucky we are not some of the people the authorities have fished into their nets."

"Don't you see, it is precisely 'the movement'"—here Johann gestured with his arms wide open—"that will catapult us out of this mess, as you call it? Communists. Jews. Gypsies. Traitors. Degenerates. Drunks. Malingers. Thieves. Low-lifes. Dangerous people, all of them. All trying to pull us down. This is a harsh world. We are right to distrust and despise what has happened to Germany before Hitler came to power. Unless we are strong, it will happen again."

She shook her head and tried to cover her ears.

He grabbed her hands. "Do you want...," Johann started to shout, "Greta and..." then caught himself. Speaking more softly, he looked into her eyes. "Do you want Paul-Adolf to grow up in such a world? Do you? With Hitler, we've established our authority, accepted our destiny, and risen to the challenge for our people in the *Sudetenland* and Austria." He let her hands drop.

She began to cry. "War is..."

"I know war. Don't tell me about war. Hitler did not want this war. He told us so himself. But we are in it. And now we must win it. For our *Volk*. Sure, I hope it has ended with Poland. The British and the French are powerless. Their time is over. But if the war continues, we will triumph. I know it. The Russians had to co-operate with us or else. Yes, we should thank God indeed. Not just for victory in Poland, my wise wife. Above all, for..."

Before Johann could add, as she knew he would, "...for Adolf Hitler!" Helga said, "It's a joke, Johann. This year's Nazi Party Rally—didn't the posters tell us, just a few months ago, about the rally for "For World Peace!"—now the rally had to be cancelled because we invaded Poland! Some peace! Instead, we have war. A big, stinking war. It won't stop with Poland. Hitler won't be satisfied with conquering an unprepared, weak country trapped between us and the Soviet Union. No. We're going to have a monstrous war. That's the world our Paul-Adolf and all the other children in Germany are going to know. Hitler aches for war."

Now Johann didn't want to listen, but Helga continued. "All these Nazi leaders love nothing so much as their guns. They remind me of little boys playing games out in the American desert, little cowboys and

WildWest hooligans against the Indians. I agree, the communists are not much better, I grant you. I was talking with *Frau* Pichler in the bakery. Her son is in Poland."

He walked over to the window and looked down on the street. "Just what has all this to do with my talking with *Herr Doktor* Brandt next week?" he asked.

"You forgot, he's a professor, too. *Ach*, Johann. Maybe everything. Maybe nothing." She sighed and stood close behind him. "Maybe he just is interested in your ideas and wants to meet a good, loyal German doctor. Maybe I should just not think so much about all this." She put her arms around him, not wanting to say any more. It had been a long time—since Greta's illness and his plans for the trip to the *Rhineland*— that she had seen him show such enthusiasm. She could not deny that 'the movement' had given him a renewed purpose and helped to restore his pride. "I'll order you a new shirt tomorrow," she said. "It will be an early Christmas present. From Bender's. It should be ready for the weekend. Now, let's just wait and see what happens with the important *Herr Professor Doktor* from Berlin."

For days before Brandt's trip to Munich, Johann was unable to concentrate on anything else. On the morning of the meeting, he boarded the earliest train. He took a taxi from the station because he feared he would get his shoes scuffed if he walked. Sitting in the backseat, he rehearsed in his mind again how he thought the conversation should go. He had formed a picture in his mind of Brandt. From photographs in the newspaper and the newsreels, he knew that Brandt's dark hair (a little longer than would be expected on a military man) was slicked back and sharply parted, not one hair out of place. Brandt had a high forehead and strikingly arched eyebrows that gave his face an animated, intelligent, boyishly exuberant look. He was quite tall, erect, athletic looking. All sure signs of intellectual depth and moral authority. That Brandt was relatively young, in his mid-thirties, Johann found inspiring, too. The man could have been taken out of a Nazi poster or a film. A perfect example of a German officer. Within an instant of seeing him, Brandt would win Johann's full confidence.

"Sit down, please, *Herr Doktor Brenner*." Brandt moved quickly to the point, looking briefly at notes written on Johann's letter. "We've looked into your suggestion for research on the relationship between sterilization and debilitating heart or lung disease."

Johann had not expected chitchat and was relieved that there was none. He sat as straight as he could, resisting the urge to lean forward and try to read Brandt's marginal notes.

"*Ja.* Quite possibly a promising suggestion, I think." Brandt made a tent of his long fingers, then pointed his hands at Johann, and studied his face. Before Johann could say anything, he continued, "Others at the Ministry had some doubts. And they have had more experience than I have with terminal heart and lung problems. In medical school I was interested more in gastroenterological conditions; at Freiburg, with *Herr Professor Doktor* Hoche, I also became acquainted with psychiatric problems. Since then, I have been more of a generalist, until I took on this administrative role for the Party. But your idea might bear looking into. We've sent a copy of your letter on to the appropriate university researchers. Perhaps they'll take it into consideration." Brandt could not help but notice how Johann's face sagged. He would not be asked to direct the project.

"I see, sir. Thank you. I just hoped that I..." Johann tried to disguise his disappointment.

Brandt cut him off. "Tell me, *Herr Doktor* Brenner, have you an interest in joining another aspect of our work on an urgent matter, something that is essential for the general improvement of the *Volk* and the *Reich?*" Without waiting for Johann's answer, he continued, "I am here in Nuremberg to help the *Führer's* Chancellery initiate a new medical service, one that, if I may say, has the highest importance for the achievement of our national goals." He sat back in his chair, folded his arms and looked directly into Johann's eyes.

"Of course, I would be interested," Johann heard himself say. "*Ja,* of course. *Herr Professor Doktor.* I would like to know what the proposal is, naturally. Does it mean leaving Nuremberg or will the service be based here? I have a wife and children. I mean a child, a son. But we could leave. Yes, we could move without too much difficulty."

"Let's not talk about too many details just now, *Herr Doktor* Brenner. There will be time for that. I need only be assured of your confidence. This is a matter of some delicacy, at least for now."

Johann nodded.

"We have investigated your career record and other matters and know we can rely on you for professional conduct. You did fine work in Koblenz in 1935. As before, we expect absolute loyalty and your absolute confidentiality in all respects, you will understand." Brandt paused, expecting Johann to do more than just nod his assent.

For a moment, the two men studied and measured each with some ideal in the core of their thinking. Instinctively, each saw in the other someone he could trust.

"*Jawohl!*" Johann said, rather too loudly. "Absolute confidentiality. Certainly. Without question, sir. *Jawohl!*" he heard himself saying again, more calmly this time.

"Fine, *Herr Doktor* Brenner. Good." Brandt smiled a smile that vanished almost as soon as it appeared. "In good time you shall learn what the *Führer* wants us to undertake."

Johann's stomach tightened. "The *Führer!*" he exclaimed out loud, unable to stifle his pleasure at hearing that the matter had originated directly from the *Führer*. His mind raced. The *Führer's* personal physician, one of the two or three most important physicians in the movement, in the *Vaterland*, is asking *me*—Johann Brenner—to join in something that the *Führer* wants us to do. He felt his palms begin to sweat and leaned forward to hear whatever Brandt was going to say. His whole life had prepared him for just this moment.

"Before we go further," Brandt said, matter-of-factly, "I am tempted to ask why you waited so long to join the Party. You joined only four years ago, just before we sent you to Koblenz. I know you did important work there on behalf of the *Volk*. So I don't question your loyalty. And I also know that you can give me any reasonable answer today, and I will have to accept it. But between us, *Herr Doktor*, I am surprised that you did not join us sooner."

"Well, it is not an answer, really," Johann stammered, "but I just wasn't ready. I was not personally ready. I had not yet let myself be persuaded. The *Rhineland* children, the mixed-race children..." Johann's voice trailed off.

"No matter, Brenner. No matter. Your record speaks for itself. Some see the light sooner. Some later. Some excellent people began to join in greater numbers, once we achieved power. Who am I to blame them? I was just a few years before you, as a matter of fact. What's important is that you have joined. We need men like you. The *Vaterland* needs doctors like you."

Brandt did not need to look up to know that Johann sat taller in his chair. "I believe I can trust you, *Herr Doktor* Brenner. We have all the information we need about you. You are, please take no offense, an ordinary German doctor—by ordinary, I mean, of course, loyal, conscientious, intelligent. We need doctors just like you to carry out our mission for the health and well-being of our *Volk*. Other obligations prevent me from going into full details of the assignment today. Suffice it to say that the *Führer* has made a commitment to the health of the *Volk* and to the compassionate, but resolute solution of its problems. We have to take action against anything that weakens us. My associates and I have been working on a comprehensive plan to help purify the German race. It rests on the will, determination and professional authority of our loyal physicians. I believe you are such a physician."

Johann resisted the urge to smile.

"That's all I am at liberty to say about our 'action' today." Brandt took a blank sheet of paper from the desk drawer, and wrote an address on it. "We are having a meeting at a villa in Berlin—*Tiergartenstraße 4*—within a few weeks. I want you to attend. My office will contact you with the particulars. And here is the address of *Herr Doktor* Horst Schumann, director of Grafeneck, an asylum in Württemberg. We are hoping someone of his caliber will participate. Contact him please. If I see him,

I will tell him to expect to hear from you. I will brief him on your credentials, but you might send him a formal description of yourself, your career, interests, your ideas about sterilization, if you wish, and so forth. I appreciate having had the chance to speak with you. *Auf Wiedersehen, Herr Doktor* Brenner."

Brandt abruptly stood up and raised his hand in the Hitler salute. Johann stood quickly and returned the salute as energetically as he ever had. When Brandt sat down and started to look at other papers on the desk, Johann said *"Auf Wiedersehen!"* and walked toward the door. Brandt replied curtly, *"'Wiedersehen, Herr Doktor,"* but never looked up.

Returning to the policlinic, Johann hardly noticed the bustle on the sidewalks and the streets. He stopped to buy a small Nazi flag for Paul-Adolf at a news kiosk. While he was standing there, a troop of Hitler Youth marched around the corner, each boy slightly younger than his son, singing loud enough to drown out the traffic. As he walked inside the policlinic, Johann saw that the waiting room was more crowded than usual. The nurse in charge told him to expect influenzas, a possible appendicitis, and a broken arm. It was a typical afternoon.

After supper and two scheduled private patients, he told Helga about his conversation with Brandt. He expected her to have many questions and he was prepared for caustic comments. Instead, she merely listened and asked him how long he would be away.

"I don't really know. Perhaps a week. I might look up Philipp in Berlin. We haven't heard from him and Christine for quite some time now."

Helga shrugged and said nothing. Before he went to bed, Johann wrote a letter to *Doktor* Schumann. When he came into the bedroom, Helga casually asked, "Why would Philipp Stein, a Jew, think he should stay in contact with us, now that you are a Nazi?"

Johann ignored her. In bed, he turned on his side and, thinking of how good it felt to be doing something important for the *Vaterland,* fell asleep.

*****

Philipp hurried across the street to meet Johann's train at the *Bahn-hof-Zoo* terminal. They walked to the station café.

"I am sorry, Johann. I've only a few minutes before I have to be back at the Jewish Hospital in Wedding. Normally I would be off from my night shift, but I have a chance to get in a few more hours. It will help us make ends meet. Later this evening, Christine and I are leaving to spend tomorrow and the next day at a little inn on the *Nordsee*, our first holiday in years. I'm sorry we can't spend more time together. She sends her greetings."

"I understand, Philipp. Helga sends fond greetings to you and Christine. You are well, I see."

"Careful, *Herr Doktor*, with the hasty diagnosis. Yes, I might look well, but this is a difficult time for me, you might understand."

"Yes. Certainly. Let's try to avoid talking about it, Philipp. We can remain friends, I hope. I have never told you that I admire and respect you, but I do."

"*Danke schön*. I am surprised to hear you say that, I must admit. Shocked, actually. You have joined the Party. You hear from Hitler and all the others"—and here Philipp smiled—"that I am an 'enemy,' a 'parasite,' a 'defiler of ...'"

"Enough. Enough, Philipp. Let's talk about something else. How's your practice?" As soon as he asked the question, Johann realized that Philipp's answer would take them directly into the heart of what he had promised himself not to talk about.

Philipp laughed a sharp laugh. "Are you joking, Johann? What practice? Here's a bit of news! Since 1936 all Jewish physicians have been banned from treating Germans. Don't tell me you didn't know. And I need not tell you, of course, that this has been crushing."

"I didn't mean..."

Philipp could not stop. "A colleague and I were planning to start our own clinic. He and his wife left Germany for Sweden five years ago now, just after Hitler declared himself *Führer* for life. They thought they would go to Canada, but they couldn't get a visa. They wanted us to go, too. I felt we must stay. I have done nothing wrong. This was our homeland, our *Vaterland*. Notice, I said 'was,' Johann. I have been robbed of my *Vaterland* by your Nazi Party."

Johann tried to interrupt, but Philipp was implacable. "Even before *Kristallnacht,* I was being threatened by your damned Party. I began working at the Jewish Hospital in Wedding because that is one of the few places a Jewish doctor is still allowed to practice. I have a few private patients."

"Please, Philipp."

"I treat everyone who comes or calls. Dangerous, but it helps. Our vacation at the inn at the North Sea is a payment from a patient, an Aryan, I must say, who was visiting Berlin when he got sick, took the risk, and came to me. There are a few Germans—excuse me, Aryans!— who remain under my care. Long-standing patients mostly, who trust me. They dare to come to a Jewish doctor. Mostly, though, I see Jews. I wanted to work with children and now most of my patients are old. Funny, isn't it? They often have both physical and mental problems, not a mystery, given the times. They cannot afford to pay much, either. I see them anyway. But this is not a practice, Johann. This is a punishment. All the Nazi 'laws' against the Jews are not laws. They are punishments."

"*Ja,*" Johann whispered softly, not knowing what else to say.

"War has been declared against us as clearly as it was declared against Poland. The *Blitzkrieg* that conquered them now is massing against us. I saw it last November here in the streets of Berlin. How else do you explain *Kristallnacht*? And it's not just war against Jews. It's against everyone the Nazis hold in contempt—Gypsies, homosexuals, whomever you Nazis despise or believe you can't trust to submit to your rule. You took the communists and the trade unionists away to Dachau and now to Buchenwald. We hear the stories. For all I know, that will happen to everyone who doesn't look or act the way you Nazis think we should." Philipp tried to calm himself. In a softer voice that was all the more accusatory for its intimacy, he whispered, "Johann, why are you so threatened by us?"

"I cannot answer for the Party's views, Philipp."

"But you support the Party. You are a member of the Party. Look at this bizarre picture we make. You in your uniform sitting here, talking with me, a Jew, a 'parasite.' I am surprised you even call me 'Philipp.' Since New Year's Day, your Nazi government has changed my name to 'Israel.' He laughed a caustic, bitter laugh.

"Philipp is still your name to me. We were friends. I hope to remain friends."

"I would have liked that, too. But it is impossible. I shouldn't have agreed to meet you. You have made it impossible for us to be friends. How can I be a friend with someone who hates me?"

"I don't…."

Before Johann could finish, Philipp said, "All this is too bizarre. Too sad. I am sorry, Johann, or I should say, *Herr SS Doktor* Johann Brenner, Nazi from Pohlendorf. Christine warned me. Still, we send greetings to Helga and your son. But now I must go. I would say *'Auf Wiedersehen!'* but I don't know why or how we should ever meet again. So *Lebewohl.*" With that, he stood up abruptly, put a *Reichsmark* on the table for his coffee, walked quickly out of the café, and was lost in the crowds on the sidewalk.

Johann remained seated for a while, then looked at his watch, walked outside, and hailed a taxi.

"*Tiergartenstraße 4*, please. In the borough of Tiergarten. It should not be far from here."

*****

The taxi eventually turned down a leafy street and stopped in front of a stately villa. A brass plaque on the gate said General Foundation for Welfare and Institutional Care. Johann announced himself to the porter and was buzzed through. A receptionist put down the telephone as he stepped toward her desk, told him to wait a moment, and then motioned toward an open a door. He stepped inside, declared his "*Heil Hitler!*" and was greeted by Philipp Bouhler, chief of Hitler's Chancellery.

Bouhler came out from behind his desk and smiled at Johann as though he were an old acquaintance. Johann noticed immediately that Bouhler's limp was more pronounced than his own.

"So, you've come from Nuremberg. So lovely there, especially in fall, but even in winter. Even in winter. My wife and I have built a home in Bavaria. Nussdorf. Lovely little village. Do you know it?" Bouhler said, taking no pains to conceal his Bavarian accent. Before Johann could reply, he continued, "We are so fortunate to live in the most beautiful part of our beautiful *Vaterland*."

Johann replied, "*Ja…*" and was about to say more, but Bouhler quickly gestured toward the door and with apologies said he would be coming to the meeting shortly. His secretary then escorted Johann to a conference room. Soon others arrived.

Bouhler began the meeting by introducing everyone. Most were physicians, but some had degrees in economics or other academic disciplines. Most of the men seemed to know each other. Johann knew none of them. He sat silent through the morning, taking in the conversation and making an occasional note. When he poured himself a glass of water from the pitcher nearest him, he was careful not to spill any. He learned that earlier meetings of this group, officially named the *Reich's* Committee for Scientific Registration of Serious Hereditary and Congenital Diseases, had developed a draft questionnaire "for the clarification of scientific questions in the field of congenital malformation and mental retardation." All children in the *Reich* under the age of three had to be registered who were suspected of "any serious hereditary diseases"— idiocy and mongolism, especially when associated with blindness and deafness; microcephaly; hydrocephaly; malformations of all kinds; especially of limbs, head, and spinal column; and paralysis, including spastic conditions.

Johann wondered how this all related to his original ideas about sterilization, but he could not find any appropriate way to introduce the topic. He had had little experience with children who displayed any of these conditions—with the exception of his Greta, whose paralysis was the result of polio, not heredity. His experiences four years earlier in the *Rhineland* were of children whose only "serious hereditary disease" was their mixed-race parentage. Nonetheless, he was inspired that his *Führer* and German medical professionals were working hand-in-hand on a problem he thought was self-evident. Medicine should reach into a patient's life, a nation's life, and make whole what was broken. And here he was, part of that noble effort, sitting in a high-level meeting in the capital of the *Vaterland*. He was not sure what would be done with the information from the questionnaires under discussion, but that would come out in due time, he trusted.

The morning focused on refining the questionnaire. Johann was most impressed with Bouhler, who, like Brandt, seemed highly intelligent, straightforward and sensible. When the meeting adjourned for the midday meal, Bouhler announced that he would be absent for the afternoon session, Johann was disappointed. Still, it was good to know that a fellow Bavarian had so much authority.

They ate a hearty stew with dumplings and drank ample wine. When the meeting resumed with Hans Hefelmann presiding, the mood was different. Some of the participants dozed off, only to awake with a start that distracted the others. Johann, more alert than most, spoke a few times. When he suggested matters of family history that might bear on a child's health— a father's work place, alcoholism, or tobacco use—he felt useful, and looked around the table for approving glances.

At precisely 5:30, Hefelmann stood up, quickly followed by all the others at the table and said, *"Danke, meine Herren! Heil Hitler!"* *"Heil Hitler!"* echoed back. The room emptied quickly. Johann hoped he would be invited to an evening gathering, but soon found himself alone in the hallway. The secretary told him how to make streetcar connections back to the train station. When he arrived there, with some time before his departure, he walked the short distance to *Potsdamer Platz*. Strung across the streets were banners proclaiming victory in Poland. Thousands of people were going home from work. He walked around slowly, admiring the liveliness and exhilaration he saw on their faces. After awhile, he found his way back to the station, decided to eat something, and sat at a table with a beer and a plate of wurst and bread, reading a newspaper. Two hours later, he boarded the night train back to Nuremberg. Although tired, he went straight to the clinic as soon as he arrived in the early morning.

When he came home for his midday meal, Helga did not seem interested in what he had had to tell her. She just shrugged when he said, "I cannot disclose what we discussed, but it was quite important." He hoped she would try to get him to tell her more. Instead, she asked about Philipp.

After passing on Philipp's greetings and saying nothing more about their meeting, he quickly shifted to what he had seen in Berlin. "*Potsdamer Platz* is amazing. It's not a city square, but rather an intersection of main boulevards. On all sides, lights, energy, noise. People scurrying in all directions. Like an anthill. Everyone going his or her separate way, with some purpose. And still, all of us Germans, all of us proud of what our country is doing. You can just feel it, Helga. It was so clear to me. I will have to go back to Berlin again in a few weeks. Maybe you can come with me. You can go to the *Kaufhaus des Westens* and do some early Christmas shopping while I am in my meeting. I shall be traveling often, I believe. Perhaps then...."

Helga pretended not to hear. "Paul-Adolf will be going away, starting tomorrow, for the next ten days," she said. "He's being sent with the *Hitler Jugend* to a youth camp in Poland. He's very excited. He'll enlist in the army as soon as he can, he tells me." She sighed. "Would you like more potatoes?"

CHAPTER SIXTEEN
𝕬 𝕯𝖊𝖛𝖎𝖑 𝕬𝖒𝖔𝖓𝖌 𝕯𝖊𝖛𝖎𝖑𝖘

My work in Berlin led to my assignment in early 1940 at Grafeneck under Doktor *Schumann.Thinking back on it now, I know that I lost my soul there, if not five years before, when I worked in Koblenz. I admit, Helga, the first months of the war energized me. I was convinced that we could do no wrong. In April, I volunteered for the SS as a field doctor.You knew I was in Denmark. I soon saw that the real war in the east was passing me by. I wanted more action.After sixteen months, I applied for a transfer.*

As you may have suspected, I was posted to Auschwitz.Yes, Auschwitz! To be honest, I was grateful to be going. It was an answer to my prayers.You know how much I wanted to do something important.

Auschwitz was at the edge of Hell. No, it was Hell itself.Working there, I became a devil among devils, all of us prodding our victims toward disgrace and death. I once had thought myself so important and my work so beneficial for humanity.What I did not realize until then was the depths to which human beings can sink to gain power over others. I soon learned that I was no different. At Auschwitz, I steeled myself to ignore the suffering I saw—and caused. It was my way of enduring. Eventually, I could endure no more. For now, know only that I may not have been the greatest devil at Auschwitz. But even a small devil can do great harm.

*****

Johann's hand was trembling when he put his pen down. Writing the word "Auschwitz" threw him into a sweat. How had a place become such a monstrous memory? How did the mere mention of it call up the names of men he could never forget? Mengele, Schumann, Clauberg, Schetzeler. And more important than any of these, Aronsohn. He had only to think of the word "Auschwitz" and he heard Aronsohn's screams. Louder than the trains. Louder than the wails of the mothers on the ramp. He could not stop himself from remembering Aronsohn.

*****

"Do you have a garden, gentlemen?"

"Pardon me, sir," Johann said.

"Do you have a garden, I ask. Do you and your wives garden? Vegetables. Cabbage. Tomatoes. Peas. A garden."

Johann looked at *Doktor* Schetzeler who was as puzzled as he was by the question. The two men had arrived at Auschwitz together by train late the day before, both newly assigned to the camp's medical staff. Now they were at trackside, waiting for a "transport" with *SS Doktor* Josef Mengele. He already knew that Mengele was important. One of the most important doctors in the camp. Why would he ask about a garden?

Schetzeler answered first. "I'm not married, *Herr Reichsarzt*. My parents had a garden when I was a boy. But no, I don't have a garden."

"My wife and I don't have much of a garden," Johann said. "A few bushes of red and black currants and some gooseberries that grow in the courtyard behind our apartment building. And a wonderful plum tree. Helga, my wife, tends the berries, but the neighborhood children usually get most of them. My parents used to have a big garden."

"No, I don't mean some bushes and a fruit tree. I mean a real garden," Mengele said. "With your seedlings neat and orderly, each in its own row, properly labeled, each tended, watered and sheltered from the wind. That kind of a garden. A garden thought out in advance. Planned. A deliberate, conscious effort to make something important happen. Just because it concerns cabbages, carrots and kohlrabi, it should not be thought that such a garden, such a plan, is unimportant."

"Yes, when I was a boy, near Munich, we had such a garden, *Herr Reichsarzt*. Not now," Johann said, still wondering how this topic had appeared.

Mengele's voice was clear and strong. He exuded self-confidence and calm, an aura of respectable authority. Where they were walking, however, there was little suggestion of a garden. The rails looked slippery and bright in the rising sunlight, with reddish rust stains on the ties beneath them. Here and there, prisoners on their knees picked cinders out of the rail bed and putting them in little piles alongside the tracks for other prisoners to collect. That alone conveyed the image of a garden, the bent men gleaning a stony, double row of steel and blackened ties in search of its remaining fruits.

"I have always maintained that gardening is essential for balance, for stability, *meine Herren*. It provides us with more than sustenance. It restores our connection to the soil. Our *Führer* tells us this, of course. But it is quite obvious. Our civilization must not forget how to garden. In gardening, you must be willing to weed. To weed! To see what is undesirable, what is noxious and disruptive of your plan, and eliminate it. Weeding is as much a part of gardening as is sowing, watering, and harvesting. In fact, if you don't weed effectively and thoroughly, you will have no harvest. Weeds will overrun your garden and rob your plants of nourishment and space. This is a fact of life." Mengele began to slow down, his lecture over. Johann and Schetzeler adjusted their pace accordingly.

"You understand this, gentlemen?"

"Indeed, *Herr Reichsarzt*," Schetzeler said. "I see your point. The Jews are human weeds. I've always thought so. Pushing themselves into our world wherever they can. Despicable creatures. Weeds, exactly!"

Johann said nothing. He thought back to his childhood, to his family's garden in Pohlendorf, to his mother bent over rows of onions. He saw himself as a small boy, pulling weeds alongside her. The weeds' fleshy, sometimes hairy, broad leaves were easy to identify among the sprouting onion tops. His mother would say, every few minutes, "Only the weeds, Johann. Only the weeds. We can't eat them."

"Why, *Mutti?*"

"We are people. We eat onions. Not weeds. Birds and squirrels will eat them. But some weeds are very pretty. For each thing, there is a reason, Johann. Our onions will grow better without the weeds shading them. The weeds have a reason to be, too. They can grow where they like. Just not in our onions."

Mengele came to a halt and stamped his foot. Johann and Schetzeler both stopped abruptly. Johann felt like a dog whose master has stepped on his leash. He turned to look directly at the *Reichsarzt,* hoping for a chance to say how important he felt their work was. How willing he was to continue the path that now lay clear before the *Vaterland*. How much he hoped to serve. He needed to say these things, not so much to impress Mengele as to reaffirm to himself his willingness to be there, now that he had seen the camp and heard some stories about what went on there.

He opened his mouth to speak, but Mengele was looking down the tracks toward the camp's main gate. A train was approaching, floating on a bed of steam. The morning sunlight flashed off the locomotive's windows. The gate swung open as Johann turned to look. He remembered a story in one of his Latin courses about a mythical, roaring gorgon that turned anyone who beheld it into stone.

As the train rolled toward them, slowing in a hiss of steam and screeching metal, the platform began to bustle with activity. Johann had been so focused on his conversation with Mengele that he had not paid attention to anyone else. Now, appearing as if some sorcerer had conjured them from the air, he saw a squad of smartly uniformed SS guards and their Alsatian dogs advance toward the slowing train. At the same time, bundles of rags now stood upright and walked close alongside the track. Some, he knew, were *Kapos*, convicts transported here from other prisons. For their brutality? Their calloused spirit? Their hopelessness?

Whatever the reason, this was where they were to continue their sentences. Others, more emaciated than the *Kapos*, he took to be Jewish prisoners who had been lured or frightened into unspeakable tasks, in the hopes of a family member's or their own survival. To Johann, they looked more like shabby train station equipment, drab and worn baggage carts and hand-trucks, than human beings. All were performing a macabre dance, shuffling back and forth in their appointed roles. Caps sat loosely on their shaved heads. Dull eyes darted back and forth in gray, stubbled faces. Striped shirts hung on skeletal bodies. Trousers looked about to fall down around their knees. Walking, grunting hunks of rags. He tried not to stare.

Mengele began to bark out orders. "Stay here, *Herr Doktor* Brenner. *Herr Doktor* Schetzeler, come with me." Schetzeler shot Johann a self-satisfied look, as if to say 'I already have made a better impression.' Johann already knew that he did not like him. Ambitious and crude. He watched as the two men strode quickly toward the far end of the platform. The glossy shine on Schetzeler's boots won't last long here, he thought.

One car stopped right in front of Johann. Some *Kapos* released the bars and locks on the doors and others yanked the doors open. Inside, a tangle of bodies attempted to unravel itself and get out. With huge liquid eyes, the captives squinted in the dazzling light. Some near the door were standing on the bodies of those who had died. It was not, however, the sight of the stunned and crazed people inside that struck him so powerfully, but the smell. The fetid air nearly knocked him over. He then noticed that the prisoners, the *Kapos*, the *SS* guards and even the dogs had learned through experience to turn their heads aside to avoid the smell.

Prisoners on the ramp pulled the corpses out and slung them like rolled up carpets onto railway baggage carts. Others pulled the living down onto the ramp. Shrieks and sobs blended into an unimaginable chorus. Mothers gripped their children so hard that they screamed. Old men tried to climb down from the boxcars with dignified authority, only to be clubbed over the head or jabbed in the ribs or groin, and fall.

The *SS* guards' dogs caught Johann's eye. Most put their tails down and pawed the ground, their eyes bulging and fangs bared. One large, black Alsatian near him had an alert, curious look, cocking his head and raising his ears, as if astonished at so much beastliness, before it, too, was jerked into an attack posture by its guard and began to snarl.

The guards barked: "Out! Out! Jews out! *Juden 'raus! Los! Los!* Fast! Fast!" 'Who would not want to come out of these stinking boxcars?' Johann thought. For the guards and *Kapos*, the pace of clearing the cars was too slow. Some of the younger people jumped off with little difficulty, others had to be pushed or pulled out, and fell to the ground.

Two prisoners pulled an old man, moaning and begging for water, out of the train and dropped him near Johann, as if to say, 'Here, you brought him here. Now do something for him.'

The image of old *Herr* Semmelberg flashed into Johann's mind. 'If the Semmelberg I saw in Nuremberg had a beard, he would look much like this. But he probably died years ago. Better if he had. What is Semmelberg to me now? That indecisive period of my life, those trivial concerns, all behind me now,' he told himself. He pulled his shoulders back to stand taller. A *Kapo* prodded the old man to his feet and pushed him back into the crowd, where an old woman and a young boy took him in. Johann was relieved.

All along the procession of prisoners, small children howled. Mothers tried to console them and not cry themselves. Old men and women stumbled. Young boys and girls found it hard to shuffle along at such a slow pace: "Where is the water? Where are our belongings? Where will we be sleeping?" There were no answers.

Pistol shots cracked out now and then. Heads turned in vain. "What was that? Was it a shot?" A guard, his hand on his holstered *Walther*, droned, "Please keep moving. Keep moving! We will register you quickly and you will be shown your quarters. There is water and food ahead. Keep moving, please. We will register you. Keep moving!"

A little boy, no more than three, jerked free from his mother with shrill, hysterical screams and ran toward Johann. He picked up the child and brought it toward the line, where a tearful woman mouthed her thanks. Turning quickly away, he resisted the impulse to shut out the shouts, wails and screams by putting his hands over his ears. Walking back to a position away from the crowd, he imagined himself at a zoo, not wanting to stand too near a cage of strange beasts for fear of being clawed into their midst.

On that first day, at least, Johann knew this was no zoo. These creatures were frightened and confused human beings. Of course, they would be desperate. For that reason alone, they were dangerous. They had to be calmed. Handled efficiently. With force if necessary. Ultimately, order would be restored.

Johann put what he saw within the context of what he knew. Jews and other undesirables were being brought to a "relocation centers for their own safety." Those arriving from overcrowded, disease-ridden ghettoes may have believed that that they were going to better living conditions. If the prosperous ones from captured western cities had been persuaded to purchase tickets for the trip, hoping that would gain them more comfort *en route,* they had probably pulled worse tricks in accumulating their fortunes. He had heard that one strategy to reassure the Jews that everything would return to normal when they reached their destination was to tell them to bring their own bed linens and cutlery. He learned later that many women, fearing that they would not be able to do their laundry as often as they wished, dyed their sheets and pillowcases blue, so dirt would not show as much. Of course, the Jews would try to hide gold and jewels on—or even in—their bodies. Weren't they age-old, cunning liars? They would have to be stripped naked and searched. Their suitcases and other belongings would have to be carted away and checked for weapons or wealth. It stood to reason.

He heard the *SS* guard recite the litany, "You'll get your belongings later. We will resolve all your problems as soon as possible." Resonating through the din was his unmuzzled dog's nervous growl.

The guards divided the captives into two groups: males, and females and children. Johann could see Mengele further down the ramp in his white laboratory coat, with Schetzeler close behind him, at the head of a column of women and children five-wide. The women were being ordered into a single file. Some, exhausted from the journey or so pre-occupied with trying to learn what would happen to them, may not have suspected the importance of the procedure. Johann noticed how the young mothers clutched their children closely, as though their tired and bewildered grip could outmatch the uniformed guards and their dogs. The captives grew silent, except for the crying of children. When the last of them passed him, Johann began walking toward the head of the procession.

Mengele, gesturing nonchalantly with his riding crop, was waving the women and children into new lines: "*Links! Rechts!* You, by truck! You, walk! Walk! You, truck! *Links! Rechts!*" His shout was staccato, shrill. Johann could see that he barely looked at the parade of prisoners passing before him until he saw a dwarf or a cripple or twins. Then he would stop the line, go closer, look into their eyes, make some mental calculation, smile broadly revealing the wide gap between his front teeth, or frown. Now and then, he offered a piece of candy to a child, or chucked a baby under the chin. "What a pretty little creature," he would say to the mother. "Tell her there's nothing to be afraid of."

The night before, a guard at the barracks had told Johann that the *Kapos* called Mengele a "white angel" because he stood on the ramp with outstretched arms, wearing his laboratory coat. A week or so later, he heard a prisoner call him the "angel of death." By then he knew why.

From where he stood, Johann saw the trucks with the red crosses painted on their doors. Those sent toward them must have been relieved—surely, this meant that they were destined for special care, a ride to their accommodations, to water and food, to a bed. Many pled to be sent to the trucks. Those made to walk were disappointed. Even angry. But he soon learned that the trucks took their passengers straight to the de-lousing showers where they were asphyxiated by *Zyklon-B* gas. And from there, their bodies were taken to be cremated in an open pit or in ovens meticulously engineered just for this purpose. How could they know that riding on the trucks meant going to their doom? That going on foot meant a chance to live longer? Later, Johann could not avoid asking himself, 'Who were the luckier ones?'

He tried to avoid looking at any one person in particular, but one incident broke into his effort to stay aloof. A young woman a few feet away on the ramp shrieked at a prisoner who had grabbed her roughly by the shoulder and pulled her out of the shuffling herd. Her little daughter had almost lost her grip on her dress and would have been trampled if the woman had not bent over and picked her up. With her crying child in her arms, she glared at the *SS* guard, shook herself free of the prisoner, and walked right over to Johann.

"This man, this… this ugly man," she said in perfect High German, pointing toward the one who had grabbed her, "says my daughter and I will both be sent to a gas chamber and killed, that I should save myself, abandon her and pretend I don't have a child!" She began to sob. Her eyes appealed for compassion and an explanation. The girl looked eerily like Greta.

Johann grew dizzy, then steeled himself. "Madam, please," he said, softly, almost in a whisper even he could not hear. He took a deep breath and began again, this time louder. Looking directly into her face, into pale eyes welling over with tears, he appealed to reason: "Madam, please calm yourself. Do you think we are barbarians?" The woman and her child fell back into the lines of people that paralleled the train-tracks. A few minutes later, he saw Mengele sending them to the trucks.

Within an hour, the whole process, from the train's arrival to the selections, was over. The platform was empty. The train was gone. The squads of SS guards marched off. The *Kapos* and prisoners dissolved into the shadows. Smoke and haze rose from the camp and dulled the sun.

Later that morning, Johann attended a physicians' staff meeting. With its grey-green walls, smooth concrete floor and high windows, its large oaken table, Hitler's picture on the wall, the meeting room was like any small conference room in a hospital across *Reich*. As Johann entered, Horst Schumann greeted him. They had not met since Johann left Grafeneck two years before. Johann was pleased when Schumann took the seat next to him. "We can talk afterwards," Schumann said. Johann nodded, looking around to see if he recognized anyone else. Aside from Mengele and Schetzeler, all the rest were strangers. He assumed most were physicians. From across the table, a major sitting next to Mengele loudly greeted a physician who was sitting on Johann's side of the table a few seats away, next to Schetzeler. Wearing thick, heavy, black-rimmed glasses, Carl Clauberg smiled broadly and bobbed his head up and down like a pigeon before returning to his conversation with Schetzeler. Johann knew Clauberg by reputation as one of Germany's leading gynecologists, and wondered what had brought him here. He hoped Schumann would introduce him. Instead, Schumann seemed deliberately to avoid looking at Clauberg. Johann wondered why but thought it could wait until after the meeting. Sitting at the table, he tried to tell himself that he was a member of an elite team whose work would benefit the *Vaterland* and bring them all great recognition. Looking around, he saw that if anyone else was uncomfortable about the morning's selection, it was not evident.

The camp's chief medical officer, *SS-Hauptsturmführer Doktor* Eduard Wirths rose to speak. After extending a warm welcome on behalf of the camp commander, he turned the meeting over to Mengele with effusive praise for his diligent energy and left the room. Mengele began with the gardening theme of his trackside conversation.

"As I was saying earlier to our newest colleagues"—Mengele's quick glance toward Johann and then Schetzeler brought everyone else's eyes toward them—"we do difficult, but necessary work. As necessary as life itself. We are the pruners, the shapers and changers of the destiny of the human race. We serve the best interests of our species here, in every sense of the word. We are gardeners, gentlemen. Gardeners."

Johann noticed how the others nodded in assent, a bored look on their faces. They had heard all this before.

Mengele was not daunted. "I welcome this responsibility, gentlemen. I even enjoy it, because our hard work, our difficult and dangerous work is essential for humanity's happiness. I see such wonderful potential from this experience." Here he looked at Johann. "We can learn a great deal from these wretches, these weeds that come here in such great numbers. I see them as a great opportunity for an experiment that will eventually reveal some wonderful truths for our cause. We can learn how to increase our numbers, by studying multiple births among our guests." Someone chuckled. "We can learn to augment intelligence, to deter birth defects, to increase longevity, to maximize physique and stamina. It is a beautiful irony, gentlemen. It makes me smile." And here Mengele actually did smile, a wide, full smile revealing his unusually even teeth with their conspicuous gap, and the tip of his moist, deep-red tongue. Johann saw how those around him were smiling, too.

"Yes, it's beautiful!" Mengele said. "A wonderful irony. From the damnable Jews, so cunning at survival all these centuries, from the filthy Gypsies, a foul stench of a *Volk*—we can learn the secrets of the human body and apply these lessons to the further perfection of our superior, Aryan bodies and minds. It is a fitting purpose to which we put these Jews, given their exploitation of our strength, our energies, our women, our children. The Gypsies may know no better, but the Jews have been our cunning enemies from the beginning." Noises of agreement filled the room. Johann recognized Schetzeler's high-pitched voice, "*Jawohl! Jawohl!*"

"I have in mind," Mengele continued, "a series of controlled experiments which will yield crucial information about fertility. I have already begun to assemble information about twins and suspect the results will be simple and straightforwardly applicable. This morning's delivery brought at least four suitable sets of twins—two identical and two fraternal—for my project. One fraternal pair in particular should prove very rewarding, as they each have a blue and a brown eye. We shall see. I am confident that learning about the generation of twins, of multiple births in general, will guarantee us the strength to control the future.

"Meanwhile, *Herr Doktor* Schumann and *Herr Doktor* Clauberg, you must work out efficient ways to effect a meaningful control on the ability of our enemies to reproduce themselves. Only with the combination of these efforts can we really be successful. I am pleased to acknowledge your two newly arrived assistant physicians, *SS Obersturmführer Doktor* Brenner and *SS Obersturmführer Doktor* Schetzeler." Mengele's applause signaled the others to join in.

Clauberg applauded louder than anyone else did. Johann saw him out of the corner of his eye, smiling and bobbing his head up and down, about to speak. Schumann, who appeared to be offended, cut him off. He interpreted Mengele's remarks to mean that his life's work was a negative, in contrast to Mengele's positive research.

"Gentlemen," Schumann said, pushing his chair back so he could stand, "when I work on refining the most suitable, most efficient scientific process to achieve effective sterilization—a sterilization that will not impede the further productivity of the individual involved—I am searching for a *positive*"—he came close to shouting the word—"method to secure full and thorough control over those individuals whose importance for the economic survival of the *Reich* cannot be ignored, at least now, in the midst of this war."

Johann heard Clauberg cackle. Schumann took a deep breath and continued. "Just as oxen are an improvement over bulls, and geldings are an improvement over stallions, for the purposes of tractability and greater work efficiency, so the sterilization of unwanted human males, whether Poles, Gypsies, Jews, or whatever, will give us enormous advantages in performing the unavoidable tasks no civilized person should have to perform." Schumann gestured so broadly with his arms that Johann had to duck. "I think of mining, for example, or working in tedious or dangerous assembly tasks," he said. "Here, thanks to the workings of Providence and the leadership of our *Führer*, we have ample and, as we say, appropriate material on which to develop and perfect our methods for efficient and reliable sterilization." Around the room, those who were listening nodded mechanically. Johann heard Clauberg clucking his tongue and drumming his fingers on the table. Others, Johann noted, seemed lost in their own thoughts. Mengele looked at the clock on the wall.

"The results of my investigations," Schumann went on, struggling to hold the others' attention by pounding his fist on the table, "will be tremendously positive. We are demonstrating incontrovertibly that X-ray castrations are positive, effective and permanent ways of preventing propagation. The treated person—male or female—retains enough vigor to be of use. I believe there is a remarkable advantage in time alone, to say nothing about the greater certainty of this sterilization process, primarily in males, compared with the chemical sterilization of females." Now Clauberg was shaking his head in disagreement and muttering something Johann could not hear.

Schumann paid no attention and extended his arms broadly in a gesture of self-confidence and pride, "That is to say, gentlemen, we can easily achieve sterilization in a male subject with X-rays in six or seven minutes. X-rays are efficient. Silent. The subject suspects nothing. Of course, there are still refinements to be achieved—dosage, appropriate duration of exposure, and so forth. Small details. I am happy to have *SS-Obersturmführer Doktor* Brenner here, as my new assistant. The first lieutenant will work with me to confirm the efficacy of these procedures." Schumann then nodded toward Johann and paused before he sat down, apparently hoping for applause or some other sign of approval.

Instead, all eyes turned toward Johann, who assumed that he was now required to make a statement of some sort, and began to clear his throat, only to have Mengele interrupt. "Yes, indeed, welcome *Obersturmführer* Brenner. Perhaps you have something you want to say, *Herr Doktor* Clauberg?"

Clauberg waited a few moments before he stood up. "Thank you, *Herr Doktor* Mengele. It is an honor and a privilege to work with you. My facilities and the conditions here for science are excellent. I need not tell you, perhaps, that *Herr Doktor* Schumann and I have some disagreements about methodology. Ultimately, one of us will be confirmed in our approach. I am confident, of course, that it will be me. I invite all of you to observe my procedures. *Herr Doktor* Schetzeler here, an accomplished gynecologist, has agreed to assist me. I am confident that our results will prove the validity of my method. Nothing else should matter for scientists, I need not say." He sat down with a smug look on his face, as the others applauded politely. Schetzeler beamed.

Looking at his watch, Mengele said, "And now, my colleagues, we have work to do. Work, it is. Yes, 'work will make us free!'" They all smiled. A few, including both Schumann and Clauberg, laughed out loud. Johann did not understand until he recalled the slogan welded in iron letters over the camp's gate. Mengele stood up, the signal for them all to do so. *"Heil Hitler!"* still echoed in the room as they filed out.

Schumann waited for Johann outside and walked with him down the hallway and into the courtyard. "I am glad you have come to join me. I can use prisoner physicians, of course, but I need someone reliable. Now that you're here, we'll show them some good medical science. There's much to do. So much to do. And so much to learn. As I said, we have ample appropriate material." Here he gestured with a broad wave of his arm. Johann followed its sweep across the path, toward the barracks and the buildings of the prisoners' hospital. In the surgery in *Block 20*, where he would do the castrations. All around them was the sprawling camp and its additions. Taller than any building, red-brick smokestacks pierced a milky blue sky. A slight wind spilled their smoke away from the two doctors toward the sun, curling its edges blood red.

"I have heard about the gas," Johann said.

"What's that?"

"I have heard about the gas. From a guard posted by our barracks last night. I asked him about the chimneys. He told me. About the selections and the gas. It's like Grafeneck."

"We did pioneering work."

"Ja, Herr Doktor. I cannot forget it. I know it was important, but...," Johann trailed off into his thoughts for a moment. Schumann waited for him to continue.

"But, I should like to see how the procedure has been refined and implemented here. Further improved. Made more modern. More effi-cient. Cleaner than..." He could not finish his sentence. Schumann started to say something but Johann continued, "Perhaps that will help me understand. Help me get...." Again he stopped. He was about to tell Schumann about his recurrent nightmare. About the injection he gave to a young boy at Grafeneck. About how the boy's eyes haunted him. He forced the thought out of his mind by wondering if progress was simply a factor of speed, if the faster things could be made to go, the better they were. He thought back to the first automobile he saw in Pohlendorf. How horses were frightened by its noise. How he was frightened, too. How, at the same time, he was fascinated by how fast it went. How it moved by itself. He remembered running after it, watching it go down the road until it disappeared. So much had changed since then. He looked up toward the chimneys.

Schumann followed Johann's eyes. "See the procedure? You probably cannot avoid seeing it. You can even count it for time served on duty with me, if you want. I'll release you for an appropriate number of hours. Prisoner physicians, as I say, can still fill in with castrations. Gassing is much larger here, naturally. A camp physician is required to oversee the site, according to protocol. You'll have a turn. Since you are working with me, however, on an experiment of value to the *Reich*, you're not required for now to do anything there. I suspect you'll not want to see too much of it. It is, well, certainly not clean, in the way I take you to mean that word. Clean it is not. Probably it can never be clean. But it is modern and efficient. Yes, beyond question, it is efficient." Schumann stopped abruptly and looked down at his smartly polished boots.

He began speaking again, almost in a whisper. "I must tell you something, *Herr Doktor* Brenner, in confidence, of course. The end result of the procedure is...." He paused. "...of the process..." then paused again, looking for an appropriate way, for what he thought would be a manly way, to express his discomfort. "It is..., it is..., well, let's just say, unpleasant."

Johann could not be sure if Schumann's voice had cracked or if it was the sound of their boots on the gravel walk. They walked a few steps without saying anything.

"No, unpleasant is not quite the word," Schumann said. Then, apprehensive he showed some weakness, some shameful residue of sentimentality, he paused again, closed his eyes, and said, raising his voice, "Distracting. Yes, that would be more like it." He stopped and looked away from Johann. "I have seen men who were otherwise sturdy and courageous and loyal, unquestionably loyal, you know, become softened and weakened by the experience. Some even become ill, physically and mentally. Raving. I have seen it. I think I can even understand it, a little.

Despite our efforts, these selections and actions are a disorderly process. The aftermath is distracting. You know what I mean. We saw that already at Grafeneck, having to pull the corpses out of the busses. Foul. Seventy-five at a time. Here we're more efficient. Faster, with greater capacity. Incineration is more effective, but still slow. There might be a better way, but we haven't discovered it yet. That's why I am interested in sterilizing the prisoners through X-rays. It reduces the need for mass gassings and gives us the benefit of additional labor. But we still have to take care of the lot. Feed them, of course. That's necessary, if we want them to work. And eventually there are too many to take care of, especially those who stop working. So, the gassings. Logical." He took a deep breath.

Johann nodded.

"But *ja*," Schumann continued, his voice again so quiet Johann could barely hear him, "the aftermath of the gassings can be grisly to those who don't keep their minds focused on our goals. It helps to have something strong to drink beforehand. That worked well enough once for me. But I don't want anything to do with the wild parties. It's understandable, I suppose, for some of the men, those who are weak, you know. But for *SS* men? For officers? I don't think so. No excuse for it. Shameful. Orgies, I'm told. No, I've seen too many naked women, in roll calls, in selections. Naked women you would never want to see naked. Revolting." He paused. Then, in a louder voice, he said, "Strong drink does help. But I don't want to see too much. I don't have time for it." He turned to look toward the chimneys. "Neither do you, *Herr Doktor*. We must not be distracted from our responsibilities. We can leave the distasteful part to the *Sonderkommando*."

"The *Sonderkommando*?"

"A special detail of camp prisoners. They do all the dirty work—pulling the bodies out the delousing showers. Loading them into the ovens. Other unsavory stuff."

"They do this?"

"They get privileges. Better food. And *schnapps*. They get to keep some of the stuff they steal from the dead. Until...."

"Until what?

"Until they no longer serve our purposes, of course. They especially must not survive."

"I see."

"They're happy enough to postpone their own fate for a month or two."

Schumann paused and looked around, as if to see who might be watching them. He continued again in his raspy whisper. "But, I say, let the others worry about that. We must be hard. I have trained myself to be. We all must be." His voice rose to a crescendo. "We are doctors, after all."

Johann watched Schumann's set jaw, saw a blood vessel swelling on his forehead. Where had he seen this determination before? In Graeber. *Doktor* Graeber, at the policlinic in Nuremberg. Schumann was neither a drunk nor an oaf, but somehow that made the similarity of the two physicians all the more worrisome.

"We must take advantage of this marvelous opportunity for medical science," Schumann almost shouted, with his arms held wide and looking from side to side. "This is a wonderful laboratory. A once-in-a-life-time opportunity!" With that, he turned abruptly and began striding down the path. He was a tall, fit, athletic man. He looked dashing in his *Luftwaffe* uniform, the epitome of a Nazi officer.

With his limp, Johann lagged behind, trying to keep up. Schumann's words, "a wonderful laboratory," tumbled over and over in his mind, their rhythm setting his pace. When they arrived at the officer's mess, beads of sweat glistened on Johann's brow.

The pungent smell of a thick stew of white sausages and potatoes filled the room. Schumann and Johann sat with four other doctors. Clauberg and Schetzeler sat a table by themselves. Prisoners served the meal. After a large helping of the stew, and some heavy white bread, and a beer, Johann felt more relaxed.

All the men at his table had been at the meeting earlier in the day, but instead of discussing it, they talked of other things. About cameras. About cheeses. And wines. The conversation turned to children. Should girls be encouraged to study medicine? "What on earth for…?" Who need more discipline, boys or girls? "Girls can be little devils…." As the conversation moved on to racecars and mountain climbing, Johann sat silently drank another beer. He knew that such conversations could be heard among colleagues anywhere after a midday meal. After a while, he was lost in his thoughts about his conversation with Schumann. Two prisoners, barely disguising their intention of swiping anything that remained on the plates, cleared the tables.

In a letter to Helga that evening, Johann wrote about the meal, the conversation and the clear, blue skies. Nothing else. As to where he was, he simply wrote, "In the *Ostmark*"—the name the Nazis had given to the land they had conquered in Poland. He finished unpacking, chatted with others in the *SS* barracks, and found some medical literature to read. He was eager to get started on the important work he had come to do. Work, he assured himself, would give him the sense of accomplishment and satisfaction that he needed to put the world of Auschwitz into its proper perspective.

Schumann wanted him to do a simple surgical procedure. In medical school, Johann's instructors had been pleased with his work on cadavers and had told him that, with practice, he could become proficient with a scalpel. Just before he and Helga were married, he took a brief rotation in a surgical clinic in Munich. He decided that he was more interested in internal medicine. His next surgical experience was in Koblenz on the mixed-race children. Now, eight years later, he was going to hold a scalpel in his hand.

Early the next day, he reported to the surgery in *Block 20*, one of the red-brick buildings that served as the prisoners' hospital. It resembled an austere apartment house on an orderly, tree-lined avenue, except for the group of sullen, frightened prisoners standing against the wall and an *SS* guard, his rifle at the ready, with his dog. The guard greeted him with a '*Heil Hitler!*' as he went inside.

Schumann was waiting for him and in a hurry. "I must leave shortly for Berlin. I'll be away a few days. Routine reporting, paper work, you know. I had hoped it could wait until next week. I wanted to be here to show you the procedure. But I trust you, *Herr Doktor* Brenner. Without question." Johann hoped his face did not reveal his apprehension.

"Just a few days, as I say. I'll be back late Friday evening," Schumann continued. "Then early on Saturday and Sunday, I'm hoping to go hunting. Saw tracks of a wild boar in the hills north of here last week. Passion of mine. That and fishing. You're in charge during my absence. We can talk on Monday. I've told the nurse. She knows the procedure quite well. And you already know the general thrust of my work. I'm confident that X-rays will achieve our goal. But we need solid evidence. We've used varying dosages. How much is too little? How much is too much? Above all, are these subjects sterile? Getting proof is simple enough. Remove the testicles. To put it crudely, we need their balls. Mind you, handle them with appropriate care. The relatively poor septic conditions aren't important. Just get semen counts and the balls."

"Don't worry, *Herr Doktor*. I will give you a report as soon as you return from your hunt. Good luck."

They exchanged energetic "*Heil Hitlers!*"

In the surgery, the low morning sunlight slanted through the barred windows and illuminated countless dust motes in the air. Johann told himself not to worry. The nurse introduced herself and helped him put on a white coat. He scrubbed his hands and arms briskly while she watched—she hummed a folksong that he had not heard in years. He smiled at her, then stepped to the operating table, asked her to adjust the hanging lamp, and said he was ready.

The nurse signaled to two Kapos standing in the hallway. They brought in an emaciated prisoner, holding him off the floor so he had to walk awkwardly on his toes. The man was breathing hard and groaning with each step. Johann had seen him earlier, standing outside nearest the door. He remembered his frightened eyes.

The *Kapos* lifted him onto the table and pushed him down. One walked around behind his head and held him by the shoulders, with his forearm across his jaw and neck. The other took up his position at the foot of the table. He quickly pulled down the man's trousers and twisted his lower body toward Johann, so his buttocks were exposed to the nurse on the other side. The prisoner began to sob and gasp for breath.

Syringe in hand, the nurse gave the man an injection near his lower spine. He continued to sob, but softer and more muffled now. Within a minute or two, his bony legs went limp. The *Kapo* at his head straightened up, but kept his hands on the prisoner's shoulders. Johann forced himself to look closely at the prisoner's face. The man's dark brown eyes, red rimmed and moist with tears, stared up at him in sheer terror. Flecks of spittle had formed at the corner of his mouth. He tried to wet his lips with his tongue, but this only spread the spittle around, making it look like he had just drunk a thick mixture of chalky water. Johann, noticing that one of the prisoner's front teeth was broken off and that his lip was bleeding, dabbed at the blood with a cotton pad until the nurse took the pad from him. She was less gentle and the prisoner jerked his head away. When he looked up at the *Kapo*, he began to wail, until he was slapped sharply across his ear. Both *Kapos* now stood by his head, each holding down a shoulder.

Johann took the scalpel from the nurse. The prisoner's eyes widened and he began to whimper in quick gasps. Then, with a deep voice, perfectly clear and surprisingly strong, he shouted in German with a Polish accent, "I am Aronsohn. Aronsohn! Daniel Aronsohn! Daniel Aronsohn! Daniel Aronsohn! From Danzig! Aronsohn!" Each time he said his name it got louder and louder. "I am a man. I am a man! I am Aronsohn! Daniel Aronsohn, a man!"

Johann told a *Kapo* to hold the patient's head still and to put something in his mouth. "Daniel Aron..." A wad of cotton muffled the rest. The *Kapos* held his head as if it were a bowling ball. Their fingers dug into the space below the man's eyes. Their thumbs jabbed into his ears. Johann was afraid they would pop his eyes out of their sockets. He looked toward Aronsohn's exposed groin.

Where a man's penis and testicles would normally have been in a nest of hair, Johann saw a matted and putrid tangle of sores, the effects of X-ray burns. Pus had dried in clots. He half-expected to see maggots feeding on the mess. Aronsohn's genitals smelled like rotting meat. The nurse appeared less troubled by the sight. She grabbed Aronsohn's shriveled penis as though it was a sausage on a butcher's table and began to swab the raw flesh around what remained of his testicles with alcohol. Aronsohn screamed and ejaculated.

"*Schwein!*" the nurse shouted, jerking her hand away in disgust.

Desperate to establish control, Johann shouted, "Quiet!" He ordered that some of the prisoner's seminal fluid be collected for a sperm count.

The nurse turned to that task with a glass slide. Aronsohn tried to shout again, but it sounded more like an animal gagging than a human voice. A *Kapo* struck him an enormous blow on his head. Blood spurted from his ear and trickled onto the table. He groaned and closed his eyes.

Johann gestured to the nurse to lift Aronsohn's penis. Light flashed off the scalpel. He made the incision. For reasons he could never determine, even though the memory of the event played over and over in his mind, the scalpel sliced through Aronsohn's scrotum and punctured the inside of his thigh. It was as though the man's flesh was too soft, too weak to impede the blade. Had he exerted too much force? Had Aronsohn twitched just at that moment? Whatever the cause, something went terribly wrong.

He had severed Aronsohn's femoral artery. Dark blood spurted like a fountain from the wound at least three or four inches into the air, over Aronsohn's midsection and legs, splashing on Johann's and the nurse's hands. Blood flowed onto the table and dripped steaming onto the floor. The nurse gasped, "*Gott im Himmel!*"

Aronsohn, adding to the panic of the moment, spit out the gag and began to scream. Then, awakened by his screams, he began to revive. High-pitched moans rose up through his throat, a combination of shrill whistling and the whimpering that one might hear from a tormented rabbit caught in the talons of a hawk. With a lunge, Aronsohn twisted himself free of the Kapos' grip and fell off the table. The nurse swore again and stepped back into the path of a *Kapo*. He tripped and fell, blocking his partner who was coming around the table to help.

Aronsohn's moans were so loud they seemed to come from thousands of Aronsohns. Slowly, they became hollow, fainter, like diminishing echoes. When the last moan and its echo were done, he lay crumpled in a heap on the floor, still bleeding, but dead.

Johann looked at the *Kapos*, who had already started to apologize for their carelessness. "Clean this up at once!" he shouted and walked stiffly out of the room, past the *Kapos* waiting in the hallway, and down the building's front steps. He stood outside, still in his white coat.

The air seemed hot, even though it was early morning. There was no wind. He looked up and saw the smoke from the crematoria chimneys curling into a dark cloud over the camp. Looking west, he imagined he glimpsed the purple fringe of the Carpathians through the haze. 'Beyond lies Nuremberg, less than four hundred miles away,' he thought. 'It might as well be on the other side of the universe.' He wished desperately to go home, to hold Helga close, to see the plum tree in the courtyard. He wished he could undo what he had just done. But he could not.

The prisoners outside *Block 20* stood silent and rigid. They must have heard Aronsohn's screams. They looked at Johann, bespattered with blood, the scalpel still in his hands. The *SS* guard and his dog showed no sign of concern. Both were frozen into a tableau of menace.

Johann took a deep breath. The air tasted bitter, heavy, greasy. After a few minutes, he went back inside. Aronsohn's body was gone. Blood-soaked rags were piled in the corner. The same two *Kapos* stood rigidly on either side of the table, as if nothing unusual had happened. He gestured to the nurse to proceed.

"This time I will use the rod first," she said, with no emotion. She told the *Kapos* to bring in the next prisoner.

Another man was lifted onto the table. His pants were removed. The *Kapos* pinned him down and turned him on his side. The nurse punched the rounded end of a thick wooden dowel into his rectum with one hand, and with the other, held a glass slide on the tip of his penis. The prisoner groaned. The nurse caught some ejaculate on the slide, and sharply twisted the rod as she pulled it out. Another groan. She put the glass slide on a small table, next to a file card with the prisoner's identification number. Turning back to the table, she gave him an injection with another swift jab, then roughly swabbed his suppurating genitals with alcohol.

Johann watched all this as though he were observing it from high in the air. He saw himself and the others standing there. He saw the prisoner clench his eyes shut and saw the guards twist him onto his back. He saw the man stretched out on the table, skeletal, his legs' blue veins criss-crossing pale flesh, a map of intersecting roads or rivers or railroad lines without any place names. He saw himself take the scalpel from the nurse, hold it like a pencil above the man's scrotum, point it downward, and, in one swift stroke, cut off the man's testicles. Saw himself arch his brows in surprise at their weight as they fell into his hand. He saw the nurse hold a porcelain soup bowl, half-filled with alcohol. Saw himself rolling the testicles into it. Saw her put the bowl on the shelf next to the man's card and the glass slide with his semen. Saw her staunch the incision's oozing blood with a gauze pad soaked in alcohol. Saw the pad turn pinkish. Saw her throw it into a can in the corner. Heard the prisoner sobbing. Saw himself signal for the two *Kapos* in the hallway to carry the prisoner to the hospital's ward. Seven minutes, start to finish. It felt like seven days.

The next prisoner was brought in. The nurse jammed the rod into his rectum, caught some semen on a glass slide, and placed it on a tray. She gave him a spinal injection. Johann castrated him. Two testicles rolled into the soup bowl of alcohol. The *Kapos* carried him to the ward. Then another man. And another. Each leaving without his testicles. Each castration quicker than the one before. It was a routine. The *Kapos* never had a break.

CHAPTER SEVENTEEN
The Wrong Time

When I received your letter about Paul-Adolf's death three years ago this month, I was surprised at how little I felt. I am sorry I could not have been with you to help you overcome your grief.

We both know that Paul-Adolf chose his fate, a soldier who wanted to give his life for Adolf Hitler and Germany. Still, how many choices did he really have? He was born at the wrong time to have choices. Perhaps I was, too. In his case, how can we blame him? I had a life before the Nazis came to power. I knew another world. I was a man. He was but a boy. He learned about the Nazis about the same time he learned to read. Everywhere he went, the Nazis were on display. His schools were a nursery for Nazis. He and his friends all played at being Nazis. When Greta fell ill, the Hitler Youth became as much, maybe more of a family to him than we were. From 1933 to 1943, the last ten years of Paul-Adolf's life, more than half of his whole life, he lived for Hitler. Now he died for him. You warned him, Helga. You warned me. Neither of us listened.

Although Johann wanted to be cut off, to face the world alone, he did not foresee how lonely he would be. When he could not sleep in his basement bunk, feeling as though the weight of the courthouse above him were crushing him, he re-read the bundle of letters Helga had sent him after he left for the war. At the time, he was angry with how little they contained. Now he saw that she was trying to express her loneliness, and comfort him in his. The one about Paul-Adolf's death was the most painful.

*****

After a week at Auschwitz, Johann wrote Helga, saying only he was safe and working. What more could he say? He wrote occasionally after that, usually for her birthday or for Christmas, but only brief notes or a postcard. She wrote him long letters, not realizing that half or more of her words were blackened or razored out by the censors. He imagined that the missing sentences were complaints or bitter accusations, giving voice to his own, unspeakable complaints. He could not bear to read the banalities that were left. For all but the highest ranking officers, the censors undercut any hope of intimacy with loved ones. Every letter was predictable: everyone was invariably healthy; the neighbors were always well-wishing; this or that gift and celebration was being planned. The letters usually closed, *"Take care and come home safe and sound."* Helga's were no different.

In March 1943, Johann received a letter from her that was not like the others. *"Yesterday,"* she wrote, *"I received a letter telling us of Paul-Adolf's death in the east. Just one sentence: 'Your son died with courage and devotion to our* Volk, *our* Vaterland, *and our glorious* Führer, *Adolf Hitler.' There is a signature by his commanding officer, but I cannot read it. Just this one sentence. And with the letter was a small box, containing an engraved wristwatch, two torn photographs and a badly tattered, blood-stained, unfinished letter that begins, 'My dearest mother and father' and goes on to mention the soldier's home town, Ebingen! It's not Karl Adolf's handwriting. The wristwatch is engraved with the initials J.S.! The photographs are of a man and woman I don't know! Just the same, I am convinced he has been killed."*

Johann saw her tearstains on the letter. He wished he could add his own, but he felt little at his son's death. He had anticipated something like this for weeks, especially when official reports on the *Wehrmacht* radio about the Russian front were so guarded. It had been an early and bitter winter in Auschwitz. Johann knew it was far worse to the east. He did not know exactly where Paul-Adolf was fighting, but anywhere in the east would have been dangerous. Anyone at Stalingrad would have needed immense luck to survive. To be captured by the Russians, Johann told himself, might well be worse than death in battle.

The boy had always been willing to take risks. Helga and Johann were astounded, even frightened by his daring. When Paul-Adolf was just nine years old, on a family's weekend outing in the German Alps, he had raced ahead and, laughing all the while, disappeared from view as he climbed onto a narrow ledge above a deep ravine. When he popped up laughing, Helga almost fainted. When he was fourteen, he rode his bicycle in races against older boys in the Hitler Youth, winning mostly because he was so reckless in the curves. Johann recalled that his son once told him, "You may be a good doctor, but I will be an explorer and mountain climber, greater than any other." He did not know what to say, except, "We'll see."

Paul-Adolf was a good athlete, tall for his age until he stopped growing at sixteen and his classmates passed him—making him all the more determined to out-do them in any competition. The Hitler Youth movement was his passion. There he gained the respect and admiration he craved. He was excited when the war began, but angry that he was not old enough to join up. He declared his eagerness to give his life for "*Führer, Volk und Vaterland*" so often that Helga demanded he stopped saying it in her presence.

"You love your Hitler more than you love your father or me," she once told him.

"No, but Hitler loves all of us, *Mutti*." He replied. "He's our Hitler, our leader. Why shouldn't we love him?"

At sixteen, he became a local Hitler Youth troop leader and, at eighteen, joined the Death's Head unit of the SS. Now, not yet nineteen, he was dead some place in the Russian snow. Among the dozens of thousands.

345

Reading Helga's brief letter, Johann hoped that their son's death was indeed "sweet." He recalled his *Gymnasium* teacher's lecture on Horace's famous line, "*dulce et decorum est*...." That was the extent of his feelings. A numbing cold had anchored itself in his body. A cold he could not escape. He saw death each day in Auschwitz and it had lost its sting— but not for the reasons proclaimed in the old Bach chorale. Death had become unnoticeable, constant.

Johann decided not to request a furlough. Given the intensity of the war and the increasing number of transports, his request was not likely to be granted. If he left, he would not want to return. What would that mean for his honor? His sense of duty to the *Vaterland*? Worst of all, how could he face Helga when she asked him what he was doing?

As to who was the rightful owner of the wristwatch, that Helga received—Johann, too, knew no "J.S." He knew that Paul-Adolf's engraved silver wristwatch was at home in the small chest under his son's bed. "For P.-A. B. Use time wisely or it will use you. J.B. / H.B. 1938," its inscription echoing the one on the gold wristwatch Johann had received from his parents on his fourteenth birthday. That watch, too, was back in Nuremberg.

*****

During the same week that Johann received the letter from Helga telling him that their son had been killed, Philipp and Christine were jubilant. On the radio they heard the somber announcement: The German army, "although courageous in its loyalty to Adolf Hitler," had surrendered at Stalingrad.

Jews were not permitted to have a radio since 1939—or private telephones since 1940—but Christine, as a German citizen, was. They kept the radio low, sitting close, listening to the BBC. Like so many others, they lived in hope, not knowing what else to do.

Christine tried to be cheerful, for fear of upsetting Philipp. And he had a secret that sustained him, even though he knew it was foolish to think it made any difference.

It was more than a year now that Jews were prohibited from using public transport. Once or twice a week on his hour-long walk to or from the Jewish hospital, Philipp stopped at a newsstand or a stationary store—always a different one—and selected a few postcards with Hitler's photograph. The clerk, noticing his Jewish star, usually gave him a strange look; a few times, he was told to go away. But most of the time, Philipp put the necessary *pfennige* on the counter and got what he wanted. With the postcards inside his coat pocket, he resumed his walk until he came to a secluded spot in a park, under a bridge, or in an alleyway. When he was sure no one was watching, he knelt down and set up the postcards as though they were playing cards, leaning one on the other to make a little house. With a cigarette lighter, he lit the corner of a postcard. He liked it best if the fire travelled slowly. It spread up across Hitler's face and ignited the others. As they fell in on themselves and the cards curled up and blistered in the flames and smoke, he chanted under his breath, "To hell with you, *Herr* Hitler! To hell with your Nazi Party! Long live Germany!" When the flames died down and the cards were smoldering, he would stamp on their ashes and grind them into the ground. The whole ritual took a few minutes. It was something. To him, it was everything.

Shortly after seven one morning, as Philipp turned the corner into his neighborhood after a nightshift at the hospital, two men came toward him. Whenever he was stopped for being on the street during curfew, he would show his working papers and usually not be delayed. Had someone seen him burning the postcards and reported him? The men blocked his path and flashed their *Gestapo* badges. One asked Philipp his name. He barely finished telling them when they grabbed him by the shoulder and pushed him into the gutter behind a black van.

"Your papers!"

"Here," Philipp said, his identification passbook already open in hand, the "J" for *Jude*, Jew, stamped in a florid, red curve over his name, bright and large, for anyone to see. Philipp stood as tall as he could, holding his hat in his hand with as little deference as he dared to show.

Immediately one of the men barked, "The Jew 'Israel' Stein is to come with us."

Philipp was pushed toward the back of the van and shoved inside. He fell to floor when the van abruptly pulled away from the curb. Others inside helped him to his feet in the darkness. Together they supported each other as the van moved on, turning right, then left, then right, and, with no warning, coming to an abrupt stop. They all fell forward. As they got to their feet, they heard a brief conversation outside. The doors opened. Another man was thrust inside, and fell to the floor as the van lurched ahead. Again those inside helped the newcomer to his feet. And so it went for another half dozen stops. The last man who was pushed inside could not fall down, the van was so full.

They were driven to a barbed-wire holding pen near the city's eastern railway yards. There was neither food nor water nor a toilet. "I'm surprised they haven't taken the air away from us, too," Philipp said to one of the men in the compound.

"Just wait, they will," the other said and pushed his way toward where he thought there would be more space.

Philipp stayed near the gate and so heard his name being shouted over the din by an SS officer.

"The Jew 'Israel' Stein. Report here. Stein! *Schnell!*"

Five men pushed their way toward the officer. Philipp reached him first.

"Who is Stein?"

Philipp was the quickest to answer. The guard immediately pulled him through the gate. The others, all named Stein, watched as he was pushed into another van along with other prisoners. After the door slammed shut, they sat in the darkness for about an hour. Outside, they could hear the crowd in the compound and the shouts of SS guards.

When they told each other that they each had an Aryan wife, Philipp said, "That must be it. The Nazis are nothing if not correct! They cannot hold us if we have Aryan wives. Or maybe the war is over."

No one laughed.

When the van lurched away, abruptly turned and accelerated, Philipp grew nauseous. 'I must not vomit,' he told himself over and over, until they jerked to a stop. He and the others were pulled out. The neighborhood was familiar. He saw the cardboard sign for the Jewish Community Center and Welfare Office, *Rosenstraße* 2-4. SS guards with truncheons prodded him and the others upstairs into a crowded room.

Christine had no idea that Philipp had been taken away. She was used to him coming home late sometimes. About an hour after he was taken away, the telephone rang.

"*Frau Doktor* Stein?"

"Yes."

A hush followed. Then the voice on the other end of the line said, "The *Gestapo* picked up your husband."

"Who is this?"

"A neighbor."

"*Frau* Ziegler? Is that you?"

"The *Gestapo*. They pushed him into a van and then drove off. Twenty minutes ago. I decided I had to tell you."

"*Frau* Ziegler?"

The caller hung up. Christine immediately telephoned the hospital but there was no answer. Growing frantic, she dialed a friend whose Jewish husband sometimes walked part of the way with Philipp each day.

"They took my Jossi early this morning," her friend said through her tears. "Pushed right into our apartment. He still had shaving cream on his face."

"I'm going to the Community Center," Christine said, unable to disguise the fear in her voice. "The council needs to know what's happened. Or maybe they can tell us."

"I'll meet you there."

Christine hung up with her friend still sobbing. She put on her coat and rushed down the stairs. The postman was putting the mail into the building's mailboxes.

"Be careful, *Frau* Stein," he said softly, looking around to see if anyone else was in the hallway. "They're picking up Jews. Tell your husband to stay inside."

She looked at him, astonished. "I don't know where my husband is," she stammered.

"Be careful," he whispered, raising his finger to his lips.

She wanted to ask him what more he knew, but he avoided looking at her and continued distributing the mail. She was amazed. A few days before, she and Philipp had decided that he was intercepting their mail and spying on them. They added him to the long list of people they no longer trusted: their landlord; their upstairs neighbors, especially the couple's fifteen-year-old son (Christine knew that the rumors about children betraying their own parents were true); the baker, actually all of the shop-keepers in their block, with the exception of the green-grocer; and the two secretaries who worked in Christine's office at the curtain factory. *Frau* Metzger, who lived across the street, was one of the few people they knew they could trust. And now the postman, whom they had suspected of spying on them, had given her a warning. She thanked him and went out onto the sidewalk. She thought of taking a streetcar to *Rosenstraße* but decided it would be faster if she walked.

Neither Christine nor her friend realized that their husbands had been taken to the Community Center. When they got there, they saw SS men guarding the doors. No one was allowed to enter the building. A few dozen women, some with young children, milled about in front of the building, not knowing what to do. The guards ordered them all across the street. There they stood, their numbers increasing all the while.

"I see someone in the window. There, on the second floor. Look!" someone shouted.

"It's my Reuben!" A woman with a small child began to wave frantically.

They all looked at the windows, hoping for some glimpse of their captured husbands, fathers, uncles, brothers or cousins. Christine thought she saw Philipp, but realized she was mistaken when a woman near her screamed and called out, "Avram! Avram!" and the man in the window waved back until he was yanked away. Whenever anyone thought they recognized someone, they shouted and waved, while the crowd cheered. After about an hour, the crowd had grown to several hundred.

"I'm not leaving until I know what's happened to my Philipp," Christine told her friend.

"I'm going back to my apartment—it's only a few blocks—to get a warmer coat. I'll bring us something to eat. We could be here a long time." As she walked away, more women were arriving.

A girl near Christine climbed onto the pediment of a lamp-post and shouted, "Sol! Solly! It's me! Look down here! Look down here! Solly!" Turning to Christine, "He's my brother. They've got my brother! That's him! In the window. There! Solly!"

"They've got my husband, too." Christine said, although she did not really know where Philipp was.

"Our mother died last week," the girl said, tears running down her face. "My father is in the Jewish hospital. Now they've got my brother."

Somewhere else in the crowd, three children, the oldest a girl no more than ten, called out in unison, "*Vati! Vati! Vati!*" They did it again and again, then looked at their mother who was crying. The two youngest began crying, too.

Four or five women began shouting as loudly as they could, "We want our husbands back! We want our husbands back!" The chant was taken up and reverberated back and forth across the street. Christine forced her way to the front of the crowd, shouting as loud as she could, "We want our husbands back!" Thinking she saw Philipp briefly by a window on the second floor, she screamed, "Philipp! Philipp!" until she broke down in tears. Still crying, she crossed the street.

"Where is my husband! Tell me what you have done to my husband!" she began shouting, as she reached the sidewalk. An *SS* guard stepped toward her and pushed her backward into the gutter. The crowd broke out into loud hissing. Christine picked herself up and rejoined them, blood dripping from her hand and knees.

Later in the afternoon, a baker's apprentice appeared and handed out some loaves of bread, which were torn into small chunks and passed around. Word spread that there were toilets in a nearby apartment building that people could use. A butcher sent some dried sausage. Someone else brought blankets. Meanwhile, they kept up their chant: "We want our husbands back!" At curfew, Christine was one of the last to leave.

The next morning, the crowd was larger than ever. Berliners on their way to work stopped to ask what was going on.

"My husband was taken. He's inside there. The *SS* have taken our husbands."

Most just shook their heads and walked on. A few stayed. The crowd stretched up and down the entire block. Although curtains now were drawn over the windows, every now and then, someone peeked out and the crowd burst into cheers and shouts.

On the second day, Christine brought a bag of apples. Someone else brought a large wedge of cheese. The baker's apprentice brought several loaves of bread. Around noon, an old woman cut up a hunk of dried meat into little cubes and handed them around to the children. The apprentice came back with more bread in the afternoon. Meanwhile, across the street, in front of the Center, the squad of *SS* guards stood at the ready, hands on their holsters. No one went in or out of the building.

The third day was like the two before, but with an even bigger crowd. Christine was among the first to arrive.

"My husband is in there, I know it," she said to one of the women she recognized from the day before. "I just know it."

"Mine, too. I saw him briefly in the window on the first day."

"They can't keep them forever."

"Who knows what they will do? Who thought this up?"

"Goebbels," Christine said. "It must be him. No one else is so cunning."

"Our dear *Gauleiter* is more of a Nazi than the *Führer* himself."

"I don't care who's behind it. I just want my husband back."

Christine began to chant, "Give us our husbands back!" as loud as she could. The woman joined her, followed immediately by dozens more. Soon hundreds were shouting. The whole day—chants, fists waving, crying. The *SS* guards grew restless. The women closest to them increased their taunts. A few thought they should defy the curfew.

"No, they are looking for an excuse to arrest us," Christine said. "As long as we stay here on this side of the street and leave at the curfew, they won't. We must come back tomorrow, though. As long as it takes." She hoped she was right. She was one of the last on the street that evening. When she urged the others to leave with her, they all did.

On the fourth day, Christine watched as the SS set up machine-gun posts in front of the building. An officer, smartly uniformed in the black and silver of the SS *Leibstandart Adolf Hitler*, the *Führer's* personal body-guard, announced that he would give the order to fire if the crowd did not disperse immediately. "Otherwise, we will shoot you!" He raised his arm as though he was going to give the signal.

The crowd hushed for a moment. Then Christine began shouting, "Murderers! Murderers! Murderers!" Others took up the chant almost at once. When they retreated into an alleyway, they continued to shout. "Murderers! Murderers! Murderers!"

Everyone expected the machine guns to begin firing. Instead, silence. At first, no one could believe it. After a few minutes, they saw the officer go inside. When he returned, the machine gun tripods were dismantled. Everyone cheered. They sensed victory of some sort. The crowd hushed. Then someone began a new chant, "Our husbands! Our fathers! Our brothers! Our sons!"

Christine joined in. The chant was louder than before. She looked back to see hundreds of people, shouting, waving their fists, babies being held high over their mothers' heads. Suddenly, the defiance and anger she saw was replaced by astonishment. A woman was pointing at the building and screaming. Christine turned to see the Center's doors wide open, men pouring down the stairs and onto the street. The crowd rushed forward to meet them. It took several minutes until Christine spotted Philipp and several more until she could make her way through to him.

After they embraced, all he could say was "Let's go home." They held hands tightly as they walked away, neither saying a word.

Back in their apartment, they locked the door behind them. Philipp went to all the windows and closed the curtains, as though there were an air raid. Then they embraced. Christine held him close, felt him tremble, heard him begin to sob.

"We should have left Germany," he said. "We should have left with Benjamin and Martha. We should have left when we could."

"But we didn't. And we'll stay until this war is over. We'll stay. I promise I will help you stay."

"I know you want to. But next time might not end this way. They won't relent until they've got every one of us."

"We're together now. That's all that matters," she said, holding him tightly so he would not see the doubt and fear in her eyes.

"Why did they release us?" he whispered.

"I don't know. What does it matter? It's all right now. It's all right."

She dared to look up at him. They tried to dry each other's tears. Christine was the first to smile faintly. She caressed his head and kissed his cheek. "Now tell me, my Lippi, why are you crying?"

He stepped back. His voice cracked. "Because it is not all right. It is not. Don't you see? You and those others stopped them. You stood up to them. They relented."

"Maybe they had other plans. We don't know. Maybe they realized it would look bad, killing a bunch of German women and their children in the street, just so they could transport a few hundred Jews to God-knows-what horrors."

"Don't you see? Whatever their reasons, you stood up to them. If you could…," he paused, "…if you could, others could have, too. Before now. Don't you see?"

The darkened room made the shadows under his eyes even darker. His face was gray, the stubble of his beard thick.

She looked into his eyes. "Philipp, I love you. Those other women all love their husbands. Those children love their fathers. Those sisters love their brothers. We could not just let you be taken from us. But most Germans, they don't…well, they don't have the same…" She struggled to find the right word. "…the same *connections*. That's it. The same connections to Jews. And to stand up for someone whom you don't love, especially now, here and now, well…that's asking a lot. An awful lot."

He shook his head. "The whole *Volk* has been caged," he said, walking to the window and peeking out quickly. He sat down and sighed. "Once, back in medical school, I saw laboratory rats kept in overcrowded cages. Too many rats for such small cages. You know what the rats did? They cowered in the corners as best they could. They trampled each other to get to the corners."

"Philipp, we..."

"And when they could not feel even a little safe anymore, they ate each other's eyes out."

"Stop..."

"They all should have attacked their keeper. Instead they attacked and killed each other."

Christine was silent for a few moments. "We're not laboratory rats, Lippi. Yes, we have good reasons to be afraid. But you must not be so quick to blame. That's just like the Nazis, blaming all the Jews. And think of how hard it is to defy them now. The price to be paid. Who can be trusted?"

He sat quietly for so long that she thought he had not heard her. Finally, he said, "I know. Yes, some Germans have tried to help. You said someone telephoned. The postman tried to warn you. Good people. Good Germans. But why not more? Why not more?"

"That's for them to say, now or later. Someday we'll all have to say."

*****

The bombings gave Philipp hope. When Hermann Goering, head of the *Luftwaffe*, declared to the German newsreel cameras in his white, full dress uniform that he would change his name to "Meier" if any enemy warplane succeeded in harming the *Vaterland*'s holy soil, Philipp sent him a postcard with Hitler's picture: *"Lieber Herr Meier! Congratulations on your new name. Long live our Vaterland!"* He signed it "Little Adolf!" and added a *P.S.*: *"You are a pompous asshole!"* It was just one of several postcards he mailed, affixing each postage stamp with Hitler's portrait upside-down, and each time using a different mailbox.

As the assaults increased in size over German cities, death descended indiscriminately on Nazis and non-Nazis alike. Since Berlin was the heart of the dragon that the Allies sought to slay, it became the prime target. When Philipp and Christine met a friend or neighbor in the evening, they wished each other *"Bolona!"*—a *"bombenlose Nacht,"* a "bomb-free night!" *"Auf Wiedersehen!"*—"Until we see each other again!"—had become too much to hope for.

Christine had come to admire how Berliners could turn something terrifying into something endurable with a bit of pointed sarcasm and wit. She told Philipp the edgy comments she heard. *"Bolona!* How absurd! This war *is* wurst! Leave it to the Berliners to make a joke of it!"

She was grateful for her bookkeeping job at the curtain factory, now transformed into producing heavy drapes and window blinds for the nightly blackouts. It brought them much needed income and gave her some distraction from the rising tensions. After Philipp was taken to the Jewish Center on *Rosenstraße*, the head bookkeeper only asked once where she had been during the week of the protest.

"I had to help my husband," she said.

"Is he ill?"

"No," she answered, not knowing how much she should tell him.

"Frau Stein, I know what happened," he said in a low tone. "I know. It's all right. I don't blame you. Now let's not say any more about it. *Herr* Meininger need never know."

Christine was astonished, just as she was when the postman spoke to her in the stairway. There were others, too, who had not turned on them. Their grocer could be counted on to give them a bit more than their ration ticket limits. After Philipp ministered to their neighbor, *Frau* Ziegler, she regularly brought them some *ersatz*-coffee; Philipp actually liked the bitter chicory taste. Christine told him that she suspected it was *Frau* Ziegler who telephoned her with the news that he was picked up.

"Sad, we'll never really know," he said.

"But she knows. That may be more important."

Another neighbor had given them a blanket, rather than hand it over to the drive for war materials, in exchange for a letter that Christine typed to a lawyer in the *Rhineland* for some advice about an inheritance. Small favors, cautiously passed back and forth, strengthened their trust.

"We're all in the same soup with the bombings," Philipp said. "Nazis or not. Goebbels and Hitler tell us how proud they are of the *Volk*. How resourceful and determined we are. Well, that's not because we all love them. Fear and hope are driving us now. Nazis or not."

Living in the *Reich*'s capital brought its special dangers. A good night's sleep was impossible. Nightly air raids, or just the sirens and false alarms meant trips to the shelters and constant fears and short tempers. The bombs touched off spectacular fires. Hapless fire brigades, their manpower diminished by the war effort, only could try to protect nearby structures.

Philipp was drawn to the fires. A few weeks after he was released from the *Rosenstraße*, he joined a crowd at the still smoking ruins of an apartment building. Two women were scrambling through the charred timbers, searching for some family treasure. Others were hunting for something they could sell or barter. They argued over who owned what and began throwing bits of the debris at each other. Paying them no heed, hapless firemen doused a toppled shelf of leather-bound books with buckets of water. When a *Gestapo* squad began pushing through the crowd, Philipp knew he had to leave. He heard one of the spectators shout, "Damn the English! Damn the Americans!" He thought, 'Maybe some other Berliner is thinking, "Damn the Nazis!"' He knew he could not hope for much more than that. He felt bad for those who suffered, but if this destruction meant the end of the Nazis, he hoped for more bombs.

In April, on his way home from the hospital, he went into a stationary store just as it was opening. He was paying for some Hitler post-cards when the local Nazi block-leader stormed in. "Why is the *Führer*'s picture upside down in the display window? What does this mean?" he shouted at the storekeeper. "On the *Führer*'s birthday! Outrageous!"

"I'm so sorry. So sorry. How stupid of me," she said. "Yesterday I learned that my husband was killed in France. My little girl is ill. I'm not thinking clearly. I'm so sorry!" She immediately went to the window and righted the picture.

"See that it doesn't happen again or I will report you," the block-leader said.

Philipp kept his back to the Nazi so he would not see the six-pointed yellow star pinned to his coat. When the man left the shop, Philipp said to the woman, "I am sorry for your loss. We both hope the war will be over soon."

"Yes," she said, still startled by the block-leader's warning. "It was foolish of me." She looked at Philipp's star, as though she wanted to say something else, but decided not to take any more risks. He could see that she was going to cry.

"We all are doing whatever we can," he said. "*Auf Wiedersehen!*"

She nodded and handed him the five postcards. As soon as he could, he darted down a deserted alley and meticulously set the postcards ablaze. After a minute or two, he began to run, until he realized that would call attention to himself. He was still smiling when he climbed the stairs to his apartment.

"Hitler's moustache burns brightly!" he announced.

"I don't understand," Christine said.

"Nothing, really. Just a line from a song I might write."

She gave him a questioning look, but he already was sitting close to the radio and listening. She knelt next to him until she had to leave for work.

"The war will be over by summer. Stalingrad proves it!" he said.

"It will be over when it is over. Don't get your hopes up."

She kissed him good-bye, and smiled to hear him whistling softly behind her.

Philipp was wrong. If the tide had turned in the war, the Nazis were determined to stretch it out as long as possible. Summer and fall only brought more bombs. The Christmas holidays provided a meager distraction.

As was the holiday tradition for a decade now, the Nazis erected a towering Christmas tree, topped by a huge swastika, on *Alexanderplatz*. A wide banner proclaiming "Peace on Earth—Good Will Toward Men" hung limply on the side of a building facing the square. The annual spectacle of thousands of electric lights had to be abandoned because of the bombing, but Berliners, Christine and Philipp among them, thronged to the dimly lit square anyway, hoping to find some holiday spirit. They shuffled between the vendors' ragged canvas stalls, searching out small straw ornaments and trinkets. Shopkeepers put out whatever decorations they had; everything metal had been co-opted for the war effort.

"Frohe Weihnachten!" "Merry Christmas!" friends and acquaintances wished each other in the same breath as they said, *"Bolona!"* But Christmas Eve was not a bomb free night. British pilots swerved and prayed their way overhead through the searchlight beams and flak bursts toward the city's center. Air-raid sirens screamed. Children still in the city (most had been evacuated to the countryside) gathered up their presents and sweets. They knew the drill as well as any adult. Mothers picked up their babies and over-night bags. Old men and women found their flashlights and helped each other down the stairs. They all knew that however dense the anti-aircraft fire, some of the bombers would reach their destination. While many bombs were intended for military installations, munitions' factories, barracks, arsenals, and bridges, railways, and canal locks, the predictable sites, everything and anything were targets. It was impossible for the bombers to see through all the flak bursts and thick smoke. If a bomb hit a densely populated apartment building instead of the factory across the street, it still served the British aim. Everyone below was the enemy. Death could come at any time. It didn't matter whether a German was a card-carrying Nazi or not. *"Ausharren!"* Goebbels ordered in his radio address. "Persevere!" There was no other choice for anyone.

Peeking through the heavy curtains of a third floor window of the Jewish Hospital before midnight, Philipp saw the surreal scene as though it was on a movie screen: shafts of search-lights waving back and forth over the skyline; barrages of anti-aircraft fire; exploding planes falling out of the sky; blasts from bombs; fires blooming around the city. He could see that this was no ordinary night's bombing.

Two nurses stayed with him to care for the patients who were too ill to be taken to the basement's shelter. The three of them gasped whenever they looked out the window. He remembered seeing the distant explosions in the first war, sitting on the vineyard-covered hillside above the hospital in France, a spectator far from the action. Now explosions were all around him.

The air-raid sirens had begun to wail shortly after dark, just after he arrived at the hospital. Christine would have gone to the bomb shelter in the cellar under their apartment house, he thought. They had a small suitcase all packed and ready by the door. Inside were some crackers, hard cheese, dried fruit and toilet paper, as well a spare pair of Philipp's eyeglasses, the silver hairbrush-and-comb set that Christine had received from her parents for her first Communion, their marriage-day photograph and some others of their family, and the poesy album she kept when she was a schoolgirl. Everyone in Berlin, in all Germany, for all Philipp knew, had prepared their *"eiserne Portionen,"* their "emergency rations," as well as a portable museum of the mundane and the rare, the most precious things that defined a life.

He was desperate to be with her. In just a few more hours, with the morning light, the terrible night would be over. They would celebrate another day closer to the end of horror. Whispered rumors told of Russian advances, of the success of the American landing in Italy, of Mussolini's flight, of rising resistance in France and Poland, even of desertions in the German army. He secretly feared that they were exaggerations, but the very fact they had started somewhere meant someone shared his hopes.

It was still dark when he left the hospital at the end of his shift. He soon saw the night's raid had caused far greater damage than any before it. Many streets were blocked. Glass and twisted metal glowed red with the heat of raging blazes. Water mains gushed into the air. Trees were shattered off their trunks. The wailing of sirens mixed with the screams of people staggering about or climbing out from under rubble. Philipp saw all of this as a blurry dream. He made his way as best he could toward his neighborhood. Going through parks and along a canal turned out to be the easiest route, although it probably took him a mile out of his way. The closer he came to his apartment building, the faster he went.

His neighborhood had been hit. Toppled buildings blocked an adjacent side street at both ends. Running around to an alley, he climbed a fence and, going around a still smoldering bomb crater, found a path to his courtyard. Or what would have been the courtyard if the buildings around it still stood. A cluster of bombs had made a direct hit. He could not be sure if the smoke all around him was from fire or just dust and ash. He heard voices on the other side, took a deep breath, and stumbled toward them and what had to be the front of his building.

People were clawing at the rubble where the bomb shelter would have been. An ambulance parked nearby had run over an old man whose body still lay underneath one wheel. His wife knelt beside him, wailing. Philipp saw that he could not be helped. He shouted, "Christine! Christine!" as loud as he could, but could hardly hear his own voice. Bodies, coated with dust, were being hauled up one by one out of a hole in the ruins and laid side by side in the street, staring like fish in the fish market, mouths gaping wide as the sun rose on Christmas Day.

An SS salvage squad commanded some Polish prisoners in the effort, but could not control the crowd and retreated to another salvage spot a few dozen yards away. Someone, careful not to be seen, spat out at them, "If it weren't for you, there wouldn't be any ruins. Why come now, when it's too late?" A newborn baby bleated in the arms of its dead mother until an old woman picked it up.

Philipp went from body to body in the street, checking for signs of life. This baby, dead. Its mother, breathing her last, choking on her own blood. This young girl, still breathing too, but with a crushed face and broken neck, hopeless. This woman, dead. Another. Another. Bodies were being brought up faster than he could look at them. Where was Christine? He climbed up on a pile of rubble and shouted her name again.

A *Gestapo* man noticed his star. "You! Jew! What are you doing? Come down here!"

"I am a doctor. I live here. My wife is...."

"Jews are no longer allowed to be called 'doctor.' Are you licensed to treat sick Jews? Show me your papers, Jew."

"There's no time for this now. These people need help. My wife is German. I am a doctor."

"Swine! Jews are not allowed to treat Germans. Come with me." He grabbed Philipp's pant leg.

"I've got to find my wife!" He shouted again, "Christine!" He kicked and twisted away.

"Get the Jew!" the *Gestapo* man shouted. "Hold the swine!"

No one seemed to hear or heed the command. Philipp ran over to where the bodies were being pulled out of the narrow hole in the rubble. Just then, Christine's appeared. They were pulling her out feet first, with someone down inside pushing her dust-covered body up toward the light. He could see at once that she was dead. Her blond hair had a deep, dark red streak that hung like a ribbon over her face. Her eyes were closed. For a moment, he heard nothing. The sirens, the screams, the shouts all vanished. He tried to reach her, to touch her cheek.

"Grab that Jew!" the *Gestapo* man shouted again and pulled him from behind so hard that Philipp fell backwards on top of him. Everyone was concentrating on pulling more bodies out of the cellar. Philipp scrambled to his feet. His assailant lay unconscious on the ground, his head near a piece of granite that he hit when he fell.

Christine's body was being taken over to the street and stretched out alongside the others. Philipp staggered toward her until he saw two *SS* men, pistols drawn, coming toward him. He turned and ran back through the dark cloud of dust that hung in the courtyard. Although he heard shots and thought he felt bullets whistling by, he kept running. He climbed a pile of rubble that had leveled a fence, jumped into the alley, and kept going. Without thinking, he ran as fast as he could toward the hospital. His coat flapped where it had been torn, the yellow Jewish star dangling from his chest.

CHAPTER EIGHTEEN
An Unfeeling Tool

From October 1943 through the summer of 1944, I continued my service in the Medical Division of the SS *at Auschwitz in the Ostmark. Auschwitz was like a vast city, having grown like fungus out of rotten wood. One of my colleagues called it "anus mundi." And yes, Helga, it was the anus of the world. Horrible things happened there. I admit, I saw—and I did—horrible things every day.*

For the most part, it was like working in a factory. We physicians had our routines, our shifts, our goals, our daily quotas, and our bosses. We even produced something—slaves and corpses, one or the other, depending on our whim. Day after day, night after night, Auschwitz seeped into me, became a part of me. I, a doctor, worked in a factory whose product, sooner or later, was death.

I was an unfeeling tool. A scalpel wielding a scalpel. As I had cloaked myself in what I thought to be scientific objectivity, as I became myself an object without feeling, it is no wonder that I saw all others as objects, as tools for our ends. I wanted to become that way. I wanted to be used.

Even when I began to realize what I had become, I did not have the inner strength to stop. For too long I gave myself to the service of Hitler's state. That so many others did the same gives me little comfort.

You may be surprised to learn that it was Philipp who inspired me to try to find the strength I needed to come to my senses. His concern for others reawakened me to my responsibility as a physician. His courage helped me find my own.

Another day of the trial. Another sleepless night. Better sleepless, he thought, than asleep with nightmares. He lay on his bed staring through the dark at the stains and shadows on the ceiling above him. Watching as they fused into agonized faces. The dead and soon-to-be-dead. The faces of those soldiers in the railway cars coming and going from the First World War. The faces of those innocents on their one-way trip to Auschwitz. All staring down at him. He closed his eyes, only to find their faces clearer, their eyes more piercing. Out of the countless faces, one loomed larger than all the others: Philipp's.

*****

Philipp, gray with ash, reached the Jewish Hospital just as *Doktor* Lustig was arriving.

"*Herr Doktor* Stein! What's happened to you?

"My wife is dead. A bomb. Last night."

"Terrible! Terrible news. Please accept my sympathies. Come inside." Lustig reached for Philipp's arm.

"No. I must resign. That's what I've come back to tell you. I must leave Berlin."

"But you must not leave. You are needed. You can be useful here. You do good work. You are most welcome to stay here. I assure you, I personally can guarantee your safety. You can live and work here, no matter what happens, until the war is over. Where else in the city are Jews safe? Come inside. You'll be safe here. Afterwards, too, of course. I have connections."

"Thank you, *Herr Doktor Doktor* Lustig." He had not expected him to be so understanding. "Thank you. But I've made up my mind. I must leave Berlin. I'll go to Bavaria. To Pohlendorf. To live there as best I can."

Lustig's eyebrows raised. "Don't be a fool, Stein. No Jew is living now. Not here and not in Bavaria. We are only surviving. You will not last a day if you try to leave. The *Gestapo* will catch you."

"I don't care. The *Gestapo* can do whatever they want. It doesn't matter anymore. It cannot be worse anywhere else. Thank you once more. *Lebewohl!*"

He walked away, down *Iranische Straße*, his torn coat flapping in the December wind. He brushed the ashes off the yellow "Star of David" and refastened it on his breast pocket, just to the left of his heart. He had no idea where to go next. When he saw a streetcar, he decided to get on, even though he knew Jews were forbidden. The conductor tried to push him off, but he got past him and found a seat. The three other passengers, an old man and two old women, only gawked. The conductor rang the streetcar's bells and refused to go any further.

A policeman on the other side of the street ran over and descended on Philipp, who tried in vain to resist. Yanked to his feet, prodded down the aisle and pushed down the streetcar's steps and onto the street, he fell face forward in a heap. The policeman pulled him up by his coat collar, twisted his arm behind his back and marched him to the next police station.

The paperwork was quick. Philipp handed over his pass with a defiant gesture. The desk officer stamped some papers, handed the policeman some keys and gestured toward a door without raising his head. The policeman pushed Philipp along a hallway into a small cell. "Too good for you, Jew," were the policeman's only words before the cell door closed with a crash. He lay down on a plank and stared at the ceiling. As a clock somewhere struck twelve, someone shoved a small lump of bread into an opening at the bottom of the cell door. Philipp asked for water. Laughter in the hallway was his answer.

An hour later, a guard fetched him and prodded him back onto the street and into a *Gestapo* van, much like the one that had taken him to *Rosenstraße*. Nine Jews huddled inside. When Philipp stumbled in, one of them said, "Now we have a '*minyan*!' Let's pray." A few laughed. No one said anything else until the van stopped in front of the *Anhalter Bahnhof*. Philipp recognized the train station even though it had been bombed.

SS guards hustled them into a cramped waiting room. Philipp saw that everyone inside wore a Jewish star. 'What a strange new constellation!' he thought, named "Scapegoat!" Two stars on a pair of men talking softly to each other were the tips of the horns. Fixed on a young woman's dress was the bright yellow goat's eye. Another man wore the star that marked the goat's beard. Two little girls, huddled together, wore stars that marked its chest. Behind them, their mother wore the star that could be the shoulder. Still more stars filled in the animal's body. He thought of how Christine would smile at hearing him describe his bizarre vision.

He wiped his tears on his coat sleeve and looked for a place to stand, eventually stopping near an old man in the corner. From where did he know him? Was he a patient? No, not a patient. Someone from long ago. A face from childhood. Although there was coarse stubble instead of a full beard, the man's nose and eyes, his high forehead, the way he pursed his lips—all evoked a long ago memory. Had the horror of the last hours scrambled his mind? He looked away, but the familiar face drew him back. He decided to speak.

The old man did not want to talk. Philipp persisted in his questions, shifting to Bavarian dialect and introducing himself. "Are you from Bavaria? I lived there, before the war. The first war. In a small town, Pohlendorf, near Munich?"

The old man's eyes widened. "You must mean my father, Mordecai. I'm Richard. Richard Semmelberg. From Pohlendorf. Who are you?"

Philipp quickly told him.

"Why yes, I knew you. Of course. I knew your whole family. Stein. You were one of the little boys in the town. Your father had a stationary shop. Amazing! But nothing should surprise me any more."

"What are you doing here in Berlin?" Philipp asked.

"That's my daughter, Ellen, over there." He motioned toward a slim, dark haired woman. "She's a nurse. I have been living with her here since my wife died. Rivka—do you remember her?—died in 1930. We had moved from Pohlendorf to Nuremberg, to be near Ellen. She then got married and moved to Berlin. My wife was ill and didn't want to live in the north. So we stayed in Nuremberg. Rivka died there." He sighed and shrugged his shoulders. "So I moved to Berlin after all. Today, a big city or a little town is best for Jews. Nuremberg was in the middle. At first, it was good there. It would have been best to stay in Pohlendorf, but who can go back in our lives? My daughter—Ellen, come here!—has been working at the Jewish hospital here."

Now Philipp's eyes widened. Semmelberg continued, "Her husband was a German. You know what I mean. What do they call themselves now? Aryan. A soldier. He was killed somewhere in the East. We heard just last week. And now she has no protection. They picked us up yesterday. Brought us here. Going who knows where."

"But you? How did you survive this long in Berlin? She protected you?"

"You might say that. I lived in her apartment. Her husband was a decent man. I didn't like him much at first. But he was a good type. He didn't mind me being there, he said, especially once he was drafted. We only saw him after that for two weeks each year. I never went outside during the daytime. I minded my own business. I tried not to be a burden. You know, old people. Ellen, come here."

She made her way through the crowd. "This is Philipp Stein, *Herr Doktor* Stein, from Pohlendorf! My daughter, Ellen. Ellen Richter, a nurse."

"*Grüss Gott, Frau* Richter! I knew your father when I was a little boy. My family is from Pohlendorf."

"Happy to meet you," she said above the noise. The guards were pushing more people into the room.

"I knew your grandfather, too," Philipp said. "Your father looks so much like your grandfather. My friends and I used to come into the candy store. Your father would give us more candy than we could pay for. Then your grandfather would pretend to scold him and tell us that we owed him lots of money. We knew he was teasing. My father was David Stein. We had a stationary store."

"You're a doctor?"

"Well, no longer a doctor, thanks to the Nazis. I have been pro-moted. '*Krankenbehandler.*' Since they believe we're all handlers, dealers, swindlers...."

He turned to Semmelberg. "She was just a little girl when I left Poh-lendorf for the war. It seems a hundred years ago. And now to see you here. What a coincidence! Actually, two. I also served in the Jewish Hos-pital."

"I think I saw you there," she said. "I studied nursing in Munich. Then I moved to Nuremberg. Then Berlin. Before the war. My husband was from here. A salesman. Then he was drafted. Yes, I nursed at the Jewish Hospital. I think I saw you once at the end of my shift. The night nurses told us you were a decent doctor. A good doctor, from Bavaria. It never occurred to me that you were from Pohlendorf." Although she had been crying, her eyes began to brighten.

"I had night duty, thanks to *Herr Doktor Doktor* Lustig." They both smiled. "I don't blame you for not recognizing me," Philipp continued. "You were just a little girl when I left for the war. The first war. Your father told me about your husband. I'm sorry." He was surprised at how absorbed he had become by the conversation.

"Thank you," she said. She saw Philipp's wedding ring. "Your wife, too?"

Before Philipp could answer, a guard opened the door and shouted, "Everyone out! Out! *Juden 'raus!* Jews out!" No one hesitated. A woman who dropped her suitcase and bent over to pick it up, was pushed out of the room by those behind her. Over the din, the guard kept shouting, "Out! Out! *Juden 'raus! Mach schnell!* Make it fast! *'raus!* Out!"

Philipp shouted, "Let's stay together. Try to stay together!" The Semmelbergs nodded. A line of SS guards, pistols drawn, herded them through the station and toward a freight train platform. As they passed a doorway, more Jews poured out of another room. And then another. All together, scores of people running toward a railroad siding. Old men and women. Mothers with little children. A few young boys and girls in their teens. A few men Philipp's age. All with their yellow stars. The constellation that he had imagined dissolving into a shower of stars, all falling toward the dark, steaming engine at the end of the platform. More SS patrolled the station with unmuzzled dogs, ordering the other passengers to turn to the wall, to cover their ears and close their eyes. The squeal of trains coming and going could not drown out the barking of their dogs.

The old people shuffled along as fast as they could. Philipp saw a woman with twin girls trying in vain to carry both children and her suitcase. Frightened and unequal to the task, she stepped out of the crowd. When a menacing guard harried her back into the torrent of yellow stars, with her children clutching their mother's skirt and running to keep up, Philipp picked up her suitcase and told her not to worry. The suitcase split open, a tangle of underclothes and photographs spilling onto the platform. He bent to pick up what he could when a guard shouted, "Leave it!" What choice was there?

He stopped again near a collapsed old woman who was being kicked to her feet by another guard.

"Mama! Mama!" shouted a young girl, who tried to stand in the guard's way. Philipp helped her raise the old woman as best he could, then hurried to keep up with the Semmelbergs.

The sooty engine loomed above them, hissing steam, its wheels huge, steely eyes. The air smelled greasy. There was no passenger car. Shuffling past several muddy, red-brown boxcars, they came to one whose heavy door yawned open. The guards pushed everyone into this hole. It was dark inside even before the door slammed shut.

Philipp was relieved that somehow he had not gotten separated from the Semmelbergs. He knew vaguely where they were going. East. How long it would be before they got there? Was what he had heard really true?

They didn't move for what must have been an hour. When the train finally jerked and lurched, some of the captives were thrown off their feet. They stood up, but each time it reversed direction, they fell down again. Without windows, no one could tell whether the train finally was going backwards or forwards. Slowly, it picked up speed, leaving behind

Berlin, fresh air, water, food and, such as it was, the thin, rent veneer of civilization.

Before long, everyone had to use a toilet. There was none. The only choice was a bucket in the boxcar's corner, near the unlucky people who stood there. It spilled over. Others could not get to it. The stench was staggering. Although December, it was stiflingly hot, but most refused to take off their winter clothes for fear of getting them soiled on the floor. What fresh air there was leaked through cracks in the walls. Those nearest the cracks defended their places with their fists.

Everyone in the boxcar was thinking, 'Surely we'll stop soon and be let out!" Each time the train slowed, the captives' voices rose with anticipation. When the train stopped on a siding, they could hear shouts and barking outside. But no one opened the door. They yelled, "Let us out! Water! We need water!" Babies and children wailed. Anyone who heard them would have thought that chained demons were inside, on their way to hell. There was little point in yelling, Philipp knew. Still, he yelled, too.

On the second day—they knew it was day from the light that came in through cracks in the boxcar's walls—the train stood on a siding for several hours. Someone briefly sprayed water on the roof. Some dribbled down the cracks. Everyone fought to get close enough to be able to lick it or soak their handkerchiefs before it reached the floor.

On the third day, someone outside opened the bolt that kept the roof's trap door locked and threw in hunks of dried bread and rags soaked in water. Not everyone got something. Philipp was pushed to the floor and kicked, but Ellen helped him stand again. She caught a crust of bread that she shared with him and her father. The old man found two sugar cubes in the lining of his coat and tried to give one to his daughter and one to Philipp. Both refused and insisted that he keep them for himself. One cube fell and was lost. Semmelberg tried to break the other, but it crumbled in his hands. Ellen sobbed.

By the end of the fourth day, some—the oldest, the youngest—were dying. Semmelberg fought for every breath. Philipp and Ellen tried to hold him up and move him near a fresh-air crack. He sagged heavily into their arms. "Let him lie down! Let my father lie down!" she screamed. In a space barely big enough for a sack of potatoes, Semmelberg fell into a heap. Philipp felt for his pulse, knowing already that he would find none. "It's over for him," he said, softly. "We still have a ways to go."

*****

At a normal train station in normal times, an observant physician waiting for his train on the platform might glance at a fellow traveler and make a mental note of this one's poor color, that one's crooked spine, another's lively step or vigor. At Auschwitz, the waiting doctors gave their glances, too. In the selections.

Along with a half dozen other SS physicians, Johann had duty on the ramp when the train carrying most of Berlin's last Jews arrived. To him it was just another train. A thousand or more captives, one hundred or so in each boxcar, coming from one place or another in Europe. Jews or Gypsies or others deemed in the way or harmful to the New Order. Enemies, parasites, the diseased and dangerous. Creatures who only resembled humans beings. With each train, he crawled deeper into his numbness.

He could not say when he had become just another man trying to get through another day. That morning, as he had done before and as he expected he would do again, he walked along the ramp, his hands in his pockets, his breath evident in the cold air, looking as little as possible at the herd moving by.

Better to think of other things, of times before the war. He remembered a day walking in the hills near Nuremberg with Paul-Adolf, then no more than eight years old. The boy wondered aloud about the loneliness of the shepherd and his flock on the meadow. Johann told him the shepherd's friends were his dog and his sheep. The shepherd knew each member of the flock and what to do to protect it from harm. The shepherd cared for every sheep, particularly the most vulnerable ones.

"Does he get a lot of money, *Vati*?"

"No. He does what he does not for pay so much as for his love of each sheep."

The arriving train startled him out of his reverie. Where is that shepherd now?

The scene of four days before in Berlin reversed itself. But the captives were changed. Eyes wild, throats parched, faces ashen, filthy from fouling themselves and each other over the days and nights of their trip, scratched and bruised, they had taken on the appearance of just what the Nazis believed them to be: vermin.

Kapos and prisoners swarmed at the open doors and clutched at the arms and legs of the new arrivals. They dragged the dead to the ground and slung them onto baggage carts, counting each one out loud. *Herr* Semmelberg's corpse made "ten," a full cartload. Two prisoners wheeled it away before Ellen could say a word. The *SS* guards' commands, the incessant barking of their dogs, the *Kapos'* grunts and chants—all blended into one age-old chorus: "*'Raus! 'Raus! Juden 'raus!* Out! Out! Jews Out! *Schnell! Los!* Quick! Fast!"

Without knowing where they were going, the prisoners began to move along the siding. A light snow from the night before was trod into a gray mush. Philipp saw that ahead of them the procession was splitting in two, a column for men and another for women and children. Cries and screams rippled back along the line. He caught Ellen's eye. What to do? Just then, he was struck by the peculiar, familiar gait of one of the white-coated men. With each step, the man threw his right leg out and forward, but slightly sideways, while his left foot did a quick, almost imperceptible hop to help him balance his stride.

"I know him! I know him!" Philipp shouted, as he broke out of the procession and rushed forward. "Johann!"

An *SS* guard dropped Philipp with a pistol blow to his head as his dog lunged at his thigh. Johann turned to see his childhood friend looking up at him in agony. Awaking as if from a deep sleep, he shouted, "*Halt! Nicht schiessen! Nicht schiessen!* Don't shoot!" and grabbed the guard's arm. The pistol fired into the ground near Philipp's head. Other guards with pistols drawn and *Kapos* rushed to the scene. Blood showed at the dog's mouth.

"Call off the dog!" Johann shouted above the others' shouts. "Call off the dog! Holster your weapons! Take this man to the *Revier*! To the prisoners' hospital! Do you hear me? The *Revier*!"

"But he touched you, the *Saujude*...!" the first guard stammered.

"That's an order! *Verstanden?*" Johann glared. "*Kapos*, you two there, pick up this man. Follow this lieutenant to the prisoners' hospital! Have this man's wounds cleaned and bandaged. I will be there shortly! Is that clear? You others, tend to the crowd there!"

Ellen saw Philipp being carried off. Not daring to go over to him, she kept walking, veering off from the men with the rest of the women and children. Johann reached the front of the line before she did. The routine was well underway. Each woman showed her identification papers and, if asked, answered a question or two. The doctor in charge of the day's selections barked out commands: "*Du...links...*to the left! *Du auch...* also left! *Du rechts...* right! *Du...*left! *Du...*right!" Within an hour, the transport was processed and the ramp was empty.

In the warmer months, Johann liked to stand and watch the train pull away. It gave him a feeling that the chaos was coming to an end. 'Someday,' he thought, 'there will be no one left to bring.' With the onset of cold weather, he left the platform as soon as the selection was over for the SS canteen and a cup of *ersatz* coffee. On that morning, he reported to the officer of the day that he had business at the prisoners' hospital.

He found Philipp lying on a straw mattress on the floor. A blood-stained bandage covered his ear and one eye. Blood had dried and flaked off his cheek. Red saliva drooled from the corner of his mouth down on to the bandage's knot under his chin. Someone had taken his coat and shoes. The deep red stains on his collar and shirtfront looked like open holes into his body. Strips of his pant-leg served as a tourniquet on his upper thigh. Another blood-soaked bandage was tied above his knee. Below it, his bare calf and foot were startlingly blue. A dirty blanket lay next to him in a heap. He was gasping for breath, coughing, and spitting blood. A small puddle had formed near the edge of the blanket.

Johann said nothing. He covered Philipp with the blanket and put some rags under his head. He took the bandage off his head and motioned to an orderly for a fresh one.

"You've bitten your tongue. Try to take deep slow breaths. Let me see your eyes." Johann pulled back on one and then the other of Philipp's eyelids. "Look up. Good. Now look down. Now over here. And here. Good." He felt for a pulse. The leg wound had stopped bleeding.

"That you are here! That you are here!" Philipp said, blood trickling from the corner of his mouth. "I am not surprised. I always knew when we met again it would be in hell. 'Where the devil says goodnight,' as my grandmother used to say. This must be it." His speech was slurred. As he focused on Johann, his eyes glowed with anger. He spat blood on the floor.

"Don't talk. Deep breaths. Now, listen to me."

"What can you possibly say to me?"

"Listen! I can help you here."

"And who will help you? *Cura te ipsum.*" A spasm of coughing stopped him from saying any more. Blood seeped out of the corner of his mouth.

Johann swabbed his chin. "Leave off your dark humor for once. I don't have time. Nor do you. Accept my help. Just listen. I can arrange for you to work in the hospital as soon as you are fit to be processed into the camp. You have to be shaved. Deloused."

Philipp tried to laugh.

Johann paid no attention. "You'll be shaved, given a number, a tattoo, and a uniform. Assigned a barrack. I cannot let them process you now. It would turn out badly, believe me. You are too weak. But in a day or two, when you are stronger, you should be fit enough. I will arrange it. I will speak for you. Then you can work as an orderly or a cleaner here."

Philipp glared. Johann knew what he was thinking. "Don't say anything," he said. "We don't have time to rehash the past."

"I will speak," Philipp said, trying to raise himself up on his elbow. "I will. How fine! I am now a cleaner. In a hospital in hell. I am, or at least, I was, a doctor. Remember? How amusing! Thank you very much, *mein Freund, mein Herr Nazi SS Doktor* Johann Brenner! You seem to have forgotten, too, that you were a doctor." He fell back, panting for breath.

Johann kneeled closer. "Stop your games, Philipp. You will work here, in the hospital. Do you understand me? You don't want to be a doctor here. You can do more good if you are not one. That way, you will not have to do what you would be required to do as a doctor in this hospital. Trust me."

"Trust you?"

"You must."

"Not likely. No." Philipp pulled himself up again and looked directly into Johann's eyes. Tears rolled down his cheeks. "My Christine is dead. A bomb. Berlin is hit day and night. She was my protecting angel. I suspect there are no angels here." He began coughing.

"Stop. You must save your strength."

"I won't stop. I already can see that this is the place where you Nazis think I should be. Where you always thought all of us should be."

"I am sorry for Christine. I hope you will believe me, Philipp. And now I am telling you what is best for you now that you are here. If you want to make it work, good. If not, I cannot help you. And no one else here will."

Philipp took a deep breath and sunk back onto the mattress. He tried to clear his throat. After a few seconds, he motioned Johann to bend down closer in order to hear him. "You want to help me, you say. There was a woman in the boxcar. Actually, you know her. Ellen Semmelberg, from Pohlendorf. I can't remember her married name. Her father and his father, too, old *Herr* Semmelberg, used to tease us. Remember? The candy store. Her father was with us in the train. He died yesterday."

"*Herr* Semmelberg? I last saw him in Nuremberg. His wife was dying. They moved there from Pohlendorf. He called me to help her. She was suffering."

The two men had begun speaking in their Bavarian dialect. Prisoners gaped at the sight: an *SS* doctor in a quiet conversation with an injured Jew.

"Ellen's husband was killed at the front. She was swept up, just like me. Our Aryan spouses were no longer our shields. She hid her father in her apartment. Poor old man." Philipp paused to spit up more blood. "She was with me on the ramp when I saw you. Where is she now? She's a nurse. I promised her we would stay together."

"Which way did she go?"

"What do you mean?"

"When she reached the head of the line, was she sent to the right or to the left?"

"I don't know. How could I know? I was on the ground. The dog was on me. I couldn't see. What does that matter?"

Johann did not answer.

"Where is she?"

"I'll try to find out."

"Her married name is Richter. That's it. Ellen Richter. Nurse Ellen Richter."

"I'll try. I must go. I'll give orders that you are to be treated here another three days, then processed, and then put to work here in the hospital. As an orderly. Do it, Philipp." Johann looked directly into his eyes. He paused, started to say something, and then looked away. "Someone will bring you something to drink. You will get something to eat later. I might not see you for a while."

Philipp said nothing as Johann rose and stretched his stiff leg. He felt something crawling up the back of his neck and into his hair. When he scratched, lice fell down into the straw mattress. When he looked up again, Johann was gone.

Johann returned the next day, worried that Philipp had been sent to the gas chamber. He was relieved to see him. He dressed Philipp's wound himself with the clean bandages that he had brought from the SS infirmary.

Philipp asked, "Did you find her?"

"I am trying."

"How hard can it be? We just came yesterday."

"You will learn how hard it is as soon as you can get up."

CHAPTER NINETEEN
𝕸𝖞 𝖂𝖎𝖑𝖑 𝖜𝖆𝖘 𝕯𝖗𝖆𝖎𝖓𝖊𝖉

When Philipp arrived in Auschwitz, he begged for mercy, not for himself, but for another. I did what I could. But I was so weary, so weak.

My will was drained. I fooled myself into thinking that I had already seen the worst. But each day was worse than the one before. Sleeping only brought nightmares. I did not know how to stop working. My routine gave me comfort. Without it, I would have lost my mind. Perhaps I did anyway.

Johann put his pen down. His letter to Helga had grown far longer than he anticipated. He still was not finished. In three days, the time he allotted himself would be over. He could not bear to write any more, but he must. A little more each day, to the end. But would it matter? Would she take him back when she knew the truth? What would he do if she did not? Where would he go?

The trial upstairs would break soon for Christmas. How much longer could it go on after that? It was already clear that things monstrous and barbaric had happened. Why stretch it out so? The accused have heard the charges, pled innocent, heard the evidence, seen the witnesses, had their lawyers cross-examine them. What more could be said in their defense? What more could be said on behalf of any one of them? He walked upstairs to another day's session. Afterwards, he would walk down *Fürthstraße* into the old city. Perhaps Meier was there, stacking bricks. Seeing him gave him courage.

*****

A few days after he first tended Philipp, someone called to Johann as he was leaving a staff meeting: "*Herr Doktor* Brenner, I would like to speak with you a moment."

He turned to see Carl Clauberg. He was surprised that the SS lieutenant general even knew his name. He knew Clauberg, though. The renowned gynecologist ranked among the most distinguished of all the Nazi physicians at Auschwitz, easily surpassing the younger Mengele in significant publications and in reputation as a medical scientist. From his first day at Auschwitz, Johann knew that Clauberg was experimenting with a technique to prevent a woman's fertility, specifically a Jewish woman's fertility. He had even heard that Clauberg was renting a spacious, modern research facility in *Block 10* with the right to have prisoners as research subjects, thanks to the indulgence of *SS Reichsführer* Heinrich Himmler himself. He had been granted unlimited authority to draw women out of the transports, to create control groups of married and unmarried women, and to subject them to experimental regimens of his choosing. The rivalry between Schumann, Johann's mentor, and Clauberg was notorious. What could Clauberg want with him?

"You work with *Doktor* Schumann on castrations, correct?"

"On X-ray sterilizations, *Herr Professor Doktor* Clauberg. I am doing surgical confirmations."

"That's what you call it, eh? I call it castrations. Shameful!"

Johann saw himself reflected in Clauberg's oversized, thick, black-rimmed glasses. Barely five feet tall, bald and overweight, Clauberg was a parody of SS standards for physical appearance. His fleshy earlobes dangled like radishes. With his beaky nose and darting eyes magnified behind his glasses, Johann thought he looked like a pink owl. He reminded him of a cartoon of a doctor in one of the satirical magazines of the early 1920s that had both amused and angered him and his colleagues in medical school.

"Anyway, Schumann tells me he wishes you were more efficient." Clauberg laughed his high, squeaky laugh. Johann did not know how to respond. "Don't take it personally, *Herr Doktor* Brenner. Schumann is wasting his time with his techniques and has to blame someone. X-ray sterilizations on the scale we require are inevitably going to be inefficient, slow and messy. My procedures, by contrast, will absolutely prevent any increase in the loathsome race. Our Jewesses will become sterile. We isolate the males. Castrate the troublemakers. Or, at our leisure, all the Jewish males for all I care. We can even use Schumann's slow procedures." He snorted with amusement at his joke. "Eventually, no more Jews! Meanwhile, we have the use of their labor."

Johann remained silent.

"Come watch our procedure, why don't you? My assistants, *Doktor* Schetzeler and *Doktor* Göbel are learning. I could use another pair of hands at the table. I can always get prisoner doctors but they are untrustworthy. The non-Jews are better, of course, but even they can't be relied on."

"Stands to reason," Johann said, but before he could continue, Clauberg cut him off.

"Göbel can fill you in on the work's background and how we've come to the Formalin dosages we are trying now. He's learned a lot for a man who is not a licensed physician. Degree's in chemistry, but he's quite useful to me. Do you know Schetzeler? He's good. Fast, but still a bit rough. We could have a contest to see who's more clumsy, you or him." Clauberg laughed his high, barking laugh. "Anyway, I could use your experience in post-operative procedures, in case we go with X-rays. Right now, I'm using dyes to detect any egg production. We need to know if eggs are actually being produced, you understand. Promising results so far. Very promising. You might be of help. Interested?"

Johann knew of Clauberg's ingratiating manner. He also had heard about his crudeness, his egotism, and his posturing. Schumann, he knew, resented his privileges at the camp and would be angry if he agreed to work for his rival. But Schumann was not using him so much of late and he was anxious that if he refused, he might be assigned to the gassings. He softly said, "*Ja.*"

Without waiting for Johann to say anything more, Clauberg continued, "So, good. *Block 10.* My laboratory. Tomorrow morning."

Johann nodded.

"I run an efficient operation, *Herr Doktor* Brenner. You'll learn something. The most recent crop of Jewesses is promising. Many had German husbands. Why, I'll never understand. Anyway, the men are gone. The women are now ours." Again, the high, squeaky laugh, tinged with a tone that put Johann's teeth on edge. "These *ladies*"—Clauberg's high-pitched voice fell to its deepest tone, followed by a smirk—"tell me that they have not had sexual relations in many cases in over a year. I have picked out a few for my studies. Good material. I'm giving them an opportunity to do something for the future of the human race. That's just one of the advantages of our work. Until tomorrow, then."

They exchanged "*Heils*" and parted. Johann immediately regretted his decision.

When he arrived the next morning, a prisoner already lay on the examination table, moaning, as a bloody discharge from her vagina widened into an apple-sized stain on the sheet underneath her. A bored-looking *Kapo* held down her shoulders, while two nurses stood on either side, chatting with each other. As he hurried to put on a white lab coat and surgical hat, he could not help but notice the surgery's set up: the array of implements, the examination table's gleaming chrome stirrups, the bright lighting (the room's windows were boarded up, as were all the other windows in *Block 10*); and the new sheeting and bandages stacked high in the open cabinets. The equal of any in the *Reich*. Clauberg and his assistant, Göbel, stood in the corner, reviewing some papers.

"*Obersturmführer Herr Doktor* Brenner, welcome. This is my assistant, *Herr Doktor* Göbel."

Johann and Göbel nodded at each other.

"*Herr Doktor* Schetzeler sent word that he had another assignment," Clauberg said. "Too bad. We'll have to get you all together another time. You just missed an easy one, Brenner. Wide open. An easy shot all the way in. She's had a lot of wear, I'll wager." He turned toward the *Kapo*. "We're done here. Take her out. Get the next *lady*." Again, the deeper voice and cackle. Did Clauberg realize how often he cackled, Johann wondered.

He was used to seeing subjects carried in, but a frail looking young woman walked in by herself, without the *Kapo*'s support. "So," Clauberg said, in his most reassuring voice, "I am glad to see that you have decided to join us. Allow me to help you on to the table."

Johann saw the woman's eyes widen. Saw the raw scrapes on her shaved scalp. Saw that a razor cut behind her ear was still oozing blood. Saw the fresh tattoo on her arm, puffy and red around the inky numbers, like Philipp's. Saw how her eyes darted around the room. The sheet she held around her body twisted and tightened as she sat leaned on the edge of the table. He heard her panting, each breath a tiny whimper.

"Twenty-three and two months, *Herr Doktor* Clauberg," the nurse said. "Married. Two children, she says. No miscarriages. No abortions. Normal periods. Last intercourse two months ago. Probably on her birthday. Subsequent normal periods. Admits to masturbating."

"Fine, nurse. We won't need this," Clauberg said, smiling, in a raised voice, as he reached for the sheet. The woman clutched at it, then let it go and closed her eyes. Clauberg took her ankles and pivoted her toward the table's stirrups, placing one foot in each and clamped them tight. "If you wish, you can pull the sheet over your head," he said, with the first of many little squeaky laughs. He took the speculum from the nurse and inserted it forcibly into the woman's vagina. A muffled groaned.

"Work much on women, *Herr Doktor* Brenner?" Clauberg asked.

"No."

"Come down here behind me. Move over Göbel. Let the *Herr Doktor* have a view. Fascinating opportunity to see their best part." Another laugh. Johann said nothing and stepped behind Clauberg.

The woman pulled the sheet over her head as far as she could. She whimpered louder now and breathed even more rapidly, the sheet swelling and falling over her mouth with each breath. Clauberg asked for the syringe. Over his shoulder, he held up the long needle for Johann to see. "Here is the solution to our problems!" He deftly inserted it into the woman's vagina and pushed the plunger, triggering a scream that may have been heard outside the building.

Clauberg began to shout, "Stop it! Stop screaming! Do you want me to send you over to Birkenau? You'll die there in a day or two, slut! Or would you rather I shoot some African's semen up your cunt? I can do it, you know! I gave you a choice before you came in here. Now shut up!"

He pulled out the syringe. The woman was gasping, body convulsing into rippling spasms. The *Kapo* held her shoulders down; the nurses, her arms.

"I don't want the solution to drain away from the cervix, *Herr Doktor* Brenner," Clauberg said. "Therefore the viscous material. Makes it stick. And no anesthetic. Might dilute the Formalin's potency. We're interested in results here."

Göbel laughed. Minutes passed. Clauberg sat a desk, made some notes, stood up, looked over the array of instruments, complained that one was not in the correct order, and then bantered with the nurses. The woman was writhing under the sheet in rhythm with her moans. Johann felt sick.

"Hold her down," Clauberg ordered. "Tighter. She'll jiggle the solution out." He looked at his stopwatch. Turning to Johann, he said, "You look pale, Brenner. I had a feeling this would be difficult for you." A muffled cackle. "Let's take a look now. Done! See, no discharge of the Formalin. It's doing the job."

He again looked at his stopwatch. "Six minutes, 45 seconds." A drop of blood slowly swelled into a *pfennig*-sized stain on the sheet underneath the woman's vagina. Then another. Clauberg took off his glasses and handed them to the nurse to clean.

"Good," he finally said. "Notice, please, the blood is not diluted. The last one was a bleeder. This one's better. Under seven minutes. Do you want to have a try, *Herr Doktor* Brenner?"

"Not yet, if you don't mind," Johann said, and stepped back from the table and leaned against the wall.

"As you wish. Take her out. Next!"

Another woman appeared in the doorway. Older. Sallow. Obviously frightened. Johann saw that she, too, had fresh scrapes where her scalp had been shaved. His eyes fastened on a dark bruise on her arm just above her tattoo. She had to be pushed toward the table by the Kapo and a nurse.

"All right, I'll take this one." Clauberg said. "Then your turn, Brenner. Then you, Göbel. You need the practice, too. Too bad Schetzeler's not here."

Göbel grunted and stepped to Clauberg's side. The woman was trembling so much she could barely stand.

"Tell us about this lady, nurse."

"Thirty-six, four months, *Herr Doktor* Clauberg. Widow. No children. No abortions. No miscarriages. Irregular periods. Last period seven weeks ago. Last intercourse, she says, was fifteen months ago, when her husband was on leave. Won't admit to masturbating."

"Thank you. Perhaps pre-menopausal. We need more data on pre-menopausal women. Let's take a look."

He smiled, then barked, "On the table! Lie down, you old sack! Bend your legs!"

The woman had to be lifted on to the table. Clauberg gestured toward the stirrups. When she hesitated, he swiftly grabbed her ankles, and spread her legs, as the nurses latched the stirrup clamps.

Johann moved closer to the head of the table. Something in the woman's eyes made him think of Philipp's appeal. Could this be Semmelberg's daughter? It didn't occur to him until this minute that she might have been conscripted into Clauberg's experiment. 'The last one was too young,' he thought. 'But this might be her.'

While Clauberg was reaching for the speculum. Johann leaned forward and asked, "Are you from Pohlendorf?" She was stunned and turned to look at him. She opened her mouth to speak but before she could say anything, Clauberg said, "*Herr Doktor,* only I speak with the subject here. If you please. Step behind me. Göbel, are you watching?"

Johann stepped back from the table just as Clauberg jabbed the speculum into her vagina. In the same instant, a grotesque scream filled the room. Clauberg began to shout and threaten, waving the syringe up above his head for her to see as he leaned in between her legs. She whimpered a moment, then screamed even louder.

"Gag her!"

From the speed with which the nurse did it, Johann knew that this was not a rare occurrence. He studied the woman's face. Her eyes were wide with terror and pain. A spasm shook her body and she fainted. Was she Semmelberg's daughter?

"Done!" shouted Clauberg, as he handed the empty syringe to a nurse for re-filling. As before, he went to his desk and wrote some notes. After a few minutes he returned to the table and looked into the woman's vagina and then at his stop-watch.

"Let's see. Five minutes, fifty-six seconds. Under six. Excellent. Not much blood, given her initial squirming. Did you see, Goebel? Brenner? A quick insertion of the syringe, the quicker, the better. It was good she passed out. Carry her out now and bring in the next lady. Ready Göbel?" Clauberg glowered at Johann. "You look ill, *Herr Doktor* Brenner. You are welcome to leave, of course. How disappointing, I must say. Not up to this work, I see."

"Yes, I'm not well. Excuse me, please," Johann mumbled and turned toward the door. He heard Clauberg snigger and curse behind him over the others' laughter. Passing the next woman in the doorway, he walked into the ward, past a row of a dozen or more terrified and trembling women destined for the procedure, to the bedside of the woman he had just seen in the operating room. She was awake.

"Don't speak," he said softly. "Just nod. Are you from Pohlendorf?"
She nodded.

"I am, too," he said. "I knew your father and mother, *Herr* and *Frau* Semmelberg. And your grandfather. You were just a little girl when I left for the first war. Philipp Stein, my friend, is recovering in the prisoner's hospital. He told me about you and your father. I am sorry."

Her eyes widened. She tried to talk but could not.

"I'll tell him you are safe. Now, do what you are told here. You will be fed well enough. *Doktor* Clauberg wants you to survive, for his purposes. I must leave before he sees me speaking with you. I will try to return."

He squeezed her hand, reported himself ill and went back to his barracks. He lay on his bunk, unable to close his eyes or get the sound of Ellen's scream out of his head.

When Johann saw Philipp again the next day, he tried not to look at the oozing tattoo on his arm and the cuts on his scalp. "You are looking better," he said, even though he thought he looked quite pale. He told him that he had found Ellen and that she was well, but he was careful to not say anything more.

Philipp smiled. "Good. Thank you, Johann."

It was the first time anyone had smiled and thanked Johann since he had arrived at Auschwitz. He looked away, out the window into an icy, gray sky out of which snow was beginning to fall.

He arranged his schedule so he could visit Philipp every other day. He brought bread, slices of apple, and a small piece of chocolate each time, pulling them out from inside his shirt wrapped in a towel that he handed to him when no one was watching. He was alarmed at how quickly Philipp was losing weight.

"Don't you eat what I bring you?"

"Not really."

"Why not?"

"Others need it more. We don't exactly have a buffet meal here. I can imagine a better soup boiled out of gravel and shoe leather. At least they use water instead of piss. Or I hope so." Philipp laughed at his own joke until Johann had to laugh, too.

The next time, Johann brought a larger piece of bread, a piece of cheese, and two apples, but no chocolate.

"Please bring more chocolate," Philipp said. "I give bits of it to those who have the worst diarrhea. It doesn't help much. But it gives them some pleasure. What's happened to Ellen?"

"She's been moved to another part of the camp. I will check in on her if I can," he said, not knowing what else to say. He had gone several times to the ward in *Block 10*, but she was not there. Johann dared not ask where she was.

Philipp only said, "I know you did what you could. Thank you."

Johann closed his eyes and shook his head.

Philipp's wounds had healed as much as they were going to under the circumstances. He had a red, jagged three-inch scar from the edge of his forehead that stretched over and behind his ear. Even if his skull had not been shaved, it would have been noticeable. The muscles in his thigh had not knit together properly and he walked in obvious pain. His prison uniform hung loosely on his shoulders. One of his front teeth was missing. Drool seeped out of the corner of his mouth when he talked. Johann thought he might have had a minor stroke.

"I know you hate me, Philipp. You have every reason to."

Philipp felt his throat tighten. He ran his tongue over the broken edge of a tooth and took a deep breath. "I don't hate you. How would hating you change what has happened? What I hate is what you have done. What you are doing."

Johann put his hand on Philipp's shoulder. "I want you to know, I am sorry," he whispered. "I know I can't expect your forgiveness, but I am sorry."

Philipp looked into Johann's eyes. "You were right. It is better that I am not a doctor here. As an orderly, I can spend more time with the patients." Maybe I am the luckier one after all. I wasn't permitted to face your choices." He turned away and began to hobble back into the ward.

Johann watched him go. After bribing a *Kapo* with a cigarette to give Philipp an extra bowl of soup that night, he left for his barracks. He visited him as often as he could, sometimes only for a minute or two, each time bribing the *Kapo* to give him an extra ration. Philipp, however, was losing weight and growing more and more distant. He seemed to be in a fog, shrinking into himself. In late March, he barely greeted Johann and seemed in a daze.

"You again. I am not surprised," he said, slurring his words. "We are doctors, after all. We will save the world."

During their last meeting, in early June, when Johann asked him how he was doing, Philipp began to cry, "I cannot help them all. They all need our help. We are doctors." Johann could not comfort him, no matter how he tried.

When he looked for him two days later, a prisoner orderly told him that Philipp was missing. "He gave me this for you," he said, handing Johann a postcard that prisoners could use to send messages to the outside world. Despite the shaky, faint handwriting, Johann recognized it as Philipp's:

"Be the doctor we both wanted to be. We can still make a better world, but it will be harder now than ever. Lebewohl! *P."*

"He had enormous courage. He wore himself out," the orderly said. "He cared for everyone. Except himself. Became a '*Muselmann.*'"

"I don't understand."

"A *Muselman*. A zombie. Looked like a skeletal, praying Arab. They waste away. Like straw in the wind. The *Kapos* pick them up and take them to the ovens. Every day there are more."

"He was my friend. From before the war."

"He did what he could for everyone here," the orderly said, looking over his shoulder at the ward. "When I saw him for the last time, he told me he didn't want me to become a 'walking shadow.' Something from Shakespeare, he said. But that's what he had become. Gave his food away." He looked out the window, toward the crematorium chimney. Johann followed his gaze upward, where black smoke was curling slowly in the bright summer sky.

Johann returned every few days to the prisoner's hospital, each time hiding food or useful items under his shirt: potatoes, lumps of sugar, chocolate, pencil stubs, needles, matches, paper. He hoped that they would be distributed to as many prisoners as possible. But he knew that whatever he did, it would not be enough.

*****

It was sunny or rainy. Nights were clear or cloudy. Moons waxed and waned. Stars and planets kept to their appointed arcs across the sky. At Auschwitz, nothing changed.

Auschwitz had two kinds of walls: one, of barbed wire strung between concrete posts that kept the prisoners where the Nazis wanted them to be; the other was the wall of hatred and denial the Nazis had built in their own minds, a wall that kept them from thinking that their prisoners were human beings. Everyone was a captive one way or another: guards as well as those they guarded; taskmasters as well as slaves; physicians as well as those they selected or experimented on. Johann recalled his mother's story about a spider and its web. He now understood what she meant: he could no more escape the web he had woven than could those helpless masses made to parade before him on the railroad ramp.

With Philipp's arrival, Johann began to see how choices—*his* choices—brought both of them to Auschwitz. That he had helped to create the suffering around them. That he deserved no mercy, compared to the mercy they deserved. As to what he deserved, he did not want to think about it.

*****

In August, Johann went with some *SS* physicians and other officers to *Reichsarzt* Mengele's private laboratory for a special demonstration about two research subjects, a father and son. Less than a week before, Mengele had picked them out during the selection that sent most of the trainload—the last survivors of the Lodz ghetto's half million Jews—to the gas chambers. He had spotted them in the procession on the ramp. Rather than send them to the showers, he selected them for himself. The father was hunchbacked and his teenage son had a deformed foot, a sure sign, he thought, of hereditary degeneration.

Doktor Miklos Nyiszli, a Jewish prisoner from Romania, who introduced himself as Mengele's assistant and Chief Physician of the Auschwitz crematoria, was escorting the group. He had examined the father and son, and then, after they had been killed, did autopsies, prepared their skeletons for display, and arranged for the day's presentation. As they walked toward the laboratory, Nyiszli told of his professional accomplishments, including his trip to the World's Fair in New York in 1939 as a member of the Romania's delegation of physicians. Johann knew why Mengele, Schumann and Clauberg would want to have Jewish prisoner physicians work for them. Many were accomplished, even excellent and well known for their specializations. Schumann, to Johann's relief, seemed disinclined to assign him to the castrations of late, having found other doctors, including some Jews, to do his bidding. Nor had he ever again observed Clauberg's procedures, but he knew that the gynecologist had persuaded other doctors, including Jews, to work for him in *Block 10*. Just how desperate would these prisoner doctors have to be? Hoping to save a family member was the only justification he could understand.

Mengele's examination rooms, medical library and laboratory were conveniently located near Crematorium Number One, whose smoking chimney Johann saw every day. It loomed over their heads as the group walked through the courtyard. He barely paid attention to what Nyiszli was saying, looking instead at the smoke's swirling shadow on the cobblestones.

With his slower pace, Johann trailed behind. Although his contact with Philipp had awakened his shame, he could not shake off the momentum of his daily routine. He slept fitfully, with recurring nightmares. One midnight he thrashed through a dream in which he was a *Muselmann*, staggering after Philipp who kept disappearing behind Auschwitz's dark brick buildings. He awoke screaming, *"Philipp! Stop! Wait! Our oath!"* His shouts echoed through the barracks, startling his comrades out of their sleep.

Little puffs of ash on the cobblestones swirled up with every step, as though the group was walking through a fog. The ash was everywhere, dusting the scorched, red bricks of its buildings and dulling the green leaves of its trees. Aside from the neatly tended flowerbeds at the homes of the camp's highest officers and their families, everything in Auschwitz was dry and dark, a city of shadows and soot. The gardens were tiny oases in a vast desert of ash. Johann caught a glimpse of ripening fields of sunflowers beyond the camp's barbed wire fence. 'How could people outside not wonder what was going on here? Weren't they curious? Or didn't they care?' Johann asked himself. High, wispy clouds of late summer floated above the chimney's smoke.

Johann felt a hand on his shoulder and turned to see Schetzeler, who had slowed his pace to talk to him. He mumbled a greeting as they walked side-by-side.

"You haven't come back to *Herr Doktor* Clauberg's surgery," Schetzeler said.

"Yes."

"Too bad. He told me you were there the morning I missed."

"Yes."

"Fascinating man, Clauberg."

"Yes."

"Fascinating work, don't you think?"

"I suppose."

"Gynecology is a delight. A real delight. You should come again."

"Perhaps."

"Later today, some of us are going for a little hike and a picnic. The last blueberries are ripe. It's a beautiful day. Want to come?"

Johann was silent for a moment, then said, "You'll ruin the shine on your boots."

Schetzeler laughed a squeaky laugh. "Some nurses are coming. We'll have *schnapps*. Or wine if you prefer that. Should be a good time. The nurses get tipsy real fast. That's why I didn't come to Clauberg's surgery that time you were there. Had a terrible hangover. Nurses probably did, too. Wild." He laughed again.

"Thank you. No. I'll stay in camp. I have duty this evening at the SS hospital. Many wounded arrived yesterday."

"As you wish, *Herr Doktor*. But I'll tell you this. Sooner or later, you'll want to find a way to imagine yourself somewhere else. In that one respect, we're no different than the shitty prisoners and the goddamned Jews." Schetzeler began whistling a little march and walked ahead to catch up with Nyiszli.

The courtyard near the crematoria was particularly grim. Nyiszli pointed out two rusting iron casks near its entrance. In those barrels, just the afternoon before, he had supervised boiling off the flesh from the two skeletons they were about to see. He had advised Mengele that was the fastest way to prepare the skeletons. They then were bleached in a gasoline bath.

"You'll see. I told *Herr Doktor* Mengele that there would be very little odor, the bones dry and white. As though bleached by the sun on the African desert. And they are. You'll see."

Johann noticed how pleased he seemed to be that his technical advice could be so helpful. He imagined the flesh bobbing in a greasy broth. The image saturated his thoughts. He overheard only bits of the conversation that followed between Nyiszli and Schetzeler.

"They really ate some?" Schetzeler asked.

"Never even hesitated…" Nyiszli replied.

"Ate?"

"With gusto, I tell you…"

"Did you tell them?"

"Why? They're tortured enough. But, yes, the *Sonderkommando* guards told them what they had eaten."

"Beasts!" Schetzeler said in disgust.

"No, just hungry."

"Beasts, I say. Serves them right, for what they do."

"What do they do?" Nyiszli asked. "They're starving Polish masons. Prisoners. After they patched up the crematorium chimney as ordered, they were hungry. They thought the flesh in the casks was food for the *Sonderkommando*. Why shouldn't they have some meat for a change?"

"Enough!" Schetzeler lagged back to walk again beside Johann. "Did you hear what he said?"

"Yes. Terrible." Johann's voice trailed off as he looked up, past the chimney, beyond the smoke, at the blue, impersonal sky.

"Sure you don't want to come this afternoon?"

"Yes, I'm sure."

They walked the rest of the way in silence.

The invited guests sat in comfortable armchairs in the laboratory's workroom. Behind the latest medical journals lined the shelves, all neat and carefully ordered. On the table by the window stood three new microscopes. Mengele greeted his colleagues with enthusiasm. His dark hair glistened with pomade. His eyes shone brightly. "Come into the dissection room, gentlemen. Come see this remarkably clear proof of congenital deformity and degeneracy."

Two bleached skeletons, smelling slightly of gasoline, lay loosely assembled and side-by-side on the marble table. Mengele fingered the father's vertebrae. He held up the youth's heel bone. Nyiszli stood in the corner, a half-smile painted on his face. His autopsies had determined that the father's curved spine was the result of rickets, and that the son's deformed foot was due to a lack of muscle, hypomyelia. Neither was a definitively inheritable condition. Otherwise, his examinations revealed nothing particularly unusual. Mengele had other ideas.

Johann looked intently at Nyiszli, at the dark shadows around his eyes. Did the assistant show pride in his professional accomplishment in order to mask his awareness of the horror of his deed? When he looked at Mengele, waving the son's heel bone back and forth in front of the assembled guests, he could detect no trace of horror. He remained silent as several of the doctors immersed themselves in an involved discussion, extrapolating from these two skeletons all the supposedly indelible Jewish racial characteristics at the root of every conceivable human flaw and crime—past, present and future.

Mengele, striding back and forth alongside the marble slab, took every opportunity to encourage his colleagues. Thanks to his study of this Jewish father and son, "priceless information has been secured.

What we are learning here will ensure the purity of the Aryan race. All other human beings will inevitably prosper."

"Excellent!" said one officer and began to applaud.

"Outstanding!" Schetzeler shouted.

"Soon," Mengele continued, interrupting the applause with a wave of his hand, "these two skeletons will be sent to the Anthropological Museum in Berlin, to become part of a perpetual exhibition demonstrating the Jews' degeneracy. Gentlemen, you will forgive me I trust if I cannot disguise my pride in our important work here." More applause. Johann noticed that Schetzeler was particularly energetic.

Nyiszli's face was wooden, his smile unchanged, but Johann thought that his eyes had an incredulous look. Under his breath, as he looked around the room, Johann mouthed the words, "we *are* barbarians. All of us. So easily."

CHAPTER TWENTY
Enormous Relief

I made excuses and pretended as long as I could. I even thought myself heroic for helping Philipp, if you can believe that. I cannot explain it, Helga. Only that I could not imagine how it could be any other way.

As luck would have it, a bomb fell on Auschwitz and I was wounded. When I was evacuated to a hospital in Berlin, I felt enormous relief. And shame.

Johann was drawn to the small square where Meier was helping clear the rubble away. He was almost certain that Meier knew who he was, but something about Meier's determination inspired him to help the old man. When he tried to pick up five bricks at once, he lost his grip. Two bricks cracked when they fell.

"That won't do," Meier said. "We need the bricks to be whole. Can't build with broken bricks."

"I know."

"Don't take so many. One or two at a time works well enough."

"*Ja.* You're right." Johann concentrated on the bricks. Gusts of a chill December wind tumbled snowflakes through the air. "Still no overcoat?" he asked.

"Not until my spit freezes before it hits the street," Meier answered with a snort. "Don't worry about me." He reached for another brick with his cane. "You've got a bad hand, I see."

"Yes," Johann replied.

"What happened?"

"War wound." When he saw that Meier wanted to hear more, he added, "Don't want to talk about it."

"Sorry." Meier stood up straight and looked into Johann's eyes.

"Nothing to be sorry about," Johann said. "I'm lucky I still can use it." He was talking too much.

"Wrong place, wrong time, eh? Like all of us." Meier said. "Do you have to wear the glove?"

"Keeps it clean. And it's not pretty to look at," Johann said, bending over for a brick.

"Sorry I asked." Meier hoisted two bricks and turned toward the stack.

The two men walked side-by-side in silence. On the way back, Meier said, "I keep thinking I met you somewhere before the war. You're from Saxony, you say. I've never been there, though. They say we all have a double somewhere, someone who looks just like us, even thinks and acts just like us. Maybe I met your double. He was a doctor. Like all them, full of himself. Sharp for Hitler, he was. Tried to warn him. That was before the war. Before the Nazis took power. Before the Depression, in fact. In Augsburg. My niece's marriage day. She married a doctor. A Jew. Nice enough fellow, though. Not many left now. Got out while they could, I suppose. My niece was killed in Berlin. A bomb. Don't know what happened to her husband. Didn't see them much after the wedding."

Johann said nothing. With difficulty, Meier dislodged another brick with his cane and bent over to pick it up. He was puffing when he stood up. "I suppose we need doctors. Broken legs. Babies. Infections. I needed an eye doctor once. Got something in my eye when I was a boy. But some of them think they're gods. Give themselves airs. Think they can cure the world of all its ills. That's what the trial's all about. Doctors who thought they were entitled to do whatever Hitler wanted them to do. If half of what the radio tells is true, they did some wicked things."

Johann made a few more trips from the rubble heap to the stack. After a while, he said, "It's getting late. My hand is hurting me. I'll come again another time. *Auf Wiedersehen*."

"Sure. Come again. Another week, ten days, two weeks at the most, and we'll be done here. *'Wiedersehen*."

Johann walked back to the courthouse. The throbbing in his hand did not prevent him from reflecting on how doctors had lost the trust of people like Meier.

*****

Early on a September morning in 1944, Auschwitz's anti-aircraft artillery guns tracked a high-flying formation of American bombers. The plane's path would take them over the labor camp formally called Auschwitz III or Monowitz, adjacent to the Buna synthetic rubber factory, with its slave laborers. The air-raid warning signals were not unusual, since Buna was an important military target. For almost three years, though, the Allies had determined that Auschwitz I and Auschwitz II (also known as Auschwitz-Birkenau)—the death and labor camps, with their staid, brick buildings, and their prisoners' barracks; their officers' quarters and electrified fences and kennels for several hundred dogs; their orderly streets, their railroad siding and ramp, their delousing showers and stockpile of cyanide crystals; their places for torture and execution by hanging and firing squad; their crematoria and open pit graves—were not worth risking a plane or spending a load of bombs. No one noticed when a lone plane, falling out of formation in the bomber squadron overhead, arched over Auschwitz I.

From it fell a speck that grew larger and larger. Johann, standing with some others outside the SS barracks, watched open-mouthed. Schetzeler, drunk and staggering toward the building from another over-night rendezvous, began to laugh. "Watch out, *meine Herren*! A bird will shit in your mouths!"

When it became obvious that the bomb would hit the barracks, the men threw themselves down on the ground. Later, Johann remembered the sequence of sounds: the bomb's metallic scream gave way to a deafening explosion; then impossible silence, in which the sky began to fall in bits and pieces—bricks and steel, sticks, shards, splinters, ashes, gore; next, a different kind of scream—piercing shrieks with short, high-pitched bleatings; finally, a pitiful wailing that gurgled from a throat filling with blood. An *SS* guard on the ground near Johann gasped in pain. Another merely muttered "Oh Lord!" and was silent. Johann's last sight before he passed out was of Schetzeler's leg in its shiny boot landing near his head.

Fifteen men died instantly. Some were crushed by falling roof tiles. Some, like Schetzeler, were torn apart by the explosion. Johann was one of the twenty-eight seriously wounded. When he raised his head out of the dirt and opened his eyes to look at his right hand, he saw that a metal fragment had pierced it clean through. Another protruded from his wrist. With his other hand, he felt the back of his neck and determined that he had only a scratch, just above his collar. Had he not instinctively covered the back of his neck, the needle-like shard would have nailed him to the ground. His leg throbbed. It seemed to be melting, warm, as though in an oily bath. Before he could raise himself up to, look at it, his eyes swam in a whirlpool of smoke and dirt and he blacked out again.

He and the other survivors were rushed to the new *SS* hospital. It was there, he assumed, that the shrapnel was removed from his hand and wrist; he had no memory of the procedure. Waking up in the ward, he looked at his lower right arm and hand, now encased in bandages wrapped so generously they might have enclosed a small melon. No amputation yet, he remembered thinking. Then he blacked out a third time.

When he awoke—hours later? days?—the throbbing in his hand was overpowering. He tried to muffle a scream, but could not, only succeeding in transforming it into a long groan, a single syllable that echoed in his head long after it had left his throat. His leg was cold below his knee. A tourniquet clamped his thigh like a vise. A shadow appeared above his bed and without a word gave him an injection. He fell back into a dark, troubled, heavy, sleep.

He awoke as he was being loaded onto a train. The rising sun slanted through the windows and reddened the car's ceiling. Darker red silhouettes, the shadows of the orderlies who walked now and then up and down the aisles, flickered overhead. The trip was bearable, mostly because it was so slow. The train moved for an hour or two, then spent several more stalled on a siding. After some time, he could prop himself up on his elbow, but doing so made him feverish. When he could raise himself high enough to look out the dirty window, he thought he was watching two motion pictures ineptly spliced together: a pastoral romance invaded by scenes of hideous devastation. Forests and fields of grain that were ripening under an unconcerned sky shifted abruptly to railway sidings that had become craters, buildings that had become rubble, a bridge slumped into the river, a church without a roof, a factory building crushed by its own smokestack. Then more trees, meadows, a distant view of a lake. With nightfall, everything faded to black.

He spoke occasionally to the wounded men on stretchers near him, all officers. He saw others propped up in the railway car's seats. The mood was sullen. Most of them had been wounded in fighting further to the east. He did not know what to say to them. His injuries seemed slight by comparison. The bandage on his right hand and wrist was smaller now; he could eat with his left. The man nearest him had no hands. While the train was stopped at a siding, Johann asked an orderly for paper and pen and tried to write a letter to Helga. His childish scrawl frightened him and he gave up. He worried that no one at Auschwitz would arrange for mail from her to be sent on to his destination—wherever that was. His injured leg was less troublesome, but still painful. Someone had replaced the bandage with a clean, looser one. He guessed that his femoral artery had been severed but had been held closed by a tourniquet that saved his life. He thought of Aronsohn.

The next morning, somewhere near Potsdam, the train stopped at a siding and stayed there two days. He saw four or five freight trains going eastward and heard others during the night. He thought of those in the boxcars. Two soldiers who had died of their wounds were carried past him and put on the siding near his window. Their bodies were taken into a small train station whose name he could not read. He thought he could pick out some features in the distance of a city's skyline through dark billows of smoke. Berlin? When he looked out a window toward the south, he thought of Nuremberg, hundreds of miles away. Somewhere in that direction was Helga. It had been nearly a month since he had heard from her. After the letter telling him of Paul-Adolf's death, she had written only a few, short notes, complaining that he had not come home on leave. He had tried to explain his reasoning in his replies. He hoped her letters to him were still in his duffle-bag. An orderly told him it was under his stretcher but said he was too busy to find them.

The train finally arrived in Berlin. Johann was taken to the military ward at the *Charité*. Two old, smartly starched nurses muscled him into a bed, despite his protests that he could move by himself. An even older looking, hunch-backed nurse caught his wounded hand, squeezed around for his pulse, found it, and then let his hand drop without warning. The sudden pain made him gasp. She scurried away, oblivious. He felt trapped in a maze of grays. Through a high, arched window, he saw the sun, a silver-white disk, trying to pierce the clouds. When he closed his eyes, they were flooded by a bloody, opaque light.

During his first night in the ward, he was kept awake by a grotesque lullaby of snores, coughs and moans. Just before dawn, a turbulent sleep grabbed him. He sweated so much that the threadbare sheet and mattress smelled of pungent naphtha. He faded into a feverish labyrinth. His mind swam through green mists and into dark holes filled with testicles and eyeballs dripping blood. He saw shadows clustering around his bed, felt the jabs of syringes, then drifted away, until the eyeballs and testicles trapped him in a cave where he could not run away.

After a week, maybe longer, his fever subsided. He opened his eyes to see the hunchbacked nurse snipping at the gauze around his hand. When he raised himself up to get a better look, she turned her back on him and kept on peeling off the bandage. He was distracted by her hump and almost reached over with his left hand to touch it. It seemed more real than did his own body. She mumbled something in a *Plattdeutsch* dialect he could not understand, turned around and held up his naked hand, only slightly darker than the white bandages that had encased it. It looked like it was carved out of a waxy, lifeless stone. An object made to look like a hand.

The nurse shifted over to High German. "Here you are, *mein Herr Doktor!* Not bad. Don't think I haven't seen worse. We have your blood poisoning under control now, too. Welcome to the living."

Johann felt compelled to say "Thank you!" He was not surprised by his hand's whiteness. Its smoothness made it look like something new, as though it had been taken off a shelf in a warehouse. But he expected to see a hole in his palm. On the train, he had dreamed he saw the moon glowing through it. There was no hole. Instead, he saw a weeping, raw-edged gash shaped roughly like a bent, jagged swastika on the back of his hand. Was this a joke? Another ragged incision stretched all around his wrist like a bracelet, decorated by neat suture marks on either side. These would scar over and shrink. But he knew that they would always be there. A scarred swastika on the back of his right hand. Another scar for a bracelet. The surgeon either had a strong sense of loyalty to Hitler or a peculiarly sadistic sense of humor. Maybe the two were inseparable.

He tried to straighten his curled fingers. His fist clenched even tighter with the effort. He relaxed when the pain in his wrist and the back of his hand signaled that he was doing something wrong. He tried again. As before, his fist tightened more, not less, his knuckles whitening with the pressure. He gasped with the pain. The nurse saw what was happening, but said nothing and left.

After a minute or more, Johann tried a third time to stretch his fingers. The same result—his fist grew tighter. He held his hand up close to his face, the swastika scar just inches from his eyes. Its sweetish, ointmented, greasy smell filled his nostrils. He studied the thin, flaking skin at the edges of the angular, purplish wound. With the forefinger of his left hand he felt over the stubbly place where the hair on his back of his hand had been shaved away. As he moved his arm, a deep, knotted pain oscillated back and forth from his head to his hand. He set his jaw and tried once more to extend his fingers. He screamed.

The hunch-backed nurse returned, followed by a short, shuffling, beady-eyed doctor in a white-coat. Johann said to both of them, looking from one to the other, "I cannot open my fist."

"You are lucky to have a fist," the surgeon said.

"Yes, but I am a doctor. I need my hands to work."

"Yes. *So so, mein Herr Doktor*," the nurse said in a mixture of High German and dialect. "We do what's best, you know,"

Johann almost shouted: "I am a doctor."

"Calm yourself. You must know that your hand is a complex instrument," the surgeon said, matter-of-factly. "I have work to do."

"How do I open my fist?"

"With time, perhaps." The surgeon grinned, then laughed. But it was not a laugh of encouragement or understanding. Nor a laugh of contempt or derisive enjoyment. Johann saw indifference in the man's eyes. A weight of despair crushed him into the mattress.

When the doctor turned to leave, Johann grabbed the back of his white coat with his left hand. He pulled him backwards toward the side of the bed and, without thinking, began to swing at him with his right hand, reflexively commanded into a fist. His fingers stretched out. Trying to make a fist had exactly the opposite effect. He stared at his open hand.

"What do you think you are doing? Outrageous!" the surgeon shouted. The nurse was speechless, astonished.

"My hand! Look, it is open," Johann exclaimed. "I want to make a fist and my hand opens. I want to stretch my fingers and I make a fist. Something is wrong. This is impossible."

After seeing Johann close and open his fist a few times, the doctor told the nurse to make a note of it on his chart. Then, with a curiosity that made him forget the attempted assault, he picked up the injured hand and commanded him to make a fist over and over again. Johann did as he was told, wincing and wide-eyed with each attempt.

"Interesting, this. Fascinating. Really, fascinating. Tendons probably cross-connected in surgery. No other explanation. Fascinating." The surgeon's eyes began to glow. "So, *Herr Doktor*, you can use your hand after all. See. You'll get used to it. A minor detail. You'll work again. Good. We need doctors more than ever."

The nurse grunted her approval. With that, the two walked away, leaving Johann to clench and unclench his fist, each time having to think the opposite in order to achieve the desired result.

When he was discharged, he had orders to report to the *Reichsgesundheitsamt*, the Office of the Ministry of Health, about a mile and a half away on *Prinz-Albrecht-Straße*. The porter at the hospital gate phoned for a car to pick him up, but when it had not arrived after two hours, Johann told him that he was going to walk. Immediately upon saying this, he thought how easy it would be to go to the train station and board any train going toward Karlsruhe and Helga—if there still was a train. He deserved a leave. He had not asked for one when Paul-Adolf was killed. Nor had he taken one when it was offered to him the year before when he was transferred to Auschwitz. He had written Helga that the war would be over soon and he preferred to be in uniform and at his post when the news arrived. Now he shook his head, thinking how stupid he had been.

The ruin around him was startling. Was this Berlin? He compared it to what he had seen in 1939. If destruction was so evident here, what would Nuremberg look like? The Nuremberg in his mind was the Nuremberg of ten years before. Banners and the flowers spilling over the timbered houses' balconies. The Party rallies each October. Surely, it must still exist, even if here in the capitol there is such grayness and despair. During his earlier visit to Berlin, the city had seemed so alive, so filled with the self-confidence and power of a transformed nation. That was when the war was beginning. Now everything reflected Auschwitz's mechanized cruelty. Smoke and dust from smashed buildings smothered every color. How can the September sun be so warm and the world so gray? How dead everything looks. How fearful the people look, walking heads down, like insects. Small, dulled moving parts in a machine that stutters on.

The more he thought about his orders, the angrier he grew. If he was not entitled to be discharged now from service, his wounds surely merited some leave for further recuperation. How much longer could this war go on? Reports from the east imperfectly hid the fact that the Russians were advancing. In the west, the American and British invasion might have stalled—at least that's what the newspapers insisted—but who knew for how long? Goebbels sounded so convincing on the daily radio broadcasts that were piped through the ward: "*Ausharren!*" he ordered! "Endure!" Looking around him at the bombed out buildings, Johann wondered how the *Volk* could endure any more. 'Willpower can overcome only so much. Goebbel's dire warnings that a defeated *Vaterland* will be turned into a desert by the merciless allies might be true enough. But the way the war is going, it's nearly a wasteland now.' He shook his head and mouthed the words of the conversation he was having with himself as he made his way toward the Ministry.

His discharge from the hospital had been delayed by a persistent blood infection. He had lost weight. His hair had fallen out in clumps. Lying in bed for several weeks had stiffened up his leg. Each step was painful. His right shoe pinched and he quickly developed a blister. He longed for a cane. The sidewalks were littered with cobblestones and rubble. Narrow paths had been cleared around bombed buildings. Smoke rose from the raids of the night before. What few pedestrians there were held handkerchiefs over their faces and kept their heads down, only looking up to take their bearings from yet another ruined façade or missing building.

As he came to a cratered intersection, Johann saw a fire still burning in what was once a warehouse, its sign lying where it had fallen in the street. A few firemen half-heartedly trained their hoses on what was left of the corner of the building. The stream of water was so weak it barely reached the gaping hole in the second floor where a bomb had hit. Feeling tired and in no hurry to get to the Ministry, Johann stood with a few others in a doorway to watch the firemen.

"Bad business, this," Johann said to the man standing nearest to him.

"Yes. We don't stop most of them even in the daytime now."

"Too many."

"And not enough of our own. In the east, they say."

"Not for long. The Russians are coming."

"*Ja*. Bastards. We should have taken Moscow. We should not have surrendered at Stalingrad. But we will stop them."

"They are past Warsaw," Johann said, just as a parapet crashed to the street in a cloud of sparks and dust. The firemen shouted to each other, moving back just in time.

"You know something?" the man asked.

"The signs are clear. We keep falling back. I don't want to be here when they reach Berlin," Johann said.

"They won't. The *Führer* won't let them."

"I wouldn't want my wife to fall into their hands. They're supposed to be monsters. And they want revenge."

The man eyed Johann carefully. "They won't get here, don't worry."

"I wish I could be so sure."

Across the street, the firemen were coiling their hoses. The fire continued to burn. Johann could not tell if the water had given out or if they thought that they could do nothing more to stop the blaze. A timber from the second floor fell and sent up another shower of sparks. The firemen did not even turn to watch. The sky above was black with smoke.

"My wife is in Nuremberg now," Johann continued. "I want her as far west as she can get. The Americans probably intend to take Nuremberg. Maybe they will. But the further west she goes the better. The Allies want to divide us up into occupation zones. I read it yesterday in the *Beobachter*. Hitler and Goebbels tell us to dig in, of course. But despite what we hear about the *Führer*'s determination, the situation is grim. Anyway, the '*Amis*' are not like the Russians. She would be safer with them."

"'*Amis*'? The Americans are doing this bombing, *mein Herr*. You speak as though you think we will lose the war."

"You don't?"

The fire blazed up and cast their shadows on the door behind them. Without answering, the man walked away. Johann left, too, making a detour toward what he hoped was a usable bridge over the canal. When he reached the end of the next block, he heard a shout behind him: "Halt!" "Halt or I'll shoot."

He turned to see a policeman aiming his pistol him. He froze. By the policeman's side was the man he had just spoken with. The policeman handcuffed Johann despite his protests and blew a whistle. Within minutes, a squad car arrived. His accuser smiled when he was told to take a seat next to the driver. Johann sat in back, alongside the policeman who arrested him, his Luger still drawn.

Inside *Gestapo* headquarters, Johann's accuser told a desk officer that he heard Johann say that Germany would lose the war and that the *Führer* could not stop it. The officer pecked out his testimony on a clunky typewriter and told him to sign it. The accuser signed where he was told. All the while Johann stood handcuffed and speechless. He was not asked if any of this was true. But if he had been asked, he would not have denied it. When he was told to sign the statement, his handcuffs were removed and he made something like a signature with his left hand.

His identification papers were taken. His pocket watch and three snapshots of Helga, Paul-Adolf and Greta were put into one envelope. When he looked up from the desk, he saw his accuser leaving the building. A short while later he was prodded through a guarded door and down a hallway into a windowless holding cell. Inside were six other men. One, in a crisp business suit with a clean white shirt and neatly knotted necktie, stood against the back wall of the cell, his arms crossed defiantly. Another, wearing a journeyman carpenter's black corduroy bibbed trousers, lay on a bench and appeared to be sleeping. The rest all sat on the floor, hunched into themselves. No one said a word. Johann gently lifted the sleeping man's feet and made room for himself on the end of the bench. When a guard came near the cell, he got up and asked for a glass of water. His answer was a grunt. The man on the bench snored.

An hour passed, maybe two. Johann, frightened and nervous, clenched and unclenched his fist. The bandage over his scar wrinkled with each attempt, revealing the edges of the reddened swastika underneath.

Finally, another guard approached and told the first to unlock the cell. Everyone looked up, until the guard pointed at Johann. He stood up and went to the door. The second guard turned him around, handcuffed him again, and motioned to another door back down the hallway.

Johann found himself in a small courtroom. The bailiff, a heavy-set man wearing a uniform that was too tight, ordered Johann to stand before the presiding judge. The judge, a balding man wearing a crisp gray SS uniform with the shoulder boards and collar of a colonel, sat behind a table upon an elevated platform. A photograph of Hitler hung on the wall. Afternoon sunlight poured in a large window, glanced off the glass of Hitler's portrait, and sent a shimmering reflection on to the floor at Johann's feet.

"State your name, occupation, birth-place and military rank," the bailiff commanded.

The judge, with a deep sigh, shuffled the papers in front of him, confirming each of Johann's statements with dramatic pencil checks in the margins of the police report. After a pause, he put the pencil down, looked up from the papers and abruptly shouted, "You are charged with treason, *SS Obersturmführer Doktor* Johann Brenner. Treason! Scandalous! A creditable witness, a loyal Party member, has sworn that this morning, just blocks away from here, on the public street, you, an SS officer sworn to be loyal to our *Führer*, maligned"—he paused, then repeated the word, louder "maligned, I say,"then paused again, only to say it a third time, drawing it out into all its syllables—"ma...lign...ed our noble *Führer*, and stated that Germany will lose the war! Outrageous! How do you plead?"

"I would like to speak with a lawyer, your Honor."

"A lawyer?"The judge's shrill voice echoed with a ping off the walls of the room. "Every loyal lawyer in the *Reich* now is fighting the enemy. We have no time for lawyers now, you weasel! You defile the uniform you are wearing. Answer my simple question. How do you plead?" Johann opened his mouth, but the judge shouted even louder, "How do you plead, *Dok...tor* Brenner? *Dok...tor!*" His exaggerated pronunciation of each syllable divided the word into two:"*Dok...tor!*"—*Ja!* That's right... '*Tor!*' Fool!"The bailiff snickered.

Beads of perspiration formed on Johann's forehead and ran into his eyes. He began to blink. He felt dizzy and sick to his stomach. He wanted to sit down. The handcuffs cut into his injured wrist, pinching and stinging at the same time. He could feel blood trickling down toward his fingertips. He looked down at his feet to steady himself.

"I was just talking, your Honor. I meant nothing by it. I have served in the *SS* as a physician. I...."

"Look at me when you are speaking!" Johann tried to, but the bright light from the window turned the judge into a fuzzy silhouette.

"You are a physician. An officer. An *SS* officer, no less! All the more reason to be responsible. You have sworn to be loyal to our *Führer*. You have sworn it! He expects much of physicians. We have heard him say that. We read it in *Mein Kampf*. Well, this valuable service from our good doctors remains to be seen, if you ask me. I repeat, do you plead guilty?"

"I have sworn...."

The judge interrupted him. "You have sworn an oath, *Herr Dok...Tor* Brenner."

"*Ja.*"

"Does that "*Ja!*" mean you plead guilty?"

"No, your Honor. I mean, Yes, I have sworn an oath. I am loyal. I am responsible. I am a physician trying to serve my country, my *Volk*. I am not a traitor."

The judge's voice turned into a sweetish whine. "I would like to believe you, Brenner. But you disgust me. Disgust me!" He was shouting again. "Where are you supposed to be now? Why aren't you with your unit?"

Johann stammered that he had been wounded and brought to the hospital in Berlin. He was released that morning. He was on his way to report to the Ministry of Health for reassignment. "That's where I was going when I was arrested. You have my orders there among my papers, your Honor."

"I see. Yes. You're from Nuremberg. I lived there once. Smug little town. Smug little people. You're a sorry story, Brenner. Imprudent! Pathetic! What business do you have, talking with a civilian in the first place? Don't you see how this can demoralize the *Volk*!" Then, in his sweet whine again, he said, "I hope you can keep your thoughts to yourself in the future, *Herr Dok-Tor*! I shall show you some mercy. It is a sunny day. We might still need you. But, I warn you, you must show complete respect for our *Führer*. Our *Führer* expects his physicians, his officers, every member of the *Volk*, to be loyal. To be responsible. Out of respect for our *Führer,* I will suspend these serious charges against you for now. Instead," he paused, glanced at Johann, and let his lips open into a thin smile. "Instead, your sentence, for loitering: one day incarceration, including time served."

The judge smirked and looked at the bailiff for approval. Johann's lower lip began to tremble.

"You should know, *mein lieber Obersturmführer* Johann Brenner," the judge said slowly, emphasizing each word while looking down at the papers on his desk, "that I intend to write to your commanding officer, strongly recommending that you be confined for another week in an SS prison and that your grotesque lapse of judgment be entered into your record." With a tiredness in his voice that he could not disguise and shaking his head, he said, "Maybe this will teach you a lesson. I would demote you if I could. That will be all. *Heil Hitler!*"

Johann instinctively tried to raise his arm to return the salute, but the attempt only tightened the pressure from the handcuffs. Instead of shouting *"Heil Hitler!"* in reply, he gasped. The judge's eyebrows went up and his nostrils flared. For a moment, Johann thought that he would get a harsher sentence. He quickly stammered, *"Heil Hitler!"* and looked at the sunlight on the floor. To his relief, he heard the judge say, "Take him out of my sight. Next!" and felt the guard grab him by the arm and walk him back inside the holding cell. When his handcuffs were unlocked, he headed for the bench. Before he could reach it, however, he fell against the wall and slid down into a heap. The guard gave him a kick and disappeared.

After a while, Johann opened his eyes and managed to get to his feet. The cell was as he had left it—but one prisoner was missing. Almost as soon as he realized this, Johann heard the staccato sound of gunfire coming from somewhere behind the wall of the cell, in what must have been the courtyard. He slumped down the wall again, dazed, staring at the floor between his legs. The handkerchief he had wrapped around his hand showed a slowly spreading stain of blood.

Precisely twenty-four hours after he had been arrested, a guard opened the cell and handed him the envelope with his belongings. Inside, he found his identification papers and his orders, along with a smaller sealed envelope from the judge. He cleaned himself up as best he could in the lavatory. When he left *Gestapo* headquarters, he was eager even for the smoke-filled air of the street. A few minutes later, he was at his destination, the *Reichsgesundheitsamt*, in the former *Hotel Prinz Albrecht*, just next door.

CHAPTER TWENTY-ONE
𝕬 𝕲reen-eyed 𝕭oy

I knew all along, Helga, that you would despise me. "Where is your con-science?" you would have asked. To do the work that I believed that I needed to do, I could not afford to have a conscience.

I know now that I was betraying everything I had hoped to become. I should have seen the harm that I was doing. But I did not. And not just at Auschwitz.

Remember my trip before the war to the Rhineland? *I joined in the effort to sterilize boys and girls who were born to German mothers and Negro fathers, thinking that they were a threat to the purity of our* Volk. *I look back now on how we feared those children and I am ashamed.*

When the war began, I was encouraged and inspired by Hitler's personal phy-sician, Professor of Medicine Karl Brandt. Later he became Generalkommissar für das Sanitäts- und Gesundheitswesen *for the entire* Reich. *Do you remem-ber, I wanted to impress him with a new shirt? I admired his determination, his will, what I thought was his idealism. After meeting him, I went to Berlin to help prepare for a still more shameful act:* Aktion T-4, *the* Sterbehilfe *program, . Yes, we 'helped' people die. We said we were providing a* Gnadentod—*a merciful death. There was nothing "merciful" about it. We murdered innocents. My first victim was a harmless, green-eyed boy. His eyes have haunted me ever since. What more proof do I need of the evil I served?*

ohann put the letter under his mattress. The twentieth day. One more day to finish it. Writing it had changed him. Made him more aware of himself. Would Helga understand? Would she take him back?

He put on his janitor's smock and went upstairs to the courtroom. A weak December sun was just rising, small and silvery through the morning's mist. Everything was in order. The day's proceedings would soon begin. Until now, Johann had dared to look at Brandt only for an instant. He could look longer at the others, but not at the *Generalleutnant*. Until now, Brandt had only to look in his direction and Johann would feel a chill and look away. 'What if he recognizes me? Will I be put on trial, too? And what if he doesn't recognize me? Am I too unimportant, too ordinary, to be remembered?' But it was more than either of these. He feared that Brandt would inspire him again. That his will would weaken. That he would yield to Brandt's logic that valued the *Volk* above an individual's life.

Until today, instead of looking at Brandt, Johann would scan the gallery, hoping to see Helga. Or study the judges at their bench and note with satisfaction that their water pitchers were properly filled and the green baize cloth hung smoothly at the corners. Or admire the determination on the face of the prosecutor and the other American attorneys. Or be absorbed by the journalists scribbling and photographers fumbling for their flash bulbs. But after a few minutes of this, he would sit with his hands folded in his lap, blankly studying the floor in front of his shoes. He had heard and seen enough of the trial. More than enough. Today, instead of looking at the floor, he decided he would fix his eyes on Brandt.

From the moment Brandt appeared between his guards in the doorway, Johann stared at him. Watched him and the others file in and stand stiffly in the defendants' dock while the judges took their seats at the bench. Watched Brandt brush a strand of hair off his forehead and fold it back into its pomaded place on his scalp as he sat down. Watched him put on his earphones with obvious distaste. Watched him set his jaw. Tense the muscles in his cheeks. Cock his head and raise his eyes to look up into the furthest corner of the courtroom's ceiling. Watched how he separated himself from the other defendants by his posture, by the stoic, intense look on his face. Watched as he arched his eyebrow and turned to focus on the proceedings. All the while, Johann did not take his eyes off him.

'He looks ill. Pale. Tired. He's probably being given enough to eat, but is he eating? Is he sleeping? The strain must be enormous. He must know that his chances of acquittal are poor. That the likely sentence is death. How can he sleep, even if he thinks he is innocent of the charges?'

Brandt must have sensed something, because he stared back. For the next several seconds, the two men focused on each other as though they were alone in the courtroom. Finally, Johann saw Brandt's eyes widen in recognition.

Johann nodded toward him. 'He knows it is me. He knows I am here. Is he thinking now of our last conversation? Does he remember what I told him about the green-eyed boy? Did he realize then—does he realize now?—how important that conversation was to me? Most of all, does he realize how I trusted him? How he inspired me? How he encouraged me by his example to do what I have done? How I might not be here if it weren't for him? Yes, he claims he is innocent. He probably still believes that he was doing good. Doing the right thing for the *Vaterland* and the *Volk*. But he's guilty of something else, too. He cannot deny that he inspired me. Inspired many of us. A model who taught us by example that it was good to do harm for the sake of the *Volk*. What he was, or what I thought he was, does not excuse me, but knowing it does help me understand how weak I was. And knowing that helps me be stronger now.'

Johann stared at Brandt through the whole morning. To test himself. To prove to himself that he would not bow his head and look at the floor in front of his shoes.

The judge adjourned the trial for the day at noon. The morning's sun was lost behind dark clouds and a windy, bone-chilling drizzle. Nuremberg's second winter since the end of the war was early and bitter. Johann got his heavy coat and went outside. He had not eaten anything. Perhaps that's why he felt a bit light-headed and noticed the cold. But whatever the reason, he felt less burdened than he had since the trials began. Less burdened than he had for years. He felt as though he could go anywhere.

He was drawn to the ruin of the *Volksbank* and *Herr* Meier, laboring at the rubble pile. As he approached, he heard the old man mumbling, "So tell me, what else should I do with my life?" Over and over Meier chanted, reaching for the bricks with his cane, bending over to pick up two, and carrying them to the roadside. Then back again. And each time the chant, "So tell me, what else should I do with my life?"

'Yes, that's the question. Now, what is the answer?' Johann thought.

But Meier did not give an answer. He just kept pulling bricks off the pile with his cane and talking to himself, caught up in his rhythm. The wet bricks glistened. They looked fresh, new. Small puddles had formed where cobblestones were missing from the sidewalk, reflecting the world in miniature.

Meier turned to Johann without a greeting, as though they had been in a conversation all the while. "I was no Nazi. But yes, I don't mind saying, even though no one now is supposed to, I did see good in some of the things they did—the work, the spirit, the enthusiasm. The *Volk* believed in itself again. People were happy enough to have a leader who promised what they wanted to hear. Hitler gave them what they wanted most. Purpose. Hope. That was all they wanted. Hope and purpose. That was before the war, of course. Some saw where it might lead. I think I did. Saw that our belief in ourselves was at the expense of others. Voted socialist. And soon after Hitler came to power, I was too scared to do anything else. Just looked at my feet, did my work, lived my life. We all did. The Nazis passed over us like this morning's wind. I knew it would have to stop sometime. I just waited it out."

"Yes," said Johann. "We lived our lives."

"But I never voted for Hitler," Meier continued. "I voted socialist. The real Socialists, not the National Socialists. And I voted for Hindenburg against Hitler for President. But politics after the first war were too loud. Too crazy. I wanted quiet. We all wanted quiet. I kept my head down. Thought little about the Jews. About anything or anyone, really.

Just baked my bread and kept my head down. It's hard to admit that. But it's true."

Johann was surprised to hear him talk so much. He had been wrong about Meier. At Philipp's wedding, he had thought that he was an outrageous, drunken oaf. Now he saw that the old man was deeper. With a forthrightness, like Philipp's.

"Used to drink," Meier said, speaking softly. "The second war cured me of that. And now, here I am, an old man. Everyone from my time has died or soon will. So, what else should I do with my life?." He took a deep breath. "…with my life?" Another deep breath. A long pause. Each of his labored breaths became misty puffs through the drizzle. Johann thought the old man looked pale. Was he going to have a seizure?

"Are you all right? Stop for a while. You must be cold. Don't you have an overcoat?"

"Don't need an overcoat. Warm enough without it." Then, in a sharp-edged whisper, he said, "Anyway, I think I know who you are."

Johann was shaken. "I told you. Westermann, from Saxony." He tried in vain to laugh.

"So you say. But let me tell you who I am first," Meier said slowly, his voice raspy and wheezing. "I live with my daughter-in-law. My son fell in France, last September. I say, 'fell.' I should say, 'was killed.' My only son." He paused so long that Johann thought he had finished talking.

After a long breath, Meier began again, "Partisans, maybe. Or just bad luck. A truck accident, the letter said. He was only forty-four. As old as the century. Now I live with my daughter-in-law. My wife died before the war, a mercy. A bomb got our only grandchild. Nine years old. Nannerl." Meier bent over and picked up a brick, then threw it back onto the rubble pile and watched roll back toward his feet. "My wife would have been heart-broken. Nannerl. Just nine. We still have her favorite doll."

Johann wanted to say something but could not find the words.

"My brother and sister-in-law died before the war too," Meier continued. "Their daughter, Christine, was killed in a bombing raid on Berlin. Her husband, a Jew, a doctor, disappeared. We can guess what happened to him. And I live on, for some stupid reason. To do what?"

"I am sorry."

"Yes. Sorry. We are all sorry now. But being sorry will not clear away this rubble."

Johann wanted to leave but could not. He bent over and picked up one of the bricks. He and Meier were a reflection of each other as they turned toward the stack behind them. Johann's leg ached. His right hand was stiff and throbbed. 'Must be the damp,' he thought. He looked up at the remaining heap of rubble. His estimate that Meier could clear it away in twenty-one days seemed ludicrous now. The pile was smaller, but by not much more than half.

"They tell me I am lucky to be alive," Meier said. "What good does that do, if I have no future?" Meier said nothing more about himself, or who he thought Johann was. He just resumed his chant. "What else should I do with my life?" Eight words. A step for each word. Thirty-two steps to the stack. Four repetitions of his question. Thirty-two steps back. Four more repetitions. A machine making the noises it must make while it does what it does.

Johann stayed with him. Carrying the bricks alongside him, he thought about what he written Helga earlier that morning. About overcoming his fear of looking directly at Brandt. About the green-eyed boy. About Philipp. About Greta and Paul-Adolf. About Helga. Meier's chant went round his head until they parted at nightfall, 'What else should I do with the rest of my life?'

The war's end had accelerated and slowed everything at the same time, like a phonograph that spun out of tempo, too quickly or too slowly. Johann could not sort out what was normal anymore. Each day at the trial, he had heard anew what he wanted to forget. A web of memories—of Koblenz, of Grafeneck, of Auschwitz—was strangling him. Until today.

Walking back to the courthouse at dusk, he thought about Meier's question. He had first faced it in Berlin, shortly after he had been released from the *Charité* in his last conversation with Brandt. It was only two years ago, when the unimaginable was happening. The war was ending with Germany's defeat.

*****

Johann was in the hallway of the Ministry of Health, looking for the room where he had to report for his next assignment. A tall officer abruptly came out of a doorway just in front of him and nearly collided with him. Johann recognized Brandt immediately. Instead of raising his arm in the Hitler salute, he blurted out, *"Herr Doktor!"*

"I beg your pardon! Do I know you?"

"Brenner, Johann. *Arzt. SS Obersturmführer.* From Nuremberg. We met. Just after the war began."

Brandt thought for only a moment. "Why yes. I do recall you. *Herr Doktor* Brenner. We discussed your participation in *Aktion T-4*. Just after the war began, I think. I suggested you work with *Herr Doktor* Schumann, if I remember correctly. You had a leg wound from the first war. And now you are an *SS* First Lieutenant. Congratulations. What brings you here?"

Johann was amazed and began to stammer out an answer. Brandt interrupted him. "Excuse me, *Herr Doktor*. I'm in a hurry at the moment. I want to personally deliver these papers. But please join me in ten minutes for coffee in the canteen."

Johann eagerly agreed.

"And relax, please," Brandt said. "Your appointment can wait a bit longer, no doubt. And there's no need to click your heels." He smiled. "I will see you again shortly," he said and gestured in the direction of the canteen as he strode away.

Johann arrived at the canteen just a minute or two before Brandt did. No one else was there. A young, crisply uniformed *SS* private showed them to a seat at a table near the window and took their order.

"You look tired, *Herr Doktor* Brenner. Are you well?" Brandt asked.

"I must apologize for my appearance, sir. I was discharged from the *Charité* yesterday morning. A bomb exploded at the *SS* barracks at

Auschwitz in September. You may have heard of the incident. I was lucky to survive." He raised his bandaged hand. "And an infected leg wound. As I say, I was lucky."

Brandt shook his head in sympathy. "Another leg wound?"

Johann continued, "Yes. I was hospitalized six weeks. Discharged yesterday. My hand is still not quite healed. There's some musculature problem. But I will get used to it, I suppose. Anyway, coming here to report for further orders, I was detained overnight in *Gestapo* headquarters. I have not had an opportunity to shave or get a clean uniform shirt. I apologize, *Herr Generalleutnant.*"

"I knew that some men who were wounded in the attack were evacuated to the *Charité.* I am glad to see you have recovered. Others were not so fortunate. Why were you detained by the *Gestapo?* And please, you may call me *Herr Doktor.* All my other titles flow from that."

"Thank you, sir. Yes, I was quite foolish yesterday. I spoke with a civilian on the street. I carelessly said I would prefer that my wife—she's in Karlsruhe—be captured by the Americans rather than by the Russians."

Brandt's eyebrows rose. "Is that so? Well, that's hardly a crime. I suppose I can understand that. I have a wife and son. If the war comes to that," he said quietly, "I would want them to go west, too."

"I must admit," Johann said, "I did imply that we would lose the war. The civilian, a good Party member, reported me. I was promptly arrested. I had a hearing before a *Gestapo* judge. He sentenced me to the night in jail."

"I see. Yes, that was quite careless of you. But we won't lose the war." Brandt stirred his coffee.

"No, sir. I regret my actions, sir. It will not happen again."

"Of course. Careless, but also quite understandable. Don't worry. No matter how disturbing things may look here in Berlin, our *Führer* is a strong-willed man. A genius. And despite what rumors you might have heard about his health, he is well. He's lucky. Like you. The injuries he suffered in July fortunately were minimal. He has recovered. There are some after-effects, of course, but nothing that impairs his judgment. Still, I do have some concerns, between us, as physicians.

There is some pronounced *paralysis agitans* of the *Führer's* right arm due to the bomb blast. Some slowness of speech, too. I have spoken with him about appropriate treatment. He is under great strain, of course. And he takes little time for himself. I regret that I cannot always be near him, given my other responsibilities. He has good advisors, especially *Reichsminister* Speer. An admirable man. Still, another doctor—or better said, a *Pfutscher*, a quack who calls himself a doctor—seems to be taking our *Führer* in a dangerous direction. I wish I were able to dissuade him from…," Brandt paused to find a word, then continued, "shall we just say, following bad advice. All this between us, of course." Brandt stirred his coffee again.

Johann marveled at the ease of their conversation. Brandt had access to the most powerful men in the land. He was one of them. And here he sat with him, having coffee and discussing the *Führer's* health. Someone watching the two from across the room would have thought they were old friends.

"And your work, *Herr Doktor* Brenner? When we first met, you were so eager to serve our *Vaterland*. With Schumann? Right? We appreciate your effort. Your sacrifices for our *Vaterland*. Your little encounter with a *Gestapo* judge is quite understandable. Of no importance. You have seen difficult duty and then suffered a life-threatening injury." He took a sip of his coffee. "So, now tell me, are there any problems that I should know about? I don't get into the field often. Even less do I have an opportunity to talk with one of our devoted physicians." It was as though a kindly boss was chatting with his trusted employee.

Johann was both awed and disarmed by Brandt's obvious sincerity and good will. "Well," he said, thinking back to the first time he came to Berlin, "I've seen a lot. In 1935, after I joined the Party, I served in the *Rhineland*, thanks to *Herr Professor* Abel. Then, just after the invasion of the *Ostmark*, you suggested I come to Berlin for a meeting at *Tiergartenstraße-4*. As you suggested, I wrote to *Herr Doktor* Schumann. That led to working with him at Grafeneck. I was eager, honored to have those opportunities. Proud that we physicians were doing something so courageous, so vital for our *Volk*. I believed in what we, what I was doing,

Herr Doktor." Johann picked up his coffee cup but put it down when he noticed his hand was trembling.

"Believed?"

"Well, much has happened since then—I am not really sure of anything anymore, sir." Johann was surprised at himself. "Please understand, *Herr Doktor*, I have seen terrible things." He looked down at the table and began to fidget with the napkin in his lap.

"War is terrible. You know that, *Herr Doktor* Brenner. You fought in the first war."

"Yes. But I don't mean the first war. Or this one. They are both terrible. I mean at Grafeneck. I arrived just after it began. *Aktion T-4*. January 1940. Six years ago next month. The grounds, the lovely trees, the beautiful old castle—you may know Grafeneck—everything was like a painting. A beautiful winter's day. Snow clinging to the branches. A park in winter. Idyllic. Calm. Beautiful. Orderly. Pure. I went inside and met *Herr Doktor* Schumann. He welcomed me warmly. We had a short conversation. He said I could be useful. For the Volk. The *Reich*. The Party. These were all things I wanted to hear. I found him inspiring. As I had you."

"*Danke.*" Brandt sat tall in his chair, which he had turned slightly toward Johann.

"*Herr Doktor* Schumann began describing the procedure to me in general terms. Told me I would be confirming and authorizing eligible cases. Paperwork." Johann thought of the black bus, windows and all, he saw coming up the drive. How out of place it looked. How Schumann turned to look at it, too. "I asked him about the bus. I was, I must say, stunned. The gas, carbon monoxide—it sounded, well, crude. 'Wouldn't a lethal injection be more humane?' I asked. He said it might be, but injections were too time-consuming, too inefficient, too dependent on the resolve of the physician. Too subject, as he put it, 'to lapses in judgment.' I did not argue with him. It was not my place to argue with the director, especially since he had invited me there. Instead, I asked how I could help."

"We knew you were the kind of man, the kind of doctor, we needed," Brandt said, looking directly into his eyes.

"*Herr Doktor* Schumann then asked if I would go up to the main barrack and help the nurses there prepare the patients who had been selected. That this group of patients already had been authorized. I agreed. I found a nurse in a nearly empty ward, standing by the bed of the only patient there. I introduced myself, told her that *Herr Doktor* Schumann had sent me, and asked if I could be of help." Without thinking, Johann had loosened the bandage on his hand under the table. He looked down into his lap. The scar was vivid red, with a slightly purple outline along its edge. He tried to pick up his coffee cup in his left hand but could not control its trembling.

When he set the cup down in the saucer, he misjudged the distance. Coffee spilled over its lip into the saucer, and then dripped onto the linen tablecloth. He didn't notice. The image of his scarred hand swam before his eyes.

Brandt, seeing that he was agitated, said softly, "Go on, please."

"The nurse said that this boy had been selected to go. I saw tears in her eyes. 'He's a harmless boy,' she said. 'The mind of a child. He does nothing but sing. Or mumble word games to himself. He sings so sweetly. Such a harmless, innocent boy.' I asked what was wrong with him. 'Nothing,' she said. 'He is small. Much smaller than he should be. Underdeveloped. Seventeen years old. Soon eighteen. Looks like he is not even twelve. Cannot read or write. No trade. Been here for the last thirteen years. Sent here from Emmendingen, in Baden, I believe. As you see, a *Mischling*. They say his mother killed herself. And he just sings. Beautiful songs he makes up himself.'"

"You remember this one boy?" Brandt asked.

"Oh yes, *Herr Doktor*. I can see the boy as though he were here now. Chocolate skin. A mixed-race boy. Broad lips. Kinky, light brown hair. Green eyes. A '*Rhineland* bastard.' But this boy already was at Grafeneck. He must have had his vasectomy right there. And now he was authorized for *Aktion T-4*. The official questionnaire was complete. He had green eyes. Clear, bright, green eyes. Startling, really. He had not eaten for several days, the nurse said. His skin was waxy, almost shiny, smooth milky brown. Most memorable were his eyes—deep-set, hauntingly green. I remember him very well." Johann was beginning to perspire. He spoke rapidly, with heavy breaths.

"Go on." Brandt put his elbows on the table and tented his hands, his fingers straightened by the pressure, his thumbs pointing at his chin. He raised an eyebrow.

"The nurse had her orders. The boy was supposed to be on the bus, with the others, she said. She gestured toward the driveway. Then she looked at me a long time." Johann heard his voice begin to quiver. After a moment, he continued. "She said that she had been giving him a sedative for several days. Demerol. Then she said, 'It would be better if he had an injection now. The last one. Better than the bus.' She looked at me. I knew what she meant. During all this time, the boy paid no attention to us. I could hear him singing softly under his breath. I told the nurse that I agreed, that an injection was better. She prepared one. I took the syringe. Then the boy noticed what we were doing. He was frightened of the syringe. The nurse began to sing a children's song. He joined in. I can see it all now. Hear them singing together. Hear his sweet, soft voice."

Johann raised his right hand now as though he was holding the syringe. Brandt saw the scar and raised an eyebrow. Silence engulfed them. Johann felt himself reach for the boy's arm. Remembered how slim it was. How his hand encircled it. How smoothly the needle slipped under the boy's skin. How, within seconds of the injection, he felt the young body tense. How saliva formed a bead of froth at the corner of the boy's mouth. How the boy's lips pulled back over his small, white teeth into a snarl. How the boy's small hand jerked from the nurse's hand, then slackened into limpness. How the boy's green eyes widened. How he died in the space of time it would take to shut a window. He remembered how he put down the syringe on the bedside table, reached over, and brushed the boy's eyelids closed. How the nurse said, "Thank you." How he saw a tear rolling down her cheek.

After a few moments, Johann told all this to Brandt as if he were in a trance. His voice was like the echo between the walls of a deep chasm, reverberating back and forth until it was lost in the roar of the rushing river below. It was as though he was the only person in the room. The only person in Berlin. In all of Germany. Europe. Earth. He had just dared to speak the deepest, most shameful secret of his soul.

"You did the right thing, *Herr Doktor,*" Brandt said loudly. "I have always held that responsible euthanasia required an injection, no matter how much time or personnel it cost. We owed at least that to those unfortunates. *SS Obergruppenführer* Bouhler, the director of the *Führer's* Chancellery and co-director of *Aktion T-4*, and I were in complete agreement on that. And Bouhler's deputy in charge of *T-4, SS-Standartenführer* Viktor Brack put it perfectly: 'The syringe belongs in the hands of a physician.' It was important to show that we ourselves were willing to do it. *Reichsgesundheitsführer Doktor* Conti and I personally injected several children in Brandenburg. I'll admit, it was difficult. Yes, quite difficult. But necessary. Unfortunately, in some cases, death was not immediate. We also tried carbon monoxide. In a sealed chamber. We could see what was happening. Difficult."

Brandt paused to take a sip of his coffee. Johann looked at his hand in his lap. "Later," Brandt continued, "when I discussed this with the *Führer,* he asked me what method would provide the quickest and least painful death. Based on some personal experience during my medical studies, I suggested carbon monoxide gas. But always administered by physicians, of course. This was a medical breakthrough of the greatest importance. Now we have refined the procedure, as you know. Much more efficient. A great service to the *Volk.* To humanity."

Brandt noticed that Johann was not listening. "I can see that you are distressed, *Herr Doktor.* So tell me, please, this boy, this undersized, *Mischling* boy....tell me, please, what benefit would his life have had for our *Volk?*"

Johann did not hesitate. "I have thought about this a long time, sir. His life, that poor boy's life, would have allowed us to show compassion. Even if there were no other reason, that alone would have been justification for his life. And beyond that, how can we know what he could have...what he might have been able to..."

Brandt interrupted him. "You are being sentimental, *Herr Doktor* Brenner. The *Volk* cannot afford sentimentality. Especially now. Our survival is at stake. Better that this boy, that dozens of thousands of such boys, if necessary, cease living, than that the *Volk* dies. That is nature's law. You must know that. He was a "useless eater." You did the right thing when you gave him the injection."

"But I know now, in my heart, that I did not."

"Nonsense. You are tired. You have been wounded. I even grant that you have seen and had to do terrible things. But none of that excuses your sentimentality." He called the waiter over. "*Bitte*, bring the *Herr Doktor* a clean saucer. He has spilled his coffee." Brandt brushed a strand of hair back from his forehead. He wiped his hands on his napkin and folded it neatly on the table.

Johann tried to compose himself. "May I ask, do you have a son?"

"Yes. Twelve years old. And you?"

"I had a son. Healthy. Strong. And strong-willed. Killed in the east. Last winter. He was nineteen."

"I am sorry."

"Forgive me, please, but I must ask you, how has my son's death, how has the death of 'dozens of thousands,' as you say, helped our *Volk*? Our healthiest youth, our precious future, has been sacrificed. We have spent our blood in a ferocious war. Meanwhile, we expend enormous resources to exterminate millions of human beings. Jews, Gypsies, Slavs, men and women whose lives may be offensive to what we think to be normal, but who are entitled to their own happiness. And who are we to say who is a "useless eater"? And for all this, is our *Volk* heathier? Is our *Vaterland*...."

Brandt stiffened. "Be careful!" he hissed.

Johann saw the fierceness in his eyes. Heard the echo of his own words mixing with Brandt's warning. Still he could not stop himself. "Must our *Vaterland*..."

"*Herr Doktor* Brenner! I advise you to stop now. I know you are under great strain. From what you have seen. And what you have done. Your son's loss. Your wounds. But what you have just said, what you are now thinking is, to put it mildly, unworthy of a German physician. I will ignore these treasonous thoughts. What we are doing is no different than what our enemies are doing. You don't suppose the Americans are not taking advantage of..."

Johann's lips trembled. Green eyes seemed to be staring at him wherever he looked in the room. "Does that make it right? When my son told me he wanted to do something just because others were doing it, I told him that was not a good enough reason. You probably told your son the same. The Americans will have to answer for what they do, just as we will. I am sorry, *Herr Generalleutnant* Brandt, *Herr Professor Doktor*, sir, but I don't want to go back to Auschwitz. I can't go back."

"I see. I see." Brandt sighed. He sat back in his chair and looked up at the ceiling. Johann thought he would be arrested on the spot. After what seemed centuries, Brandt spoke so softly that Johann could barely hear him, "Well, *Herr Doktor*, I can reassign you here in Berlin. Yes. You have the right to make this request, to be sure. Always have. Always have, you must know. Others have refused. From the very start of *T-4*."

Johann sat, drained and speechless.

"Our work at Auschwitz will be done soon in any event," Brandt continued. "It has been quite useful. Imperative and useful. But it will soon be finished." He assumed a professorial tone, sitting as tall as he could in his chair and looking up again toward the ceiling, as he began what might have been the introduction to a formal lecture, "It is in the national interest to determine optimal conditions for survival for our troops in extreme combat conditions—pilots downed at sea, sailors overboard, severe nutritional deficiencies, and the like. The Americans and the British have no doubt been doing the same kind of medical research. They may even be ahead of us. It is urgent for the war effort, for the *Volk*'s very survival. We have had an exceptional opportunity, with so many specimens from the east available for study. We can vary temperature, altitude exposure, diet—medical science will be dramatically enhanced by our efforts. I am encouraged by it all. It represents the best that our medicine can do. I have told the *Führer* this."

Johann stared blankly at him. Just as Brandt was about to go on at greater length, he stood up at attention and quickly said, "I don't want to go back to Auschwitz, *Herr Generalleutnant.* I ask respectfully that I be reassigned."

"Yes, as you said. Sit down, please. I see that you are tired, *Herr Doktor* Brenner. To be sure, I can well imagine that some of the work is distressing. The camps are cesspools of disease. There are bound to be unfortunate occurrences. Prisoners by definition don't always cooperate. We...."

"Please!" Johann said, before he realized he was interrupting.

"Fine. I will arrange it. You have done what we have asked of you, *Herr Doktor* Brenner. You have served our *Vaterland,* served our *Führer.* Your son has fallen for our cause. I understand. In some ways, I must say, I envy you. You have done your duty. I still must do mine. Whatever the cost. And now you must excuse me." With that, he stood up abruptly and extended his arm—"*Heil Hitler!*" He did not wait for Johann to return the salute as he strode away.

An hour later, while he was waiting in an anteroom of the Ministry for his appointment, a messenger handed him an envelope. Inside was a typed statement reassigning him to the medical staff at the *Charité* in Berlin. He looked at Brandt's signature. It was nothing more than a dash of a pen, a slash of ink. He felt as though he had been rescued from a deep pit.

*****

Johann's next few months in Berlin were blurred by smoke and chaos. His duties at the *Charité* kept him in a state of near-exhaustion. At first, he had twelve-hour night shifts. These expanded to fourteen, then sixteen hours, seven days a week. The injured arrived constantly, from the front and from the city streets: gunshot wounds, burns, limbs blown off, infected field amputations, chests or skulls crushed by falling debris. All this, besides the routine admissions—appendectomies, bleeding ulcers, gallstones, pneumonia, births, heart attacks, strokes.

At first, Johann did post-surgical care. Stomach wounds were the worst. There was little he could do except order morphine and recommend additional surgery. Many died of trauma and sepsis. His gratitude at not having to go back to Auschwitz and his enthusiasm for his new assignment kept his spirits up. He spent all his time in the wards, by the bedside of any patient who needed him. Essential supplies—gauze, needles, morphine—were running out. Berlin, indeed Germany, was the patient now—and the prognosis was poor.

When he had learned how to control his injured hand more predictably he accepted a surgical assignment from *Doktor* Ferdinand Sauerbruch, chief of the division. Johann knew that Sauerbruch was among Germany's most distinquished surgeons. He would have liked to assist him with some of his legendary operations, but he knew he should be grateful that he was assigned relatively uncomplicated procedures. When they first met, Sauerbruch noticed the scar on Johann's hand and said nothing about it. Johann had heard he was a supporter of the regime. Later, he learned that Sauerbruch had sharply chastised the surgeon who did it. Johann found a tight-fitting leather glove in the hospital's collection of cast-off items. He took the glove off only when he was sleeping.

He tried to work unassisted on amputations. During the first dozen or so, he was too tentative and hesitant. His hand trembled. A nurse even dared to ask him if she should call another surgeon. Worst was a double amputation he performed a week before Christmas on a young soldier who had already lost both feet and ankles. Johann severed both of the man's legs above the knees, taking another ten inches off each of the gangrenous stumps. When the soldier regained consciousness, he begged Johann to kill him with an overdose of morphine.

"No," he said, trying to make his voice its most reassuring. "You can still lead a meaningful life, even if that seems impossible now. Give yourself time, man. Wait a week, at least. We can talk again after a week."

"Please, *Herr Doktor*," the soldier begged, "I don't want to live like this."

"Wait a week, I tell you," Johann said, looking him in the eye. "Things might look different then." Later that afternoon, he sent a letter by special courier to the man's parents, who lived not far away, urging them to visit their son. He was relieved when the soldier seemed to change his mind.

Once he assisted the old surgeon who had worked on his hand. During their scrub, the surgeon expressed an interest in Johann's progress with hand and muscle control. "Yours is an interesting case. I can operate again and see what might be done to re-arrange the tendons. Might work, might not. Would make a good topic for a journal article."

"No, thank you. I am learning how to adjust, *Herr Doktor,*" Johann said.

"As you wish," was the curt reply.

Johann assisted him in an operation on a soldier with an infected, ulcerated bowel. Johann admired the old man's methodical approach—no wasted movements, no hesitancies, no doubts. "You may close now, *Herr Doktor,*" he said to Johann. "I have saved this man's life. See that you don't spoil my work." He clicked his heels as he walked away. Was there a smirk behind that surgical mask? Although he watched to see if other surgical patients had swastikas similar to his carved upon their wounds, he never saw one. The old nurse who was so rough in unwrapping Johann's bandaged hand was absurdly deferent and willing to do whatever he asked of her. He avoided working with both of them as much as he could.

Some younger nurses tried to celebrate Christmas. One brought the patients little squares of chocolate that must have come from the black market. Another brought a bottle of red current juice, poured tiny portions in small paper cups meant for pills, and handed them around. A third placed a tiny sprig of evergreen on each patient's pillow. A small choir of nurses and doctors sang "Silent Night," going from ward to ward with the noise of the war outside. Johann just listened.

No one talked about how the war was going. There was no need. The quickening pace of arriving wounded and of the round-the-clock bombings were clear enough signs. Bombs fell all around the hospital. One started a fire on the roof that miraculously went out. But shortly afterwards sections of the building's walls collapsed, leaving gaping holes into a ward. The electricity repeatedly failed. A burst water main below the street threatened to flood the ground floor. Drinking water had to be drawn from the Spree, carted to the hospital, and boiled. Food was in short supply for patients and staff alike. Anyone who could be was sent to facilities in Berlin's western districts. Or simply turned away.

January was colder than usual. The hospital's dwindling supply of coal was supplemented through the black market. Windows were boarded up. People, usually with family members in the wards, brought in blankets and food. Air raids constantly interrupted every routine. Severely wounded patients were left in the cellar shelter, rather than be taken back and forth to their beds. One by one, the hospital staff began to disappear, hoping to escape the growing chaos.

When mail deliveries throughout the *Reich* were suspended, Johann knew that any effort to contact Helga would be in vain. At the same time, all long-distance passenger trains leaving Berlin were cancelled. 'We're being choked to death. But at least I'm here, and not at Auschwitz,' he kept reminding himself. He looked often at Helga's letters and the postcard from Philipp. He vowed to stay in the capital as long as he could. In February, the heaviest attack by British and American bombers to date announced the death throes of the Third Reich to all but the most fanatical Nazis. A bomb hit another wing of the hospital. Among the dead was the surgeon who had operated on Johann's hand.

He helped move the injured into the remaining, already overcrowded wards. From the growing numbers of people needing treatment for burns, he knew that fires were raging throughout the city, especially in the working-class districts of Nollendorf, Kreuzberg, Wedding, and Prenzlauer Berg. He knew why. The bombers were aiming for the factories and their workers' huge apartment complexes. Why bomb the outlying wealthier neighborhoods, with their villas surrounded by spacious gardens and parks?

The front was growing nearer. 'The Russians will throw thousands of men into the assault. Maybe millions,' he thought. 'And what will Hitler do? What can he do? He'll grasp at every straw. Goebbels will urge him on. Or Himmler. Or Goering. It doesn't matter who is our *Führer* now. We have been lied to. Led and lied into an abyss.'

He stood by the cot of a boy, no more than thirteen, his voice just beginning to break, his arm shot up so badly that it had to be amputated below the shoulder. The boy told him that he had joined the *Volkssturm*.

"What's that?" Johann asked.

"A *Volkssturm!* Our *Volk* will storm over our enemies, just as we did over Napoleon. Don't you know that? Our *Führer* calls for us. All of us. All boys between twelve and sixteen, and all old men, over sixty-five. All of us! A true *Volkssturm!* We will save our *Vaterland*. We will fight to the death to defend our 'Fortress Berlin'! Defend us from the stinking Bolsheviks! From the stinking Jews! Girls and old women will help, too."

"Calm down now, lad. I want to change your dressing," Johann said, as he peeled off the bloody bandage. He could not stop himself from thinking out loud, "So, you boys will do what the army cannot do?"

"Yes! Of course! We are heroes. We're the *Volk*'s true heroes. We will triumph. We have to! For our *Führer!*"

Johann could only shake his head and say, "No. We don't."

More wounded children staggered in. He examined a blinded sixteen-year-old. He stroked the boy's hair and held his hand until the nurse called him. She pointed to a twelve or thirteen year old girl whose face had been lacerated by flying glass. Together they removed several shards from her forehead and cheeks. A boy no more than twelve and an old woman carried in another youth on an improvised stretcher made from a broken ladder. He had bled to death before they arrived. When the nurse and the old woman began to weep, Johann put his arm around them and helped them find a quiet place to sit down. Then he went back to the receiving room. The blinded boy was whimpering. The girl, her face bandaged so completely she could barely see, made her way over to him and tried to console him. More wounded were arriving as the nurse returned to help.

Johann had heard the promises on the radio. "Secret weapons!" "Imminent reversals!" And he had heard the warnings. "The end of civilization!" "Russian brutality!" "Merciless fiends!" All the while, the wounded flooded in. Most died. Each day gave more proof of his powerlessness, but he soldiered on, not thinking of the past or the future.

CHAPTER TWENTY-TWO
𝕴 𝔐𝔞𝔡𝔢 𝔪𝔶 𝔠𝔥𝔬𝔦𝔠𝔢𝔰

Oh, Helga! I now see that I was caught up in the unbridled patriotism that drove us into the wars. When the first one ended, I was angry and anguished over Germany's loss and the unjust peace. Frustration and disappointment festered in me and propelled me toward the Nazis. We sought revenge. A New Order. A Thousand Year Reich. How absurd it all seems now. Some handled those terrible times better than I did. It gives me some comfort to know that there were heroes amongst us. Against Hitler and for Germany. Some even for the Jews. For all those we thought did not deserve to live. For the causes that I should have championed.

Other demons were at work in me, too, hatched out of the arrogance that I learned during medical training. I was so certain that doctors were superior beings. And that patients were but a collection of symptoms. Of body parts to be dissected and manipulated in our hospitals and on our laboratory tables. We worshipped German science. We were so convinced that our profession would improve our race and the world.

I had choices, but they were limited by my narrow understanding, by my unwillingness to explore any other way of thinking. So, I chose to join the Party. I chose to go to Koblenz, where I sterilized helpless children. I chose to go to Grafeneck, where we killed those we thought were "living lives not worth living." Then I went to Auschwitz. I took part in its abominations. Selections. Castrations.

I closed my eyes to what was happening all around me. I had been warned. By my mother. By Philipp. And especially by you, Helga. I did not listen. Instead, I betrayed you all.

The prosecution finished building its case. They had introduced thousands of pages of evidence, notwithstanding the challenges of the defense attorneys. The judges had passed the documents back and forth. Had consulted with each other and decreed what was valid and what was not. Witnesses had displayed their wounds and told their stories. Experts had testified about medical conditions. About medical ethics and practices in Germany and elsewhere, especially America. Through it all, Johann had sat in his chair as the trial carried him along in its roaring, painful current.

Brandt was of no importance to him now. He knew that there had been 'crimes against humanity.' That the defendants, especially Brandt, were guilty. That he himself was guilty, too. Once he realized that, only Meier's insistent question dominated his thoughts: "What should I do with the rest of my life?"

What he hoped for most of all was to be with Helga. To live with her in whatever happiness they could find. To rebuild their lives together. If he could, he wanted to resume his practice. He knew he could not do this as Johann Brenner. Perhaps as Heinrich Westermann? Perhaps, if he left Germany. If he stayed, he might be recognized. Brandt would not accuse him, he now realized, because any testimony he could give would support the case against him. But someone else, a victim, might see him and turn him in. No, if he wanted to practice again, Helga and he would have to leave. They could go to Spain or South America. If she was willing, they could even go to Africa and set up a clinic in the jungle for the natives there. He thought about the need for good medicine, the warm sun and exotic landscape, the bright colors, the huge butterflies and tropical birds. That would be a good and satisfying life. A chance to make amends. And if Helga rejected him? Unbearable as that might be, he could still leave Germany by himself and practice medicine abroad. Or take up another occupation—be a baker, or a janitor.

Most of all, he wanted to live. At only one point, when the prosecution described the dimensions of *Aktion T-4*, had he thought of killing himself. Several times after that, he contemplated confessing to the authorities and hoping for mercy. 'But what good could I do in prison? And when I was released, I probably wouldn't be able to practice again. Maybe I would not be released. Maybe I would be sentenced 'to life,' or executed.' Round and round his mind went. 'It all depends on how Helga reacts to my letter,' he told himself. 'She has to see that I need her and love her. That I am sorry for what I have done. When she sees that the old Johann Brenner did in fact die, that I am a different man now, that I tried to help Philipp, that I did good work in Berlin…when she learns that I stayed there as long as I could, helping others…maybe she will believe in me again.'

Near noon, the chief judge announced that the trial would adjourn until January. All rose as the judges left their bench. Johann watched the defendants file out. Watched Brandt as the guards escorted him through the doorway. Watched the lawyers and their assistants put their papers in their briefcases and leave, talking to each other in low tones. Watched the translators put down their earphones and move toward the exit, behind the journalists and photographers hurrying to file their stories. Watched as the gallery emptied with murmurs and footsteps. After a few minutes, the courtroom was silent. The only sound came from gusts of wind, rattling the windows and pelting them with large drops of rain.

Johann stood up slowly, exhausted and relieved at the same time. He went to the judges' bench and gathered their water pitchers and glasses. He folded the green baize tablecloth. He put the chairs out of the way and slowly swept the polished wooden floor. When there was nothing more for him to do, he closed the courtroom door, went down to the basement, sat on his cot, and, to his great surprise, began to weep. His thoughts wandered back to Berlin in the last days of the war. It was still fresh in his memory.

*****

April 21, 1945. The day after Hitler's birthday. There was no miracle. Soviet mortars smashed louder and closer than ever. For over a week Johann had been able to do no more than watch people die. There was no food, no water, no medicine. Still, he thought, it was safer inside the hospital than outside. He had learned his way around the old complex of buildings: where he could catch a quick nap in the basement; where a draft of fresh air rose in a stairwell; where, from an upper-story window, he could glimpse the sunset. But if he was going to see Helga again, he knew he had to leave the *Charité* and Berlin. He planned to go to the railway yards outside the city, hoping to find a train that would take him west.

After seeing his patients one last time, he put on his uniform, packed a small bag and walked out a back door—or what had been a door, until a bomb blast had made it three times wider. Partially covered bodies lay under debris on either side of the alley. When he heard gunshots ahead, he crawled inside an overturned, burned out streetcar. He wondered if he should go back to the hospital. After a few minutes, he decided he had to take his chances while he still could. Stumbling through the mortally wounded city, he thought the world was ending. He smelled bloated bodies floating in the canal. He saw rats feasting on the carcasses of horses and their riders. He tripped over the headless body of a child, its head being pawed and rolled down the street by a dog.

Gangs roamed the streets, or what was left of them. Looters picked through the remains of bombed out stores. Gunfire snapped like whips and echoed off still standing walls. Every now and then, he saw dazed and wounded soldiers in groups of twos and threes, helping each other toward some non-existant haven. He knew that they were being driven back into the city from the east by the Russian advance. He ducked into doorways, hid under bridges and in bombed-out ruins, trying to avoid contact with anyone. Roving bands of Nazi diehards, "Werewolves," were accosting anyone they suspected of disloyalty to the *Führer* and hanging from lampposts those they deemed traitors. He walked by some of their victims. When he saw five or six boys a few hundred feet ahead of him line up two unarmed soldiers at gunpoint against a bullet-pocked brick wall, he lay down in the gutter and pretended to be dead, hoping they would not come his way. After the pistol fire, he looked up to see the boys chalk something on the wall over the soldiers' slumped bodies and then run away shouting. After several minutes, when he dared go past the bodies, he read the word "*Verräter!*" "Deserters!"

He turned down an alley and nearly bumped into a drunken woman. He tried to turn away but she staggered toward him, fell to her knees at his feet and began to retch. He knelt beside her to help her up, but she rolled over on to her back, put her arms around his neck and tried to pull him on top of her. When he freed himself and stepped back, she pulled her skirt up over her hips and beckoned him, "Come to me! Why not? Are you afraid? Why not? For two cigarettes, *Mein Herr Offizier!* Just two cigarettes. Or maybe some *schnapps*. Right here! Come to me." She began to vomit. He thought back to Schumann's comment at Auschwitz about naked women at the selections. To Clauberg's maliciousness. To Schetzeler's remarks about the orgies. He felt like vomiting, too. Walking down the alley as fast he could, he could still hear her calling to him, "Come to me! Come back to me! *Liebchen!* Don't leave me to the Russians!"

For weeks, he had heard that Berliners, with or without alcohol and drugs, had sought each other out in bomb shelters, in basements, under bridges, and in ruins to escape their fears in brief ecstasies. People who would have never imagined being seen together were giving themselves up in frenzied lust. From Schetzeler, he knew that there had been wildness at Auschwitz, too, but he had never been tempted. Nor had he tried to find escape, as some had, in solitary drinking or even in an occasional walk alone in the hills above the camp. 'At least,' he thought, 'I have not lost control of myself entirely.' He pitied the woman in the alley. And when the Russians finally came, invading the city over the bodies of their own dead by the hundreds of thousands, it would be unspeakably worse.

The alley opened on *Unter den Linden*, the old, lime-tree-lined boulevard, promenade of Prussia's kings, of Germany's chancellors and emperors. He thought he was hallucinating when he saw a herd of goats materialize out of the smoky air between the street's blasted stumps. 'Can goats run now where Frederick the Great rode in his golden coach? Have I gone mad? Has the world gone mad?" He decided to cross the boulevard and find another alley.

At every turn, everywhere he looked, death was defeating life. No one knew what would come tomorrow, only that it would be worse than today. While he was still working in the hospital, he had heard that a piece of family silver could be swapped for a few cigarettes or a bottle of *schnapps*. That housewives smashed their antique chests, their bedsteads, their picture frames into firewood. That animals at the zoo were slaughtered for food. That vegetable gardens that had been harvested months before were explored inch by inch in the desperate hope of finding a fugitive carrot or potato. That weeds, dried linden leaves, bones of no known origin, and empty gunnysacks were boiled into a soup. Now he saw old women hacking at the shredded, tangled camouflage netting that had been strung over streets. 'Do they try to make soup from that, too?' He saw them on their knees by the train tracks, looking for crumbs of coal. He walked by butchered draft horses, rotting in the streets where they were killed, maggots crawling around in the sockets of their eyes and what was left of their intestines. He knew that the living were desperate to keep living. And that the dead did not know the indignities they were subject to. That funeral directors sold coffins for firewood, after having sold them two or three times before, and disposing of the bodies in a bomb crater or a nearby canal. The stench of death made him stagger. He wished he had a pistol and civilian clothes.

After eight or nine hours, he had gone less than a mile and was exhausted. He mouthed the words, over and over: 'This must be how the world ends.'

He hoped he could sleep safely in a subway- station's bomb shelter. He soon saw that hundreds had the same idea. Instead of claiming a corner of one of the crowded pallets, he walked past the throng and along the tracks into the dark tunnel. He stopped when the shelter's torchlight behind him had become a dull, orange glow and he couldn't see anything in front of him. With his back to the wall, he lay down to rest, if not to sleep, careful not to put his legs anywhere near the rails, though he doubted any train would come. As his eyes grew accustomed to the darkness, he noticed a shape on the other side of the tracks. There was no sound. Nothing. He felt compelled to speak.

"Have no fear. I only want to sleep here. I need to sleep."

No answer.

Then, a bit louder, Johann said, "I am just going to sleep a bit."

Still no answer.

"Are you all right? Answer me, please."

Still no answer. At first, he thought he should move away. 'But maybe there's nothing there. Maybe it's just my imagination. Maybe just a bundle of rags or a pile of sand.' He dared to toss a small stone at what he thought were the shape's feet. Nothing. Then a larger one. Still no sound or movement. After a few minutes, he talked himself into crossing the tracks. The shape did not stir.

Lighting a match, he saw why. It was a man's body. He had been dead for no more than a few hours, barely cold, his face yellow gray in the flickering light. Blood from a gash on his forehead had already dried. Johann assumed that the man had died of a heart attack, and had hit his head when he stumbled. He was still clutching a small, mechanical flashlight in his hand. Johann cranked its handle and was happy to see that it worked. He found the dead man's identification papers in the vest pocket of his suit coat: *Heinrich Westermann; born May 1, 1900; 1.78 meters; no identifying scars; home city: Dresden; unmarried; clerk; Protestant; wounded veteran—exempt from military service.* The smudged pass-photo showed what must have been sandy, graying hair, light, widely set eyes, a high forehead, a straight nose, a thin moustache, and an unremarkable chin.

'With a moustache, and in these times, I could pass for him,' Johann thought. 'My great luck!' It took him several minutes of tugging and lifting of the corpse. He had to stop several times to crank up the flashlight. Finally, he took off his uniform and put on Westermann's clothes. 'The shirt collar is big and the pants are loose, but whose aren't nowadays?' He tightened the dead man's belt around his waist. After resting a few minutes, he began dressing the corpse in his uniform as best he could. He was careful to put Helga's letters, his three photos of her, Greta and Paul-Adolf, and the postcard from Philipp with Westermann's other clothes in the dead man's brown-leather suitcase. In its place, he put his own canvas bag and papers by the body. He rested for a few minutes before he picked up the suitcase, walked back across the tracks and went further down the tunnel, away from the station where he had entered the subway. The flashlight helped him see a narrow path alongside the tracks. The cadenced echo of his limp gave him courage.

Eventually, he saw the glow of another subway-station shelter. Before he reached it, he decided to lie down under a narrow ledge. He slept fitfully, his dreams filled with the horrors he had seen during the day. When he awoke, he went as quickly as he could through the station and climbed the stairs to the street. It was dawn. He found his bearings, zigzagged through the ruins, hid when he saw anyone, and, just after mid-day, clambered over a broken fence down into the train yards.

Without worrying where he was going, Johann hoisted himself up into an open boxcar, strained to close its door behind him, sat in the corner, and anxiously waited. 'No train will go east. Even if this one doesn't take me anywhere, I am safe enough here for a while,' he thought. He tried not to think about food. Every now and then, he heard voices. He did not know what he would do if the door opened.

After dark, the train slowly began to move. Johann peered through some bullet holes in the boxcar's wall. Exploding mortars and fires illuminated the skyline. He could see that he was leaving the city. He slept in fits, jerking awake with each bomb blast. 'Here I am, having escaped hell only to die on a bombed train!'

At dawn, he could tell that the train was heading south, not west toward the *Rhineland*, as he had hoped. He found that the boxcar door had not locked when he pulled it shut, pried it open and tried to jump off, but the train was going too fast. He slumped back down in the corner. 'Still better than going east,' he thought. 'Anywhere would be better than Berlin.'

He was amazed at the calm countryside. Forests were greening. Five or six cows were grazing in a broad field as the morning mist rose around them. At one railroad crossing, two children and an old woman on a bicycle waved as the train passed. He heard the noon bells as the train passed a village.

Trying to forget his hunger, Johann dozed through the afternoon. The train swayed and rocked, the rhythm of its wheels a soothing lullaby, and he dreamed of Pohlendorf. He was walking to school with Philipp on an early morning. Shopkeepers greeted them as they went down the main street. The bells chimed out seven and Philip and he began to run, their school bags bouncing on their backs. They got to their seats just as the teacher—"Old Schmidterl" entered the room and began his history lecture about the Ostrogoths and Visigoths. This faded into Johann having his mid-day meal at Philipp's house. Philipp's mother gave him an extra portion of her cucumber salad, his favorite, and a big slice of bread with butter, to go with his stew. When he asked for more, everyone laughed. Philipp and he walked back to school, talking about how the Ostrogoths fought the Romans. On the way, they climbed a tree and pretended they were Red Indians. They were hunting buffalo and when they got back to their village there would be a great feast and dancing and happiness for days and days. Pohlendorf's chief—"Old Schmidterl" again, now wearing a bonnet of eagle feathers!—would declare them valiant braves and give them great honor at a ceremony in the town square.

Johann woke up smiling from the best sleep he had had in days. For a few moments, he could not understand why he was in a boxcar. Pohlendorf, Philipp, everything and everyone in his dream seemed so real. So good. 'But it was just a dream,' he thought. 'A dream of the best world I have ever known.' He shook his head. With a great sigh, he got to his feet to look through the bullet holes. The sun had set, silhouetting the trees on a distant hillside. Something told him he was near Nuremberg.

When he sensed that the train was slowing down, he pushed the door open and tried to judge where he could safely jump off. The train rounded a curve. He threw his suitcase and jumped at the same time. He landed hard and tumbled down a weedy embankment. When he tried to stand up, he found he had sprained his ankle. His suitcase had split open, but nothing seemed to be missing. He gathered everything together, closed it, and began to hobble. His stomach groaned with hunger. 'There must be a farmhouse or a village near here,' he thought.

At the edge of a field, he came to a dirt road, with lights in the distance. He had not gone a hundred yards before he was captured. A patrol of four American soldiers had seen him coming, took cover in the brush on either side of the road, jumped out and surrounded him. Johann dropped his suitcase and put his hands in the air before he knew what was happening. They checked him for weapons, took his papers and marched him another two hundred yards to a barbed-wire compound. Inside it, a hundred or more men and boys, all in civilian clothes stood around in small groups or lay on the ground. Some, he saw, were standing in line for soup and bread.

"*Namen?* What is your *Namen? Wie heiss Du?*" a soldier asked in broken German.

"Westermann, Heinrich. *Ich komme aus Dresden.*" Johann replied and handed over his papers.

The soldier wrote "Westermann, H." on Johann's suitcase with a piece of chalk and put it near a pile of others. When he pointed toward two guards who opened a gate and motioned for Johann to go inside, Johann did not hesitate. He reached the soup line just before it shut down. He took a tin cup and held it over the nearly empty kettle. Before a soldier could fill it, he pulled it away and took a deep swallow, then handed it back for more. The soldier laughed, ladled it full, and handed him the last slice of bread off a tray. A Red Cross nurse at the end of the table smiled and handed him a blanket that he tucked under his arm.

When he walked to an open spot near the edge of the compound, Johann could make out another barbed-wire enclosure some fifty yards away, in which a thousand or more uniformed soldiers were confined. Jeeps shone their headlights all around them through the night. Moths and other night insects fluttered around the lights. He found the low drone of the engines was reassuring. He wrapped himself in the rough blanket, lay down on a grassy patch of ground, and fell asleep almost immediately. In the morning, he found the latrine. A cold shower behind a curtain of blankets. A cup of hot coffee and another piece of bread. The day was clear and warm. He felt safe for the first time in several weeks.

Ten days later, when the American troops fired their rifles into the air and cheered, Johann and the others all knew what had happened, even if they didn't understand English. In the evening, everyone got mashed potatoes and some pressed, canned meat with carrots, beside their tin of soup. All around, spring was slowly unfolding on the distant hillsides.

Early the next morning, Johann was assigned to a work detail. He hobbled toward the waiting trucks. Twenty minutes later, he gasped at the sight of his beloved Nuremberg, crushed almost beyond recognition. 'Thank God Helga has left,' he thought. His truck stopped at the Palace of Justice, one of the few buildings that had escaped destruction. The old courthouse had some blown-out windows and a few hundred shattered or missing roofing tiles. But overall, damage was minimal.

He was told to push a wheelbarrow filled with new tiles from pallets by the roadside around to the back where other men were carrying them up a makeshift scaffold to the roof. Johann filled his wheelbarrow as full as he thought he could manage it. He had not taken many steps when it tipped over. Almost all the tiles tumbled out and broke.

An American sergeant came over. "*Nicht* good. *Nicht* good."

Johann tried to explain that his limp and sore hand kept him from being able to grip and balance the wheelbarrow when he was walking. The sergeant understood. "Go there! Go there!" and pointed toward the main entrance to the building.

Johann limped in that direction.

The sergeant shouted to another soldier in the doorway. "This guy's no good out here. Use him inside."

The American gave him a small brush and pointed to where he could get a bucket of soapy water. Johann set to work scrubbing the main staircase. It hurt to kneel on the stone steps. Three hours later, a whistle blew. The Red Cross dealt out what was probably turnip soup and handed each worker a hunk of bread, a cup of coffee, and a small square of chocolate. Johann thought of Philipp. Twenty minutes later, it was back to the staircase. At the end of the day, the trucks drove them back to the compound. The next day brought the same routine, but on another stairway. The next, more stairs and a hallway. The day after that, another staircase and toilets. Each evening, soup, bread and coffee. An extra blanket helped to soften the ground underneath him. Tired and sore, Johann fell asleep almost as soon as he lay down. Each morning, awake at dawn. A shower. More coffee. The truck ride. And the scrubbing.

Johann did not complain. He had to get up off his knees every few minutes to keep from getting stiff. His shoulders ached. His left hand was red and swollen. His right hurt from having to brace himself. But at least he was left alone. He tried to look calm. To act normal. To do as he was told. Now the war was over, "Zero Hour," as the Germans called it, he knew he had a chance for a new beginning. Spring's fresh, sweet smelling air melted into June's warmer days and nights. Birdsong awakened the compound. Most days the canvas cover on the truck that transported him and the others was rolled back. Soon, Johann answered instinctively to "Westermann." He turned conversations away from where he had been before the war or what he had done during it. No one questioned it. They did the same.

In early 1946, along with other civilians from the compound, Johann was brought before a denazification panel. He rehearsed all the information he had filled in on the questionnaire: 'I am a refugee from Dresden. I never married. My only brother was killed in Poland, early in the war. My sister-in-law and her children have been missing since the Dresden firestorm. I lived in my parents' home. My mother died of influenza at the end of the first war. My father died in 1934 of heart disease. I have no living relatives, save a widowed aunt I hoped to find in Nuremberg. I fear she died in the war. I did not serve in the military because of a leg wound in the first war. I was a clerk in a warehouse. I injured my ankle just before I was captured. I voted for the Center Party, even though I was raised a Lutheran. I finished middle school and worked in the kitchen staff of the Zeiss Optics factory until it was destroyed in the Dresden fires.' Johann thought to himself, 'A whole life. A good life. I wish it had been mine."

His biggest worry was his hand. If he had to take his glove off and explain the swastika-shaped scar, he would say that it was the result of a gang that held him in Potsdam, where he had gone after Dresden was bombed. That they had beat him up, cut his hand and robbed him because he was not a Nazi.

It went more easily than he imagined. No one asked him to remove his glove. A clerk stated the questions and a translator, a young American soldier with a strong accent, spoke them in German. When Johann said he was from Dresden, the translator said with a broad smile, "My uncle lived in Dresden, too. Came to the States after war. First war. Neumann. Peter Neumann. My mother's brother. Uncle Pete. Maybe you know him?" At the same time, the clerk asked Johann if he had been a member of the Nazi Party. Johann shook his head "no" to the translator's question, who then said to the clerk, "Don't worry, this old guy's no Nazi. He was a simple clerk, for Chrissakes." The clerk rubber-stamped his passbook as an "exonerated person."

'If only it were so easy to escape the past,' Johann thought. 'Denazification is no more difficult than waiting in line at the soup kitchen.'

For a while, he did not allow himself to think about Helga. He was certain that she had gone to Karlsruhe to be with her sister. Then it dawned on him that she might have been notified that he was dead when his papers were discovered with Westermann's corpse. 'Perhaps I should have died, along with the Germany I served. For now, Helga is better off without me.' He tried to forget the immediate past, especially his life as a doctor. 'To practice medicine again—would that mean having to have the same hopes again? Having to suffer the same disappointments?'

In late summer, to his surprise, he was assigned to be chief janitor for the Palace of Justice. He was grateful for his new place in the world. It meant a bunk in the courthouse basement. A regular routine. Fixed responsibilities. Responsibilities that he could meet each day. Doing something tangible, something useful. For the while, he wanted nothing more. 'Amazing,' he thought, 'how we can become used to things that we never imagined could happen.' If asked, Johann might have said he was happy.

But a few weeks later, as the preliminary activities of the International Military Tribunal began, he sensed the coming danger. He felt as though he were being dragged back onto a freight train that would take him into his past. When the trial began, he felt trapped. His nightmares began. He lost much of the weight he had gained since the end of the war. He yearned to escape, but did not know how. 'Even better now that Helga is in Karlsruhe,' he thought. "But I don't dare write her. They are reading the mail. I will be discovered. And she will find out what I have done. How will I be able to face her? How?' When the International Military Tribunal ended, he felt relieved. Felt that he was in clear. A few more months, at the most, by Christmas surely, he could leave Nuremberg. Could find Helga and begin to live again.

But the Doctors' Trial was worse than the International Military Tribunal. Far worse. It brought the man into the courtroom whom Johann had most admired. The chief defendant, *Herr Professor Doktor* Karl Brandt, sitting in the very same chair where Hermann Göring had sat. He thought of their last conversation. The peaceful weeks of last summer, before the trials began, he now saw were just an interlude, and not the new beginning he had hoped for. In order to reach that beginning, he would have to relive everything that had happened. Everything.

Awake to this newest nightmare, he forced himself to listen as others reminded him of what he had done. His terrors nearly overpowered him. Seeing Helga was painful. Worse still was not being able to go with her. Writing his letter had helped him to steady himself. There was not much more he could add to it. The twenty-one days had run out. He sat at the little table next to his bunk in the basement. Before him were the several sheets of his letter. There was just room for a few more sentences:

I don't believe I'm evil, Helga, even though I have done evil things. These were evil times. In a different time, a different place, I might have been a better man. I have let myself be used. But that is no excuse. I should have been stronger. Or at least more aware of my weaknesses. And guarded better against them. I have been too human.

Please help me, Helga. Let us begin a new life together. I need you and love you. As always,

Your husband, Johann.

He folded the pages and put the letter in his overcoat pocket. He felt as though a huge load had been lifted from his shoulders. The trial was adjourned. He could leave, could take a morning train to Karlsruhe. Could hand the letter to Helga himself. The thought made him anxious. 'But at least I will know where I stand. I can be there by Christmas Eve.'

He packed his suitcase, wrote a note to the porter to tell him he was going away for the holiday, and began to walk to the train station. The ruined *Volksbank* was on his way. As he hoped, he saw Meier and some others sorting the rubble.

"*Guten Morgen, Herr* Meier. I want to wish you a 'Merry Christmas.' But it's much too cold today. You should have a winter coat."

Meier was bent over his cane, looking at the bricks at his feet. Just as he started to speak, he looked up at the sky and collapsed. Johann knelt down quickly by his side and felt for a pulse. Faint and fading. A heart attack! He loosened the old man's shirt and shoes, wrapped him in his overcoat and shouted to the two nearest girls working on another pile of rubble: "Help! Get help! Quickly!" He rolled Meier over to lie face down, turned his head sideways and stretched out his arms above his head. He straddled the old man's body and began putting rhythmic pressure on the center of his back. It had been a long time since he practiced this in medical school. He was afraid he would crack his ribs. He shouted again for help.

The girls ran towards the street and stopped a passing jeep. They pointed toward Johann and Meier. The American soldier called on his walkie-talkie to call for an ambulance. After two or three minutes of pumping on Meier's back, Johann stopped to feel for a pulse. Still there, but weak. He began the rhythmic pressure again. Others who were clearing rubble nearby ran toward them. Johann saw the commotion out of the corner of his eye. After a few more minutes, he decided that

Meier would breathe easier if he were on his back. When he rolled him over, he saw that the old man's eyes were wide open. Meier, breathing rapidly and groaning, was paler than before. Johann pulled his coat tighter around him.

"Easy now. Easy. Breathe slowly. You'll be all right. An ambulance is coming."

Meier grunted with pain. "I ..., I ..., I know...," he stammered.

"Easy. Don't speak."

"I know...who...you...are." Meier said, in clear, deep gasps between quick breaths.

"Don't speak," Johann repeated.

"You are...a doctor. You were...at my niece's...marriage. A witness. Like me. Our wives. Augsburg. I remember you. You are...a doctor. Brüning...? No, he was Chancellor, I think. Brehmer...? No. You are...Brenner. Yes, that's it....Brenner. *Herr Doktor*...Brenner. You welcomed...Hitler. I remember." Meier took several more labored breaths. He grimaced with pain. His eyelids fluttered. Then his eyes bulged briefly and closed. Johann thought he had died.

'Had anyone else heard him?' He looked nervously at the girls standing on either side. He snugged his overcoat around Meier's chest. He cradled his head and held his hand. He was surprised to find a pulse. Just then, a Red Cross ambulance arrived. Johann described what had happened as the driver and his helper put the old man on a stretcher. Johann asked if he could ride with him in the back.

When they reached the hospital, Johann walked alongside the stretcher down the corridor toward the emergency room. Johann held the swinging door open. Inside, he saw the bluish, suffused light that came through its high, whitewashed window. The familiar smell of alcohol and naphtha nearly made him unsteady on his feet. The hallway's green walls and white-tiled floor began to spin. Rooms like this flashed before his eyes. An operating room in the *Rhineland*. The ward at Grafeneck. *Block 20* and Aronsohn, bleeding to death in a heap on the floor. The Prisoners' ward, where he last saw Philipp. Clauberg's surgery in

Block 10 and Ellen Semmelberg. His mind tumbled backward through his past.

'This is not any of those hospitals,' he tried to tell himself. 'This is the hospital in Nuremberg where I worked before the war. Before the Nazis came to power. Where I saw patients from the policlinic and my private practice. Those other hospitals, those other wards were then. From another life. This is now. This hospital tries to help people. I once tried to help people here. Even my own Greta. And later, at the *Charité*. I tried to help.'

He felt himself leaning back on the doorframe. Meier was carried inside. The swinging doors closed. He found a chair and collapsed into it, dazed and speechless. He could not have said how long he sat there before a young nurse came over to him.

"Excuse me, please. You were with the old man in the ambulance," she said in a North German accent.

"Yes. His name is Meier. From here, he told me. Lives with his daughter-in-law in the city. But I don't know where."

"I am sorry to have to tell you that he has died. We could not do anything for him. His pulse when he arrived was barely detectable. He never regained consciousness. He may have had another heart attack, or could not survive the first one. I am sorry."

"Thank you. I met him by chance some weeks ago. I liked him. But I don't know where he lives in Nuremberg. He only told me that his wife was dead. And that his son was killed in the war. He was living with his daughter-in-law here somewhere."

"He had no identification papers," the nurse said. "Only a letter in his overcoat. He seems to have written his wife a letter. A long letter. No address, no envelope. Only the letter. His wife's name was Helga. 'Dear Helga…' he writes. Signs it 'Johann.'"

"No. No. You see that letter…that letter…." Johann stammered and began to perspire.

"The doctor and I read the letter. He was a doctor. His name was not Meier. He used an alias. Called himself 'Westermann.' His real name was

Brenner. Johann Brenner. Did you know he was a doctor? Are you sure he lives here?"

"My coat…" he began, but then he quickly realized that claiming the overcoat would link him to the letter. He shook his head.

"The letter tells that he worked at Auschwitz," the nurse continued. "Did terrible things there. Elsewhere, too."

"Why did you read the letter? Give it to me, please," Johann said, his voice rising.

"Are you a member of his family? The letter should go to his daughter-in-law," the nurse said, firmly. "You say he has a daughter-in-law. If his wife and son are dead, his daughter-in-law should have it. But he writes it to his wife, Helga. His wife—or daughter-in-law, if his wife is really dead—should have it. A family member. You say you're not a member of his family. We must alert the police in any case. When he doesn't come home, his wife or daughter-in-law will probably go to the police. They'll send her here. We probably should give the letter to the police. I'll ask the doctor in charge."

"I want to have that letter," Johann said sharply. "I can give it to his daughter-in-law, once she comes to the hospital to claim his body. If, as you say, it is shocking, she shouldn't be given it just like that. Look, I knew the old man. We talked while he was helping clear the rubble from the *Volksbank*. I knew him. *Herr* Meier. His name was Meier."

"Terrible things," the nurse said, as though she had not heard anything Johann was saying. "Just like the things we read in the newspapers about the Doctors' Trial. I can't imagine it. The newspapers tell us what those doctors were doing, and now this man's letter says he was doing the same things. Auschwitz. I can't imagine it. He was a doctor at Auschwitz." She started to walk away.

"I want that letter!" Johann shouted. "Where's the letter?"

The young nurse turned and stared at him. A guard standing in the lobby walked over as another nurse came toward them.

"What's going on here?" she asked.

Johann began to stammer again, "It's my… It's my…."

Before he could finish his sentence, she said, "*Herr Doktor* Brenner? You are *Herr Doktor* Brenner. I can't believe my eyes! Your wife told us you had been killed. Your wife told us you were dead."

The first nurse looked confused. "Who is this man?" she asked her colleague. "Do you know him?"

"Of course. He's *Herr Doktor* Johann Brenner. He used to be affiliated with our hospital, before the war." Turning to Johann, "But your wife said…"

"Did you write this letter?" the younger nurse interrupted. Johann tried to step away from the two women and the guard, but he was standing too close to his chair and fell back into it. An American military policeman got up from a seat near the hospital's door and walked over to see what was going on.

"Your wife worked here after the war ended," the older nurse said. "She left us less than three weeks ago. Told us she had to go to Karlsruhe. Does she know you are here? Don't you remember me, *Herr Doktor* Brenner? We worked together at the policlinic for a while. Then I transferred here. We saw each other occasionally afterwards at the hospital. I remember when you left for the war. We even gave you a going-away party. You were in uniform."

"Are *you Doktor* Johann Brenner?" the first nurse asked, standing over him. "Did *you* write the letter? Were *you* at Auschwitz?"

Another guard approached. The military policeman put his hand on his holster. Johann looked up into their faces. He didn't know what to say.

Afterword and Acknowledgments

History must be told.

—Eugen Rosenstock-Huessy

This novel has a history and I believe it is worth telling, if only briefly. It grew out of my determination to understand the participation of physicians in the Nazi regime. As a professor of history at the State University of New York at Plattsburgh, I focused on Germany's intellectual, social, and cultural energies, especially in the last two centuries. During this period, philosophy, literature, law, music and the visual arts, the social sciences and the natural sciences, especially medical science all flourished in Germany. Its citizens' achievements were remarkable in all these domains. It many ways, they embodied the essence of Western Civilization before Hitler came to power. How could such a state give rise to Nazism? How could its educated elites lend themselves to its vicious policies and practices? In particular, how could so many of its physicians, having sworn the Hippocratic Oath to "do no harm," become so enmeshed in the state's cruelties?

History provides us with a mirror of what is possible. Studying it reveals the best and the worst in all of us. What was possible in Germany, especially the Germany of the early twentieth century, is, I believe, possible anywhere. What happened there, given comparable situations, could happen wherever compassion and humility are outweighed by arrogance, ambition, greed, pride, hatred, or fear. Events since the Holocaust, alas, prove this true.

My original intention was to research and write a history of medical ethics and practices in Nazi Germany. Privileged to receive a Senior Fulbright Scholar/Teacher Award for the 1985-1986 academic year to study medical ethics in Germany between 1880 and 1945 and with a generous invitation from Professor Manfred Heinemann, I was appointed as a visiting guest professor in his unique *Zentrum für Zeitgeschichte von Bildung und Wissenschaft* ('Center for the Contemporary History of Education and Scholarly Studies') at the *Universität Hannover*. While based there, I worked in twelve major archives in the Federal Republic of Germany and in the German Democratic Republic; I also explored the rich holdings of the Welcome Institute for the History of Medicine in London, England. During the year, I interviewed medical personnel from the Nazi era and others with first-hand knowledge of my topic and had frequent conversations with German historians of medicine. I presented some of my preliminary research to seminars at the universities in Hannover and Bochum, West Germany, and, with the generous invitation of Paul Weindling, at St. Antony's College, Oxford University.

A flurry of psychological and historical works in English on the history of medicine in Germany began to appear even while I was still doing archival research, beginning with Robert Jay Lifton's widely praised study, **The Nazi Doctors: Medical Killing and the Psychology of Genocide** (Basic Books: New York, 1986). Other excellent books by Robert Proctor, Michael Kater, Paul Weindling, Michael Burleigh, and Henry Friedlander soon followed. Henry Friedlander's later study, **The Origins of Nazi Genocide: From Euthanasia to the Final Solution** (University of North Carolina Press: Chapel Hill, NC, 1995) and, two books by Ulf Schmidt—**Justice at Nuremberg; Leo Alexander and the Nazi Doctor's Trial** (Palgrave MacMillan: New York, 2004) and **Karl Brandt: The Nazi Doctor; Medicine and Power in the Third Reich** (Continuum Books: London, 2007)—became especially important to me; both scholars treat their subject with the clarity, thoroughness and sensitivity that I hoped to achieve. And many outstanding German historians and researchers—for example, Götz Aly, Angelika Ebbinghaus, Heidrun Kaupen-Haas, Claudia Huerkamp, Ernst Klee, Fridolf Kudlien, Stefan Liebfried, Benno Müller-Hill, Christian Pross, Karl-Heinz Roth, Reinhard Spree, and Florian Tennstedt, to name only the ones whose works I consulted the most—provide compelling descriptions and analyses of the public lives, careers and impact of academics, physicians and nurses in the years before and during the Nazi regime. In particular, Ernst Klee, the prize-winning journalist of *Die Zeit*, has done pioneering, indefatigable research on the "euthanasia program" and other Nazi medical atrocities; it is most regrettable that Klee's many excellent books have not been translated into English.

I soon saw that any historical account I could offer would neither be as detailed and comprehensive, nor as analytically incisive as any these scholars had written. I lacked the intellectual stamina and self-confidence one must have to confront these atrocities as they had. I also saw that archival research alone was not going to provide me with answers to my questions.

Generally, historical attention has tended to focus on the most prominent, most notorious Nazi doctors. They were at the pinnacle of the bureaucratic and medical apparatus and as such, left a historical trail. Essential as it is to document and analyze the conduct and motives of the chief perpetrators, I wanted to know more about the "ordinary" Nazi doctors—not the apparent psychopaths like Josef Mengele, or the self-righteous opportunists like Carl Clauberg, or others, whether sadists or delusional fanatics. What about the "ordinary" idealistic doctors, acting with at least some measure of "good will," who volunteered their services for the "euthanasia program," or participated in the sterilizations and experiments, or joined in the "selections" in the concentration camps? Driven by idealism, ambition, personal experience, arrogance, pride, fear, and whatever other emotions, they slid slowly, deeply into these horrors. To some degree, they were encouraged by Westernized medical philosophy and practices, to say nothing of the prevailing cultural arrogance and prejudices, nor of the militarism and xenophobia to be found in industrializing nations world-wide; anti-Semitism was, of course, not unique to Germany.

I saw signatures on documents authorizing sterilizations; I read trial transcripts that reflected career-choices and deeds. This, however, did not "open windows into the souls" of the lower rung of Nazi doctors? Why had they done such harm while thinking they were doing such good?

Even more importantly, why are there still such doctors today, still willing to serve in situations where they violate the Hippocratic Oath? And not just doctors, of course. What leads men and women of good to violate fundamental ethical principles? How do they justify their behavior? Are we all capable of such acts? And if so, how can we guard ourselves from making these choices? These are the questions at the heart of my endeavor.

In 1990, when I realized that I could not add anything significant to the formal scholarship on medical ethics in Nazi Germany, I decided to write a firmly grounded historical novel. There I could more creatively explore, could try to imagine, if you will, the mind and motives of what I believed to be an "ordinary" Nazi doctor. My novel describes such a doctor, able, for a while, to justify his actions and believe he was still fulfilling his sworn responsibilities to "do no harm." It tells the story of his descent into this abyss. And it allows me to raise two questions: first, what, if anything, can a perpetrator do to redeem himself? and second, what should society do if it becomes aware of his deeds?

I have tried to make Johann Brenner plausible as an ordinary human being. Although he is fictitious, he has many of the characteristics of typical German physicians in this era, indeed of physicians wherever Western medicine was practiced. These men—the vast majority were men—believed in racial categories and hierarchies, in the benefits of positive and negative eugenics, and in the inevitable benefits of medical science. Johann Brenner and others like him in German-speaking Europe, of course, went even further in welding their medical views onto their submissive loyalty to Adolf Hitler and Nazi ideology. Philipp Stein is fictitious, too, representative of countless German physicians deemed by the Nazis to be a "non-Aryan." Except for that seal on Philipp's fate, the fate of nearly all the Jewish doctors who could not escape the Nazi maw, to say nothing of his compassion, he and Johann are more alike than they are different.

It is important to note that the typical Nazi doctor did not demonstrate Johann Brenner's sense of shame or remorse. Most escaped punishment, often resuming their practice and dying in their beds long after the end of the war. Some achieved fame and praise for their work from an unaware or unconcerned public. Relatively few of the most nefarious or influential were apprehended, brought to trial, found guilty and executed—Karl Brandt is the most prominent example. Others received prison sentences of varying lengths, but these were often commuted. Still, I fervently want to believe that at least one had a "change of heart" and came to see that his arrogant self-confidence in his medical skills, his unequivocal devotion to his *Vaterland*, and his hate-filled acceptance of racial ideology inexorably led him to do evil.

I have tried to be as faithful and attentive to historical events as I can be. Still, a novel is a contrivance, a creation of characters placed within settings, all according to the will and inclinations given them by the author. Its coincidences might be rare in real life, but in fiction, they give a story its dynamics, its tensions and twists that propel it toward its ending. My novel is no different. Everything in it either did happen or, I believe, could have happened. I want it to evoke an historical reality— from the experiences Johann Brenner and Philipp Stein might have had in their childhood, to their involvement in the First World War and its chaotic aftermath during the fourteen years that "Germany tried democracy," to the impact of the Nazi regime on their lives and choices. These are crucial *public* events, affecting everyone who lived through them. The novel's more incidental facts, too—from the color of the American automobiles in Nuremberg in the immediate aftermath of World War II, to the improbable herd of goats in the streets of war-ravaged Berlin, to the slaughterhouse next to the train station in Freiburg—are drawn from my study of the sources, from reading other historical accounts, and from my personal experiences. With regards to chronology, though, I should note that the Nazi Doctors' Trial actually began on December 9, 1946; my narrative has it beginning a week earlier, allowing for the nineteen days before Johann decides to leave Nuremberg to be in Karlsruhe at Christmas.

The novel's *private* events, of course, are my own imagining. While many of the characters in the novel are factual, its main characters are fictional. In addition to Johann Brenner and Philipp Stein, I have imagined their wives, families, colleagues, neighbors and friends, including Luise Seligman, Pelcher, Schetzeler, Scharff, the Semmelberg family, the "green-eyed boy" and his mother, Aronsohn, Meier and others who appear through the story.

In two instances, I have quoted actual dialogue. The first is the witness testimony quoted in Chapter One, taken from the official English translation of the transcript of the Nazi Doctor's Trial in Nuremberg, Doc. NO. 819, which can be found on-line, thanks to the *Harvard Law School Library Nuremberg Trials Project; A Digital Document Collection* at <http://nuremberg.law.harvard.edu/php/pflip.php?caseid=HLSL NMT01&docnum=120&numpages=12&startpage=1&title=Affidavit. &color_setting=C> accessed most recently on September 7, 2010.

The second instance of actual dialogue is Johann's comment to a terrified woman on the ramp—"Madam, do you think we are barbarians?" In "Genocide," one of the programs in the "World at War" documentary by Thames Television (1974), Rudolf Vrba tells of having heard this dialogue spoken by an *SS* officer at Auschwitz; see Vrba's memoir, *Escape from Auschwitz*, New York: Grove Press, 1988, for the powerful story of his experiences at the hands of the Nazis and his daring flight.

In order to flesh out some of the historical reality of the novel, I offer brief descriptions of some of its actual individuals, places, circumstances and events, in most cases with a reference to recent scholarship on a website designed for this purpose:

<www.shadowswalking.com>

Here is a list of this website's entries:

The website also includes a select bibliography of additional scholarly studies that helped me provide background and context for my
story. Most of these have bibliographies for those interested in further
reading in English or German.

*****

Every author's book is a special experience in his or her life, a span
of time, usually spent apart and alone with one's self. More than I ever
imagined when I began it, over twenty years ago, this book has shaped
me, forced me to learn about myself, as much or more than I have
shaped it. Whatever merit it might have derives from the inspiring confidence and patience of so many who have helped me conceive it, persist
in writing in, and now decide, after fourteen earlier drafts, that I must
declare it finally done to the best of my ability. With a sincere hope for
my reader's indulgence, I welcome this opportunity in print, at last, to
express my gratitude to so many of my teachers, colleagues, students,
friends and family members. Many of you will see your names below,
but even if you don't, please know that I appreciate you all for the love
you have shown me.

I have had many professors—especially Fred Berthold, David Roberts,
William Ruddick, Frank Ryder, T.S.K. Scott-Craig, Thad Seymour, and John
Williams at Dartmouth College; F. Edward Cranz and Hannah Hafkesbrink
at Connecticut College; and William Church, Tom Gleason, Stephen
Graubard, Burr Litchfield, Bryce Lyon, Tony Molho, Donald Rohr, Dietrich
Rueschemeyer, and my especially patient dissertation advisor, Norman

Robert and Ann O'Brien were like loving parents to me. Through
them, I was privileged to meet and learn from Professor Eugen
Rosenstock-Huessy after his retirement from teaching at Dartmouth
College; he set me on my life's course of trying to understand the
past in order to learn our responsibility to the present and the future.
With Rosenstock-Huessy's guidance, I went to Germany and lived in
the family home of Franz and Bertha Schürholz, whose extraordinary
kindness resonates in me to this day.

460

Rich, at Brown University—who encouraged me and helped me to see how fulfilling a teacher's life could be, beginning with my energizing high school journalism teacher, Jerome Weiner. I also was privileged to know Harvard Professor *emeritus* Robert Ulich, whose understanding of the history of education has inspired me throughout my teaching career. I have tried to be for my students what they and so many others have been for me.

Four members of SUNY Plattsburgh's History Department and their spouses became my mentors and friends: Allan and Elsie Everest, Hans and Vera Hirsch, Eugene and Beulah Link, and George and Elizabeth Pasti. They always found a way to guide and cheer me on. Even now, George still does, with every sunrise.

I am grateful to the Fulbright Commission for the opportunity to begin the research in Germany that underpins my novel. Manfred and Gerda Heinemann were my gracious hosts in Hannover. Klaus Wiese and Ilona Wiese-Zeuch generously welcomed me into their home in Berlin. It gives me great pleasure to express to you, Manfred and Gerda, and to you, Klaus and Ilona, my heartfelt appreciation for your lasting friendship. During that year I also received huge doses of tender, loving care from my beloved mother-in-law, Rosalie Schaudt, and from my wife's and my dear friend, Rosemarie Wild. Their inspiring lives in the face of great hardship reminded me daily of the good that is in the world. And I was privileged to join the countless admirers and benefactors of the scholarly achievements and generosity of Georg and Wilma Iggers; thank you for your continuing interest in my work.

While still doing archival research in Germany, I received patient guidance from archivists Klaus Dettmar and Monique Kriescher-Fauchs, and from Professor Gisela Miller-Kipp. And at SUNY Plattsburgh, Gordon Muir always offered me more bibliographic references than I could master. I hope my effort, even if different than you must have imagined, assures you of my deep appreciation.

Shortly after I began to conceive the novel, Margaret Gibson and David McKain listened to my rambling plans with such palpable enthusiasm that I was propelled beyond just thinking about it. And Hobart and Jean Mitchell, our "spiritual parents," continue to inspire Margaret,

David, my wife and me with our memories of their steadfast devotion to each other, so I cannot express my gratitude to you, Margaret and David, without thinking of the spiritual gifts that Hobart and Jean have given all four of us.

More than anyone else, Tom Moran, Founding Director of the Institute for Ethics in Public Life at the State University of New York at Plattsburgh, with his constant good humor, patience and thoughtfulness, has encouraged and stimulated my endeavors, and renewed my self-confidence on countless occasions. It is a great privilege and an honor to thank you especially, Tom, for your belief in me and in the importance of my work.

Margaret Lavinia Anderson, with characteristic devotion and thoroughness, offered me a detailed, penetrating critique of an earlier draft. Her suggestions forced me to re-write substantial portions and pushed me to a greater awareness of my purpose in writing. Peggy and her husband, James Sheehan, have helped me, as they have helped countless colleagues, scholars and students perceive the nuances of Germany's history. It is a great privilege to be counted among your friends.

Nick Woodin, despite many more important things that he would have rather done, helped me make me the novel clearer and smoother by reading several drafts. I can't expect you to read it again, Nick, but if you do, I hope you will see how I have followed so many of your suggestions. To you and to Daui, my deepest gratitude for your support and friendship.

Over the past fifteen or more years, our "First Sunday Evening Writers' Group" in Plattsburgh has suffered through my innumerable efforts to get the novel "right." Ann Tracy, our energizing founder, Mary Dossin, Tim Myers, Laura Palkovic, and Vera Vivante, as well as others, listed below, and some less-frequent participants all listened to my concerns with patience and wise advice. Your own fine writings have helped me raise my standards for mine.

Suzanne Moore continually inspires me with her sensitive, evocative writing. Thank you for pushing me toward a stronger understanding of my subject and how to convey it to others, and for your constant support.

Herbert Savel, using photographs as his guide, has carved hundreds of powerful *bas relief* portraits in wood of victims of Nazi brutality. With plans to do hundreds, if not thousands more, his website shows and tells about his work and where it can be seen: <http://www.holocaustcarv-ings.com/> You, Herb, and Isabel, your wife and helpmate in the most beautiful sense of the word, have a rare combination of determination and genius that has often pulled me back to my writing with renewed zeal.

Beth Cederstrom's capacity to see and create beauty has helped me preserve and nurture my hopefulness. And when I encouraged Ingeborg Sapp to tell her own poignant stories of her life in Germany under Nazi rule and then under Soviet domination, which she has done brilliantly, I knew I had to follow my own advice and persevere. Thank you both for your inspiration.

Many of my colleagues in SUNY Plattsburgh's Department of History have had good reason to doubt the progress of the novel, having heard many times that "its done!" when it still wasn't. In particular, Chuck Bashaw, Vincent Carey, Kevin Dann, Gary Kroll, Ben Morreale, Jessamyn Neuhaus, Richard Schaefer, Connie Shemo and Stuart Voss indulged me in extensive conversations about the issues I was attempting to understand and/or read portions of various drafts. Many others—in some cases long before I began this project—have inspired me with their devotion to teaching and research: Bethany Andreasen, Adnan Abu-Ghazaleh, Robin Balthrope, Amy Bass, Sylvie Beaudreau, Suzanne Buckley, David Glaser, Wendy Gordon, Martin and Ann Hasting, Jeff Hornibrook, Bill Husband, Ed Judge, Martha Lance, Carol Leonard, James Lindgren, Dixon Miyauchi, Jack Myers, Stan Nadel, Anita Rapone, Corky Reinhart, James Rice, Larry Soroka, Chandar Sundaram, Monica van Beusekom, and Altina Waller. It has been a privilege to know you all, both as colleagues and as friends.

David Mowry, Founding Director of SUNY Plattsburgh's Honor's Program, has provided my colleagues and me with a wonderful setting to teach small groups of energizing students, many of whom, mentioned below, read earlier versions of my novel and gave me thoughtful criticism;

my colleagues and I are in your debt, David. Two more treasures of SUNY Plattsburgh's faculty, Richard Robbins and J. W. Wiley, have shared their enthusiasm, insights and wisdom with me over the years. Another dear colleague, Lary Shaffer, has given me a life-long model of excellence and creativity. James Armstrong and Mark Cohen, two members of SUNY Plattsburgh's outstanding Anthropology Department, have enlivened me with their passion for learning and teaching. Two successive Deans of Arts and Sciences, H.Z. Liu and Kathleen Lavoie, and College Provost Robert Golden tried in vain to protect me from distractions of my own making; and, Bob, your reading of early chapters helped me immeasurably. And thank you, Norman Taber, for your skill and patience in designing the book's cover. I appreciate and admire you all.

Being with Tom Moran over the past twelve years in the "guided inquiry" seminars and lunchtime discussions of SUNY Plattsburgh's Institute for Ethics in Public Life has allowed me to share my thoughts with each semester's triad of Fellows; not only have you all listened to my struggles, you generously offered constructive criticism and kind encouragement. I particularly want to thank Beth Dixon, whose perennial question, "What do you mean by that?" forced me to find the most appropriate language to express my thoughts. Jürgen Kleist gave me valuable advice and encouragement in structuring the novel. Lauren Eastwood's close reading of an earlier version gave me a renewed burst of energy at a particularly difficult time. Jean Ann Hunt and David Stone cannot know how much they have sustained me with their compassion and interest in my well-being. Anna Battigelli and Paul Johnston inspired me with their profound devotion to literature and its highest goals. Susan Mody generously engaged my thoughts and greatly enhanced them with hers. Mark Beatham, Tracie Church-Guzzio, Monica Ciobanu, Mark Holden, Jin Kim, Ray Johnson, Stewart Denenberg, and Jonathan Slater stimulated me with their insights and interest in my work. And John Yardan faithfully listened to all of us and gave generously of his own; I know I am not alone in missing him each Wednesday. I thank you and all the other Fellows and participants in our weekly seminars who indulged my questions and challenged my responses; some have already been mentioned above: Deborah Altamirano, Anne Bongiorno, Robert Cabin, Rodney Cavenaugh, Peter Conrad, Jose deOndarza, Helen Deresky, Ellen Fitzpatrick, Lonnie Fairchild, Diane Fine, Jon Gottschall, Kurtis Hagen, Bob Harsh, Kim Hartshorn, Holly Heller-Ross, Bryan Higgins, Hiroshi Itoh, Kate Joyce, Thomas Konda, Daphne Kutzer, Martin Lubin, Steve Mansfield, Thomas Morrissey, Margaret Morrow, Amy Mountcastle, Faten Moussa, Priscilla Myers, Connie Oxford, Tim Palkovic, Douglas Perez, Bill Pfaff, Shakuntula Rao, Jennifer Scanlon, Lynn Schlesinger, Heidi Schnackenberg, Richard Schnell, Doug Selwyn, Charles Simpson, Laurence Soroka, William Tooke, and William Teter. Exploring ideas about ethics and civic responsibility with all of you in the Institute has been an invaluable, invigorating tonic for me. What a blessing the Institute is for our College!

How can I possibly mention every student every student who has had to hear me hold forth on the historical foundations of my novel and allowed me to describe why I think the issues it raises are important? Inevitably, some stand out in my mind: Phil Allen, Erin Barnard, Fred Cole, Chris Davies, Kevin Days, Brian Didier, Larry Dolan, Andrea Downing, Charlene Dubuque, Bill Duffany, Shaun Errichiello, Brad Fahsel, Nick Favicchio, James Fennessy, Jana Fitzpatrick, Dan Galimidi, Woody Groves, James Guberman, Greer Hamilton, Alonna Haseltine, Zachary Hoffman, Briana Holland, Orlando Illi, Sarah Jensen, Avram Kaufman, Monique Kirenga, Ryan Kivett, Christopher Levendos, Jessica Levine, Krystal Lugo, Melissa Mansfield, Marie Mitchell, Matt Minor, Russ Mitchinson, Joy Morgan, Kate Morris, Marie Nacht, Norman Radow, Yeshe Richman, Sandra Ortsman, Tim Sarrantonio, Owen Smith, Stephen Stolarcyk, Ed Svec, Jordan Wallance, and Carrie Woodward. My indelible memories of Carl Kegel, who shared his intense energies and extraordinary talents so enthusiastically with everyone who knew him, remind me of the fragility of our lives and of our responsibilities to each other. And Laura Perras has made an indelible impact on me and so many my colleagues, teaching us all anew that we must cherish the sublime gift of each and every day. Four more outstanding former students—Colleen Pope Lemza, Blake Harrison, Kevin Husselbeck, and

Doug Sloan—and their respective families continue to inspire me and bring me great joy long after my teaching career has concluded. All of you, and so many others whom I cannot name here, embody my fervent hope for a kinder, more compassionate world.

I also am grateful for dear high-school friends—Frances Brown, Tom Coroneos, Steve Day, George Hessenthaler, Erin Silva, June Totten, and Chris Trumbo—who have helped me with the novel's form and ideas. After more than fifty years, we still sail the Argo.

Two of my college classmates and life-long friends, DeWitt Beall and Bruce MacPhail, gave me advice and much appreciated encouragement just when I needed it. DeWitt, I hope you would be proud of your first "roomie"; and Bruce, I hope this is a worthy addition to your marvelous library.

My publication team at CreateSpace have been outstanding from start to finish. I take great pride in offering each of them my sincerest thanks for their exceptional efficiency, patience, and understanding in helping me to complete this work.

Finally, my grandparents and my mother sheltered me as best they could from the hardships they endured; my father's turbulent life constantly reminds me of the blessings of my own. Their love for me has helped to teach me how to treasure every day for the gift it is. My son and my wife, although they have been thoroughly mystified from start to finish by my determination to devote so much time and energy to this project, unquestioningly have given me the strength and courage that only loved ones can give. I have no words that fully express my gratitude and love, Andrew and Evelyne.

Photo by Mitchell Tomar Skopp

Douglas R. Skopp graduated from Benjamin Franklin High School in Los Angeles in 1958. After two years at Dartmouth College, he took a year off to learn German and study at the *Albert-Ludwigs Universität* in Freiburg-im-Breisgau, Federal Republic of Germany, then returned to Dartmouth and received his B.A. in 1963, majoring in history and minoring in German. He earned an M.A. in Medieval Studies from Connecticut College in 1964, and a Ph.D. from Brown University in 1974, focusing primarily on modern German history. From 1972 until his retirement at the State University of New York at Plattsburgh in 2006 with the rank of Distinguished University Teaching Professor, he taught aspects of European history, particularly modern Germany, as well as the Middle Ages, the World Wars, the Holocaust, education in Western Civilization, and historical research methods and skills. In Fall 1998, he was an Inaugural Fellow in SUNY Plattsburgh's Institute for Ethics in Public Life. He continues to assist each semester in the Institute's "guided inquiry" seminars on ethics, ethical practices and the curriculum, and serves as SUNY Plattsburgh's College Historian.

Made in the USA
Lexington, KY
18 May 2012